OUT

OF

HOPE

ELENA AMBROSE

Editor: Susan Gaigher

Cover Design: Lynn Andreozzi

Cover Images: Ovidiu Iordachi/Adobe Stock & canjoena/Abobe Stock

Internal Design: Lorna Reid

ISBN-13: 979-8-218-61305-1

1

JUNE 1995

The image of the city skyline had disappeared from her rearview mirror hours ago, but Hannah could not stop herself from glancing back and hoping to see it. The mile markers flew by outside her window as she drove down the interstate. With the passing of each one, uneasiness rose in her stomach, knotting her up inside. She was getting closer to her destination and farther from where she wanted to be.

Her usual views of high-rise buildings and the Lake Michigan shoreline had been exchanged for the sprawling, never-ending scenes of corn fields and countless miles of flat land that now formed her horizon. In all the years since Hannah had left, she could never have imagined returning to Hope. She was still in disbelief at the sequence of events that had led her here on this sunny, early summer afternoon. She was driving back to the place she swore she would never return to. A place she had left the moment she was able to.

Her thoughts wandered to the past, but she was brought back to the present by the whoosh of air from semis streaking by. It didn't feel like she was driving slowly, but the other vehicles on the road were zooming past her. Usually, she would be fighting for space in the left lane using her city driving skills to finish the trip as quickly as possible, but today she had no desire to reach her destination. Every extra minute she spent on the road was another minute she wouldn't be in Hope.

When she approached the sign for her exit off the interstate, her heart dropped. The off-ramp was long and curved, and as her car came to a stop at the top of the hill, she considered going straight and speeding right back onto the highway. Reluctantly, she put on her left turn signal and slowly made the turn. The journey she had spent the last fourteen years trying to avoid had finally been completed. She was home.

Hannah quickly lowered her speed as the limit dropped from forty-five to thirty-five miles per hour and finally to twenty-five miles per hour within a few blocks. She no longer had in-state plates, and she guessed that it was still the town police's mission to catch outsiders speeding. Before she had time to prepare herself, the whole town came into view. It sat on a small hill surrounded by fields and farms. The hardware and supply store still sat on the right, the post office on the left. At the top of the hill, the court-house loomed above a grove of trees, and a few blocks to the right stood the town's one church. Nothing had changed since she left. She had been gone for so long, but at first glance, everything ap-peared to be exactly the same.

She rolled down her window and took a deep breath. The air smelled the same—a hint of soil, livestock, and stagnation. With one inhale, she felt as if she were eighteen again. The last time she had smelled these familiar scents she was on this very road. How-ever, that day she had been on the other side of the road. Hope had been in her rearview as she stared out into the horizon that unfurled in front of her. It had held a future of possibilities away from this place. She remembered taking a similar deep breath that day and telling herself that she would never have to smell these smells again. How wrong she had been.

The closer Hannah got to the heart of town, the more a sense of déjà vu overtook her. As she passed the familiar sights of her youth, she could not help but replay in her mind the events that had driven her from this place. Just a few hours ago, all her memo-ries of this town had seemed like a hazy dream, but now that she was back in Hope, they were all rushing up to the surface. The scenery outside her car blended with her recollections of it, and before she realized it, she had already reached the turn for her street. The corner was marked by the tallest point in all of Hope, the steeple of Holy Trinity Church. It towered over the rest of the town. Not that there was much to tower over in Hope. The church served as the centerpiece of the community. Being that it was on the end of her block, it had always served as an easy visual of where to turn for her house. She braked at the stop sign and put on her signal to turn right onto Pace Avenue. As Hannah turned her head from right to left, checking for oncoming cars, she saw him for the first time.

Hope was a small town, and she was quite sure she knew pretty much everyone that lived there. Although she hadn't been back in a long while, her mother had kept her updated on all the comings and goings over the years. There was no way she would not have mentioned this man. He was a little older than her but similar enough in age that she would have remembered him from school. Hope High only had two hundred students when she attended, so it was easy to know everyone. She searched her memories for anyone resembling him even remotely, but she couldn't place him. He most certainly wasn't from Hope.

The man was mowing the grass in front of the church. The sun was high in the sky, and even though it was early summer, Hannah could feel the heat radiating through the windows of her car. He was wearing a tank top and shorts, both wet from sweat, and his arms and legs were marked with streaks of dirt and grass. His face was half hidden under a flop of shaggy, reddish-brown hair. Sweat dripped down the curls that fell over his forehead. Hannah strained to see his features more clearly. Usually, she made it a habit not to stare, but right now she couldn't help herself. The sweat on his body made it glisten in the bright sun, and for a few moments, she sat in disbelief at what she was seeing.

The man continued with his work as she sat unmoving in her car. When he paused for a second to move the hair up off his forehead, she was finally able to catch a glimpse of his full face. She was so caught off guard by the sight of this handsome man that she momentarily forgot all her other fears about being home. The knot of anxiety that had formed in her stomach on the drive into town loosened as quickly as it had formed. She didn't know who he was, but there was something about him that made her feel at ease. They had never met, but she felt drawn to him—that was undeniable.

Hannah wasn't sure how long she had been sitting at the stop sign, but it was long enough for her to get honked at. The sound of a car horn blasting behind her jolted her out of her daze. She looked away from the church as her cheeks flushed bright red. *The man must have looked up at the honking,* she thought. Hopefully he hadn't noticed her. She turned down Pace Avenue and did her best to keep her eyes forward as she passed him on her left. During the short drive down her street, Hannah felt a small flash of positivity growing inside her. Maybe this summer wouldn't be as awful as she had expected. Maybe things could change in Hope. The beautiful stranger she had just seen was proof that the place was not completely unalterable. For a few moments, she felt optimism instead of anxiety about her return home.

As she approached her childhood home, she could see that her mother Julie was sitting outside on the front steps. As Hannah looked at the house for the first time in so many years, she could see that this was another thing in Hope that hadn't changed. The house was the same pale blue color it had always been. The front door was now an even more faded light yellow. She pulled into the driveway and tried to prepare herself for the giant step she was about to take. Before she opened her car door, she looked out the window at Julie. The house might have been roughly the same, but Julie looked different from when Hannah had last seen her a few weeks earlier. She looked paler, thinner, and more tired. The brief spark of possibility and hope Hannah had just been feeling was snuffed out as suddenly as it had been lit.

2

MAY 1995

Her mother had called her in April to tell her she wasn't feeling well. At first, Hannah had not been all that worried. In fact, she had been in the middle of making dinner and hung up on her mom rather quickly. Julie had been nervous about telling Hannah about her diagnosis and couldn't get the words out before Hannah excused herself from the call. She'd been halfway through making dinner and was too preoccupied with getting to her workout class on time to really listen to what Julie was trying to say. Two days later when her phone rang and it was her mother again, Hannah sensed that something was wrong as soon as she heard Julie's voice on the other end. Julie rarely called so close together. Once Julie began to talk, Hannah's fears were confirmed. She could only vaguely remember the call. What she did process, she wished she could erase from her memory. Cancer. Terminal. These words stuck out amongst all the other things her mother said between sobs. The carefully crafted world Hannah had created for herself came tumbling down around her. Years of building walls and distance between herself and where she came from were all washed away by a single tsunami.

Hannah had insisted that her mother get a second opinion. She even brought her up to Chicago to see a highly regarded specialist, but the prognosis had been the same. Julie had the option to get experimental treatment that could buy her a few extra months.

The treatment would leave her weak, sick, and nauseous. It would also keep her three hundred miles from her home. The other option would be to go home and have a couple of mostly normal months before the end. Hannah of course wanted her mother to fight and not give up. She pleaded with Julie during several teary-eyed conversations. Yet Julie seemed weirdly at peace despite the dire options that were available to her. Hannah couldn't comprehend why her mother didn't want to fight.

Julie was clear that she wanted to be at home living her life, not spending her last few months getting poked and prodded, living on Hannah's couch. She wanted Hannah to go on with her life; she did not want to be a burden. Eventually, Hannah had no option but to accept Julie's choice. By the time Julie left to return home, Hannah had begun to accept her decision not to get any further treatment. However, when she saw Julie's car turn the corner at the end of her block and disappear from sight, Hannah knew there was one part of her mother's wishes she couldn't accept—not Julie's choice to refuse treatment, but her choice to work through it alone. Hannah waited a few hours until she was sure Julie had made it home, and then she called her.

"Listen Mom, I'm coming home. I'm spending whatever time you have left with you in Hope." Julie wanted to argue, but she didn't.

The next day, Hannah went straight to her department chair and asked to go on sabbatical. The spring term would be over in a week, and she was supposed to teach a summer class and then a full roster of classes in the fall. She loved her work as a history professor, but she wasn't sure how long her mother had. Part of her was still holding out hope that the doctors had all been wrong. She wanted to believe that Julie had longer than three months, so she asked for both the summer and fall semesters off. After explaining the situation, and due to the chairperson having just gone through a similar situation with his own mother, she was granted her request. Hannah was so grateful, but the support of her coworkers made leaving even harder.

With work sorted, she turned her attention to convincing her fiancé Noah that this was the right decision. As she made her way to the train after leaving the university, her mind was preoccupied with thoughts of how to address the situation with him. She should have told him that she wanted to stay with Julie the minute she had the idea. Most certainly, she should have told him before she arranged time off from work. She wasn't entirely sure why she hadn't told him yet. Perhaps it was because she was conflicted about her decision to return to Hope, and any protest from Noah might be enough for her to abandon her plan.

She boarded the train and sat in her usual seat by the windows. Normally, the ride seemed to take forever, but on this day, it flew by. The buildings that lined the train tracks all blurred together, and she didn't hear the announcement for her station. Noticing where she was at the last second, Hannah hurriedly jumped up from her seat and out the train doors onto the platform right before they closed.

On her the walk to her apartment, she tried to take in all the sights and sounds of the city. The honking of horns, train and bus announcements, and chatter of conversations from the sidewalk cafes. The sounds all vibrated off the concrete and stone buildings, blending to form the beautiful hum of the city. She had lived here since the day she left Hope, and she had planned to never leave. The circumstances left her with little choice, though. It wasn't Julie's fault that Hannah was going to leave. She was all Hannah had left.

When she finally made it home, she was glad to see that Noah wasn't there. She needed time to prepare her explanation. A few months earlier, when they moved in together, it had seemed like the right move. Noah was working long hours trying to make his way up at an investment firm, and Hannah was a full-time college professor. They rarely had time to see each other, so moving in together made sense. At least they could spend the hours they were home together. Now she wished they had waited. The fact that they were living together was sure to make her absence seem more acute to him.

Noah didn't know much about Hannah's past in Hope, except that she had never wanted to go back. Hannah herself tried to remember it as little as possible, so she rarely shared stories from her past. She always thought it was ironic that she studied and taught history but tried her best to never reflect on her own. Now, suddenly, she was going to tell Noah that she not only wanted to return home but that she planned to live there, completely putting their lives on hold.

She started making dinner, hoping a nice meal would help ease them both into the conversation. The smell of garlic and tomato sauce had filled the apartment by the time Noah came home from work. He was surprised, as he usually got home first on Tuesdays, since Hannah taught an evening class.

"Hey babe, you're home already?" he called from the foyer as he removed his shoes and set down his bag.

"Yeah, I got off early. I made us dinner." Hannah tried to sound as normal as possible.

Noah washed up and came into the kitchen. He was greeted by a fully set table, lasagna, salad, and a bottle of wine. At first, he thought maybe he had missed an anniversary or birthday, but when he saw the look on Hannah's face, he realized something else was going on.

"This looks so delicious, but are you okay? Why aren't you at work?" His voice was full of concern.

Hannah had hoped that they could at least sit down and have a little wine before she explained herself. Clearly that was not going to happen. She had practiced her speech several times while cooking, but when it came time to speak, her mind went completely blank. For several seconds she could do nothing but look down at the table and fidget with the embroidered edge of the napkin in front of her. She took a deep breath to center herself.

"Noah, you know my mom is very sick. So, I have decided something… I need to go home and be with her. She doesn't have much time, and I couldn't live with myself if I let her spend those months alone. Work already agreed to let me take a sabbatical."

At first, Noah was caught off guard. He wanted to be sensitive, but they had spoken at length about this before Julie left, and she had been explicit about not wanting Hannah to come home with her. Hannah had always been uninterested in returning to Hope, even for a short visit.

"Did you talk to Julie about this?" he asked cautiously.

"I did, and she agreed." Hannah still couldn't look up to meet his eyes.

"Well, of course I'll support you if that's what you want, but I'm worried about you going back home. I can tell even talking about that place makes you uneasy. How are you going to stay there for months?" Hannah could hear the concern in his voice. If she was being honest, he was right to be concerned. She wasn't sure how she was going to handle it. But her mother needed her.

She reached out and put her hand over his. Then she took a deep breath and tried her best to sound reassuring.

"You are right, but Julie was never the reason I left. Staying away so long probably wasn't fair to her. I have a chance to make up for some of the time we were apart and support her. I feel like I need to do this."

Noah hesitated before responding. "I just wish you had discussed this decision with me. And I wish that I could come with you." He sighed. "But my work would never allow it."

"I know," Hannah replied. She nodded her head as she considered what to say next.

"I'm sorry this means we might be apart for a while." Hannah had been trying to stay strong but could no longer hold back her tears. In a few quick steps, Noah was by her side, and he pulled her into his chest.

"We will be okay. Everything is going to be okay," he whispered as he held her.

She wanted to believe his words. She wanted to believe that the distance between them would not make a difference, and that they were strong enough to survive being apart. She wanted to believe that she was strong enough to survive a summer living in Hope and her mother's illness. Only time would tell whether Noah or the unease growing inside of her was correct.

3

JUNE 1995

Hannah finally opened the door and took a step out of the car. Julie stood up. She began waving, and a smile lit up her face as she walked towards the car.

"Welcome home, honey. You know you didn't need to do this, but I'm glad you're here."

The sincerity in Julie's voice gave Hannah comfort that she had been correct in coming. She smiled back at her mom and tried to sound clever. "Pfft. This is the longest vacation I have had in ten years."

They both had a short laugh and began to unpack the car. Hannah tried to shoo her mother away from carrying anything heavy, but Julie insisted. They each carried two suitcases as they walked into the house. Hannah was again struck by how things were still just as she had left them. The foyer had the same blue and white striped wallpaper overlayed with tiny pink bows in circle patterns. The same wooden bench and coat hanger greeted her as she came through the door. Something in the living room caught Hannah's eye, however. It was certainly something that had not been there before. Where their couch used to be, she saw a hospital bed.

Hannah turned towards the living room and motioned at the bed. "Are you sleeping in the living room?" She tried to sound calm, but she was panicking. Maybe her mother was already feeling worse than she had let on.

Julie tried to reassure her, but the words fell flat on Hannah's ears. Her mother explained that as of now, she could still walk up the stairs to her bedroom on the second floor, but soon that would become difficult. She wanted to be prepared. Although Hannah had long been aware of her mother's diagnosis, seeing a hospital bed in the living room suddenly made the situation all the more real. Hannah's thoughts raced, and she wasn't sure which emotion to process first. She hadn't even had time to adjust to being back in Hope, and now she was also confronted with the hard reality of her mother's illness. It hit her like a slap across her face. Hannah asked for a few minutes to get packed and settled upstairs. She needed time to calm her nerves and catch her breath. Julie obliged and offered to make a late lunch.

"Thanks Mom. I just need a few minutes. And I need to call Noah and let him know I arrived," Hannah responded, trying to sound reassuring.

As Hannah carried her bags up the stairs, she realized she needed to let go of the notions she had about how this summer would go. The feeling of unease grew inside her again. With each step up the stairs, the tension inside of her increased. It was as if her body was warning her that nothing good was going to happen here. Her mind and heart, however, fought against the rest of her body's protests. She needed to be there for Julie. She needed to be strong for Julie. She couldn't let herself break down every time things got hard. The sight of a bed could not undo her. She dialed Noah's number, and thankfully he picked up. She updated him on her drive in and how her mother was doing. They parted with the promise to call every night.

Delaying her inevitable walk back downstairs, Hannah took her time unpacking. Even though she hadn't been home in over a decade, her room was so familiar. There was a new comforter and sheets on her bed, but the rest of the room had remained largely untouched. Her walls were still adorned with faded posters of Paul McCartney and Rick Springfield. She had taken her radio with her when she left, and its spot on her dresser was still vacant. There were old trophies, art projects, and other remnants of her childhood arranged from wall to wall. Sitting in her room, in her mother's house, it was as if no time had passed since she had last been there. The scratches and scuffs were still on the back of her door from the time her friend Katie tripped into her bookcase, causing it to fall and hit the door. The only line her father had drawn on the door frame to mark how tall she had grown was still there. She traced it with her fingers. So much in her room seemed familiar, yet it also felt like it all belonged to someone else.

Growing up, she had always felt separate from her hometown. Hope was a small town where everyone knew everything about each other. Sometimes this was an asset, especially when people came together to help a neighbor or lend support during hard times. In her experience, however, it often had the effect of being a negative. Her father was born and raised in Hope, but her mother was not. This had been the original problem with her family in the eyes of their neighbors.

Hannah had never really tried to fit in, which was why she received nothing but judgment and suspicion from the townspeople. There was no room for even a degree of difference between how you were expected to behave, what you believed or became, and what was acceptable in Hope. Perhaps things would have been different if her father were still alive, if she had cared more about what they all thought and tried to change, but since she was little, the only thing she had cared about was leaving.

Hannah had wanted to go away to college, to travel, and to live in a big city. She never considered getting married young and having children right away. After her father passed, his parents had to close their family business, as there was no one to pass it on to in their older age. That was how most of her friends had built lives for themselves in Hope—by taking over the family business—but for her that was not an option. Every time she or her mother went somewhere in town, it was as if the winds would change. A cool breeze of sideways glances and whispered words would blow their way. She often felt like she was walking into a room where everyone had been talking about her. It baffled her that her mother had stayed all these years and didn't want to leave even now.

If Hannah was going to stay this time, she would need to give her room a good decluttering. There were a few boxes sitting in the corner of the room, which she assumed Julie had left her. The posters were the first to go, followed by all the other remnants of her teenage life that served no purpose to her now. By the time she finished, she had carefully packed away all the evidence that this room had last belonged to a teenage girl in 1981. After placing the lid on the last box and sliding it into the back of her closet, she took a deep breath. She had successfully overcome her first obstacle of being back. For just a moment, she felt like maybe she could leave the past packed away with the posters in her closet. As Hannah was shutting the closet door, she heard Julie call out that lunch was ready. Hearing her mother's voice calling from downstairs pulled her past right back into the present.

Hannah and Julie spent lunch catching up on all the details of Hannah's move home. She recounted Noah's support and how he had helped her prepare for her move so quickly. They had decided to put their wedding plans on hold for now, but both made promises to move forward with things once the summer was over.

"Hannah, I'm so sorry that you have to go through all this." Julie started to tear up.

"Mom, please, I already told you I want to be here." She placed her hand over Julie's. They sat in silence for a few moments before Hannah got up to take the dishes to the kitchen. The doorbell rang, and it was a welcome interruption.

Hannah hurried from the kitchen to answer the door. There were only two people in this town that ever came over for a visit to Julie's house. One was whoever the priest was at the time, and the second was Jane Russell. Jane and Julie had been best friends for as long as Hannah could remember. Jane's husband had left her to start a family with a woman in the next town over. As a divorced woman who never remarried or had children, she didn't fit in here either. She had helped raise Hannah. Jane was there for every holiday, every school concert, and every time she or Julie needed anything. Hannah had missed her so much over the years. One of the bright spots in her childhood memories was opening the front door to see Jane warmly smiling back at her. Jane was always kind and patient, and most importantly, the most fun adult she had known as a child. Sure enough, this time was no different. When Hannah swung open the front door, she was greeted by Jane's smile and squeal of joy as she threw her arms around Hannah.

"Welcome home love! We have missed you so much!" Jane exclaimed.

Hannah hugged her in return.

"I have missed you as well."

4

After he finished up the yard work outside the church, Patrick went in and showered. He made himself an early dinner and then set about cleaning the dishes. As he washed the last dish, he pondered what he should do next. Admittedly, there wasn't much to do in Hope, and he rarely left the rectory for anything personal. But there was something about the warm summer air this Friday that caught his attention. It seemed to buzz with possibility, compelling him to want to do more than simply read on the front porch.

He pondered his options. The nearest theater was a thirty-minute drive away. It was early enough for him to get a good seat. He grabbed the newspaper and looked at what was playing, but nothing caught his eye. He wished he had someone to ask to go with him, but he had been in Hope for almost eight months and hadn't managed to make any friends yet. Two older ladies from church would invite him over for Sunday lunch after Mass, and that was the extent of his social calendar. The people his age in town mostly had children and their own set group of friends. They didn't seem too interested in hanging out with their priest. If he had been home in New York City, he would have had things to do, friends to call on. Whenever he felt a longing for the city, he tried to remind himself why he had asked to be sent to somewhere far from it. Even though he felt a longing for his childhood home from time to time, it was no longer a good place for him to be.

He rarely regretted his decision to leave, but on this beautiful summer night, he yearned for conversation and camaraderie. He might not have any friends here, but that wasn't going to stop him from doing something by himself. He settled on walking into town and getting a drink at the town bar.

***

Hannah enjoyed catching up with Julie and Jane as they cleaned up after dinner. Overall, her first day back was going as well as she could have hoped for. Being with her mother and Jane, in the safety of their small house, transported Hannah back to the good times of her childhood.

Julie and Jane went out to enjoy the cool evening air and relax on the back porch, so Hannah decided to take inventory of the kitchen. When they were making dinner, she had noticed that the pantry and fridge were both mostly empty. If she was going to make food for Julie, she would need to go into town and buy some groceries. She contemplated what recipes might be best and then made a list of the items she needed. By the time she had finished, the sun was already starting to set. Hannah grabbed her purse and headed for the backyard to let her mother and Julie know she was leaving. As she walked onto the back patio, she saw that Julie had dozed off in her lounge chair. Jane assured Hannah that she would help her mother to bed and ushered Hannah to carry on.

***

Hannah drove down the street headed back towards Holy Trinity. She knew that the man who had been doing yard work at the church earlier would surely not still be working at this late hour, but she couldn't help but look for him. Her curiosity about the handsome stranger had been growing since she saw him. Thoughts of him were a welcome distraction from everything else going on around her. As expected, he was not there, and she made the right turn onto Route 36 to head into town. A few blocks later, she was pulling into a parking space in front of The General Store. It was in fact the only grocery or pharmacy in town, but still, she had always thought they could have tried harder with the name. As she grabbed her purse and opened the car door, she noticed a commotion outside the building next to the grocery store. There were several people carrying on, laughing and smoking in front of CC's Tap—the one bar in town.

"Of course," she muttered to herself.

It was naturally crowded since it was a Saturday night, and the sound of music and voices flowed out from the bar onto the street. On the weekends growing up, she and Katie would ride their bikes down this street and watch the ridiculous adults stumbling home from an afternoon or early evening of drinking. They had both vowed if they were ever to stumble out of a bar someday, it would be in a much better place than downtown Hope.

Hannah kept her head down as she walked into the store. She wasn't ready to run into any old acquaintances. Seeing her mother in her current condition was enough stress for one day. She quickly gathered the items on her list. It was lucky nothing had been rearranged in the store since she had last shopped there, so it didn't take her long. When she went to check out, she was thankful that the clerk was a high school girl she did not recognize and who did not recognize her.

Grateful that her trip had been uneventful, Hannah left the store and headed back to the car carrying her two bags of groceries. When she reached the back of the car, she set down the bags and began looking in her purse to find the keys. She should have known better than not to have her keys out and ready. She would have if she was in the city. As she was searching her purse, Hannah didn't notice someone quietly approaching her.

When she finally went to put the key in the trunk, she was caught completely off guard. Before she could react, she felt someone grabbing her wrist and spinning her around. In the skirmish, she kicked over one of the grocery bags, scattering her purchases all over the pavement. At first, she was too stunned to process what was happening. Now that she was face-to-face with the person who had grabbed her, she knew exactly who he was. The sight of him made her sick. Her stomach turned.

"Well, look who decided to show her face again. I heard your mom was sick, but I didn't think you would have the nerve," he growled.

He grabbed her other wrist and pushed both her hands onto the top of the trunk, pinning her in place. Startled, Hannah tried to gather the courage to fight back or at least scream for help, but he exhaled, and the smell of liquor and cigarettes on his breath made her stomach turn again. She had to resist the urge to vomit. He moved his face back ever so slightly, and she finally centered herself enough to do something.

"Colton, let go of me. You're drunk!" she yelled through clenched teeth.

"I saw you go into the store. I was waiting for you to come out," he whispered into her ear, moving his face close again. Close enough for his lips to brush her ear.

She recoiled back from him and tried to pull away, but he held on tight and slammed her hands back into the car. She let out a pained cry. Hannah's mind was racing. Where were all the people who had been outside the bar minutes ago? Why was no one helping her?

"Go ahead and scream. No one believed you then. No one will believe you now." His voice dripped with disdain.

He was still close enough that she could feel the warmth of his skin. The smell of liquor on his breath stung her eyes and throat. She closed her eyes and tried to pull as far back from him as she could. All she could do was pray someone would come to her aid.

5

Patrick was half a block from CC's when he saw a slight commotion in the street. He quickened his pace to see what was happening. Nothing of interest ever happened in this town, so it was unexpected to see any kind of scuffle happening. From where he was on the other side of the street, a small group of men was blocking his view of what was occurring. One of the men leaned over slightly to snuff out his cigarette. That gave Patrick just a second to see what was happening behind the ring of onlookers. He saw Colton Hayes pinning a woman to the back of a car. At first, he thought it must be a joke. However, right before his view of them was blocked again, he caught a glimpse of her face. She was terrified. Her eyes were closed tight, and she was recoiling from Colton as he held her hands pressed to the trunk, his body against hers. Patrick quickened his pace and moved across the street towards the woman. He was at Colton's back in only a few seconds.

A shudder went through Hannah's body as she braced for whatever Colton planned to do to her next. Then, unexpectedly, she felt Colton's grip suddenly loosen, and she heard a new voice.

"COLTON, WHAT ARE YOU DOING? LET HER GO!" a man's voice ordered assertively.

She opened her eyes and tried to take a deep breath now that she didn't feel Colton's breath on her face anymore.

"Oh, just catching up with an old friend," Colton said, laughing. He stumbled a step away from her, finally releasing her wrists.

Free of his grasp, Hannah suddenly felt lightheaded. The sound of his laughter rang in her ears. She slumped down against the car. The man who had told Colton to let her go pushed past him and was now kneeling beside her. He gathered her in his arms, holding her up. She looked up at his face. It was the man she had seen in the church yard earlier. Half stunned by him, half stunned by what had just happened, she was unable to speak. She wanted to thank him, but all she could do was cry.

"Miss, are you okay? Are you hurt?" he asked reassuringly.

She could feel him checking her hands and wrists.

"You're developing bruises on both your wrists. Do you want me to call the police? Miss, do you want me to call for help?" He was almost shaking her, trying to get some response as she sat motionless, still in a complete fog.

Hannah could still hear Colton laughing with his friends and heckling in the distance. "She isn't hurt, we were just catching up." She could hear the group of men she had seen outside the bar join in tauntingly, "Yeah, she's fine; just can't handle her own grocery bags."

"Are you okay?" the kind stranger asked again. "Do you want me to call for help?" His voice was growing more concerned.

Hannah knew that would only make things worse for her. She shook her head no. He insisted again, "Are you sure?"

"Please do not call the police," she whispered.

He nodded, then got up to confront Colton and his friends. "Go home Colton! You're drunk. She doesn't want me to call the police, but if you don't leave right now, I will!"

At the threat of involving the police, Colton and his friends finally stumbled off.

"Okay, okay. We are going." They were still laughing and carrying on as they walked away.

Once Colton and the group had walked far enough away, the man was back by Hannah's side. He gathered the dropped groceries, placing all the items back into the bag. Hannah couldn't move herself off the ground next to the trunk of her car. She could barely process what had just happened. Had Colton just attacked her again?

When she tried to get up, she found that she was still too unsteady on her feet. Her legs would not hold her weight. She had to clumsily sit back down on the ground. The man offered to walk her across the street and into the park to make sure she was okay. She agreed, and after a few minutes, she had calmed herself enough to walk. He helped her slowly move out of the street. They walked past the bushes that lined the sidewalk. After a few more steps, the man sat her down against a tree just beyond the bushes. Hannah was grateful for the privacy. Even though they weren't completely out of sight, they were partially hidden from the prying eyes on Main Street.

Hannah was shaken, and her head was spinning. For several seconds, she tried to say something, but nothing would come out of her mouth. It was as if her mind had been wiped clean. She could do nothing but shake and cry. The man held her close in his arms. He was whispering words of reassurance and slowly rubbing her back.

"It's okay."

"You're safe now."

"Just breathe."

She was extremely grateful, but it took her a while to say anything in response.

"Thank you so much for helping me."

He began speaking again, and she wasn't sure if he was asking her a question or simply thinking out loud.

"Are you sure you're okay? I don't feel right not calling the police. I don't understand why no one else stopped him?"

Hannah wanted to answer him because she did KNOW why no one else had helped her. Other questions were of more interest to her, however. She wanted to know who this man was and why he had helped her.

"What is your name?" she quietly asked.

"Patrick," he responded.

"Why did you stop to help me?"

"How could I not?" His voice was soft and reassuring. Yet, he seemed surprised that she would question his motives for stepping in.

He put his hand under her chin and brought her face up to meet her eyes. Her whole face was wet with tears and streaks of mascara. He used the bottom of his shirt to wipe under her eyes. It was the first time since he had seen her from across the street that he was able to really see her face. In this town, a new face stood out. Hers even more so. She had shoulder-length brown hair that collected in waves around her face. He could see the bright blue of her eyes and the gentle curve of her lips. She was exceptionally beautiful, even red-faced with tear-stained cheeks.

Patrick knew he should have told her the truth. His name wasn't just Patrick. If he had been honest with her, he would have said his name was Father Patrick. Why had he omitted that part? He had been introducing himself that way for so many years now. Why was this different? When he had seen Colton pressed against her, trapping her against her car, instinct had taken over for the first time in a very long time. He didn't feel like "a priest" who was expected to behave in a certain way; he just felt like a regular man. It had been so long since he felt that way, without the barrier of his priesthood inhibiting him. Now that he was holding her in his arms, looking into her soft, misty eyes, he wasn't ready to give up that feeling.

They stared at each other for several moments, taking each other and the situation in. Hannah could now see that he was even better-looking than she had been able to make out through the windshield of her car. His face was accented by reddish-brown stubble, highlighting every handsome curve. He had gentle eyes that looked at her with so much concern she thought her heart might burst. She wished her momentary wonder at him could last longer, but it quickly dissipated as she remembered what had just happened. She couldn't stop the tears from falling again.

Patrick wanted to ask for her name, but as he was about to speak, she laid her head on his chest. He decided it was better to just hold her and to let her cry for as long as she needed to. He occasionally wiped her tears away and stroked her back. When she finally started to compose herself again, she pulled back and silently stared at him.

Hannah still had no idea who Patrick was. She knew every person that lived in this tiny town, but she couldn't place his face. He clearly had no idea who she was. He would never have helped her if he did. As she looked into his eyes, she felt something entirely unexpected given the situation.

She felt safe.

The secret of what happened to her had eaten away at her every day of the last fourteen years. It had pushed her to leave this place and never return. She never told her mother or Jane. She never told her fiancé or her best friend. She wasn't sure why she suddenly felt that she wanted to tell a practical stranger; why she wanted to tell Patrick. They didn't know each other at all, but he had just seen what Colton was capable of. He had seen Colton for the monster that he could be.

Hannah wanted to tell Patrick the story. Over the years, she had come close to telling someone so many times: her best friend in college after a night of drinking, Noah after she realized she was falling in love, her mother the night after the summer festival. It had never felt right though. Something inside her always stopped her. The shame, the trauma—she wasn't ever quite sure what—but the words always died on her tongue before she could get them out.

Tonight was different, sitting under the stars with this kind stranger. Her wrists were still aching from where Colton's hands had pushed her against her car, but the secret inside of her was hurting her more. It was threatening to explode through her skin if she didn't let it out.

Patrick looked at her intently, sensing from her expression and the look in her eyes that she had something serious to say.

"Can I tell you something about what just happened?" she asked cautiously.

"I was hoping you would," he replied immediately.

She thought it would be hard to recount the details, as she had never spoken the words out loud. But somehow, with this stranger, they flowed out of her as easily as any words ever had.

"The summer after my senior year of high school, something happened. I have never told anyone...but I think it might explain what you walked into tonight." He nodded and listened.

The words came out in waves as Hannah explained what Colton had done to her at a party in their senior year. Then what Colton's now-wife Jackie had done to make it so much worse the next day. Hannah had kept her secret for so long that she had deluded herself into believing she had moved past it; that she didn't need to tell anyone the truth. It was becoming clear to her as she spoke that that wasn't the case at all. With each word that left her mouth, the weight of the secret she had kept for so long began to lift from her. The heaviness that had been bearing down on her for the last fourteen years slowly started to disappear. By the time Hannah had finished speaking, she felt as if she was floating. The only thing keeping her tethered to the earth was Patrick's gaze, his hand on top of hers.

Patrick sat in silence for a few moments, considering everything she had just told him. He was heartbroken for this beautiful girl he just met. She had kept a terrible secret for too long. She had let everyone blame her for a situation in which she was in fact the victim. He wanted justice for what she had gone through then and justice for what she had gone through just a few minutes ago.

"With what you have just told me and what I witnessed tonight, I would go with you to the police and corroborate your story. I heard what Colton said right before I pulled him off you. I have been in this town for several months. I knew that it wasn't perfect, but I never guessed... Jackie, Colton... I'm so sorry." Patrick's voice shook as he spoke.

He could have never imagined that this sleepy town could hold such a dark secret. The Hayes didn't seem like the perfect family, but Jackie regularly helped him at the church. Their kids went to Sunday school. They were two of the most established members of the town. Colton had always seemed rough around the edges and maybe a little quick to anger, but nothing like what Patrick had seen him do tonight. His mind spun at everything he hadn't picked up on about his parishioners. Had he been engaged enough? Had he been paying attention?

6

Hannah felt exhausted but also relieved. Someone finally knew the truth. She barely knew his name, but he now knew the most hidden part of her. The comfort she felt from his willingness to believe her was overwhelming. It gave her hope that perhaps one day, she would have the courage to tell her mother and to set the record straight with everyone else as well. But tonight was not the time for that. She had only just begun to adjust to the feeling of one person knowing the truth and certainly couldn't handle anyone else knowing just yet.

"Thank you so much for saving me, for listening to me, and for believing me." She looked up at him with gratitude.

"Of course," he replied.

"You can't tell anyone else, though. I don't want anyone else to know." Her voice was firm and resolute.

Patrick wanted to argue, but it was her decision, and he wanted to respect it.

"I understand, but if you ever change your mind, I'm here for you." He tried his best to give her a reassuring smile.

The air had felt dense before. It had been suffocating her as she tried to catch her breath. Now it seemed light and filled with anticipation. She couldn't describe it, but there definitely was something happening between her and this man—Patrick. The fear and shock Hannah had been experiencing only a few minutes ago was transforming into new emotions. Now she felt nervous, a sense of anticipation, and thankful that what had happened led her to meet this man.

Patrick's guilt over concealing the truth about himself was growing. Especially considering she had just been so vulnerable with him. But every time he tried to start, the words stopped short. He was frozen in the moment, in awe of her beauty and sincerity. When they went their separate ways, he would be Father Patrick again. He would no longer be Patrick the man who rescued her, or the man she shared the most secret part of herself with. Patrick tried to center himself, realizing that he was dangerously close to crossing a line. But he wanted to stay in this moment for as long as he could. He wanted to know more than just her worst secret. He wanted to know what made her happy, what made her laugh. For now, he would have to settle for knowing her name.

"You still haven't told me your name," he whispered.

Hannah heard his question. At first, she thought she must have mentioned it as she recounted the events from her past. After scanning her memories, she realized that somehow, she had conveniently left her name out of the story. She didn't know what to do. She wanted him to know her, but she was also becoming more aware that it wasn't the only thing she wanted from him. None of it made any sense.

The emotions were all mixed up inside of her. She had the urge to cry for joy about meeting him, but she also wanted to cry in anguish about what had just happened. She wasn't sure which sensation would win out. Her eyes locked onto Patrick's hand on top of hers. She followed his hand to the bend of his elbow, up the rest of his arm, past his shoulder, and finally settled her eyes on his face. It was kind yet strong, most assuredly the most handsome face she had ever seen.

She should have just given him her name, but her eyes had moved on to his lips, and a different thought was taking over her mind. As soon as she realized what she had been thinking, a guilty panic overtook her. What was she thinking? Kissing a stranger? She was engaged to Noah. A hot wave of embarrassment swept across her body.

She needed to leave before she did something she would regret.

She was glad she hadn't given him her name. She pulled back and hurried to her feet. In her haste to get up, she lost her balance. Patrick, who had been startled by her quick, unexpected movements, also stumbled as he caught her. She ended up in his arms, her face buried in his chest. When she looked up, she saw him gazing down at her. Their faces were practically touching, their lips only a breath apart. Both of them knew they should pull away, but for a few seconds, neither moved.

Hannah knew it wasn't right to relish how her skin tingled in all the areas he was touching her. It wasn't right for her to want the small distance separating their lips to disappear. She could feel his breath on her face, and it was almost enough for her to forget herself and lean in and kiss him.

Patrick hadn't been this close to a woman in years. It had been forever since he had experienced the wave of sensations that were radiating through his body at this moment. He could feel the rise and fall of her chest against his, and it was enough to undo him. As he looked down, all he could see were her lips. They were so close to his. With only the smallest movement, his lips would be touching hers. Of course it would be wrong, but he couldn't overcome the sense that he didn't care; that it would be worth the consequences.

As quickly as they had fallen into each other, however, they both came to their senses and pulled away. Patrick straightened out his shirt, while Hannah tucked her hair behind her ears, trying to look more presentable. Neither spoke at first, both embarrassed by the thoughts they had been having.

Hannah spoke first. "Thank you for everything tonight," she said quickly. "Please don't tell anyone what I told you… I…I need to go."

Patrick was still caught off guard by what had just happened. He was ashamed of the desires and longings that still filled his head. He wanted to protest her leaving, but fear that he might not be able to stop himself from acting impulsively held him back.

"Are you sure you're okay?" he called after her as she quickly sprinted to her car.

"Yes, thank you!" she called back, not even turning to face him while she responded. When she reached her car, she rushed to throw the groceries that were still sitting on the street into her trunk.

"Wait, you never told me your name!" Patrick called out to her. With all that had happened between them, he still didn't know the most basic detail about her.

Hannah heard him but didn't stop or respond. She got in her car and pulled out to head back home. If he didn't know who she was, maybe they would never see each other again. Maybe she could forget what had just happened. But as she drove the few blocks back to her mother's house, she knew she was lying to herself. She would never be able to forget. All she could think about was how much she still wanted to kiss him.

Patrick gathered himself and started his walk back to the rectory. In all his years at the seminary and as a priest, he had never felt so tempted. He had never had any trouble keeping his vows. Now, not only had he lied to her about who he really was, he had almost kissed her. Even worse, he still wanted to kiss her. He thought about lying to himself. He could try to make himself believe that it was just a fleeting thought, not something that still had his body buzzing with sensations he didn't even recognize. He knew it wasn't possible, though. Not only did he want to kiss her, but he also wanted to do so much more. He wasn't sure what it was about her that was affecting him so deeply. From the moment he caught a glimpse of her face, feelings had emerged from deep inside him. Feelings he had hidden away years ago when he decided to become a priest.

As he opened the front door of the rectory, he finally had to face reality. He was a priest, no matter what parts of him she had reignited. Nothing more could happen between them. He didn't know her name. He certainly couldn't ask around hoping someone had seen them together and knew who she was. For both their sakes, he had to hope and pray that no one had seen them together. He knew that if he saw her again, he would be in serious danger of losing himself again. There was only one thing he could do.

First thing in the morning, he would make up an excuse and ask to be transferred to a different parish as soon as possible.

***

When Hannah arrived back at her mother's, she unloaded her bags from the trunk and went inside. Her mind was still spinning from everything that had happened since she had crossed into the city limits of Hope. She saw her mother asleep on the bed in the living room. Julie looked so peaceful. An outside observer would not have been able to guess that she was sick. Her long hair, still thick and curly, cascaded down her shoulders. She had avoided the sun most of her life, and it had paid off. She looked ten years younger than her age. Julie really was a beautiful woman, and her kindness only made her more so.

After she put away the groceries, Hannah headed upstairs, stopping on her way to kiss her mother's forehead and whisper, "Goodnight."

She was exhausted from the day. Her interaction with Colton had left her uneasy. But she also felt drained from sharing her truth with Patrick. That combined with her conflicting feelings towards him was more than she could process tonight. She should have showered and washed away all traces of Colton's hands on her, but she was tired. The other thought she couldn't shake from her mind was that Patrick had also touched her. She didn't want to erase his touch from her body. The places he had held her, where she had felt his breath on her. The very thought of him made her body shudder. Showering would have to wait until tomorrow. She changed into pjs, flipped the lights off, and hopped into bed.

As tired as she was, Hannah had trouble falling asleep. For a long while, she lay staring at the ceiling, replaying the events of the evening in her mind. Seeing Colton had been worse than she anticipated. Simply being in the same room with him would have been challenging. She could never have imagined he would put his hands on her again. She should have been a mess, but by some miracle, that wasn't the case. Her thoughts about the man who saved her overwhelmed her mind. They overshadowed any emotions she had about Colton. All she could think about was the feeling of Patrick holding her. After the day she'd had, a smile was the last thing that should have been on her face. Somehow, she dozed off with one anyway.

7

"Hannah, breakfast is ready!" Julie called from downstairs.

Rolling over, Hannah glanced at her alarm clock. Nine a.m. She hadn't slept so late in forever. She had hoped sleep would help to clear her mind from last night, but unfortunately, both Colton and Patrick were in the front of her mind. She slipped into a pair of slippers and plopped down the stairs. Her mother had made a full breakfast for her—pancakes, eggs, and bacon.

"Mom, I'm supposed to be taking care of you!" she teased.

"I plan on living my life as normally as possible for as long as I can. Right now, I feel fine. I don't need you to take care of me. I need to take care of my daughter. My daughter who is home for the first time in years. Do you know how long I have wished for this day, the day I would hear your footsteps coming down the stairs in the morning?" Julie wiped away the tear that had formed in the corner of her eye.

Hannah wasn't sure how to respond. After last night, it was obvious that she had made the right choice in not coming back sooner, but seeing the joy on her mother's face right now still filled her with guilt.

"I know. I'm sorry it took so long. We have all summer to make up for it." She tried to sound reassuring as she walked over and hugged Julie. Could one summer make up for fourteen years away? Of course, she still saw her mother a couple of times a year, but Julie always came to her. It wasn't the same, she supposed, as having your child back in your home. Desperate to change the subject, she asked Julie what she had planned for the day.

Julie's eyes dropped to the floor. "I meant to mention it yesterday, but then I fell asleep. I invited Father Murphy over so that you both could meet." She hesitated as she spoke, assuming Hannah would be displeased with the idea.

As quickly as the guilt had come over Hannah, her emotions switched to that of an annoyed teenager. "Seriously Mom, I haven't even been back for one full day yet!" she responded with exacerbation.

"Well, there is something I want to talk to the both of you about, and I think this is the best way to do it. I think you will like Father Murphy." Her mother gave her a guarded smile.

Hannah wasn't sure why she felt so irritated at the notion of having to have lunch with their priest. Maybe it was that she'd hoped to simply spend today adjusting to being home with Julie. Maybe it was the thought of having to sit across the table from a priest for an entire meal, knowing how she, an engaged woman, had almost passionately kissed a stranger in the moonlight last night. Perhaps that's what was making her more uncomfortable about her behavior than she already was. However, there wasn't much point debating it in her mind. Just like all those times growing up, Hannah had no say in this matter. Father Murphy would be there in a few hours, whether she liked it or not.

Over the years, Julie had frequently invited the different priests from Holy Trinity over for dinners or lunches. The meals consisted of Hannah getting hour-long lectures on "Kids Today" or historical lessons about life before the town had running water. Hope was a small town. Holy Trinity was a tiny parish. They never had young or dynamic pastors. Father Carter, Father Boyle, and Father Randolph had all been over seventy-five when they started there and had gone into retirement soon after. Hannah had always thought they already seemed to have a foot into their retirement while they were still working in Hope.

Hannah didn't want an argument on her first full day home, so she acquiesced. "Ugh. It doesn't sound like you have left me a choice in the matter then. Can't wait." She tried to end with a positive tone in her voice, but she was sure her mother saw through it.

"Great. He will be here at noon." Julie smiled, satisfied that she had gotten the last word. Although she didn't want to fight with Hannah, the familiarity of a mother-daughter disagreement gave her comfort. The house had been quiet for too long.

Julie had worked as the parish secretary for the last thirty years. Besides having Hannah, it was what gave her the most joy in life. When Julie had found out that the previous pastor, Father Randolph, was retiring, she was sad at first. She had enjoyed working for him. He had always been a kind man and easy to get along with. Eventually, when she heard who was replacing him, her sadness changed to optimism. Hope had always had older priests. They always had trouble engaging younger members of the church. The new priest was supposedly younger than the previous three. Julie remembered chuckling to herself, thinking that probably meant the new priest was sixty-five instead of seventy-five.

Hannah had no interest in making forced conversation with her mother's new boss, but she decided not to waste any more thought on it. She headed upstairs to shower and get dressed. Her mom was already cooking by the time Hannah came back downstairs. She set the table and tidied the kitchen as she waited for Father Murphy's grand entrance. As she worked, she tried to remain present in the moment. She tried to think about Noah, their wedding, the work she was missing, anything besides her mysterious hero from last night. It was harder to do than it should have been. Her thoughts kept drifting to how close she had been to Patrick, to how much closer she still wanted to be. It was better she never saw him again, but somehow, she knew their paths would eventually cross again. After all, Hope was a VERY small town.

8

When the doorbell rang a few minutes later, Julie called to Hannah, "Can you please get that dear?"

Hannah walked to the front door, pausing for a few moments to put a smile on her face before she opened it. When she had the door halfway open, she caught a glimpse of the man standing on the other side. As quickly as she'd opened it, she abruptly slammed the door shut again. Hannah's heart was pounding, and her mind was racing. Julie had heard the door close and emerged from the kitchen, wiping her hands on her apron.

Puzzled, she asked Hannah, "Why would you slam the door on him?"

Hannah tried to speak, but her mind was blank. She didn't know how to process what she thought she had just seen.

"If you aren't going to let him in, please move so I can. You're being rude," Julie demanded.

She walked in front of Hannah and re-opened the door. Hannah was still too stunned to say anything. Standing on the front stoop was Father Murphy, dressed in black slacks and a black button-down short-sleeved shirt with a white collar. Julie welcomed him in, remarking on how red his cheeks were as she ushered him in.

"Welcome Father Murphy. Please come in. Come in!" Julie shut the door behind him.

Hannah stared at him. He looked uncomfortable. His cheeks were indeed a bright shade of red, and he was fumbling with the bouquet of flowers he had brought for Mrs. Marshall.

"I brought these for you. Thank you for having me." Father Murphy's voice cracked as he spoke.

"You didn't have to, but thank you." Julie took a step to the side so that he could see Hannah. She put her hand on Hannah's back and nudged her forward.

"I would like to introduce you to my daughter, Hannah."

Father Murphy reached his hand out slowly, and Hannah eventually stretched hers out as well. Their hands met briefly before they quickly moved away from each other.

"Nice to meet you, Hannah." He tried to sound as normal as possible, but the words caught in his throat.

"You as well," Hannah replied.

"Would you look at your cheeks, Father!" Julie exclaimed. "It must be hot out today. They are completely flushed. Let me get you something to drink. Hannah, please show Father Murphy the living room." Julie pointed towards the living room, then left for the kitchen.

Hannah stood still in the foyer of her mother's house, staring at the man who had come for lunch. She had expected an elderly priest, but that was not who was standing in front of her now. Her head was spinning, and she wasn't sure if she had taken a breath since she first saw him through the crack in the door. Although he looked a little different in the daylight dressed in black, she recognized him instantly. It was as if from their one interaction, he was imprinted on her forever. Neither moved nor spoke. Silence lingered in the air between them.

Father Murphy dropped his eyes to the ground and fidgeted with his belt. He tried to take a few deep breaths and lessen the redness that still flushed his cheeks. Hannah could not take her eyes off him. She still wasn't sure how this could really be happening.

Finally, she broke the silence. "FATHER Patrick, would you like to have a seat in the living room?"

He nodded and followed her into the next room.

Once they had both taken a seat, Patrick finally worked up the nerve to try and explain. "About last night... I'm so sorry, I should have said..."

Hannah cut him off. "What you should have said is that you

were a priest, before you held me, before I spilled my guts to you…before we almost kissed?!" she hissed at him. The disbelief inside of her was transforming into anger and disappointment.

This town really was trying to crush her. She had come a breath away from cheating on her fiancé. She had felt a deep connection to a total stranger, and he hadn't been honest about who he was. She felt like a fool for feeling so seen by him. She knew nothing about him.

He finally responded so quietly that Hannah could barely hear him.

"I'm so sorry." Before he could say anything more, Julie swooped into the room with a pitcher of lemonade.

After they drank their lemonade, Julie directed them into the dining room, where they shared a lunch of tuna salad on croissants. Hannah barely touched her food as Julie carried most of the conversation. She rambled on and on about all the things Father Murphy had done to liven up and reinvigorate their parish and connect with people.

Hannah remained silent, expect when she mumbled under her breath, "Oh, I'm sure he is great at connecting with people."

Julie was too far away to hear, but Patrick heard, and his cheeks went red again. Hannah was grateful that the conversation had been very surface level so far and that Julie had done most of the talking. Once Hannah could no longer fumble with her food, she offered to clear the table. She took her mother's plate first, then Patrick's. He tried to hand it to her, but in the process, their hands got tangled. For the briefest second, their skin was touching before she pulled the plate away. As betrayed as she felt, the same spark that had gone through her body when he touched her last night shot through her again. She knew it was wrong, and she was still angry, but at least she knew she hadn't imagined what she had felt last night.

Hannah left for the kitchen, and Patrick could finally breathe. Every moment since he had walked through Julie Marshall's front door had been suffocating. The very sight of Hannah was almost too much for him to bear. He knew not telling the truth about himself had been wrong. Yet now, face-to-face with Hannah, it was even more clear why he had done it. When their hands touched a few moments ago, the same wave of sensations had taken over. It was something he had never felt before; something he desperately wanted to feel again. He drifted, lost in his own thoughts, when the sound of Hannah entering with dessert jolted him back to reality.

She was carrying a pound cake and strawberries. She served her mother first and then Patrick. The minutes could not pass fast enough. They were both embarrassed for their own reasons. Yet even more worrisome was the fear they both had that Julie would notice there was something between them. They were afraid she would notice they were not strangers. Although they both tried to put all their focus on Julie, every so often they couldn't help but glance at each other. The pull was too strong to ignore completely.

As they finished their last bites of cake, Julie announced she had something to say to them both. Her voice wavered as she began. "I asked you here today, Father Murphy, for another reason besides our usual lunch get-together."

Patrick watched as Julie talked. Her tone of voice told him that something was wrong. Both Hannah and Patrick held their breath, unsure what Julie was going to say next.

"Father Murphy, I know you are aware that I've been sick. However, I didn't share with you how sick I actually am. I have cancer, and it's terminal. There is no treatment that would make much difference. So, I've decided to spend the time I have left at home. Hannah left her life behind to come stay with me during whatever time I have left."

Patrick was stunned. He had known something was going on with Julie, but he had no idea how serious her condition was. She had always been so kind to him; she most certainly did not deserve this fate. As he tried to process what she had just said, he couldn't help but notice Hannah. She was looking down and fiddling with her fork.

As saddened as he was to learn about Julie's condition, another thought streamed through his mind. When Julie introduced

Hannah earlier, it should have occurred to him then, but he had been too caught off guard to put it all together. Julie's daughter Hannah was…engaged. Julie and Jane had told him all about it. For days after the engagement, he had humored nonstop wedding talk from both of them. The realization almost pushed him over the edge. He would have to deal with that later, however. Right now, Julie needed him.

"Oh Julie, I'm so sorry…is there anything…I mean, I'm just so sorry to hear this," Patrick said tenderly. He was genuinely shocked that Julie had kept this from him. They worked together every day, and she had not let on how serious her condition was. She had been a mother-like figure to him from the first day he arrived in Hope. From helping him with all the ins and outs at Holy Trinity to inviting him to meals at her house with Jane, Patrick had come to depend on Julie. He felt awful for not having realized what she was going through.

"Please, do not be sad," Julie said. "That is not why I told you. Right now, I feel okay, and my daughter is finally home. I only told you now because I think it's better that I stop working at this point. I'm not sure when I will get worse. I don't want to have to step away suddenly. I was hoping you could do me a favor."

"You don't need to worry about work, but I can absolutely do you a favor. Anything you need," Patrick reassured her. He reached out to place his hand on Julie's arm.

Julie smiled warmly at him. "So I'm going to have to step back from my job at the church—"

"Of course, don't even think about that," Patrick responded before Julie could finish her sentence.

It was Julie that cut his off this time. "Yes Father Murphy, thank you, but that isn't the only thing I was going to ask. I would like Hannah to take over my position for as long as she's here."

Patrick and Hannah looked at each other, both surprised by Julie's request. Hannah couldn't help but feel blindsided by her mother's idea. She had come to spend time with Julie, and now her mother was essentially proposing to send her away for half the week.

If that wasn't bad enough, she couldn't imagine having to work that closely with Patrick—Father Murphy. She wasn't sure what to say.

Hannah finally spoke up. "But Mom, I came to stay with you and spend this time together. We don't know how much time you have left. I don't understand why you want to have me working away from home thirty hours a week? It makes no sense!" Her tone was exacerbated.

"Hannah, I can't have you fussing over me all day," Julie explained. "We will spend a lot of time together, but you're used to working and having your own interests. Right now, despite some fatigue, I still feel okay. I don't need to be watched all day," Julie insisted.

Hannah tried to interject. "I won't be 'watching over you,' but I can spend time with you."

Julie held up a hand, silencing her daughter. "Hannah, you don't have any friends in town. You have no one you can lean on here in Hope for support while we go through this. It's upsetting enough to me that you had to put your wedding on hold. I can't trap you in this house with me for an entire summer. And Father Murphy, I don't mean to come across as rude, but besides our church lady lunches, you never have plans outside of church business. I think you could both benefit from having someone your own age to talk to. Maybe the two of you will even become friends." Julie smiled, clearly pleased with her plan.

"We aren't five years old, Mom. I don't need you to arrange friends for me! And besides, I'm a college professor. What do I know about running a church office?" Hannah objected. She looked to Patrick for support. However, there was an expression on his face that she couldn't read.

After several seconds, he took a deep breath and turned to Julie. "If Hannah agrees, that would be fine with me."

At first Hannah was too surprised to respond. Had he just agreed to Julie's ridiculous plan? How could they work together after what had happened between them? Her exasperation was growing. She couldn't stop herself from raising her voice.

"What? You're okay with this proposal of hers? I was supposed to—"

Julie cut Hannah off mid-sentence. "Hannah, do not get upset with him. This was my idea. I know you don't like it, but it would mean a lot to me if I could hand my work over to you. I have spent the last thirty years taking care of Holy Trinity. I wouldn't entrust it to just anyone. And thank you, Father Murphy. It means the world to me that you would honor my request. I will bring Hannah with me on Monday, and we can start the transition."

Hannah sensed she was outnumbered in this argument. There was no way she could say no to a request that clearly meant so much to Julie. Monday she would go to Holy Trinity and begin working as the secretary. She wondered how long her mother had been concocting this plan and why she hadn't at least mentioned it to Hannah before this lunch. Perhaps because she knew Hannah would protest, just as she had.

Hannah sat listening but not comprehending as several minutes of conversation passed between Father Murphy and Julie. She remained silent, feeling like she was invisible to both of them. She could hear the words they were saying, but her mind was clouded by the thought of working so closely to Patrick every day. Finally, when they looked to her for input, all she could utter was a string of sures and okays. When the discussion wrapped up, Julie asked Hannah to show Father Murphy out.

Hannah led Patrick into the hallway. She opened the door. He paused to put his shoes on. She was upset about everything that had happened from the moment he had shown up on her mother's doorstep. She had told him her deepest secret—she had wanted to kiss him—and she was quite sure he had wanted to kiss her as well. Now she would be alone with him, and her conflicted feelings for him, four days a week. Her mother would be home by herself. As the church secretary, she would be forced to see and speak with so many people she had spent her adult life trying to avoid. She tried to come up with some clever dig to make him feel guilty for agreeing to Julie's proposal, but she settled on, "I guess I'll see you Monday."

Patrick hesitated before he replied. He knew he should just leave it alone, but he couldn't stop himself. "Hannah, you're engaged?"

The words barely made it out of his mouth. He wasn't sure if he was relieved or disappointed. He felt guilty about his dishonesty. However, what right did she have to be so angry at his omission when she had omitted something as well? The moment between them had been wrong on both their parts.

Hannah heard the hurt in his voice. She hadn't been fair to him earlier because she hadn't been honest either. Her omission seemed like the less significant one, but it was an omission nonetheless. She felt embarrassed and didn't look at him as she softly nodded her head once.

"Uh, I see. Um… I'm sorry I agreed with your mother. However, I promised her I would help with whatever she needed. I didn't know what she would ask. When I met you last night, I didn't know who you were, or that you were…engaged…" The last word lingered in the air between them before Patrick spoke again. "But I should have been honest with you about who I was."

The look of hurt on his face was almost more than Hannah could bear. She wanted to reach out to him. She wanted to ask him to forgive her and bury her head in his embrace. She also knew she wouldn't ever get to do that again. A priest and an engaged woman don't usually have happy endings.

"I think it's better if we don't talk about it anymore. Can we just forget last night ever happened?" She was sure tears were about to fall, so she turned her face away from him as she spoke.

There was no point in disagreeing. It was the only practical way of handling the situation. Patrick nodded in agreement.

"Yes, of course. Sensible plan." He turned and stepped through the door.

Hannah couldn't close the door behind him fast enough. She took a moment to gather herself before she went back into the dining room. When she did, Julie was sitting in the same spot at the table, looking quite content. *At least Mom is happy,* Hannah thought. It was one consolation in an otherwise untenable situation.

Julie had thought a lot about how to handle having Hannah come home. She had also thought a lot about stepping back from her position at the church. She had been in the role for so long that she felt a strong sense of ownership over it. She didn't want just anyone to take over her position. She knew Hannah would only be in Hope for a limited time, but it still seemed like a good idea. The support Hannah would receive from Father Patrick would surely help her through the difficult months ahead. Hannah was used to working and having her own life. As a university professor, she was certainly overqualified for the role of church secretary. Yet it would be better for her to have something to occupy her time instead of only sitting around the house as Julie slowly declined. Julie even imagined that Hannah could help modernize things at the church. That would make it easier for someone else to take over at the end of the summer. There hadn't been a fresh set of eyes on her files or processes since Julie started working there.

Even though she didn't want to admit it to herself, there was also one more petty reason she had wanted Hannah to take over. Julie was getting older, and there had been speculation in town about her retirement. Father Murphy had asked her about it when he arrived at Holy Trinity. Other members of the church had brought it up as well. One person always seemed to be the most interested in her plans, and that person's name was Jackie Hayes. Of course, the remarks she made were always couched as jokes or kind suggestions that Julie deserved a break after so many years of service. Julie didn't appreciate the comments, however.

Jackie was a girl Hannah had known from school. She had begun filling in for Julie on her days off and was always making herself available to help. Jackie had not shown much interest in Holy Trinity before Father Murphy took over in October the year before. Yet now she was a constant fixture around the church. Julie suspected Jackie's new enthusiasm was mainly due to their new pastor. Julie understood the appeal. Besides being easy on the eyes, Father

Murphy was kind and engaging. He had brought new life and energy to their aging parish. Julie knew Jackie would jump at the opportunity to take over the position as soon as she learned of Julie's condition. It was one of the reasons Julie had been so close-lipped about her illness.

Something about Jackie had never sat right with Julie. She could never shake the feeling that Jackie had been awful to Hannah in some way. Hannah never confirmed her suspicions, but she had remained cautious when it came to Jackie anyway. It made her nervous to hand a job so vital to the community over to a woman she didn't trust. Once Hannah had decided to come home, Julie realized she could deny Jackie by having Hannah take the position. The next few months would be difficult for Hannah, and Julie wanted her to have a friend to lean on. Noah was too far away to help her with her day-to-day, but Father Murphy was right here in Hope. He needed a friend as well.

At first, she had felt nervous about sharing her idea with Hannah. As the day of Hannah's arrival had approached, she decided she would ask her in front of Father Murphy. She wouldn't give Hannah the chance to say no. Today at lunch, her plan had gone exactly as she had hoped.

9

The walk back to the rectory was the longest two blocks Patrick had ever walked. He was still raw from the events last night. Now he had to contend with the fact that the mysterious woman he had wanted to kiss was going to be very close to him for the foreseeable future. He had been to Mrs. Marshall's house so many times. How had he not noticed Hannah in the pictures that were scattered around? The photo Julie had on her desk at work was from before Hannah's father passed. Hannah was only two years old in the picture, and there was no way he could have known what she looked like as an adult. He also hadn't noticed that she was wearing an engagement ring.

Mrs. Marshall was the most welcoming person he had met in Hope. She had helped him get settled with the church dynamics and everything else that she could. There was no way he could say no to her request, especially given the circumstances. He wondered why she hadn't mentioned any of this to him before. Why hadn't she given him any warning of the seriousness of her illness or her daughter returning? She had always been quiet about her personal life, but he was surprised that something so significant had not come up in one of their many conversations. Guilt, sadness, embarrassment, and a surprising feeling of jealousy filled him. He didn't know which emotion to address first.

He was obviously saddened to learn about the seriousness of Julie's illness, but he was also hurting from the realization that Hannah was ENGAGED. He had no right to feel betrayed, yet he couldn't shake the feeling. Hannah could never be his—he knew that. Didn't he? He would have to resolve to think of last night as nothing more than a dream he thought back on from time to time. He would have to find the will to let go of any romantic notions regarding Hannah. Since last night, he had been praying for forgiveness for his actions and clarity on his feelings.

He had been searching for a reason to explain why he was so profoundly affected by a woman he had just met. After learning of Julie's illness, the answers he was searching for seemed more within his reach. He knew that Julie and Hannah would need his support in the coming months. Maybe his and Hannah's connection wasn't meant to be romantic. Maybe it was meant to be something else entirely. He would have to try and convince his heart and body of that. Starting Monday, he would have to try and see her like any other parishioner that needed his help. She would have to become the woman who worked in the church office, not the beautiful woman he had held and almost kissed under the stars.

***

Hannah tried her best to forget what had happened the night before. She also wanted to erase the truth she had learned today from her memory. She needed to keep busy and spent the rest of her Saturday helping Julie. First, they cleaned up after lunch. Then they both spent some time reading and napping on the lounge chairs in the backyard. Hannah put together a quick dinner, and they ate early. They hadn't talked much since Father Murphy left. Hannah was lost in thought about Patrick and how she was going to handle being so near to him, and Julie didn't want to push her luck with Hannah. It had been years since they had spent more than a couple of days together. She knew Hannah was not happy with her proposal. She didn't want to push her away when she had just returned home.

The thought had occupied Julie's mind all afternoon. When Hannah was a child, Julie had never been fully honest with her about why things were the way they were for them in Hope. She had hoped Hannah would have an easier time fitting in than Julie herself had. Even after Hannah left, Julie had held out hope that someday, her heart would soften to this place. It never had, though. Many times over the years Hannah was away, Julie felt as though she had made the wrong decisions when it came to being upfront with her daughter. She should have pushed her more about what happened right before Hannah left fourteen years ago, and she should have been more forthcoming with her story as well. Maybe Hannah's perspective would change if she understood the past. Julie didn't want the cloud of all the things she had never said hanging over them for whatever time she had left. She came up with her second plan of the day. She would finally tell Hannah their family story.

Hannah had just finished washing the dinner dishes when Julie came into the kitchen asking for help in the basement. She said she wanted help sorting boxes and gathering items to donate.

At first Hannah started to protest. She was tired from all the events of the last two days and didn't particularly want to spend the rest of the evening in the dusty, dank basement sorting through all their memories. Julie insisted and then tried to explain herself.

"This way, when I'm gone..." Julie started to say. Hannah immediately stopped her mother. She couldn't handle the thought of her mother not being there, at least not today.

"We can organize the basement, but only if you don't finish that thought." Hannah tried to sound teasing, but the words cut her as they left her mouth.

Hannah thought rummaging through a lifetime worth of junk in the basement sounded like a grim idea. But the thought of going through all their memories without Julie seemed infinitely worse. They started with the things in the front of the basement and slowly worked their way back. It was a daunting task, but they were making progress as they opened portals to an earlier time, sharing memories both good and bad. One box had high school projects and year books, another the outfit Hannah wore to her first dance recital. There were many boxes full of pictures that never made it into albums and boxes of Christmas decorations from her grandparents that they had never used.

It seemed like half the boxes were things from her grandparents that Julie hadn't felt like dealing with after they passed. Both Hannah's sets of grandparents had passed before she turned six, and her father Matt passed when she was only two. Hannah's mother and father had had no siblings, and neither did Hannah. There had been no one else to collect the things her grandparents had left behind. Julie had been a young widow with a small child and no space for dealing with processing her and Matt's parents' belongings. Hence the mountains of random things Julie had chosen to take from their houses before donating the rest.

Hannah couldn't remember a time when it wasn't only her and her mother. Soon it would be only her. For the first time in her life, the thought of the future was more upsetting than remembering her past. After making a good start on sorting and emptying several boxes, Hannah needed a break. She had had enough of past reminders for one day. She was about to tell her mother they should stop when Julie stumbled across a box of her father's things. Julie must have known it was down there, but she seemed genuinely surprised by its contents.

"Hannah, would you look at this!" she exclaimed while she pulled a man's motorcycle jacket out of the box. It looked well worn, with faded edges and a few small rips. Julie held up the jacket and looked at it lovingly. She then pulled it close against her body and breathed in the smell of it.

"I want to tell you what really happened between me and your father," Julie said, her voice wavering as she spoke.

Hannah was surprised that her mother wanted to talk about it. Growing up, she had begged for stories about her father, but Julie always kept them short and sweet. She rarely spoke of her grandparents or how they settled in Hope. She had never given an explanation as to why they had stayed even after her father had passed. At a certain point, Hannah had stopped asking. It wasn't Julie's fault that it was difficult for her to talk about it. On some level, Hannah understood, but it had made it easier to leave when she did. She never felt any connection to this place she had to call home.

"I asked you so many times growing up, but you never wanted to talk about it. Why now?" The reason seemed obvious, but Hannah still wanted to hear Julie's explanation.

"I know I should have told you earlier. I thought I was protecting you, but now I realize that I just pushed you away."

"Mom, you aren't the reason I left. You know that, right?" Hannah had never heard her mother talk this way. It hurt Hannah that Julie thought she was the reason Hannah had stayed away. It wasn't true. She searched for the courage to tell her the truth as she had with Patrick, but she still couldn't, remaining silent instead.

Julie wanted to say yes, but she couldn't shake the feeling that her choices had been one of the reasons Hannah had left and why she never came back.

"Well, I certainly didn't give you any good reasons to stay. I'm sorry I wasn't more open with you, but I want to be now. Let's go and sit outside. We will be more comfortable there."

10

They left the stuffy basement and headed upstairs. Julie went to the kitchen and grabbed a bottle of white wine from the fridge. Hannah poured them a glass each, then they went outside, settling into the lounge chairs on the back porch for the second time that day. They could hear the crickets chirping and the rustling of leaves, but little else. It was so much quieter than what Hannah was used to in the city. The stars were so clear. Drowned out by the constant glow of city lights, the stars weren't even visible where she lived.

Julie took a large drink of wine, then began. "Hannah, I know that you have felt like we never fit in here. That is my fault. I chose not to tell you everything because I wanted you to be able to form your own opinions of this place. Your father was the star quarterback for the Hope Huskies. He even received a scholarship to play at Indiana University after his senior year. Then the Huskies won the State Championship in his senior year. That part of the story you know. The night we met, we flirted, and he asked for my number, even though he was seeing someone else at the time. For the record, when I met him, I didn't know he had a girlfriend. I know it sounds unlikely, but there was something about him that night we met. I was only eighteen, but I just knew he would be important in my life."

"Love at first sight?" Hannah joked, giving Julie a skeptical grin.

"I know it sounds silly, but it really was," Julie responded. Then she went quiet, lost in a memory.

"Mom, I don't think it's silly. I was just joking with you." Hannah reached out and put her hand on Julie's shoulder.

Hannah's touch brought Julie back to the moment.

"After we met, we talked on the phone every day for weeks. We became very close very quickly. Unfortunately, we didn't live near each other. We weren't sure how we could see each other again. My parents were very strict and would never have let me meet up somewhere with a boy. We were both supposed to go to IU in the fall. Your father was going to study business, and I was supposed to study pre-law, following in my father's footsteps. We hatched a plan to meet up at IU under the guise that we were touring campus and getting things ready for our fall term. We spent the week together instead, staying on the couch of one of my friends who was a year older. We walked the whole campus, stayed up all night talking, and fell deeply for each other. By the end of the week, we knew that what was between us was so much more than a summer high school fling."

Julie paused, lost in her memories again. Hannah tried to imagine her parents young, happy, and TOGETHER. Julie took a few more sips of wine.

"When our week at IU was over, we returned home. College would start in six weeks. We couldn't wait to be together again. A few weeks before school was due to start, I began to feel sick. I eventually got up the nerve to take a pregnancy test. It was positive. I was scared and nervous, but I called your father and told him. I shouldn't have been surprised by your father's response, but it was more than I could have hoped for. Things moved very quickly after that phone call. Your father said it obviously wasn't what we had planned, but he loved me and the baby. He proposed to me on the spot.

My parents were furious, of course, and refused to pay for college if I didn't give the baby up. That was never an option for us. Matt's parents were also furious and tried to convince him that I was trying to trap him. At first, we thought Matt should at least stay in school, but we didn't know how we would support ourselves if he did that. He would have had to stay in a campus dorm because of his scholarship, and with football and school, he would have no time for a job. We tried to come up with a better plan, but neither of us could find a solution to pay for school and the baby. We were only kids. Maybe with either of our parents' support, things could have been different."

Julie began to tear up. Her voice cracked as she spoke.

"Despite my protests, Matt decided to give up his scholarship. I dropped out before school even started. We got married—to the horror of both our sets of parents. Our two closest friends were the witnesses because both our families refused to attend the ceremony. We didn't have any money for rings or a reception, but we got married on the day of the town's summer festival. So we decided that would be our wedding reception. That night, we danced together under the stars in front of Matt's family and the rest of the town."

Again, Julie had a wistful look on her face. How had Hannah never heard any of this from her mother? It was becoming clear that she didn't know much about her parents' time together. But there wasn't really anyone who could have told her. It had been too hard for Julie to talk about. Jane and Julie didn't become friends until after her father had already passed. Julie's parents all but disowned her after she got married. Matt's parents were disappointed in how things had happened and never approved of Julie. She'd had no relationship to speak of with any of them.

"Your father was determined we would make it though. He was able to rent a small apartment in town, from the parents of a friend. His father eventually agreed to let him work for the family auto-repair business. After you were born, we saved up and bought this house. We had only moved in two weeks before your father died. We loved each other, and we loved you." Julie had begun to cry.

"You see Hannah, your father was supposed to be something. He would have been the first to go to college, and on a full scholarship, no less. I was an only child, and my father was a third-generation lawyer. I was his one chance to continue with the family law firm. He couldn't let go of the fact that I ruined his dream. When my parents passed, they left all their money to charity. They couldn't forgive me, even at the end."

Hannah sat quietly for a few moments, considering what her

mother had told her. She knew her father had been a good football player, but nothing about his scholarship. Her mother had never mentioned joining her grandfather's law firm. Hannah had always wondered why she only saw her mother's parents a handful of times before they passed.

"My parents could never let go of the should-have-beens. And the whole town had trouble letting go of the past as well." Julie paused, considering how much Hannah needed to know.

"Like I said, I didn't know that your father had a girlfriend when we first started talking. Maybe I would have felt differently about him if I had, but he only told me when we spent the week together at IU. He had been with her all through high school. He knew it was wrong to ask for my number while he was still dating her. After the first time we talked on the phone, he broke up with her." Julie looked ashamed.

"There is nothing to be embarrassed about, Mom. It was high school, and Dad broke it off as soon as he met you." Hannah was confused as to why Julie had grown so serious.

"Well…Hannah, the thing is...his girlfriend was your classmate Jackie's mom, Barb. She always thought I stole him from her. I did meet him while they were still dating, but their relationship was never serious. Your father told her that their breakup had nothing to do with me, but of course she didn't believe him."

Hannah considered what her mother had just said and suddenly realized something.

"Wait…is that why Mrs. Jenkins has always been so awful to us? Because Dad dated her thirty years ago?" Hannah asked with surprise. "That can't really be why, can it?"

"I wish I could say no, but I think so. I think that's why so many people in this town always seemed to keep their distance from us. In their eyes, your father was supposed to be something more, and people saw me as the person who ruined that. I messed up his relationship with the most popular girl in town. I messed up his college and football opportunities," Julie answered, her tone tinged with pain.

Hannah remembered all the sideways glances and cold shoulders she and her mother had gotten throughout her youth. It all seemed so ridiculous. She wasn't sure whether knowing this made things easier or harder. They had been ostracized for something that happened so long ago, and with regards to Barb, it all seemed so trivial. Barb Jenkins had been holding a grudge for decades, even after she had gotten married herself. The reason behind their treatment was so ridiculous. Her father had made his choice, and to hold it against Hannah and her mother was just plain cruel.

Julie reached over and grabbed Hannah's hand. "Hannah, you need to know that your father was happy. Although we gave up a great deal when we got pregnant so young, we were satisfied. Your father was proud to be a mechanic in his father's business. We loved each other, and we loved you very much."

Hannah understood why they had decided to live here initially, but after her father died, why did Julie never leave? Especially when she knew they were being treated poorly for such a stupid reason.

"Thank you for telling me all of this, but I'm still a little confused. Knowing we were never welcome, why did you stay all these years? Why did you keep me here growing up?" Hannah asked.

"Maybe it was the wrong choice, but I didn't feel like I had a different one. Your father was the love of my life. This is where we were together. This is where we agreed to raise you. I always hoped things might be different for us here. I never told you any of this before because I didn't want it to cloud your judgement of this place." Julie smiled warmly at Hannah as she continued.

"I also know you have always been very skeptical of how dedicated I am to Holy Trinity. After your father passed, I had no income, and I had to support a two-year-old. My parents refused to help. Your dad's parents helped where they could, but it wasn't enough. I went to speak to the pastor at that time, Father Boyle, for guidance and comfort. He created the job of secretary specifically for me. Then, while you were little or on school breaks, he would let me bring you to work with me. He literally saved us. I have only been trying to give back what was given to me."

Hannah remembered spending her days out of school playing in the church office. She had always hated going there because it was so boring. Hearing the reality of the situation, she couldn't help but feel grateful for Father Boyle's kindness. Julie had endured sideways glances and whispered insults for years in Hope, all to stay close to the man she loved. For the first time, Hannah saw her mother not as a woman who had been too afraid to leave, but as someone who had been strong enough to stay.

Jackie and Barb Jenkins had always been subtly and overtly rude to her and her mother. She had always wondered what she had done to draw Jackie's ire. Now she was seeing the complete picture. Jackie had been shaped by her mother Barb's animosity.

Hannah and Julie sat on the back porch for a while longer, sipping their wine and breathing in the cool night air. Julie felt relieved that she had finally come clean to Hannah about their past. Hannah felt closer to her mother than she had in years. When they finally headed to bed, Hannah thanked Julie for sharing what she had always kept to herself. Perhaps, Hannah though, one day she would be able to share with her mother the secret she had been keeping in return.

"Thank you for telling me your story Mom. I needed to hear it."

11

Although Hannah hadn't been home in years, she knew her mother's Sunday routine. Mass was at 9:30 a.m., so her mother would start fasting at 8:30. Accordingly, there were no lazy sleep-ins at their house on Sundays. Julie would be up early so that she would have time to drink her coffee and eat breakfast. Hannah awoke to the sound of dishes clinking in the kitchen. She rolled over to check her alarm clock. It was already 8:20 a.m. If she wanted to eat, she would have to go downstairs quickly. She tossed a sweat-shirt over her pajamas and headed to the kitchen. Julie already had toast, eggs, and coffee ready. Hannah buttered some toast while Julie poured them a cup of coffee each.

Yesterday had been such a heavy day; Hannah hoped today wouldn't be as emotionally draining. As she started eating, she noticed a dull ache in her head.

"Two glasses of wine is apparently one too many for me," Hannah joked.

"For me too. I slept until eight. That hasn't happened in years. We must be getting old," Julie responded with a chuckle.

They both finished their breakfasts and headed up to get dressed. Going to Mass had always been one of Hannah's least favorite parts of the week growing up. She would be forced to sit among so many people that were never very kind to her or her mother. It always burned her up inside to watch them nod in agreement with the sermons and sing along with the songs. As if this made them better people somehow. The whole performance seemed hypocritical, nodding along to messages about treating your neighbors as you wished to be treated, only to do the opposite in your actual life.

Today, however, she was less concerned about seeing her old classmates and neighbors. She was more concerned about seeing Patrick, Father Murphy. Even though she wanted to forget her feelings for him, they were always simmering in the background. She had tried to distract herself, focus on other things. She had even called Noah and asked him to visit as soon as he could.

It would have been hard to erase what she had felt that night if she never had to see him again. It seemed an impossible task now that she would be working for the church. They were going to see each other almost every day. Patrick had hurt her when he wasn't honest about himself. It made her feel foolish that she had shared part of her truth so openly. She knew it was wrong to be so hurt by his omission, as she had not been completely honest either.

When they arrived at Holy Trinity, Hannah insisted they sit in the back row. She kept her head down and hoped that no one would notice her. Jane came in a few minutes later and sat down next to them. She gave Hannah a warm hug.

"Ah, the three ladies of Pace Avenue finally back together again." Jane let out a sigh of satisfaction as she smiled and reached around Hannah to pat Julie on the back.

A few seconds later, the sound of the church organ filled the space, echoing off the stained glass and the high-vaulted ceiling. The music increased Hannah's sense of anticipation. She would see him any second. Sure enough, by the time the intro to the hymn had finished, Father Murphy began the procession into church with the altar servers. Once he made it to the altar, he turned to face the congregation.

Hannah didn't want to look at him, but she also couldn't help herself. She felt so many intense emotions when she thought of Patrick, which only seemed to be heightened by the sight of him. As he continued with the Mass, her vision narrowed in on him, and the rest of the church faded into a blur. She felt ashamed of her thoughts and the feelings she had for Patrick. Yet somehow, those sentiments seemed to get drowned out by the intensity of the other emotions roiling inside of her.

Desire. Longing. Curiosity.

She had never experienced these feelings so intensely before. Of course there was the physical desire she felt for him. The desire to know the feel of his lips on hers, or the touch of his hands pulling her face towards his. The electricity that had been in the air around them still prickled the boundaries of her skin when she closed her eyes and imagined being near him. Even now in church, surrounded by people who made her uncomfortable, she felt unexpectedly at ease in his presence.

The desire she had for him was so much more than physical, though. She longed to know everything about him, his every wish, hope, and fear. She wanted to know what he thought about world events, what his favorite foods were, and how he liked his coffee. Her curiosity about him had no limits; she wanted to know every aspect of him. It was like nothing she had experienced before. She started to feel completely out of control, and she had no idea how she was going to get ahold of herself.

When it was time to take communion, she remained seated. She hadn't been to church in years, and she knew her mother would lecture her after Mass if she went up to receive it. At the end of the service before the processional, Patrick began to make a few announcements. The first couple were about benign things such as remembering to turn in collection envelopes and information about signing up to volunteer for the summer festival. Hannah had been lost in thought, anxiously awaiting the end of the service. But as Patrick introduced the final announcement, there was a change in his voice that caught Hannah's attention.

She looked up at him. Patrick was staring right at Hannah and Julie. This caught Hannah off guard because for most of the service, it had seemed to her that he was intentionally avoiding looking in her direction. As he began to speak, she realized what he was about to say. He announced that her mother would be retiring due to an illness and that Hannah would be taking over as the church secretary. Suddenly, all eyes in the room turned to Hannah and Julie. Hannah felt her whole body go red and hot.

She nudged her mother and asked, "Um...did you okay this announcement?"

"Yes, we all talked about it at lunch yesterday," Julie responded, slightly annoyed. "Don't you remember?"

Hannah did not remember, not in the slightest. Of course, she had heard her mother and Patrick talking about plans for the transition, but she must have been more zoned out than she realized. She had occasionally tuned in to the conversation, but she hadn't picked up on the fact that they had decided to make a public announcement.

Thankfully the hymn started playing, and the procession began down the aisle, drawing attention away from Hannah and Julie. Hannah couldn't wait to run out the doors at soon as she could. She got up from her seat, but the people in the rows around them had already begun to gather around Julie. Hannah was stuck.

Offers of help, questions, and concerns about Julie's condition flooded in from every direction. The faces that encircled them were all familiar, but Hannah could see the years that had been added to them in her absence. People she remembered as children now had children of their own. Brunettes and blondes had gone grey, and deep-set wrinkles had infiltrated what used to be smooth skin. Hannah was starting to feel overwhelmed when, out of the corner of her eye, she saw Jackie headed towards them. Hannah attempted to maneuver through the crowd, but she was blocked in her pew. In a few seconds, Jackie was right in front of her, hugging Julie and offering her concern and prayers.

"You know you could have asked me to take over for you Julie. You didn't have to have Hannah come home," Jackie chided jokingly.

It made Hannah sick to see Jackie hug Julie and to see them speak so cordially to one another. Of course, her mother didn't know the truth of what had happened all those years ago, but Jackie did. Hannah didn't understand how she could act as if she had never done anything wrong.

Julie thanked Jackie but reassured her that Hannah had come home to spend time with her. Hannah's taking over as secretary had only been arranged after. Julie explained that she wanted Hannah to have something to do besides fussing over her while she was home. Hannah felt very uncomfortable. Being so close to Jackie brought all the pain she had caused back to the surface. Again, Hannah nervously searched for a way to walk away from the conversation. Jackie had started to speak again when Hannah felt a hand on her shoulder. At first, she recoiled, unsure of who was touching her.

Then she heard a whisper from the person standing behind her. "How are you doing?" The sound of Patrick's voice washed over her, and she immediately felt more at ease. The panic that had been rising inside her was halted by his presence. He could not get into the aisle to stand next to Hannah, but he ushered her to the side so that he could enter the conversation.

Patrick assertively took over the conversation, stopping Jackie mid-sentence.

"Thank you, Jackie. Julie and I are both very grateful for all your help these past months. Hannah will be starting on Monday and could use that same support. How is Colton, by the way? I saw him last night, and—" Jackie's face went pale. She responded quickly, preventing Patrick from saying more.

"Yes of course. And yeah, Colton is fine. He just wasn't feeling well this morning, so he stayed home from Mass. Thank you." There was a tinge of irritation in her voice. Her face hardened as she flashed a tight smile and excused herself from the conversation.

Patrick had saved her once again. Hannah turned to look back at him. He gave her a knowing smile. She mouthed, "Thank you." He mouthed back, "Anytime."

Their circumstances were not ideal. Her feelings for him were definitely wrong, but maybe their presence in each other's lives was not. She had never believed in fate or signs, but it was hard to ignore how he had come into her life at the exact moment when she had so much to deal with. Maybe they would become friends after all. Maybe that would be enough.

12

The alarm buzzed at 7 a.m., and Hannah rolled over to turn it off. It was her first day of work at the church. She could hear her mother already moving around downstairs. Knowing that Julie was excited about bringing Hannah with her today made her a little less apprehensive. Sluggishly she pulled herself up out of bed and headed downstairs for a cup of coffee. As Hannah had predicted, Julie was as excited and impatient as a child on Christmas morning.

"You're not dressed yet?" Julie had already put away all the dishes from the night before and was fully dressed, eating the last bites of her breakfast.

"Mom, we don't have to be there for an hour. I think I have plenty of time."

"You don't want to be late for your first day," Julie quipped as she motioned for Hannah to go back upstairs.

Grabbing coffee and a slice of toast off the table, Hannah headed to the bathroom to get ready. It was too early, and her nerves were too shot to pick a fight. It had been years since she and her mom had a go at each other, but she remembered the usual result. It was better to simply keep her mouth shut. Besides, she wanted to look nice. She tried to tell herself that it was only because she wanted to make a good impression on her first day and that it had nothing to do with Patrick. After putting on three different outfits, she finally settled on a simple blue sundress with a jean jacket and sandals. Julie was already waiting on the front stoop by the time Hannah went downstairs.

The walk to the parish office was over in a quick two blocks.

It was in fact the shortest commute to work Hannah had ever experienced. At least that aspect of her position would be pleasant. She had plans to use her lunch break to go home and check on her mother each day, although Julie had protested at the idea. As they approached the office door, Julie withdrew a set of keys from her purse. She paused for a moment before inserting them into the lock, turning to Hannah.

"I have had these keys for twenty-five years. After today, they will be yours." Julie spoke with a somberness in her voice.

They filed up the short staircase to the second floor, where the office was located. Hannah noticed that not much had changed since the last time she had been here. A new ficus plant grew in a pot by the window, but the furniture and furnishings were the same. Her mother had a small brown desk with a large filing cabinet behind it. There were a few mementos on top of it, including a family picture with her father in it. Hannah couldn't help but think that it was no wonder Patrick didn't know who she was. The only picture her mother had of her was from when she was a toddler. There was a couch and table by the front door with a water cooler and coffee maker against the wall behind it. Across from the desk was the door to Patrick's office. The last time she had been here, the name on the door had read Father Randolph. Now, in bold black letters, the name across the glass read: Father Murphy.

Julie spent the next hour giving Hannah a tour of the storage room, including where they kept the extra toilet paper and paper towels. Having to stock the church bathrooms was one of the less glamourous aspects of an already unglamourous job. Even though they had arrived at 8 a.m., Father Patrick didn't come in to the office until 9 a.m. on most days. Julie started to clear away the few personal things she had in the office, placing them in a bag she had brought with her. She asked Hannah to feel free to make the space her own. Hannah hadn't planned on having any kind of workspace to "make her own" while she was in Hope. The only thing she had brought with her was a photo of her and Noah from when they had gotten engaged. She set it down on the desk where her baby picture had been sitting. She hoped that seeing Noah all day would distract her from thoughts she shouldn't be having of Patrick.

Julie had kept everything in good order. The files were neatly organized, and her calendar and appointment book were up to date and easy to read. All in all, Hannah felt confident that she could do the actual day-to-day work. However, the clerical duties weren't the part of the job that had her stomach twisted into a knot. She hadn't had to interact with anyone yet, and Patrick still hadn't arrived.

Just as she had that thought, the door to the office clicked open, and Hannah's heart jumped in her chest. She tried to look as though she wasn't eager to see him.

"Good morning, ladies." Patrick smiled as he greeted them. "How are things going so far? Anything I can help with?"

"Morning. I think we are just fine. My mother seems to have everything under control," Hannah replied rather curtly.

"I guess we are just fine, Father Murphy," Julie said with a chuckle. Hannah was going to need to improve her people skills for this job.

Patrick nodded and went into his office. Julie gave Hannah a short lecture on being a bit more friendly. She explained that people came to this office either for happy things such as baptism and wedding arrangements, or for sad things like funerals and anointing of the sick. In either category, Hannah's demeanor would affect people greatly and reflect on the parish. Hannah already knew this, of course. It was one of the reasons she hadn't wanted this job in the first place. She had enough of her own emotions to deal with. There wasn't any space left inside of her to deal with the emotions of others.

Julie showed Hannah her script for answering phone calls and how to use the messaging system. They reviewed the filing system and what forms were needed and when. By lunchtime, Hannah felt capable of handling the details of her new position, and Julie was starting to get tired. Hannah used her lunch break to walk Julie home and then headed back to the office.

When she entered, she was taken aback to see Patrick sitting on the couch in the reception area.

"Welcome back." He smiled warmly at her.

"Thanks." She hesitated. "Did you need something?"

"No, not necessarily. I just thought...well...I thought maybe we could talk properly now."

Hannah didn't really want to talk. She wanted to pretend nothing had ever happened.

"I thought we agreed to forget everything," she responded.

"We did, but before I can...forget it...I want to address it. I'm sorry about the other night. I should have told you. I got caught up in the moment. I have never done anything like that since I became a priest. I just wanted you to know—"

Hannah cut him off. She didn't want to hear anymore. "Please, we don't have to...um, what I mean to say is, I can't explain what happened between us. It was a traumatic moment for me. I got swept up in it. My emotions got away from me. I'm sorry as well. I should have told you that I'm engaged. Can we just forget whatever we thought we felt? Please?" Her tone was pleading, and she wasn't sure if she was trying to get through to Patrick or herself.

"Yeah. I understand. Then we are agreed. It shouldn't have happened. I think that's probably best—especially since we must work together now," Patrick responded.

"Yes. Agreed."

They nodded at each other in final agreement, then Patrick went back into his office. Hannah sat down at her desk.

That was how things remained for most of the next two weeks. They offered professional greetings to each other and interacted only when necessary. They both started to believe that whatever had sparked between them on that summer night was an anomaly—something that would never be repeated.

Hannah and Julie had gotten into a routine of having breakfast together, lunch during her break, and then making dinner together. Some evenings, Jane would join them. Each night after dinner, Hannah would call Noah and catch up on his life in Chicago. Then, sitting under the stars in the backyard at night, Hannah and Julie would have a few sips of wine and share stories from the past or ideas for Hannah's wedding. It wasn't the summer she had expected, but Hannah finally started to feel like she had made the right choice to come home. She wouldn't have traded the time she was having with her mother for anything.

13

After two weeks of work without major incident, Hannah began to feel cautiously optimistic about how things were going. She felt more at ease each day she spent in the office. It even seemed as though she had started to get her feelings towards Patrick under control. She had created a morning routine for herself. First, she would water the office plants, check the mailbox, and then check the church answering machine. Patrick would arrive before nine, and they would exchange their typical professional greetings. Then he would go into his office and shut the door.

Today was no different. Patrick had arrived and was already in his office when the phone rang. Hannah answered.

"Good morning, Holy Trinity Parish. How may I help you?"

The voice on the other line was not a voice she had ever heard before. The man sounded older and had a discernable accent. She guessed he was from the east coast, maybe New York. He asked to speak to Patrick, not Father Murphy or Father Patrick, which Hannah immediately found odd. She transferred the call to Patrick's desk. From her side of the door, she could hear Patrick raise his voice for a few sentences. Then she heard the phone slamming down. Seconds later, he was out of his office and tearing through the front door. He was a few steps out the door when he turned to her and mumbled a few words about needing some air.

Hannah wondered what could have set him off, but she also wanted to stay true to their commitment to keeping things professional. The minutes ticked by, and soon he had been gone for over an hour. She knew she had no right to worry, but she couldn't help herself. As she was lost in thoughts about Patrick, the phone rang again.

This time, it was a more familiar voice on the other line. Bev Joseph was a woman she had known since she was a child. Bev and her family were kinder and more open than the other people Hannah knew in Hope. Hannah could tell something was wrong as soon as Bev began speaking. She explained to Hannah that her husband William had a heart attack a few hours ago. He was in the ICU at Community Hospital in Franklin, a town near Hope. The doctors didn't think he would last the day. She was desperate for Father Murphy to come and give him the Sacrament of Anointing of the Sick. Hannah pulled out the script for this situation, but as she tried to read it, it felt like it was not personal enough. Instead, she assured Mrs. Joseph that she would get Father Patrick there as soon as she could. Hannah hung up the phone, nervous that she had promised something she might not be able to deliver on. She had no idea where Patrick was.

Hannah wrote a quick note to post on the door, then grabbed Patrick's bag, her keys, and purse. The hospital was at least thirty minutes away, and she still had to find Patrick. She knocked on the door of the rectory and peeked through the windows. He wasn't there. She did notice that his car was still parked out front, so he couldn't have gotten too far away. She wasn't sure where to look next, but she thought perhaps her mother might have an idea. She could cover more ground if she had her car, so she ran home. When she rushed inside, she startled Julie.

"Hannah, what is going on?" Julie asked.

"Will Joseph had a heart attack. Father Murphy left the office and didn't tell me where he was going. I have to find him and get him to Franklin. Do you know where he could have gone? I already checked the rectory." Hannah was frantic.

"I'm not sure. He never left without letting me know where he was headed. I can call the office every few minutes to see if he picks up while you go look for him. He can't have gone too far. You will find him." Julie tried to sound reassuring.

"That would be great. Thank you." Hannah grabbed the car keys off the rack and jumped into her car.

She headed out on the road, driving up and down the blocks nearest the church. There was no sign of Father Patrick. She wracked her brain trying to think what his phone call could have been about, or any place he had mentioned liking to go. In all honesty, she quickly realized that she barely knew him. They had chosen to keep their distance from each other for good reason, but in this instance, it was a detriment. She eventually turned down Main Street. If she didn't see him walking somewhere along the street, she would have to get out of the car and start asking if anyone had seen him.

After driving down the length of the street, she still hadn't located him. She turned around at the end of the block and reluctantly pulled into a parking space on Main Street that was very near where she had parked that first night in Hope. She tried to push all thoughts of Colton and Patrick from that night out of her mind. She needed to find Father Murphy. That was all she had time for right now. As she grabbed her purse from the passenger seat, her eyes caught an image in her rearview mirror. She didn't see Patrick, but she did see the bushes and the tree they had sat behind the night they had met. She wasn't sure why, but she felt compelled to check there first. She looked for traffic and then ran across the street. When she made her way around the bushes, she saw him. He was sitting under the tree they had both sat under a few weeks ago.

Putting aside the feelings seeing him there stirred in her, Hannah tried to refocus on the task at hand. The Josephs were her priority, and she wanted to fulfill her promise to Bev. She took another step forward, and the sound of her footsteps caught Patrick's attention. He looked up abruptly as she approached him, clearly startled by the sight of her.

"Why are you here?" he demanded.

Hannah wanted to return his attitude, but this wasn't the time. "Mrs. Joseph called. Will had a heart attack. They don't think he has long. We need to go."

It took Patrick a minute to process what Hannah had told him. He tried to apologize for his initial rudeness.

"Sorry if I snapped at you. I just got a call I wasn't expecting—"

Hannah interrupted him. "It doesn't matter. We need to go NOW." They didn't have much time to make it to Mr. Joseph before it was too late.

Patrick nodded and followed her back to her car, pausing before opening the door.

"I need to grab my bag."

"I know. I brought it," Hannah responded.

They were ten minutes into the drive to Community Hospital before either of them spoke again.

"Hannah, please let me explain why I left early. I think you deserve an explanation."

Hannah was sure she heard sadness in his voice, but right now she couldn't handle anything other than getting to Franklin. She sped down County Highway 21. This job had always seemed so trivial to her when her mother was doing it. Filing paperwork, answering phones, opening mail... But right now, it seemed so important and consequential.

"We can talk after. Let's just focus on getting there in time," Hannah responded. They sat in silence for the rest of the car ride.

When they arrived at the hospital, Hannah dropped Patrick off at the main entrance. Then she went to find a parking space and rolled down the window. She wasn't sure how long he would be, and the summer heat was stifling so early in the day. The adrenaline that had gotten her to this point was starting to fade. Hoping that Patrick had reached Mr. Joseph on time, she reclined her seat and closed her eyes.

The first image that flashed across her mind was of Patrick with his back leaned up against their tree downtown. Of all the places to go to, he had chosen that one. Even though they had agreed to forget that night ever happened, it HAD happened. She had tried to tell herself it was all a fluke, that Patrick couldn't possibly have felt what she did. She had repeated that mantra to herself many times.

She had told herself it made no sense that he would care for her as intensely as she thought she cared for him. And that what they had felt was only because of the heightened situation with Colton. What if she was wrong? What if it was real?

At some point she dozed off. A knock on the passenger door brought her out of her slumber. It was Patrick. He had a solemn expression on his face. She unlocked his door, and he got in. Hannah waited for him to say something.

"We made it in time. Will isn't doing well, but we made it in time." His voice was heavy.

"Thank goodness." Hannah felt a wave of relief wash over her.

"It was very sad, but all his family were there. It was a very healing moment for all of them, I think."

"I am so glad you could be there for them," Hannah replied.

For the first time, Hannah fully realized the impact her position and the church itself could have on someone. She had only ever thought of the hypocrisy and showiness of it all. But today, she heard desperation in Mrs. Joseph's voice when she called, and it made Hannah frantic to help. There is so little one can do in situations so dire, but this was something that could be done to offer comfort and hope. There was purpose in that.

They both buckled their seatbelts, and Hannah started to drive out of the parking lot. But before pulling out, she braked. It was almost lunchtime, and she was very hungry.

"I was wondering if you would mind if we stopped and grabbed some lunch before we drive back? I saw a diner when we came into town," she asked with reluctance.

"That sounds perfect," Patrick replied.

14

They slid into their respective booths at Joni's Diner. When the waitress came over, they ordered, but they had yet to say any other words to each other since entering the diner. Hannah fumbled with the wrapper from her straw. Patrick focused his attention on the cars passing in the street outside. After a few minutes of awkwardness, they looked up and started speaking at the same time. Hannah tried to insist, "You don't have to explain—" but Patrick had already begun to say, "Let me explain—"

Laughing at their miscommunication, they both felt some of the heaviness in the air lift.

"Hannah, you see, my father called this morning. I will spare you the long story, but he is getting remarried. I got very upset, and I just needed some time to clear my head." He looked embarrassed.

"Like I said, you don't owe me an explanation. I am just glad we got there in time." Hannah wanted to know more, as there was clearly a great deal he wasn't sharing, but it wasn't her place to pry.

"I know Hannah, but…where you found me." His cheeks flushed bright red.

Hannah couldn't help but look away. She was embarrassed but also strangely happy that she had found him there.

"I don't really know how to explain it. I know we are just coworkers now, that's what we agreed. But that night… When I was upset this morning, I went out, and then I just wound up there. I don't want to make you uncomfortable. I am sorry."

This time, it was Hannah's cheeks that were turning red.

"I am not uncomfortable. I can't explain why either, but I

completely understand." She knew she shouldn't have responded that way, but for some reason, in this moment, she didn't care.

When the food arrived a few seconds later, it was a welcome interruption. After lunch, they got back into the car and began to drive back, sitting quietly except for the occasional small talk. It was hard enough to be in the office together alone, but in Hannah's small sedan on a hot June day, the feeling between them was impossible to ignore. Their two-week détente was coming to an end. As they approached the city limits of Hope, the wind streaming through the car windows, Hannah and Patrick both secretly wished the ride could have been a few minutes longer. As they pulled back into the church parking lot, Hannah suddenly felt emboldened.

"Someday, will you tell me why your father's news upset you so much?" she asked.

Patrick had never wanted to share that painful part of his past with anyone before. He was sure he felt like Hannah had on that first night. For some reason, she was the first person he had ever met who he wanted to share everything with. He wanted her to know him completely.

"Yes. Someday."

15

The next week at work, things were different between Hannah and Patrick. They shared a friendly conversation every morning before Patrick went into his office, discussing stories in the local paper, how Julie was doing, or church business. They had developed a natural, easy rapport. Hannah felt more at ease in her position and around Patrick. He was starting to see a future for them as friends and coworkers. Knowing the depth of his feelings, he wanted to keep her in his life in whatever way he could.

Julie came to visit the office and was surprised at the change in dynamic between them. The initial reservations Hannah had about taking the position seemed to have melted away. When Julie reached the front door at the top of the stairs, she paused because she could hear them both laughing. She couldn't help but smile and feel proud that her plan seemed to be working better than expected. Hannah had been reserved since she came home. Even the bits of conversations Julie had overheard between Hannah and Noah lately seemed subdued and perfunctory. She was happy to finally hear Hannah's laughter again.

When Julie opened the door and walked in, she saw Father Patrick jump up off Hannah's desk. Clearly, they were becoming friendlier with each other.

"Good morning! I thought I would stop in and see how things were going?" Julie swore she saw them both blush a little.

Patrick moved back, putting even more space between himself and Hannah.

"Morning Julie. It's so good to see you. How are you feeling?" Patrick walked over and gave her a warm hug.

"I am doing well, but even better now that I see you and Hannah getting along so well. She mentioned things were falling into a good routine, but I am happy to see it for myself." Julie gave them both a self-satisfied smile.

"Yes, we have definitely found a routine. Hannah picked up everything very quickly. Holy Trinity is lucky to have her, as it was lucky to have you." He took another step towards his office. "I have a few things I need to attend to, though. Lovely to see you, Julie." Smiling, he turned the knob on his office door and went inside.

Hannah and Julie stared at each other for a moment before Hannah tried to change the subject. Hannah was afraid that Julie would see there was something more between her and Patrick. They had just started to find a way to enjoy each other's company without guilt and angst. Julie knowing the truth would take that away.

"Hannah, I am so happy that you two are getting along so well. I thought you would."

Hannah breathed a deep sigh of relief. Thankfully, it seemed Julie only saw two people getting along and working well together.

"Yeah, things are going well. Father Patrick is easy to talk to. I feel like we have known each other longer than we actually have." Hannah felt good sharing a small piece of her feelings with her mother, even if it was only half the truth.

Julie beamed and gave Hannah a hug.

"Oh honey, I am so glad. You know what, why don't you invite him over for dinner tomorrow night? We haven't had him over in a while. Noah will be in town as well, and I think it would be nice for them to meet."

Julie waited for Hannah to object to the idea. Hannah waited for herself to object. She shouldn't have wanted to see Patrick outside of work as much as she did, and she definitely didn't want Patrick to meet Noah. The thought of them together filled her with dread. Yet, the person she was becoming when she was around Patrick was so different from who she had been before knowing him.

She liked who she was becoming. It was hard not to want to be around him more, even in awkward circumstances. When she was finally done wrestling with her feelings, she surprised Julie with her simple response.

"Yeah, I think that would be nice. I will ask him."

16

The same routine from Patrick's first visit was playing out in the Marshall home again. Julie prepared dinner. Hannah got ready and tidied up. Hannah's mood was much different this time, though. She was counting the minutes until Patrick would arrive at her mother's front door. She had been nervous to ask Patrick to dinner after her mother left the office. What if he said no? She knew they were trying to be friends, but was this too much? Was it wrong that she wanted to spend more time with him? Did she even care if it was wrong? She had so many questions running through her mind as she prepared to ask him. Her fears were quelled when he smiled and said, "Of course, I would love that."

Now she was putting on makeup and fussing over her outfit to wear to dinner with her priest and her fiancé at her mother's house. She couldn't help but smile at the absurdity of it all. Yet, it wasn't really more absurd than anything else that had happened in the last few months. She should be married, living in Chicago, working at a job she loved. Instead, she was in Hope, spending time with her dying mother, and working at the church. Whatever happiness she could find given her circumstances couldn't be wrong. Right? At least, that was her justification for allowing herself to feel the way she did. In a few months, this part of her life would be over, and she wanted as many happy memories of this time as possible.

Noah arrived while she was getting ready. He headed upstairs to see her. When he got to her door, he knocked. "Hannah are you ready? Can I come in?"

"Yeah, I am. Come in." She tried to sound casual.

Noah was surprised when he saw her so made up. "You know we are just going to your mom's backyard, right?" he joked.

"Yeah, I just felt like dressing up," she said with a smile. He put his arms around her and kissed her neck.

"Well, you look beautiful. I've missed you," Noah said as he hugged her tighter.

A wave of guilt swept over Hannah. She was dressed up, but it wasn't for Noah.

***

Patrick fumbled through his closet, looking for something to wear. He considered wearing his normal black pants, black shirt, and collar. He was fighting with the urge to dress in something more natural and casual. He wanted freedom from the restriction he felt when dressed in the outward symbols of his profession. Cursing himself under his breath for having so few casual clothes, he finally settled on khaki pants and a blue polo. Glancing at the time, he realized he had taken far too long to get ready and was already late. He ran a comb through his hair and headed out the door.

This time when the doorbell rang, Hannah couldn't answer it quickly enough. She paused for just a second to cool her anticipation before opening the door.

"Hi. Good to see you. Please come in." She moved back and ushered Patrick into the foyer. He smiled at her and walked inside.

"Thank you. Good to see you as well." As he moved past her in the doorway, he stopped for just a second. Hannah was unsure what he was doing, and in a moment of awkwardness did the first thing that came to her mind. She leaned in to hug him, and he returned the embrace. As they stood in the foyer, their bodies pressed together, Julie came around the corner. As quickly as they had come together, they moved back from each other.

"Good evening, Father Patrick! Thank you so much for coming," Julie exclaimed.

Patrick moved quickly to hug her as well. This was going to be more complicated than he had anticipated. The moment Hannah opened the door, he had been struck by how beautiful she looked. She was wearing a flowery dress, with her curled hair flowing down over her shoulders. In that moment, the sight of her had caught him off guard. He hadn't expected her to hug him, but he was happy that she did.

When Julie led him out onto the back porch, he saw Noah for the first time, and he understood why Hannah would have been drawn to him. Noah was tall, with thick brown hair and strong features. Noah walked up to Patrick and introduced himself.

"Nice to meet you Father, I am Noah, Hannah's fiancé." He reached out and shook Patrick's hand as he spoke.

Patrick felt embarrassed by the thoughts he had just had about Hannah but tried to play it cool. "Father Patrick. Nice to meet you as well. I have heard a lot about you."

The four of them sat around the table sharing a delicious roast Julie had spent all day cooking and a few too many glasses of red wine. Julie entertained them all with silly stories about Hannah's youth. After asking for a refill on her drink, Julie turned her attention to Patrick.

"Father Murphy, I know you are originally from New York, but I don't know anything more about you before you arrived in Hope. I also feel guilty talking about myself and Hannah all the time when I know so little about you." Julie was clearly feeling the boldness that comes with having too much wine.

Hannah could tell that Patrick was becoming uneasy as Julie spoke. He looked away from her and was nervously swirling the wine in his glass. Hannah considered trying to change the subject, but she was curious as well. He knew so much about her, but she knew so little about him. She was also pretty sure the man that had called and upset Patrick a few weeks ago—his father—had been from New York. It only made her more interested in what happened on their phone call.

Patrick took a deep breath and slowly exhaled. "Well Julie, I'm from New York City. My father still lives there, but my mother passed when I was a teenager."

Noah, Julie, and Hannah all offered their condolences at once. Julie looked embarrassed to have broached the subject, not expecting this answer.

"Thank you, but it's okay. It was many years ago now. I went to a small college in Iowa before entering the seminary. My mom's cousin is a priest as well. He was like an uncle to me growing up. My mom took me to his church every Sunday. After her passing, it was where I felt closest to her." Patrick seemed to get lost in that thought for a moment before continuing.

"Well, anyways yeah, my cousin had a good friend that was the bishop of this diocese. He helped me find a church to sponsor me, and I went to seminary near here. After that, I went back to my home parish an hour or so from here for my year of "internship." Soon after I was ordained, I was assigned to Holy Trinity." Patrick took a large gulp of his wine.

Hannah couldn't help but feel that Patrick was holding back. What reasons would make him move so far away from home? She wanted to ask him many more questions, but the expression of discomfort on his face made her hold her tongue.

"Thank you for sharing, Father Murphy. Do you ever get a chance to see your family from back home?" Julie asked, not picking up on Patrick's reluctance to talk about himself.

"Um...not really. I'm not very close to my father, and I don't have any siblings. I do still speak to my cousin, though." Again, Patrick took another large sip of wine. It seemed to Hannah that he was trying to wash the words about his past out of his mouth as soon as he spoke them.

Hannah quickly tried to change the subject.

"Mom, why don't you tell Noah the story of you and Father Murphy trying to fix the leak in the church basement?" Hannah suggested.

Thankfully, Julie shifted back into storytelling mode and abandoned her questioning of Patrick. She shared what had happened with the plumbing, and then shared a few other humorous stories about things that had happened at the church the past year. One story had them all in stitches. One of Hannah's old classmates had gotten married, and during the ceremony, the brother of the groom had stood up to protest the marriage. He revealed to everyone that he had been having an affair with the bride. The bride had taken off down the aisle, followed by the groom, his brother, and their parents. Halfway, she slipped on her train and fell, and everyone that followed behind her ended up colliding one after another, until they were all on the floor tangled in her dress. Once it was clear that no one was hurt, Patrick and Julie had tried to break up the squabble, both working hard not to burst into laughter. After they had cleared the church out, both of them laughed so hard that they started crying.

After sharing a few more comical stories, Julie suggested it was time for dessert.

They all agreed. Julie asked if Noah could help her inside with getting the dessert ready to bring out. He agreed, and they went into the house together.

Once Hannah heard the click of the sliding door closing, she suggested that she and Patrick go sit in the more comfortable chairs at the edge of the lawn. They sat down, their backs to the house. For a few moments, they sat quietly, unsure what to say next, the air around them buzzing with anticipation.

"I'm sorry for my mom's questions earlier. I know you didn't want to share about your past," Hannah said softly.

"Don't be sorry. I should have told you more about myself already. You have been so open with me. I wanted to tell you, I just didn't know how," Patrick replied. Hannah could hear the hesitation in his voice.

"You don't have to tell me anything you don't want to. I'm grateful that you listened to me, but it took me fourteen years to find the courage to tell someone about that. If you ever want to tell me anything, I'm here for you, but you don't owe me anything," she tried to reassure him.

Patrick took a deep breath. His voice shook as he replied. "You see Hannah, things with my father are very complicated. My mom didn't just pass away. She committed suicide, but I'm the only one who knows."

Hannah could see the pain on Patrick's face as he uttered the words. A few tears began to run down his cheeks. Before she had time to think, she had reached over and wiped them away. He placed his hand over hers and held on.

She moved from her chair to kneel in front of him. "Oh Patrick, I'm so sorry."

He reached his other arm out and pulled her up into an embrace. For a moment, he forgot where he was. He was lost in her touch. The release of sharing the truth about his mother struck him harder than he had expected. Saying the words out loud made it real all over again. He hadn't told anyone in all the years he had known the truth. For the first time in forever, he allowed himself to feel the weight of the secret he had been carrying.

They had both shared the most guarded parts of themselves with each other. The closeness they felt after only knowing each other for such a short time was undeniable. When the sliding door clicked open, they didn't pull back immediately. It took them a second to remember where they were. Hannah released her hold on Patrick and slowly returned to her chair. She hoped that her mother and Noah hadn't noticed anything. Patrick wiped the last tears from his face.

"Dessert is here!" Julie called, stepping onto the patio.

She didn't see Hannah at first, just Patrick's back in one of the large lawn chairs in front of her. In a blink, Hannah was standing next to Patrick. Julie wasn't sure what she had seen. Noah followed Julie outside. Hannah walked back to the table, and Patrick followed behind a few seconds later. Now all four of them were standing around the table once again.

Noah set down the plates and forks. He walked over to Hannah and put his arms around her for a hug, kissing her briefly on the lips. She had tried to move away, but she was trapped between Noah and the patio table. With Patrick standing just a few feet away, it didn't feel right to have Noah kiss her.

"Why are you so jumpy?" Noah asked Hannah.

"I mean, my mom is right there." Hannah tried to sound light-hearted. What she really wanted to say was that Patrick was right there.

"She is going to see us kiss on our wedding, but okay, have it your way," he said with a chuckle.

Patrick was already raw from just having shared his secret with Hannah. They had been embracing only a moment ago, but he was quickly brought back to reality when he saw Noah kiss her. Even though he felt so connected to Hannah, they could never share anything like what she and Noah had. They would never have a real relationship, just secret glances, hidden embraces that were over too quickly, and guilt. There would be no public kisses, acknowledgement that they were together, or carefree touching in front of family and friends. Being faced with such a stark reality was too much for him. He suddenly lost his appetite.

"Julie, thank you so much for dinner. Dessert looks lovely, but I think I'm going to head home actually." He tried to sound calm and convincing.

Julie, Hannah, and Noah all protested, but he again insisted that he needed to go home. Julie asked Hannah to show him out. She wanted to protest but imagined that would only draw more attention. As they moved through the house, Hannah and Patrick said nothing to each other. Hannah moved in front of Patrick to open the door, pausing in the same spot they had hugged when he first arrived. She wanted to say something, anything, before he left to break the tension and address what he had shared with her earlier. Her hand was on the doorknob when she stopped and looked up to meet his gaze. After a few seconds, she still couldn't find any words. He reached out and put his hand on top of hers to turn the doorknob and pull the door open between them. Their eyes were still locked on each other, but neither spoke. The air around them was now heavy with unsaid words and unexpressed feelings.

Finally Hannah whispered, "Patrick, I'm sorry."

"Sorry for what? he asked.

"I'm sorry about your mother, and...I'm sorry about Noah." Hannah looked down and tried to fight back her tears. Patrick reached out and placed his hand under her chin, lifting her face to meet her eyes.

"There is no reason for you to be sorry about kissing your fiancé." Patrick tried to sound convincing, but Hannah could hear the strain in his voice.

"I will see you Sunday at Mass." He gave her a warm smile and then disappeared out the door.

Hannah watched him fade away into the darkness of the night. She held back her tears until he was out of eyesight. She let herself cry for just a minute before drying her face and fixing her makeup. The sounds of Julie and Noah's conversation outside floated in through an open window as she tried to put herself back together and pretend like nothing was wrong.

17

As he walked away from Hannah, Patrick felt his eyes begin to well up again. Crying twice in one night certainly was a record for him. He picked up his pace, hoping to make it back to the rectory before he began to cry again. The moment he was inside and the door was shut behind him, he could no longer hold back. He had never told a single person the truth. He had foolishly thought he could leave behind what had happened by moving away. There were a few occasions when he had wanted to admit the truth to his cousin, but every time he started to talk about it, his words would fall short. With Hannah, it was different. As painful as it was to say the words out loud, keeping it from her was hurting him as well. He wanted her to know everything about him with no secrets separating them.

The peace he had felt after telling her the truth was so quickly interrupted. It had been jarring to see Noah in person. Before tonight, Patrick could think of him only as an idea, not as a real flesh-and-blood person. When he saw Noah kiss Hannah, a hot wave of jealousy had rushed over him. He had never felt so caught off guard in his life. He felt possessive of her. He knew she could never be his, but that didn't stop his heart wishing for it.

The rest of the weekend went by quickly. Patrick had a baptism on Saturday. Noah helped Hannah with a few projects around the house. Then she took him on a tour of the town, since he had never been to Hope before. They cooked dinner on Saturday night with Julie and had a wonderful time. Noah's presence reminded Hannah of the connection she had always felt with him. Their relationship was still easy and comfortable. With Patrick she felt many things, but nothing about it was easy or comfortable. How could feelings like that ever grow into something good?

Sunday morning as they walked to Mass, Hannah held Noah's hand and hoped she would be able to control her emotions better when she saw Patrick this time. When Mass started and Patrick began to walk down the aisle, Hannah kept her eyes down on her hymnal. Even when he began to speak, she tried to avoid looking at him. They were only friends. That was all they would ever be. She needed to focus on the people in her life that made sense—her mother and Noah.

After the service, Hannah would have preferred to leave quickly, but Julie stopped to talk to a few ladies who were inquiring how she was doing. She stood with Noah at the back of the church, waiting for her mother to finish. Hannah's back was turned when she felt a tap on her shoulder. She turned to see who it was and jumped a bit when she saw Jackie.

"Hannah, who do we have here?" Jackie asked as she reached out her hand to Noah. "I am Jackie, one of Hannah's friends from high school."

Noah reached out his hand to take Jackie's.

"Nice to meet you. I am Noah Bailey, Hannah's fiancé."

Hannah could do nothing but stand frozen in place. Had Jackie really just told Noah that she was her friend? The panic was rising inside of Hannah again. After all this time, she still couldn't stand up to her.

"Well, Hannah never mentioned having a fiancé. Hannah—keeping secrets, are we?" Jackie shot a smirk at Hannah.

Noah was completely oblivious to Hannah's growing discomfort.

"Hannah never mentioned she had a girlfriend here still. She always said that she didn't have any friends left in town. I'm glad she does because as far as I can tell, the only person she has been hanging out with is Father Murphy," Noah said teasingly.

"Yes, they have been spending a great deal of time together." As Jackie spoke, she gave Hannah a suspicious look.

Noah looked down at Hannah and grinned. "Well, it's a good thing he is a priest then." He gave Hannah a playful nudge.

Hannah had heard enough. Just as she was about to finally say something, she felt the subtlest brush of fingers on her back. She couldn't see him, but she knew it was Patrick.

"There you are, Jackie. I was hoping to catch you before you left."

Jackie changed her demeanor as soon as she heard Patrick's voice.

"Oh, good morning, Father Murphy What do you need?" she replied in the kindest, friendliest voice.

"Would you mind coming with me back to the office for a few minutes? I was hoping to see if you would help us with some of the planning for the end of summer festival?"

"Of course, that would be no problem." As she left, she offered one final pleasantry to Hannah, Noah, and Julie.

"It was nice to meet you, Noah."

Patrick gave Hannah a quick smile, then turned to Noah. "Do you head home today?"

"Yeah, I'm driving back after lunch."

"Have a safe drive." Patrick smiled and extended his hand to Noah.

"Will do. Keep an eye on my girls for me." Noah shook Patrick's hand. Hannah could see the flush in Patrick's cheeks as he responded.

"Always." He directed his smile at Hannah for the briefest moment.

"If you will excuse me now. Jackie, shall we?" And with that, Patrick and Jackie were on their way to the office.

Hannah knew that Patrick previously had no interest in involving Jackie in any of the festival plans. It amazed her how he had responded. He must have known she was uncomfortable even though he had been standing half a church away. Noah hadn't noticed, and he had been standing right next to her.

Noah gave Hannah a quick embrace. "I'm glad you have a girlfriend here. Of course, Father Murphy seems very nice as well. But

I feel better knowing you have some additional support." He kissed the top of her head. She didn't have it in her to tell him the truth about Jackie. Julie was finally ready to leave and suggested they walk home for lunch. Hannah was happy to agree.

18

Before Mass, Patrick had been conflicted about wanting to see Hannah. He had known that Noah would still be with her, and that made him even more anxious. He managed to avoid looking at them during most of the service, but the uneasiness he felt about seeing Hannah had fallen away when he noticed Jackie talking to her and Noah. Even from a distance, he had been able to see the tension in Hannah's body. She had been clenching her jaw in discomfort. He had moved as quickly as he could to interrupt the conversation and get Jackie away from Hannah. He had been struggling with his thoughts towards Jackie and Colton. What they had done to Hannah was so wrong and cruel. He knew he should try and forgive them, and in turn, try to guide Hannah towards forgiveness, but he was finding it extremely difficult to do so.

Jackie had been eager to help with the festival. She was always eager to help. Patrick always had some hesitation around her even before Hannah had told him what Jackie had done. He sensed that her motives were not always altruistic. As soon as he had met her, it seemed to him that Jackie was the type of person that wanted to be the center of attention. In a town like this, being active in the church was one of the most visible ways to be acknowledged by the community. It made sense to him that she would want to be involved. Now that he knew what she was capable of, he was even more cautious around her. He offered to let her chair the dance portion of the festival. She would get to select a DJ and oversee that portion of the evening. On short notice, it was the best he could come up with. He knew that Hanna wouldn't want her involved, but he could deal with that later.

The walk back home after Mass gave Hannah a much-needed chance to catch her breath. Julie was talking Noah's ear off about some gossip she had heard after Mass. As Hannah walked behind them, watching them laugh and talk, she couldn't help but feel distant. Their encounter with Jackie at the church had made her feel even more disconnected from them. Neither knew how much Jackie had hurt her; only Patrick knew the truth. It wasn't Noah's fault he hadn't been able see how uncomfortable she was. It was her fault for never being honest. She considered telling him as soon as they got back the house. She could ask him to go on a walk with her before lunch, and she could explain the whole story to him. Part of her wanted to be free of her secret and be open and vulnerable with him. The relief she felt from Patrick knowing the truth was overwhelming. She wasn't sure it would feel the same telling Noah. She feared that revealing the truth to him now, after so many years together, might feel like a betrayal to him because she had never been fully honest. Also, if she told Noah, there was no way Julie would not find out. Hannah did not want to burden her mother in her condition.

Back at home, Julie went to the kitchen to put together lunch. Hannah helped Noah pack. As much as her secret burned inside her wanting to come out again, she settled on not telling Noah, at least not today. It was just easier to leave things as they were. When her mother passed, she would reconsider.

Once lunch was ready, they all ate together at the table on the patio. After lunch, Hannah got up to clear the dishes, but Noah asked her to wait. There was something about his tone of voice that got her attention. She set down the dishes she was holding. Noah got up from his chair and walked around the table, stopping to stand face-to-face with her. The serious look on his face made Hannah uncomfortable.

"Noah, what are you doing?" she asked cautiously.

Before responding to her, he got down on one knee and pulled a small box from his back pocket. Hannah's face went red with embarrassment as he opened the box to reveal her engagement ring.

Noah gazed up at her and began to speak. "I found this in a drawer at our apartment. I know you left it because you wanted to focus on your mom, but you should have it back. Being at Holy Trinity today, I couldn't help but think how perfect it would be if we got married there this summer. I know you wanted to wait, but this way, Julie can be involved in the wedding. We would be getting married in the church your parents were married in. Please say yes." His tone was hopeful.

She should have been touched, or happy, or grateful. His gesture was extremely sweet and romantic. Of course she wanted her mother at her wedding, but she was completely caught off guard by this proposal. She and Noah had agreed on a plan, and now he was changing everything. Not to mention he was doing it in front of Julie. Hannah closed her eyes and tried to take a deep breath. It had been so easy to say yes when he asked the first time. Now it didn't feel right. She couldn't get the word out of her mouth.

When she came to Hope, they had put the wedding planning on hold because she couldn't process both her wedding and Julie dying at the same time. Now she felt guilty saying yes because her heart was so conflicted by her feelings towards Patrick. She had hoped to put Hope and Patrick behind her before she would have to revisit getting married.

Hannah again tried to speak but could not force herself to say what she knew both Julie and Noah were waiting for. Yes. All she had to say was yes. She couldn't say it, though. She loved Noah and could see their whole lives play out in her mind. It was the future she had wanted for so long. But deep inside her, there was one feeling that had taken over. It stopped her from answering. She could no longer ignore it. She had tried denying it for weeks. In this moment, she could no longer hide from it.

She was also in love with Patrick.

She felt sick with the realization. Slowly, she became aware that she had been taking too long to respond. Both Noah's and Julie's eyes were set on her. The thought of it made her cheeks turn a brighter shade of red. The thought of Patrick marrying her to someone else was inconceivable. Her mind raced with the image of her walking down the aisle of Holy Trinity with both Noah and Patrick waiting for her at the altar. It was a scene out of a cruel dream. She loved Noah, and she did want to marry him, or at least—she had wanted to marry him. Noah was waiting for an answer from her, but she still couldn't speak. When she tried to speak a final time, all that came out were tears.

Noah got up, put his arms around her, and apologized for bringing it up again. Julie also came to Hannah's side and offered her reassurance. Of course she would love to be at Hannah's wedding, but there was no rush. Their concern only made Hannah feel guiltier. She was the problem, not them. She was letting them both down, not the other way around. Finally, she was able to compose herself enough to give an answer.

"Noah, I'm sorry. I was just caught off guard. Let me think about it."

They didn't discuss it again. When Noah left later that afternoon, Hannah waved goodbye as he drove off. When she went back inside, Julie was waiting for her with a glass of wine.

"Why don't you tell me what is really going on?"

Hannah tried to skirt the conversation by telling Julie that she was tired. But Julie pressed her again.

"You have been distant all weekend. Now you don't say yes to Noah's completely romantic proposal. What is going on, Hannah?" Julie's tone was firm.

Hannah wanted to tell her mother the truth, but there was no way to tell either of her secrets to Julie without hurting her. The partial truth would have to be enough.

"Umm…sorry, I just have a lot on my mind. Friday after dinner, Father Murphy told me the truth about what happened to his mother. She committed suicide. He was very distraught. Please don't say anything about it. He said he never tells anyone." Hannah took a large swig of wine and waited for Julie's response.

"Oh, what a relief!" Julie exclaimed.

"Mom, what—?" Hannah tried to interject, surprised by her mother's response.

"Sorry, of course that's terrible about his mother. I won't say anything, and I'm glad he felt he could confide in you. I thought maybe there was something more going on," Julie said with a laugh, trying to lighten the mood.

"What do you mean more?" Hannah asked quickly, bracing herself for Julie's response.

"Oh nothing; forget I mentioned it." Julie tried to sound nonchalant.

Relieved, Hannah responded, "I didn't turn down Noah's offer. It was just a lot to process..." She tried to continue, but she trailed off as tears returned to her eyes.

Julie put her arm around Hannah.

"Let's not talk about it anymore. It's your decision. I'm sorry I questioned you."

Hannah didn't want to hide things from her mother, but she couldn't tell Julie the truth. It would be too much for both of them.

19

While Hannah walked to work on Monday morning, she replayed the events of the weekend in her head. The moment of intimacy between her and Patrick, Noah's visit, the run-in with Jackie at church, and of course, Noah's re-proposal. She still didn't know what she was going to do, and so many questions were troubling her mind. Had her mother noticed something between her and Patrick? She still wasn't sure what Julie's vague comments about "something more going on" meant. Perhaps she was being paranoid, but if Julie sensed something, could other people sense it as well? How long could they hide their connection? And the question that scared her the most: Did he love her too?

She wasn't sure she wanted to know the answer. If her feelings were one-sided, then it was simply a crush she needed to move on from. If he felt the same, would it make any difference? She knew he was a priest and that it was wrong to even think about him this way. But he was also just a man. A man who had made her feel safe and seen. A man who could set her whole body on fire with a simple glance. Could something so profound really be wrong? After she arrived at the office, she resolved to put all her questions aside for the day. She had work to focus on.

Hannah checked her phone messages, started a pot of coffee, and reviewed the schedule for the week. Planning for the end-of-August summer festival was getting busy. It was only seven weeks away. The fact that she had already been in Hope for a month was crazy to her. It was the beginning of July, and the summer was flying by. Thankfully, so far Julie's health was stable, besides some fatigue. Hannah feared what was to come. It seemed as if each week that passed was borrowed time.

When the door clicked open, she took a deep breath. Every time Patrick entered the room, she felt like she might burst. Part of her wished that her feelings would fizzle out as quickly as they began, but the other part of her dreaded the day she would no longer feel so alive. She looked up from her desk as he greeted her. She tried to take part in their usual morning banter, but instead, the pit of her stomach dropped. All the questions that had been swirling in her head flooded through her. Patrick saw the look on her face and rushed to her side. He kneeled in front of her and put his hands on her knees.

"What's wrong? Please tell me," he asked with urgency in his voice.

Hannah was at a loss for words again. When she tried to speak, nothing came out.

"Is it Julie?" Patrick asked.

Hannah shook her head no.

Patrick paused for a few seconds, trying to think what to say next. Hannah started to cry.

"Jackie or Colton?"

She shook her head no.

"Noah?"

Hannah once again shook her head no.

Patrick hesitated for several seconds, trying to think what could possibly be wrong. After a long pause, he quietly asked, "Is it...me?" He braced himself for her answer.

This time, she nodded her head yes. He was the reason she was crying. To be so close to him but never truly with him was unbearable. Experiencing small moments of intimacy with him while knowing that those moments were all that would ever exist between them was impossible to process.

Patrick didn't know how to respond. He understood why she would say that he was upsetting her. Even with all the other issues in their lives, his conflicted feelings towards her kept getting in the way of everything else. None of it made any sense. He still couldn't find the right words to say, so instead, he put his arms around her. Hannah let herself cry, and Patrick held her.

After several seconds, Hannah pulled back a little. Patrick remained close, his hands on her face.

"It's my feelings for you that have me confused," Hannah said between sobs. "That's why I said YOU are what is wrong. But that isn't true. You aren't what is wrong. My feelings for you are. Noah wants us to get married—this summer—at Holy Trinity—and for you to marry us."

Patrick wasn't sure what he had expected her to say, but it most certainly wasn't this. He was again confronted by the reality of their situation. She was an engaged woman. He was a priest. He wiped away her tears. She continued trying to explain.

"After lunch yesterday, he proposed again. I didn't answer him. How could I? You can't marry us. I mean that is unthinkable, but how can I say no to him without drawing suspicion?" Hannah waited for Patrick to respond. She wasn't sure what she wanted him to say. Her heart felt torn in two.

"Oh Hannah. I'm so sorry," Patrick said as he teared up as well. He knew the answer he should have given her, but he was unable to get the words out. Marrying her to another man was unthinkable. The thought made him sick. He pulled back from her and wiped his eyes. Hannah began crying into her hands. He looked at her and was amazed at how beautiful she was, even in this condition. But it was also clear that no matter what was going on between them, it was hurting them both. He had to be the voice of reason. Whatever they felt for each other, it wasn't doing them any good to pretend that things could be different. They could never truly be together.

He grabbed her hands and pulled them away from her face, drying her tears with his shirt sleeve.

"Listen Hannah, do you love Noah?" he asked cautiously.

"I mean yes, but what does that—" Hannah began before Patrick interjected.

"Then I think you should marry him. I understand if you don't want me to marry the two of you, but—" This time Hannah cut Patrick off.

"I don't understand...what about us?" Her head was swirling. What was he suggesting? She knew he felt the same way; she could see it in his face when she told him about Noah's proposal. Why would he tell her to marry Noah?

"We both know there can never be an us." The words crushed Hannah. Saying them crushed Patrick.

Before either of them had time to say anything else, the office door clicked open, and Jackie walked into the room. She saw Patrick kneeling by Hannah, her face covered in tears. At first, she was taken aback by the scene. As soon as she had processed what she was seeing, jealousy kicked in. She tried to mask it by pretending to be concerned.

"Is everything okay?" she asked, hiding her annoyance.

Patrick and Hannah moved back from each other slowly. More slowly than they should have, Jackie thought.

"Yeah, Hannah was just having a moment about her mom," Patrick said as he slowly got up. He pulled a tissue from the box on Hannah's desk and handed it to her.

"Yes, I'm just having a bad morning," Hannah added.

"I can come back later if that would be better, Father Patrick." Jackie offered.

Hannah wanted to scream at her to never come back again. How did this keep happening to them? Friday night and now this. It seemed like they never got a chance to finish a conversation.

Instead, she choked back her tears and told Jackie it was no problem. She gave Patrick a forced smile, ushering them both towards his office.

"You can come in Jackie." Patrick opened his door, and they both walked inside.

Hannah was left alone sitting at her desk, replaying what Patrick had said to her. How could she agree to Noah's plan? How could Patrick just dismiss what was happening between them? She felt like she was sinking into quicksand, reaching to be pulled out, only for Patrick to push her right back in.

20

The rest of the week Hannah and Patrick spoke very little. They had returned to their purely professional pleasantries and kept their distance from each other. Hannah hated it, especially because Julie was having a hard week. She could have used the comfort of Patrick's company, but she didn't know how to approach him. Noah had called several times, and she continued to dodge giving him a final answer. For the first time that summer, Julie was experiencing more than fatigue. She had a few fevers and body aches too. Seeing her start to decline made Hannah's decision even harder. As much as she had tried to deny what was happening to her mother, she knew it was inevitable. That didn't make it easier to decide.

On Sunday, Hannah went to Mass alone. Julie was feeling too ill. Patrick saw Hannah sitting by herself in her usual back pew, and his heart sank. He knew Julie never missed Mass. Hannah had not seemed herself all week, which he had assumed was about him. How could he have been so self-absorbed? Was Julie struggling, and he hadn't even asked?

After the service, Hannah left quickly and headed home, hoping to avoid seeing or talking to anyone. She hadn't wanted to leave Julie in the first place, but her mother had insisted. When she was halfway home, she started to hear the patter of footsteps behind her. It seemed like they were getting closer, so she stopped and turned to see who was headed towards her. She was surprised to see Patrick following her. He ran towards her and slowed down when he saw her turn around. Her heart skipped a beat, but then she remembered what he had said to her earlier in the week. Every day she had waited for him to come to her, to tell her he had made a mistake by telling her to marry Noah. He never did.

"What are you doing?" she asked.

"I...I wanted to talk to you." He was trying to catch his breath and placed his hands on his knees to center himself.

"About what? You haven't spoken to me all week. After what you said to me on Monday, I'm not sure what is left to say between us." She sounded colder than she had intended.

"I know, I'm sorry. We do need to finish that conversation, but today I was wondering if Julie is okay? She missed Mass." Patrick realized he hadn't thought through what he was going to say once he caught up to Hannah. He didn't know exactly what he could say to make things better between them, but he was genuinely concerned about Julie—and Hannah.

"That's why you followed me...I mean..." Hannah was caught off guard. "Yeah, she hasn't felt well all week. She is still in bed." Hannah was happy that Patrick had finally realized something was happening with Julie, but she also felt an overwhelming wave of disappointment. He must not have changed his mind about them.

"I brought communion for her, if she wants it," Patrick offered. It hurt him to see the pained look on Hannah's face. It took all his strength not to gather her up in his arms to kiss her and beg her to forgive him. Instead, he stood still and silent, waiting for her answer.

"I'm sure she would appreciate that." Hannah turned to finish her walk home, and Patrick followed behind.

21

Hannah asked Patrick to wait outside for a moment while she went inside to make sure Julie was decent and up to receiving a visitor. She helped her mother sit up in bed and combed her hair. Julie was grateful that Father Murphy had noticed her absence at Mass. It was comforting to know that someone was looking out for her.

When Hannah let Patrick in, the energy between them was so different than it had been a week ago. She called out to her mother and Patrick to say that she would be in the kitchen if they needed her. Having Patrick so near but also so distant made being around him too painful for her.

After Patrick had finished praying with Julie and offering her communion, he sat with her for a few minutes, holding her hand. He could see the change in her. Her coloring had changed, and she seemed to be uncomfortable just lying still.

"How are you, Julie?" he asked, intending to wait until she told him the whole truth.

"I felt good until the last few days. I deluded myself into thinking that maybe the doctors were wrong. It has been such a joy to have Hannah home and to spend this time with her. But I fear we may not even have as much time as they promised."

"I'm sorry to hear that, Julie. Please let me know if you need anything." Patrick was saddened by the resignation in Julie's voice.

"I'm where I want to be. I feel at peace with what will happen next. I do worry about Hannah, though. Do you know why she hasn't given Noah an answer yet? Has she said anything to you? I don't want to rush or push her, but I also don't want to be the reason she puts her wedding on hold." Julie looked at Patrick, hoping he could make some sense of Hannah's mindset.

Patrick didn't know the exact reasons Hannah had hesitated to move forward with the wedding before she came to Hope, but he was confident in at least some of the reasons she was delaying now.

"I'm not sure. This week we have been so busy that we haven't talked much." Patrick tried not to make eye contact. He was afraid Julie would see right through him.

"Would you do me a favor, Father?" Julie implored him. "Please ask her about it. She won't talk to me about it. I can't help but worry that she's delaying because of me. I'm afraid she will regret not doing it before I pass." She began to tear up.

"Of course, yes, I will talk to her." Patrick placed a hand on her shoulder and tried to keep his own tears from falling.

After sitting and talking with Julie for a few more minutes, Patrick got up and walked to see Hannah in the kitchen. She was fumbling with the dishes, nervously opening and closing cabinets. The noise of slamming drawers echoed through the whole house. He wasn't sure how to start the conversation. As he approached her, she swung around, still holding a freshly cleaned casserole dish. It was clear she hadn't heard him come in. As she turned to face him, he noticed she had headphones in. A startled look flashed across her face as she saw him standing in the doorway.

"You're still here? I thought you had left..." Hannah trailed off.

"Yeah, um...your mom wants us to talk," he said softly.

"My mom wants us to talk...about what?" She sounded annoyed and suspicious.

"Can we go somewhere together? Somewhere we won't be interrupted?" he asked cautiously.

"I'm not sure I want to go anywhere with you."

Her words hurt him more than he expected. He tried his best to offer a rebuttal.

"For your mother, then."

Hannah was frustrated by his request. All week they could have spoken, but he had instead chosen to hide in his office and avoid her. His distance had hurt her more than she wanted to admit.

Finally, she nodded yes. "You can follow me."

She set the casserole dish down on the kitchen table and walked to the front door. Patrick followed her but remained a few steps behind. The hurt in her voice had been clear. He felt guilty for not talking to her sooner. The truth was that he had been afraid to. He was not able to control his emotions around her. He was nervous he would break the second they started talking. He wanted to beg her not to marry Noah, but he had nothing to offer her besides friendship. How could he ask her to give up her life? It wasn't right, and it wasn't fair.

As they left, Hannah called up to her mom to let her know she would be back soon. Hannah led Patrick to the end of the block and then into a patch of trees that ran around the outer edge of town. They still weren't speaking as he followed her deeper and deeper into the greenery. Throughout all the months he had lived there, he had never noticed the small path winding through the grove of trees. After a few minutes, they stopped at the edge of a small creek. There were several large stones lined up at the water's edge, forming a bench.

"My mother showed me this place when I was a kid. She said my father would take me here on walks when I was a baby. Whenever I wanted to feel close to him as a kid, I would come here." Hannah ran her fingers down the line of large boulders before finally sitting down on the last one in the row.

Patrick sat down beside her. It was midday, and the sun was high in the sky, but they were nestled under a thick cover of trees. It was cooler and darker in the grove than it had been out on the street. Scatters of light darted through the canopy of leaves when the wind blew. They sat in silence for several seconds, adjusting to the scenery around them. Hannah was recalling her trips to this place from her youth. Patrick was taking in the beauty before him for the first time.

When the silence finally broke, it was Hannah who spoke.

"I'm not sure what you wanted to talk to me about, but I have something I've been wanting to ask you all week." Her voice started to shake. "Do you honestly think I should marry Noah? You said it so definitively. I know how I feel about you, how conflicted I am. But you...it's like I don't matter to you at all. Do you have feelings for me? It has been killing me all week. I thought..." She kept her head down as she paused, trying to figure out how to finish her question. "I thought there was something between us..." Hannah's voice trailed off as she spoke. She was embarrassed but also relieved to have spoken her thoughts out loud.

Patrick wanted to deny it to her, but would that really help? In the end, denying the truth would only hurt Hannah more. He reached out and put his hand over hers.

"Of course there is something between us. I'm so sorry I made you feel that I didn't care about you. But what can we ever be besides this?" Patrick said somberly.

Neither wanted to move. They sat listening to the trickle of the creek. The whole world carried on outside the edges of the grove. Yet here, hidden by the canopy of the trees, it was as if they were the only two people that existed. Their minds raced with all the words they still wanted to speak to each other. There was so much more that could be said. But for just a few moments, they simply sat in the truth that they both had deep feelings for the other. Whatever was said next would surely shatter the momentary joy they felt at knowing the connection between them was real and reciprocated.

Hannah began to cry quietly. Patrick reached out and pulled her into him. They held on to each other until she had calmed herself. Hannah didn't want Patrick to say anything more; she wanted to stay next to him on the rocks by the creek forever. She tensed up when he pulled away and turned to look at her.

Even though he knew he would regret saying the words out loud, one of them had to. His voice cracked as he began to speak.

"There is something between us, Hannah, and I will never be sorry for that. Never in my life did I think I would feel so strongly for another person. I'm so thankful you came into my life, but we must face reality. You are engaged, and I am a priest. There is no future for us besides as friends and coworkers. No matter how much we want it. You should marry Noah if you love him." His heart sank as he spoke. This was the one woman he had ever loved, and he could do nothing but break her heart.

Hannah hesitated before she responded. She knew what he was saying was true. Whatever was happening between them was wrong and could never be. What good would it do to make it more dramatic?

"I know…I know you're right." Her voice quivered as she responded. Marrying Noah made the most sense. It was better for everyone, especially her mother. Before Patrick, marrying Noah was all she had wanted. Maybe with time, she could want it again. At this moment though, her heart was broken. She had somehow managed to keep herself together for weeks, but not now. The truth that Patrick felt the same as her but that there was nothing they could do about it was the final straw. It was as if all the pieces of her broken heart were floating away down the creek in front of her. She was losing Patrick, her mother was dying, and she would be lying to Noah. She would leave this place with less than she had entered with.

"I will still always be here for you, whenever you need me." Patrick couldn't bring himself to say anything more.

They sat side by side for another minute. Hannah finally stood up and turned to walk away. Patrick reached out and grabbed her arm.

She was still facing away from him. It was taking all her strength not to break down.

"Please just let me go," she pleaded.

"I am sorry," he whispered as he reluctantly let go of her arm.

Hannah wanted to walk away. It seemed like the only logical thing to do. She wanted to put one foot in front of the other and keep going. But no matter how hard she tried, her legs would not move. She was stuck. How could she just walk away from him? He hadn't said the exact words out loud, but when he had spoken of his feelings for her, she could tell he was in love with her as well.

She turned towards him, and he stood to meet her face-to-face. Although she had been unable to walk away from him, her body was quick to move towards him. Unlike the first night they met, she wouldn't stop herself this time. She threw her arms around him and kissed him deeply. Patrick put his hands behind her back, pulling her closer. Hannah's fingers slid through his hair and grabbed at the collar of his shirt. If this was the only moment they would have, it didn't seem wrong to kiss goodbye.

Hannah tried to remember everything about being so close to him. She wanted to remember his smell, his taste, the feel of his stubble across her face as their lips moved together, and the pressure of his hands pulling her face to his. It felt as if she were truly alive for the first time. Sensations she had never felt before flooded her body and touched her in places she hadn't even known existed.

After a few seconds, they stopped and took a step back from each other, facing each other again. She wanted to scream at the ridiculousness of the situation. He was obviously hurting. She was as well. It seemed so unfair to have come into each other's lives just to be ripped apart as quickly as they came together.

Hannah was the one to apologize this time. Her voice caught in her throat as she spoke. "Now I'm the one who is sorry. I know I shouldn't have kissed you." Her eyes dropped, and her cheeks flushed with embarrassment. She turned to walk away for the second time, but again Patrick reached out and grabbed her wrist. He took a step forward, his body almost touching hers.

"You have nothing to be sorry for." His voice was low and raspy. "I wanted to kiss you. You have to know that."

Patrick was so close behind her that Hannah could feel the warmth of his breath on the back of her neck. The sound of his voice and the words he spoke sent another wave of heat through her body. He rested his forehead on the back of her head and grasped her wrist tighter. His fingers pressed into her skin was all she could think about. Even though they were barely touching, it was the most sensual thing she had ever felt. She longed to touch him more than she had ever wanted to touch anyone before. Her mind was unable to focus on anything but his touch on her body. It was almost too much, the longing she felt for him.

Hannah was grateful when Patrick finally moved to stand beside her, releasing his grip. He slid his hand down her wrist and interlaced his fingers through hers. Neither of them spoke while they walked back along the path towards the street. As they neared the end of the path, Patrick slowly removed his hand from hers. Their fingertips lingered before he moved a step away, finally separating them. As he did so, the wind around them seemed to change. A breeze wafted between them, moving through the space Patrick had created between their bodies. Now that they were back on the street, it was as if all the intimacy they had shared just a few moments ago was swept away by the wind.

22

When Hannah called Noah that evening, she tried to sound excited. She should have been excited. Yet, moving forward with the wedding was a reminder that her mother was ill and that whatever spark had been lit between her and Patrick would be snuffed out for good.

"Ah! Hannah, I'm so glad you said yes! If you were here now, I would kiss you!" Noah's voice was filled with excitement and affection.

Hannah was glad she didn't have to tell him in person. She couldn't help but wince at the enthusiasm in his voice, knowing she was faking hers. They talked through many of the details and planned half the wedding in one phone call. At work the next day, Hannah would check for a date at the church. They would take it from there. The reception would be small, held in Julie's backyard. After the phone call, Hannah took a few deep breaths and tried to pep herself up to tell Julie. It would be much harder to convince her mother of her excitement, especially since she would be standing right in front of her.

"Mom, I said yes to Noah..." Hannah was only able to get those few words out before Julie lost herself in delight. She squealed with happiness.

"Wonderful news, just the most wonderful news!" Julie yelled. She rushed up to Hannah and wrapped her in an embrace.

"I have to go get you something!" Julie exclaimed, then headed to the basement. She started digging through the boxes she had set aside when they organized the basement. Eventually she found what she was looking for. She emerged triumphantly from the basement with a white lace dress in hand.

"I know it will be hard to find a dress in such a short time. Would you want to try on mine?" Hannah could sense the hope in Julie's question.

The truth was that Hannah didn't want to go wedding dress shopping. She didn't want to do any wedding planning. All the pomp and circumstance seemed trivial compared to what Julie was facing. If wearing her dress made her mother happy, then it would make Hannah happy as well.

"I would love that, Mom," she answered with a warm smile.

Hannah took the dress to her room and slipped the simple lace garment over her head. As it fell down the sides of her body, the wedding became even more real. It was a tea-length white lace dress that was sheer across her shoulders. The waist was cinched by a silk ribbon that tied behind her back. In truth, it fit perfectly. It did not need a single alteration.

Julie quietly knocked on Hannah's door. "Can I come in?"

"Yeah, come in," Hannah responded.

Julie's face lit up when she saw Hannah in the dress.

"Oh wow. You look stunning." Julie couldn't help but start to tear up. "I was so worried I wouldn't get to see you in a wedding dress, but here you are looking beautiful in mine."

Hannah was grateful to see how happy Julie was. It helped remind her of the importance of her decision to move forward with the wedding. In the back of her mind, though, she couldn't fight the feeling of dread that had started to settle over her since the moment she had said yes to Noah.

In only one night, her dress was picked out, and they had a reception venue in Julie's backyard. Now she just had to secure a date for the wedding. She already had an idea of what date might work. If she remembered the calendar correctly, there was a Saturday in a few weeks with nothing on the books. It was also three weeks before the summer festival. Even if she needed a few days off for the wedding, that would still give her and Patrick time to finish all the last-minute planning. Everything seemed to be moving so fast. She had been engaged for months already at this point, but now it felt like she had put her foot on the gas pedal, accelerating towards the finish line. The quicker the wedding happened, the less time she would have to change her mind. It was also more likely that Julie would still be around to see it happen.

23

Monday morning, Hannah woke up earlier than usual. She quickly got ready and headed out for work before Julie got up. She needed the extra time to prepare herself to see Patrick again and tell him about the wedding. Once she got to her desk, she immediately flipped open the church date book. She had been right in thinking Saturday July 27 was available. When Patrick arrived, she would confirm with him, and then it would be official. She would be getting married to Noah in three weeks.

The anticipation she usually felt prior to Patrick's arrival was today replaced by a sense of uneasiness. Her feelings towards him were as intense as ever, maybe even more so now that she knew that he felt the same. But she needed to move on. Noah deserved her commitment and love. Hannah resolved to try to put her romantic feelings for Patrick out of her mind, and—to the extent that she could—her heart.

By the time Patrick arrived at nine, her stomach was in knots. She felt like she was betraying him, even though he had told her to marry Noah.

Patrick smiled at her and tried to act as if nothing had happened between them the day before. But his expression changed when he saw the tension in her face.

"Morning Patrick…Father Murphy. Can I double-check something with you?" *Better to just rip the Band-Aid off,* she thought.

"Mm hm. Of course." He gave her a warm smile and tried to sound reassuring.

"The calendar is open on the 27th. Can I schedule my wedding that day? In the afternoon, around 3 p.m.?"

He took a deep breath. All the same arguments he had been having with himself flashed through his mind before he answered. No matter what he wanted, he knew there was only one answer he could give her that made sense.

"Yeah of course. We can spend some time going over the ceremony this afternoon if you want?" He smiled and tried to hide how much this was hurting him.

"Thank you. That would be good." She smiled back.

Patrick turned and headed into his office. Usually, weddings were a joyful part of his duties, but he couldn't shake the sensation that this wedding felt more like a funeral.

Hannah scribbled, "Hannah and Noah Bailey wedding, 3 p.m." in the empty box for July 27th on her desktop calendar. She sat and stared at the words for longer than she should have. When Noah had first proposed, she had been so happy. Why didn't she feel that way now? Nothing had changed with Noah. He was the same sweet, kind, and thoughtful man he had always been. It was Hannah who had changed. So much had happened since their engagement six months ago. Most of it she couldn't even put words to. The feeling she got the first time she looked Patrick in the eyes, the sensation that cascaded through her body when he touched her, how her heart dropped every time she saw her mom sleeping in the bed in the living room. Words could not describe any of that.

The truth she could articulate, however, was that soon she would lose both her mother and Patrick. In different ways surely, but they would both be gone from her life by the end of the summer. Noah, however, would still be there, offering the same safe landing he had always offered. She did love him. Did her whole body start to burn from the inside out when he walked into the room? No, but she felt safe and supported when she was with him. She wanted to be that person for him as well.

24

Hannah tried to get on with the rest of the business she had to take care of that day, keeping busy to keep Patrick from her mind. It was difficult to do, knowing he was only one room away from her. Her mind finally started to settle. She had immersed herself in a mailing project when the phone rang. As soon as she heard the voice on the other end, she recognized it.

The man on the other end of the line sounded quite distinct from the people who usually phoned the parish office. He had the same thick east coast accent she had heard a few a weeks ago when he phoned asking for Patrick.

"Good morning, is Patrick Murphy, I mean Father Murphy in this morning?"

Hannah wasn't sure what to do. The last time she transferred Patrick's father's call, it had upset Patrick greatly, but she couldn't hang up either. Deciding on a compromise, she asked the man to hold, and she went to knock on Patrick's door.

"Come in." She could hear the hesitation in his voice.

"You have a call on hold."

"You can send it in," he replied, looking at her with confusion. She didn't usually ask before transferring his calls.

"Well, I wanted to ask because I think it's your father again." Hannah could see discomfort flash across Patrick's face.

"Oh…in that case, please tell him I'm not available," Patrick said curtly.

"Yes, of course."

The next few days, Hannah and Patrick continued to keep

their interactions formal. They managed to awkwardly finalize the details for the wedding and get several things done for the festival, but they shared no personal conversation. Hannah was even grateful when Jackie came to help one day because it gave Hannah a good excuse to leave early.

Patrick's father continued to call all week, with Patrick giving the same instructions to Hannah each time: "Tell him I'm unavailable."

Hannah wanted to press Patrick on why he wouldn't at least talk to him, but she felt it wasn't her place. The situation between them was already almost untenable, and she didn't want to complicate things even further.

She didn't usually work on Friday mornings, but she decided to go in to finish up a few details for a baptism that was taking place that Saturday. When Patrick came in later in the morning, he was startled to see her at her desk. It was clear he had not expected to see her. She couldn't help but feel a little hurt. He looked almost upset to see her. They shared pleasantries, and he went into his office. A few minutes later, someone came in through the office door. It was Hannah who was caught off guard this time.

"Good morning miss, I'm looking for Father Patrick Murphy."

As soon as he spoke, Hannah realized who he was—Patrick's father. He was a handsome, well-dressed man. Nicely groomed, with the same reddish-brown hair as Patrick, only it had grey scattered throughout, which made him look even more distinguished. Hannah felt very torn about how to feel towards him. Patrick clearly wanted nothing to do with his father, but as he stood in front of her desk, she couldn't see why, based on his appearance and manners alone. He seemed to have a very gentile nature. Although she knew who he was, she wanted him to think that she didn't.

"May I inquire who is asking?"

"You can tell him it's his father, Matthew Murphy."

Hannah nodded. "You can take a seat while I check if he is available." She motioned for him to sit down on the couch.

She didn't bother to knock before she swung open the door to Patrick's office and quickly moved inside. He started to speak. She put a finger to her lips, gesturing for him to keep quiet, and quickly shut the door. She rushed over to Patrick and leaned in close to his ear. This was the closest they had been all week, but she couldn't focus on that right now.

"Your father...he's here...in the waiting room," she whispered to him as quietly as she could.

Patrick sat back in his chair, considering what she had said. Hannah moved back from him and studied his face and body language, looking for signs of how he was feeling. The color had left his face. He looked almost ill. After several seconds, she still had no idea how to handle their unexpected visitor.

"What do you want me to do?" she asked, her voice full of urgency.

Patrick's mind was racing. He tried to avoid his father at all costs. If Hannah knew what had happened between them, she would understand. After he told her about his mother, he had thought he would have so many chances to tell her the rest of his story. Things between them became complicated so quickly that he never had another opportunity.

From the first time his father called, he had wanted to tell Hannah the truth about why it upset him so much. He often wondered what she thought about him being so indifferent to his father, when she never had the opportunity to know hers. He would have to struggle with that later, however. He had to handle something else right now. He had to deal with the fact that his father was sitting just outside his office.

"I guess I have no choice but to see him." Patrick hung his head in resignation and walked out to greet his father. Hannah followed behind him and went back to her desk.

As she watched Patrick and his father walk into the office, a feeling of uneasiness settled over her. During their time together, she had only seen Patrick that affected a few times before. She could see how uncomfortable he was in his father's presence. He had been there for her when she needed him. This was her opportunity to be there for him now. She sat at her desk, poised to go to Patrick's assistance if needed. After a few minutes, she heard their voices rising a little at first, then growing louder and louder. She hadn't ever heard Patrick raise his voice, except on that first night with Colton. Hannah knew she had to act. Without knocking, she swung open the door and interrupted the argument.

"Sorry Father Patrick, but we need to leave for the Edwards right now." She tried to sound firm and decisive.

Patrick looked at her, puzzled at first. Then she saw a look of realization dawn on his face.

"Ah yes, the Edwards. Sorry Dad, we will have to finish this later." Matthew looked confused and irritated.

"You're going to leave right now? I came all the way here to see you." His tone was cross.

"We will have to finish later. I have an appointment I can't miss." Patrick grabbed his bag and was heading out the door of his office before Hannah even had time to move out of the doorway. They practically collided.

"Hannah will show you out. I need to leave. I'll meet you in the car, Hannah," Patrick instructed.

Hannah motioned for Patrick's father to follow her. She walked him to the office door and opened it for Mr. Murphy to leave. He was grumbling under his breath as he headed for the door. Before he walked out, he paused and turned to Hannah.

"Would you please let my son know I will be in a town for a few days and that we WILL be finishing our conversation before I go home?"

Hannah nodded yes in reply.

25

Once he was gone, Hannah quickly shut the door. She grabbed her keys and switched the lights off. She wasn't sure where Patrick was planning to go, but she doubted she would find him in his car. When she reached the bottom of the stairs outside the office, she saw Mr. Murphy get into a black sedan. At least he was gone. She didn't see Patrick in the parking lot, so she headed for the rectory. When she got to the screened front porch, she saw Patrick pacing back and forth. The look of conflict and distress on his face made her stomach drop. It was the start of the day, but he already looked exhausted. His reaction to his father made her more desperate to know what had happened between them.

Hannah opened the screen door and walked onto the porch. Patrick was still pacing back and forth. He hadn't even acknowledged she was there. She waited for him to say something. Finally, he stopped pacing and started to speak.

"I can't believe he had the nerve to just show up here. I wouldn't take his phone calls. Why would I want to see him in person?" He was saying the words out loud, but Hannah wasn't sure that they were actually meant for her.

"Patrick, are you okay?" He didn't respond but just started pacing again. She tried to get his attention by yelling, "PATRICK?" This finally got his attention. He stopped again and looked up at her.

"You need to tell me what is going on." Her tone was firm but kind.

She waited for him to respond, but instead of saying anything, he started to cry. When she saw his tears, her first instinct was to go to him and hold him. She wanted to fight the urge, but it didn't seem right, given the situation. She pulled him in for an embrace. He held on to her, burying his head in the crook of her neck.

He hadn't seen his father since he left New York. His father was, after all, the reason he had left in the first place. Their relationship was one of the main reasons the priesthood had appealed to him. It was the reason Patrick had come to this small town so far from his childhood home. He had never been fully honest with anyone about all the things that had happened when he was a teenager. The person who knew the most was his mother's cousin, but even he only knew part of the story. His mother's cousin George was a priest and had helped Patrick through his mother's death. Cousin George was who had first inspired Patrick to consider the priesthood as his vocation. Yet as close as they were, Patrick had never fully opened up to him either. Like everything else that had happened with Hannah so far, this would be another first. He pulled back to look at her.

"I will tell you everything. Let's go inside. Are you comfortable with that?" he asked as he reached for her hand.

She had been hoping he would invite her inside someday. She wanted to see where he lived and the things that made up his life. In this moment, she also wanted to know what had happened with his father.

"Yes of course," she replied.

He grabbed her hand and led her through the front door. They should have been worried that someone might see them, but right now it didn't matter. Hannah tried to prepare herself. She had no idea what pain Patrick's story would hold, but she could tell it was significant. She couldn't help but wonder whether that was why they felt so connected to each other. They were two broken people who found each other in the most unlikely place.

Once inside, she noticed that the house smelled like Patrick, woodsy and cool. It was plainly decorated, littered with stacks of books and empty coffee mugs. The staircase that led upstairs was in front of her, the kitchen to the right, and the living room to the left. For a split second, she imagined herself and Patrick together in the house. She could see them, cooking together and reading books next to each other on the couch; the coffee cups that were scattered about—half hers and half his. No good could come of her being here. She knew it, and she was sure he knew it as well. But he had asked her to come inside, so she had. It was no more complicated than that.

"Please have a seat. I'll make us some coffee." Patrick motioned towards the kitchen table.

She sat down as he moved around the kitchen, opening and closing cabinets, running water, and putting the kettle on the stove. When Patrick came to the table with two hot cups of coffee a few minutes later, Hannah's heart was still racing. Despite her best efforts, she hadn't been able to stop herself from imagining the life they would never have.

Patrick sat down across from her and blew on his coffee before taking a few sips.

"I've wanted to tell you my story since the day we met." He hung his head, not making eye contact.

"The day we met? After everything with Colton?" Hannah was puzzled by his admission.

"Yes. I know it sounds crazy, but you had just shared your deepest secret with me. I felt like I had found someone I could finally share my secret with as well. It didn't make sense to tell you at that moment. You had just been traumatized again, and I didn't want to burden you with my baggage. I never thought we would see each other again, so I figured there was no point in thinking about it anymore. But now, so much more has happened between us. The night I told you about my mom, I was going to tell you the full story, but then we were interrupted. I thought it was another sign that I should keep it to myself. I wasn't expecting my father to come here. I can't deal with this alone anymore. I know it's selfish with everything you are going through, but—"

"You can tell me anything. Please. I want to know," Hannah spoke over him. She reached out to put her hand over his. They looked at each other for a few moments, neither moving their hand away. Patrick began to tell her what happened to his family all those years ago, only letting go of Hannah's hand occasionally to wipe his tears away.

Patrick was from New York City. His father was a wealthy banker. They lived in an impressive townhouse on the Upper East Side. His mother Sandy was beautiful, fun, and several years younger than his father. They had met at a fundraiser she had been working at, and they quickly became very serious. She became pregnant with Patrick shortly after they started dating. They decided to get married after only knowing each other a short time. From the outside, they looked like the perfect family.

For a time, they were happy, but eventually, his father started having affairs. Once Patrick was old enough to understand why his parents were always fighting, his mother had already started to decline. The affairs and betrayals had sent Sandy into a depression. Patrick would hear her threatening to leave his father, but it would have hurt his reputation to be divorced. So, in turn, his father would threaten her with taking Patrick away from her or not paying her anything. They both thought he didn't hear them, but he often did.

Patrick tried to make his mother happy, but nothing he did seemed to help. She would sleep all day and rarely left the house. He tried to get his father's help, but he seemed unconcerned and always too busy. One day when he was sixteen, Patrick came home from school to find his mother lying in bed. At first it seemed like any other day she had simply slept through. As he got closer to her, however, he realized she was not okay. When he tried to wake her up, she didn't respond. Her body was cold. He panicked. He tried turning her on her back and was going to start CPR, but he realized there was no point. Her skin was waxy and pale. Her lips were a pale shade of blue.

Patrick called 9-1-1, but his suspicions were confirmed. It was too late to help his mother. While he waited for the paramedics to arrive, he saw a small piece of paper sticking out from under the bed. He hadn't noticed it when he first entered the room, but he hadn't been looking for it either. He picked it up and turned it over.

It was a note in his mother's handwriting. As he read it, his heart sank.

Patrick quickly realized that his mother's death hadn't been an unexpected tragedy after all. She had done this to herself. He only had a minute to decide what to do before the paramedics arrived. On the one hand, he wanted to show his father the note. He wanted his father to know exactly what his behavior and callousness had caused. On the other hand, though, he wanted to protect his mother. Being Catholic was very important to her. Although church teachings had recently changed on the matter, there was still a stigma against Catholics who committed suicide. He also wanted to spare her the gossip. To die tragically at a young age was one thing, but to be the subject of speculation and unkind chatter was something else. He didn't want his mother's name to be dragged through the mud. So, he decided to put the note in his pocket and tell no one what he had found.

The paramedics showed up a few minutes later. They confirmed that she had already passed, as he had feared. They took her away, and the police came in and searched her room. They found a bottle of sleeping pills in her bathroom. Eventually, his mother's cause of death would be ruled as an accidental overdose. Even if his father hadn't directly killed her, Patrick couldn't forgive him for what he had put her through.

Hannah's heart was breaking for Patrick. The same emotions she was going through now, he had already experienced. Patrick had watched his mother suffer with a terrible illness when he could do nothing to save her. She squeezed his hand as he continued.

"I kept this note all these years. I never showed my father or anyone else." He let go of her hand, got up from the table, and walked over to the bookcase in the living room. When he came back, he handed Hannah a small, yellowed piece of paper. She opened it and read it.

Michael,

I want you to know you have led me to this. Please tell Patrick it wasn't his fault. I tried to be strong for him. I hope he can forgive me someday. I hope this haunts you forever.

- S

"You never showed anyone this?" Hannah asked.

Patrick didn't respond. He kept his head down, lost in his own thoughts.

"Why didn't you at least show your cousin?" she asked more forcefully, and this time, the sound of her voice jolted Patrick out of his distraction.

"I didn't want anyone to know," he said. His voice was low, and he still hadn't taken his eyes off the piece of paper. "At first, I thought I was protecting my mother. Over time, I've come to regret that decision. Of course, the people around her knew she was depressed, but I don't think they understood the extent of it. My father should have known the truth. He needed to face his actions and how they affected her. His actions hurt me too, and he has never taken accountability for any of it." Patrick was unable to hold back the tears he had been fighting.

His tears started slowly but quickly began to cascade down his face. Hannah didn't know what to do. She was used to Patrick being the one comforting her; now the roles were reversed, and she was unsure how to react.

She got up from her chair and moved to his side of the table. Once she reached him, she wrapped her arms around him. He buried his head in her chest and held on as tight as he could. They remained like that for a few minutes before Patrick slowly pulled away. Hannah was caught off guard by the expression on his face. He was laughing to himself.

Patrick looked up at her. "You know what the craziest part of this whole situation is? I am here—I met you—because of what happened. But also, I became a priest because of what happened.

The irony has not escaped me." The humor in his tone had turned somber.

It was true. The events in their lives that had led them to each other were also the very things that would prevent them from ever being together. Patrick became a priest because he wanted to get away from his father. Hannah was rushing to get married in part because her mother was dying. That's how they had both ended up in Hope.

She had often wondered why Patrick became a priest. She saw how good he was at it, but he could have helped people in so many other capacities. When she thought about it, she wanted to be angry with him for his choice and ask him why he hadn't waited for her. But what good would that do?

Today she had been given one more piece of the puzzle that was Patrick Murphy, but she still felt like she didn't fully understand his reasons. Now didn't seem like the right time to ask him those questions. Maybe the right time would never come. The weight of his words hung heavy in the air between them. Finally, Hannah responded.

"I'm so sorry, Patrick. You should never have had to keep all this to yourself. You should never have had to go through that alone…" She trailed off, this time fighting the tears back herself.

He reached for her hand and lifted it to his lips, kissing it ever so briefly before letting it go.

"It's enough that you know the truth now," he said, giving her a small smile.

26

As Hannah walked home, she couldn't help but feel overwhelmed by what she had learned. In her mind, she was the broken one, the one Patrick was helping to put back together. But they both had hurt in their past. She didn't only need him, he also needed her. Before she left the rectory, they had agreed on a plan for Patrick. He would finally show the note to his father. It was time he knew the truth. Hannah had offered to be with him when he spoke to Matthew, but Patrick had insisted he needed to do it on his own.

They both assumed Matthew would most likely turn up to the office again in the morning. Hannah would make sure they had the privacy they needed, taking the phone off the hook and turning away any visitors. As awful as the whole situation was, in a sense she was grateful for it. The longer she could focus on Patrick's situation, the longer she could avoid dealing with her own.

When she arrived back home, she saw Jane's car in the driveway. She hadn't even realized how long she had been at the rectory. It was already early afternoon. Hannah had forgotten that Jane had offered to come over and cook dinner. Julie had been more fatigued the last few weeks, and the rushed wedding planning was pushing her more than was probably best. Hannah had objected to her overworking herself, but Julie could not be stopped.

As Hannah walked in the front door, the aroma of Jane's chili wafted over her and instantly sent her back to childhood. How had she been back for so many weeks and not had Jane's chili yet? Growing up, Jane would come over almost every Sunday evening and make dinner with Julie. Half the time it would be chili, but it was so good that somehow, it never got old.

"Hannah darling, come in. We are having a drink!" Jane threw her arms around Hannah, then grabbed a glass of wine from the counter and thrust it into her hand.

"What gossip are you two ladies spreading?" Hannah asked with a smirk. They all laughed. So many times, Hannah had walked into the room, interrupting a deep conversation about what color someone had dyed their hair or who was divorcing whom. It was one of her fondest memories of home, the two girlfriends laughing and chatting. Her mother was always at her happiest when she was with Jane. She considered her family, an aunt—not a neighbor. All the years Hannah was away, she was always grateful that Julie had Jane. She knew her mother was never alone.

The rest of the afternoon, they enjoyed each other's company, sharing laughs and stories. As the afternoon turned to evening, they could see that Julie was looking tired, so they helped her get ready for bed and said goodnight. Hannah and Jane headed out to the back porch for one more glass of wine.

"Hannah, now that we are alone, I wanted to talk to you about your mom. This last week I have really seen a change in her. I think she's starting to decline. I don't think she wants to say anything with the wedding coming up next week, but I just wanted you to know." She took a large gulp of wine.

Hannah had noticed the same change in her mother, but she had tried to block it out. They had been having a great summer, in fact, it was the best time they had ever spent together. She was having trouble accepting that it would soon end.

"Yeah. I noticed as well."

"I must tell you Hannah, she's so happy you are home. It has given her peace. Now with the wedding to focus on, she has even more to look forward to and keep her busy. No matter what happens in the future, you need to hold on to how happy you have made her." Jane put her arm around Hannah's shoulders, pulling her into an embrace.

Hannah knew she was right. It had been the best decision to come home, and agreeing to the wedding had been the right decision for her mother. She was still unsure whether it was the right decision for her, but what would be the point of stopping it? She could never be with Patrick, and if he wasn't in the picture, she would have been thrilled to marry Noah. Her life needed to move on from this place. The summer would soon be over. Her mother would be gone, and she would be back in the city, without her mother or Patrick. She winced at the thought of losing either and wrapped her arms around Jane in return.

27

When she unlocked the office door the next morning, a feeling of unease swept over her. She knew that Patrick's father would most likely be coming soon. They had made a good plan to deal with him, but actually following through on it was an entirely different thing. Jane's words from the night before were still echoing in her mind as well.

"I think she's starting to decline."

Hannah had called Noah before bed, and that had made her feel a little better, but deep down, her first instinct was to want to speak to Patrick about it. She wasn't entirely sure why she was so drawn to him. But from the first time their eyes met, she had felt safe and seen. It was as if they had known each other their whole lives. His presence was the comfort she needed more than any other.

She tried to put all thoughts of Julie and Patrick out of her mind and focus on a little work before Patrick arrived. The coffee was brewing and all the mail had been sorted by the time she heard him open the door.

"Morning." She smiled at him reassuringly.

"Morning. Any sign of my father yet?" he asked cautiously.

"Not yet."

He nodded at her and began walking to his office.

"You know I'm here if you need me," she offered.

He gave her a small smile and nodded again before disappearing behind his office door. Thirty minutes went by, but it seemed like much longer. They sat at their desks, contemplating their individual struggles, both wanting to go to each other but staying planted where they were.

Patrick was nervous, rapping his fingers on his desk, anxiously checking the time and staring at the note he had set out on his desk. It seemed so odd to him that over the years he and his father had so rarely spoken about his mother. In truth, they rarely spoke about anything, so it shouldn't have been surprising that they never spoke about Sandy. He had heard his father say a few times that he didn't want to bring her up because he was afraid it would upset Patrick. But what his father didn't understand was that he was already upset. Not talking about it didn't erase the fact that Sandy had died.

When the door finally opened at 9:40 a.m., Hannah didn't even need to look up to know who it was.

"Good morning Mr. Murphy," she said as she raised her gaze to meet his.

"Good morning miss. Is my is son in this morning?"

Before she could answer, Patrick flung open his door.

"I'm here. Please come in."

After they had moved inside, Hannah got up and locked the main door. She also clicked her office light off and took the phone off the hook. They had decided to pretend as though no one was in to give Patrick some privacy. She sat at her desk, straining to hear what was being said on the other side of his door. Several minutes passed before Patrick and his father emerged from his office. Hannah hadn't been able to hear much of what was said, but she also hadn't heard any yelling or raised voices, so she took that as a good sign. The first person through the door was Patrick. When she looked up at his face, she could see the traces of tears left on his face.

Patrick walked his father across the room towards the exit. Before his father left, he patted Patrick on the back. Then they both smiled briefly at each other.

"See you in a few minutes," Patrick said as his father left.

Hannah waited a few seconds to make sure Matthew had walked out of earshot before speaking.

"How did the conversation go?" she asked with some hesitation.

"Difficult," Patrick, said shaking his head in disbelief. "I should have told him earlier. I don't know why I kept this secret for so long." He walked towards her and sat down on the edge of her desk. Hannah moved back in her chair to make some extra space between them. She could not be so close to him and not be driven to distraction.

Even at a greater distance, he was still close enough for her to feel the warmth from his body. While he was talking, she could hear the words, but she wasn't taking anything in. After a few sentences, he noticed that she wasn't responding.

"Hannah, are you okay?" he asked with concern in his voice.

She was lost in her own thoughts. He had crossed his arms over his chest while he was talking. For some reason, her thoughts were stuck on that. When they had kissed two days earlier, she had touched his chest in the same spot his arms were now resting. When she didn't answer him, he got up and walked around the desk to face her. His movement finally broke her trance.

"Oh, sorry. What were you saying?" Her cheeks flushed as she spoke.

Once he was in front of her, he was confused by the odd expression on her face.

"I was just saying you were right. I should have opened up to him earlier. Are you okay? I feel like you aren't listening to me?" Patrick's voice slowed as he spoke. He was still unsure where her head was at.

"Yeah, I'm okay. Sorry, I got lost in thought for a moment. I'm glad you were finally able to tell him." Hannah tried to brush off his concern. The truth was that she was not okay. The small bit of him that she had only made her desperate for more. It seemed the most natural thing to reach out and hug him—kiss him.

Again, he was confused by the look on her face and reached out to put a hand on her shoulder. At the feel of his touch, she drifted even farther from the conversation they were meant to be having. Radiating from the place his hand rested on her skin, a wave of heat streamed down her body. She tried to move her chair back from him, but her will was not as strong as it should have been.

"Hannah, what are you thinking?" he pressed her again.

"Um. Yeah, sorry. What were you saying?" She couldn't remember the last thing either of them had said before he touched her.

"I was just saying that you were right, about telling my father?" It was a statement, but he posed it as a question.

She shook her head and tried to free herself of the thoughts she was having.

"Yes, that's good. I'm glad it went well." She wasn't thinking clearly when she decided that hugging Patrick was the next thing she should do. She got up from her seat and leaned in to embrace him. Patrick was not expecting her approach, and when he started to lean forward to return her embrace, they awkwardly collided into each other. Their arms became tangled up as they ineptly attempted to hug one another. When they pulled back, the embarrassing interaction had rendered both their cheeks bright red. They laughed out loud.

"Well, that didn't go as planned," Patrick said as he fumbled with his collar, a smile on his face.

"Should we try again?" Hannah offered, raising one eyebrow playfully.

This time when they leaned in, it was seamless. Hannah knew she should let go, but when she tried, Patrick held her in place. He moved his head into the curve between her neck and shoulder. She swore she felt him breathing her in, the way she was doing to him. Time stood still for a few seconds. Finally, Patrick let her go. When Hannah looked up at his face, she could see he was still flushed. This time, it was not from embarrassment. They both took a step back, and a deep breath. After a few seconds, Hannah finally refocused on the conversation they were meant to be having.

"Sorry, I just have a lot on my mind about my mom. Please tell me what happened with your dad. I want to know." She directed all her attention to his response.

"Well…he apologized for everything. He had no idea about the note. Of course, he admitted he had fears that her suicide wasn't accidental. He never wanted to share them with me because he thought it would hurt me even more. All those years we didn't talk about my mother, he thought he was protecting me from the pain of remembering her. He acknowledged all the pain he caused me and my mother because of his selfish actions. He says he is trying to be a better man. We obviously have a long way to go, but that was the most honest conversation I've had with him in twenty years. I could never have done it without you. Thank you, Hannah."

"I'm so glad."

"I hope you will still be happy after I ask you for a huge favor." Patrick had an anxious look on his face. "The reason he was so insistent to speak to me was because he is getting remarried this weekend. He had written me letters, and obviously he has been calling the rectory, but I've been ignoring him. He wants me to attend. I don't know if I can trust him yet, but it seems like he is trying to change. I cautiously want to give him a chance. I know we have—"

"Don't worry about a thing here, that isn't an issue," Hannah cut him off. "I can handle all our appointments. I can call Father Simmons from Delevan to fill in on Sunday. He is always looking for a chance to say Mass. Are you sure that you want to go to his wedding though?" she questioned.

"I'm nervous, and I'm not ready to completely forgive him yet. I haven't seen much of my family in years, though. He said he will help me tell everyone about the note. He was willing to bring down the mood of his wedding to be honest with everyone. If I don't take this chance to believe him, I think I'll regret it." Patrick tried to sound sure of his answer.

"Then I think you should go." Hannah smiled at him.

Patrick returned her smile. "Thank you so much for covering things here. I know we have some things to work on for your wedding and the festival as well. I'm so sorry about the timing; it's awful."

"We can finish next week. Go, have a good time and reconnect with your family. I promise everything is covered here." Hannah then ushered him towards the door.

Patrick was so grateful for her. There had never been anyone in his life he could rely on so completely. Yes, they worked together, but he knew that was not why she was so willing to take care of him. Without thinking or hesitating, he leaned down and kissed her on the lips. As quickly as he had done it, he moved back, his face the picture of embarrassment.

"I'm so sorry, I should not have done that. I'm not sure what came over me—"

Hannah hushed him by putting her finger to his lips.

"Shh. Stop." They stood like that for a few seconds. For weeks, all Hannah had wanted was to be near Patrick. After their kiss on Sunday, the thought of being able to touch him again had consumed her thoughts.

"The only thing you need to apologize for is if you don't kiss me again." Her voice was full of urgency. She looked at him achingly.

Obviously taken back by her request and her bluntness, Patrick didn't move for a moment; Hannah's finger was still pressed to his lips, distracting him. He pulled her into his body and kissed her, the same way they had kissed by the river. They held onto each other tight, each lost in the short moment they shared. Hannah ran her fingers through his hair and up and down his back. Patrick tried to memorize the feel of her touch and her smell. After a minute, they slowed down and reluctantly pulled back from each other. Patrick rested his forehead against Hannah's.

"We shouldn't keep doing this. We agreed that whatever this is is over," he said with resignation in his voice.

"Just let it be a kiss," Hannah replied softly. "Nothing has changed." She smiled at him. They stood forehead to forehead for another second before Patrick turned to look at the clock.

"I'd better get going; my father is waiting. Are you sure you'll be okay for the week? That we are okay?"

"Yes, and yes. Go! I'll see you next week." Hannah tried to sound confident.

Patrick went into his office to grab a few things and then headed towards the door. He stopped and turned back to Hannah, then walked back to her side with a few long strides. When he reached her, he stopped and kissed her forehead.

"Thank you again. If it wasn't for you, I would never have had the courage..."

Hannah knew how he felt; she felt the same way. He didn't need to explain.

"I was only repaying the favor."

Once Patrick was gone from the office, Hannah could finally take a deep breath. Everything around her was spiraling out of her control. Julie was getting sicker, her wedding was happening so soon, and her feelings for Patrick were becoming untenable. For weeks she had controlled herself, but now that she knew she loved him and that he felt the same way about her, she was more lost than she'd ever been. She felt the intensity of their feelings every time she was near him. She had felt it just now in his kiss. They didn't need to say it out loud. The feeling of joy she had when she was with him was overwhelming. Even under the trying circumstances, Hannah couldn't shake the feeling that, as painful as it could be, their relationship was a gift.

28

It took Hannah several minutes to compose herself before she picked up the phone to call Father Simmons, the associate pastor at a church in a larger town a few miles away. He rarely got to say Mass anymore and was always willing to help out. He picked up on the first ring.

"Good morning, Father Simmons speaking."

Once Hannah had the weekend Mass covered, she set about rescheduling the few appointments Patrick had on his calendar for the week. The Clancys would need to move their meeting about their newest baby's baptism, and the Smiths would have to come a different day to discuss becoming parishioners. Besides those, Hannah could handle the rest of the business herself. She owed that much to Patrick. They did have quite a bit of work to do confirming vendors and volunteers for the church festival, but she would handle it herself. She went into his office to retrieve the festival documents she needed. While she was inside, she couldn't help but linger for a few seconds. The whole space smelled like him. She closed her eyes and remembered the kiss they had shared earlier. She tried to let go of her pain and guilt and instead hold on to the gratitude she felt that they had come into each other's lives.

When she emerged from his office, she was startled by two women standing in front of her desk.

"Oh hello. Good afternoon." She tried not to sound nervous as she welcomed them. She wasn't sure why she cared, however, since Mrs. Jenkins and Jackie had always been two of the most unwelcoming people in the whole town. Hannah now knew what had happened with Barb and her father, but that didn't excuse all the times she had been awful to Hannah and Julie. It made sense now how Jackie had turned out to be a bully, considering her mother was the original mean girl in Hope. She had no interest in dealing with either of these women, but she had promised Patrick she would cover for him. That was more important to her.

"What can I help you both with?" she asked, gaining confidence in herself with each word.

"We were actually hoping to see Father Patrick. Is he in?" Jackie was cordial, but Hannah could see the effort it cost her.

"He actually had to leave very abruptly for some personal business. He will be out all week. Can I schedule you an appointment for—"

"How irregular. There was no announcement that he would be out," Barb interrupted curtly.

Hannah wasn't going to let them dominate the conversation like she had let them dominate her childhood.

"As I said, it was quite unexpected. He left just a short time ago. I haven't had time to post the change yet."

Visibly annoyed, Jackie and Barb exchanged glances.

Jackie spoke up this time.

"Well, I guess we can speak to you about this then. My mother and a few of her friends normally have set areas they oversee for the festival. They haven't been contacted about anything yet, and the festival is getting closer by the day. We know that you are new to this position, and it's also Father Patrick's first time coordinating the festival. We just wanted to make sure we were listed as volunteers in those areas and that nothing has changed. It's obvious that it's a lot for you to handle. If you need, we can step in, since we have done it before." She tried to make it sound like an offer of help, but Jackie's tone made it clear that her words were meant as a reproach.

There was no way Hannah was going to allow Jackie and Barb to take over any part of the festival. She had let them ruin her last festival in Hope so many years ago, and they would not have that privilege again.

"Actually, thank you for the offer, but I was just about to do that this week. My mother kept the list of all the past year's volunteers. I was going to reach out based on that." She smiled at them as warmly as the chill of a February breeze. Hannah reached down to pick up the festival-planning book Julie had assembled. Hannah and Patrick had literally been going through it step by step.

"Everything is in here, so I don't think we need any additional help with planning right now."

Both women seemed caught off guard by Hannah's directness.

"Oh good… Well, please let Father Patrick know we stopped by, and tell HIM of our offer." Jackie made sure to emphasize that Patrick should make the decision.

"Will do. Thank you for stopping by." Hannah didn't even wait for a response before she sat down and picked up the phone to call the first name on the list. Jackie and her mother walked out the door, clearly annoyed. Hannah was proud of herself. She had never stood up to either of them. She had kept her cool and professionalism, not shrinking in their presence.

The rest of the day flew by. There was so much work that needed to be done. She couldn't deny that she welcomed the distraction. The situation with Patrick was still confusing, and with every day that passed, her mother looked less like herself. The wedding had given her a burst of life, but underneath that, Hannah could see the dark circles growing under Julie's eyes. She couldn't ignore the fact that her mother looked pained every time she walked or sat down. The large work checklist she had was helping to keep the panic at bay about what lay ahead. She was once again grateful her mother had forced this job on her. It really was a blessing.

She remained at the office as long as she could. The sun had already begun to set when Hannah finally locked up. She had accomplished many things, calling volunteers and vendors and getting started on the map of where each booth would be located. She had even called Jackie to confirm that she had secured a local band for the night's entertainment. She felt proud of how much she had done by herself. She had always hated the festival, as it was also the second worst night of her life, and now she was planning it.

When she stepped outside, the summer air was thick with humidity. It made her skin sticky before she even began walking. It hadn't rained in weeks, and the grass had begun to turn brown. It had been a very hot day, and the smell of the warm asphalt from the street still lingered in the air. All those things brought her back to the last summer she had spent in Hope. That summer had already been on her mind all day after seeing Barb and Jackie and because she had been working on the summer festival the entire day. On her way home, she couldn't help but reflect on how different this festival would be from the last one she went to—and how different she was now as well.

29

AUGUST 1981

Hannah hadn't even wanted to go to the end-of-summer party at Jackie Jenkins's. Her best friend Katie had begged her to go for several days, and in the end, Hannah had finally given in. She had avoided the other end-of-senior-year parties over the course of the summer. She felt guilty saying no to Katie for this final one. Hannah and Jackie had never gotten along, so she didn't want to go to her party, but Katie had been insistent.

Jackie lived on a farm at the edge of town, with a large backyard and a pool. Katie convinced her that they could avoid Jackie once they got to the party. When they arrived, they found a spot on some lawn chairs out in the yard away from the larger crowd. They had a beer and shared some laughs. A few other kids they usually hung out with also were there, so Hannah finally started to feel at ease. The night was going better than she had expected, until she had to use the bathroom. She left Katie and her other friends to go into the house.

She asked one of the first people she saw inside where the bathroom was. They pointed upstairs. She cautiously went upstairs and checked the first few doors that she saw. Neither was the bathroom. Finally, she opened a third door to discover a bedroom with an en-suite bathroom. She didn't see him at first, but when she was few steps into the room, she noticed a boy stand up from the bed. She stopped and started to apologize for intruding.

"Excuse me, I was just looking for the bathroom." She was planning to turn and leave, but the boy was staring at her. Of course, she knew who he was. She knew everyone in Hope. His name was Colton, and he was Jackie's boyfriend. He had never been mean to her, but to be fair, he had never actually talked to her either. Even though their school was small, he was in a group that didn't mix with kids they didn't think were cool.

He finally responded to her. "No, please go ahead." He motioned for her to pass him to get to the bathroom.

She did really have to pee, and she had no reason to be suspicious of him. She took a few more steps into the room. As she got closer to Colton, however, she could tell he was very drunk. He moved towards her but stumbled at his first step. When he tried to speak again, his words were slurred, and she wasn't sure what he was trying to say. Hannah got a bad feeling about the situation. She decided to leave and go back downstairs. It all happened so fast after that. When she turned to leave, he reached out and grabbed her arm, forcing her to stay.

"Colton, let me go! You're drunk!" she yelled at him.

She tried to push him away, but he held on to her arm tight.

He leaned in as he spoke, stroking her cheek. "Why does Jackie always say nasty things about you? Did you know that she does that? She says the rudest things about you. Sometimes I think she does it because she knows I think you're hot," he murmured as he pulled her deeper into the room and away from the door.

She tried to fight him, but he was bigger and stronger. Colton grabbed her other arm and pushed her up against the back wall of the room. He held her in place with his forearm across her chest. With his other hand he touched her face, her breast, and then grabbed her butt. She screamed at him again.

"You're hurting me. Stop!" She sounded frantic. She could hear the music downstairs. It was so loud that she feared no one could hear her screams.

"Let's see if what Jackie says about you is true," Colton whispered into her ear.

The words sent a wave of fear through Hannah's body. She could only imagine what deranged untrue things Jackie might have said to him. She assumed something along the lines that Hannah was easy. She had to get away from Colton. She struggled and continued to scream at him to stop, but he wouldn't let her go. She started to panic as he shoved his hand down her shirt and tried to undo her jeans. Again, she yelled at him.

"Stop! Get off of me Colton!" Her tone was now more panicked than before.

But he didn't stop. Hannah tried futilely to push him away. He shoved his fingers into her mouth, and she bit down hard. He pulled back in pain just for a second, giving Hannah just enough time to break free from his grip. She tried to run away and managed to escape the room, but he caught up to her and grabbed her at the top of the stairs.

They scuffled again, and as she broke free, Colton tripped and fell down the stairs. He was too drunk to catch himself. He twisted and turned the whole way down, landing on his arm as he crashed onto the tile at the bottom of the stairs. His pained scream was so loud that it drew a small crowd to the bottom of the stairs. As Hannah processed what had happened, she saw Jackie standing just down the hall. She had been near enough to hear everything, and she had most certainly seen Colton grab Hannah before he fell. Jackie stared at Hannah without saying a word. Eventually she pushed past Hannah and went downstairs to help Colton.

Hannah was in shock. She ran down the stairs, fleeing past Jackie and the others that had gathered. They were all helping Colton up off the floor. Everything around her seemed hazy. She was having trouble getting her bearings and catching her breath. The sounds of the party seemed muted, but before she could make it out the front door, she heard Colton yell out at her angrily.

She didn't stop or slow down, running the two miles home in her flip flops. When she was finally safe inside, she realized both her feet were bleeding from the sandal straps. Her mind was spinning with what had just happened. She knew she should tell someone what Colton had tried to do. She should have found Katie. She should go up and wake her mother. She should have gone to the police. But she wasn't going to do any of that.

Hadn't she been lucky that she managed to fight him off? He was just a dumb drunk boy, right? She hadn't done anything wrong, so why did she feel so ashamed? In a week, she would be at college, leaving this town and everyone in it behind. That was reason enough for her not to stir up a mess with Colton and Jackie. She made the decision to go upstairs, shower, and try to pretend nothing had happened.

The next day was the summer festival, and her mother insisted she go. Julie was working at the corn booth and had signed Hannah up to help her. She tried to get out of it, but eventually gave in, mostly to get her mother to stop asking her what was wrong. Once she arrived at the festival, she knew she should have tried harder to get out of going. All around her she could hear the whispers about how Colton had fallen and broken his arm at a party the night before. There was speculation about his football future and what a shame it was that he had gotten injured. Every comment hurt Hannah, even though it had been her decision not to tell anyone the truth. She tried to hide in the back of the booth, shucking corn and staying out of eyesight.

Most of the night, she was successful at avoiding seeing anyone from her class. At one point, she had to duck down and pretend to be cleaning up a mess on the floor to avoid being noticed. However, towards the end of the night, she caught a glimpse of Jackie and Colton approaching the booth. She tried her previous hiding tactic, but Jackie spotted her anyway. They both walked up to Julie at the front of the booth. Hannah remained with her back glued to the rear wall of the tent. Colton was wearing a cast and sling on his right arm. Julie began offering her sympathy to Colton.

He stood practically stone-faced as she talked, glancing angrily towards Hannah. It sent a shiver up her spine. She was taken aback by how Colton seemed to feel no shame or remorse for what had happened. Midway through Julie's well wishes, Jackie began shaking her head. At first Hannah was hoping Jackie would apologize or that she would have some kind of reprimand for Colton. Hannah didn't have the strength to vocalize what had happened on her own, but if someone else started the conversation, at least the truth would be out. By the end of Jackie's first sentence, Hannah knew her hopes had been misplaced.

"Thank you, Mrs. Marshall, but you need to know what really happened. Hannah tried to start something with Colton! When he rejected her, she pushed him, and he fell down the stairs!" Jackie screamed her accusation more than once, yelling loudly enough for everyone nearby to hear.

Julie tried to defend Hannah, but her voice was drowned out by the whispers and admonishments of all the townspeople who had gathered around. Jackie began crying and lamenting how unfair it was that Colton would most likely lose his football scholarship. Sensing there was no reasoning with the crowd, Julie grabbed Hannah and led her out the back of the tent. They briskly walked home, not slowing down until they reached their front walkway.

Hannah was still in shock about being attacked, but hearing Jackie lie about what had happened was more hurtful than the actual attack had been. Everyone thought Hannah was the one who had hurt Colton. As they were leaving, she heard the chatter around her growing, calls for the police and accusations that she had assaulted him drifting into the air. Jackie had seen what happened. She knew that Colton had attacked Hannah. Why would she lie? Why would she stand by him? Although Jackie hadn't helped her and had stood by and watched, Hannah hadn't thought she would actively blame her; that was unthinkable.

Once they were inside the house, Julie slammed the door and locked the deadbolt. She sat Hannah down on the front bench and kneeled to look at her face-to-face.

"What really happened Hannah? I didn't even know anything happened at the party last night."

Seeing the concern on her mother's face brought tears to Hannah's eyes, but she couldn't speak. She couldn't tell her. Maybe she could never tell anyone. She felt such shame, guilt, and trauma. All she could do was weep. Julie held Hannah until she stopped crying. Julie reassured her that she knew Jackie was lying, and that it was okay if Hannah didn't want to talk about it. Hannah nodded and hugged her mother.

The next week, Julie tried to bring up what had happened a few times, but Hannah immediately changed the subject. Julie decided to leave Hannah be and let her talk about it when she was ready. Hannah stayed in the house all week, always coming up with an excuse to stay in, like cleaning or organizing something. When she left for college the next weekend, she hugged her mother and hoped she wouldn't bring up Colton and Jackie ever again. Of course, Julie tried one final time to find out what had happened, but Hannah again refused to talk about it. When she drove away, she glanced in her rearview mirror. She caught a glimpse of Julie standing alone in the driveway. When she looked back at the road ahead, she planned to never look back at Hope again. For fourteen years, she kept that promise to herself.

30

JULY 1995

Hannah finished her short walk from the church to home. As she turned to walk up the driveway, she couldn't help but think about how much had changed since the summer of 1981. She had spent so much time away from her home and from her mother. Yes, they talked on the phone once a week. They saw each other several times a year, but Julie always had to come to Hannah. After she left for college, her mother had tried to get her to come home on many occasions. Hannah always found a reason not to. Whether it was an internship, school work, or later her job or friends, she always found an excuse not to come home. After a couple of years, Julie stopped asking. The distance between them grew, and they settled into their separate lives.

How much time had she let Colton and Jackie take from her? The number of holidays, summer get-togethers, nights drinking wine with Jane and Julie in the backyard... There were too many to count after fourteen years of being away. She walked into the house, expecting to see her mother up watching TV or reading a book, but she was lying in her bed in the living room, asleep. Hannah studied her for a few seconds. Julie's face was illuminated by the last light of the setting sun. There were now lines around her eyes and mouth that hadn't been there when Hannah left all those years ago. Small grey hairs poked through her otherwise dark-brown hair. Her skin looked greyer than it had at the beginning of the summer. Her cheeks were hollower. In her heart, Hannah knew her mother did not have long. Even when she heard that her cancer had already metastasized, Hannah had held out hope that it wouldn't come to this. But here she was, watching in real time how easily a person full of life can be taken down.

Hannah felt guilty all over again. All the years she had spent away from Julie meant she had years full of memories never made. Her mother had to have wondered why Hannah withdrew so completely and suddenly. Didn't she deserve to know the truth? She had told Patrick, and the burden she had been carrying had lightened greatly as a result. If she told her mother, maybe she could be rid of it completely.

She approached Julie and gently patted her shoulder. Julie's eyes opened and looked up at Hannah. Looking into her mother's eyes, however, Hannah realized she still wasn't ready to tell her.

"Mom, I just wanted to let you know that I'm home."

"Thank you. Glad you're back," Julie murmured as she fell back asleep.

31

The rest of the week went by quickly. Hannah was in the office for long hours, working late each night. Jane stayed with Julie during the day. Hannah felt grateful for all her help. Thankfully, there weren't any repeat visits from Jackie or Barb. She had been able to work mostly uninterrupted. Once the community found out that Father Murphy was out of town, there was little reason for anyone to call the office. Hannah's mind often drifted to how Patrick was doing in New York. She hoped that his father had been genuine in his remorse. She also wished more than once that he would call to let her know how he was doing. As the week stretched on, it seemed less likely that he would. The distance between them was also for the best.

She wanted the days to pass quickly until he returned, but each night, she wanted time to slow down. Her mother seemed to be fading a little more each day. They still spent their evenings talking or playing cards, but Julie was getting tired more quickly. She was going to bed earlier and sleeping in later. Most mornings, Julie was still asleep when Hannah left for work at 7:45 a.m.

The week turned into the weekend. Hannah was grateful that she had so much to do for her wedding as well as the festival. Saturday and Sunday were busy with wedding planning and preparation. Noah had come to help clean and prep the backyard for the reception. Hannah had protested, but Julie insisted on cooking dinner on Saturday night. They shared a relaxing meal with Jane. After dinner, when Julie was feeling too tired to walk back inside, Noah offered to carry her. At first Julie balked at the offer, but she eventually gave in. Hannah wanted to cry at the bittersweetness of the moment. Noah had always been so thoughtful. He never needed prompting to step up when he was needed. Remembering one of the reasons she was most drawn to him helped to calm a bit of her apprehension about moving forward with the wedding.

Sunday night, Noah left to go back to Chicago. Hannah felt a renewed sense of hope. She had survived the week without Patrick. In fact, she had thrived. It would be difficult to leave him; the thought still made her sick, but she could do it with Noah by her side. As she drifted off to sleep, for the first time since she had agreed to the wedding, she felt a small sense of excitement about it.

Monday morning started as so many others had that summer. Hannah completed her usual tasks of plant watering and checking the answering machine. She also organized all the work she had done while Patrick was away. As the minutes ticked by, she started to get the same sense of nervous anticipation she always got before Patrick arrived at work.

When the door finally swung open, Hannah took a deep breath and looked up at him. *Right on time,* she thought. She had wanted to be cool and most certainly more professional than she had been before he left. She had spent the past weekend reconnecting with Noah, and she was getting married to him in a week. But when she saw Patrick, all the strength she had been feeling slowly fell away. He looked better than she had ever seen him. He had a fresh haircut and looked well rested. He seemed lighter to her, almost younger. It was clear that his secret had been weighing him down. Now, he was no longer encumbered by that burden.

"Good morning, Hannah." He flashed a large smile her way.

She couldn't help but smile back.

"Good morning. How was the trip?" It was a question she had been wanting to ask him for the last week.

"It was as good as I could have hoped. My father and I had so many necessary conversations. We shared what happened with my mother's family as well. It was good for me to see them and have them know the truth. My father and I are still in an uncertain place.

I want to see that his resolve to be better isn't just a momentary thing. But by the time I left, it felt like we were at least in a place we can start that process from." Patrick's voice was full of hope.

He continued telling Hannah about his week. He had seen all the family that he hadn't spoken to in years and had even met up with a high school friend for dinner one night. He had also seen his mom's cousin, who had helped him become a priest. As he was finishing detailing the events of the week, he grew more serious.

"I told my cousin about you, Hannah." He dropped his head, and his cheeks flushed. Hannah thought she heard embarrassment in his voice.

Hannah blushed as she wondered what that meant. Had he told his cousin that they were friends or that they were "friends?" Her eyes once again settled on his lips. She couldn't stop herself from thinking about what had happened the last time they were in this office. The feeling of his mouth on hers, his hair in her fingers, the warmth of his body pressed against her... She suddenly felt very self-conscious.

"ALL about me?" she asked hesitantly.

Patrick chuckled. "Well not ALL about you. I told him I met an amazing woman who helped give me the strength to finally tell my father the truth. He might have picked up on my feelings for you, but he didn't let on if he did."

Hannah was simultaneously relieved and saddened. Part of her desperately wanted someone, anyone, to know the truth about her and Patrick. The practical side of her understood the implications of that honesty. No one could ever know. Who would even understand what was between them? It didn't even make sense to either of them.

"Well...I'm glad that it went so well. You deserve some happiness after everything you have been through with your family." Hannah was being truthful. She was happy that Patrick had reconnected with his family. Their time together would end soon, and this way, she knew he would have other people to lean on for support. She imagined that was how he felt about her marrying Noah.

He couldn't be with her, but he knew Noah would take care of her.

"Thank you. I never would have had the strength if it wasn't for you." He paused and smiled warmly at her, but then his demeanor changed.

"Well, enough about me. I believe we have a wedding we need to work on this week, don't we?" He winked at her playfully.

She knew that his lightheartedness about her marrying someone else shouldn't hurt her, but it did.

"Yes, I suppose we do. Let me fill you in on all the things I got done for the festival first." Hannah grabbed the lists she had compiled the previous week and followed him into his office. She couldn't help but feel something else had changed with Patrick. It was more than just the relief of his family knowing the truth. He seemed more distant than the week before. The details he had offered her about his trip home were very sparse, and then he had immediately switched gears to work. She wanted more from him. She wanted to know every detail of his trip—and more about the other people he had seen, like the friend he went to dinner with. She could tell Patrick was holding back.

Instead, they went over a few details for her wedding. They then moved on to the festival. Eventually their discussion reached the topic of festival volunteers, and she told him about her run-in with Jackie and Barb. It wasn't especially relevant, but she wanted him to know in case they brought it up with him. She hoped he would approve of her behavior. After she finished recounting the incident, Patrick started laughing.

"I'm proud of you. You stood up to them."

"Thank you. I wasn't too rude?" she asked, half serious, half joking.

"After how they have treated you, I think you were exceedingly cordial."

Hannah breathed a sigh of relief and sat up a little straighter in her chair. She was proud of herself too. When the conversation turned back to her wedding, Hannah felt the familiar tension slowly move through her body. Patrick gave her some paperwork to fill out and had her approve the final list of songs and readings for the ceremony. He promised to take care of the wedding certificate and coordinating the church musicians. These were usually things she would do, but he insisted that she shouldn't have to do it for her own wedding.

After discussing the wedding plans, Hannah retreated to her desk. The rest of the day dragged on for her. She was growing anxious to get home. An hour before she was supposed to leave, she asked Patrick if it was okay for her to go home early.

"Of course, you deserve it. Thank you for all the work you did last week."

Hannah enjoyed her walk home. The fresh air was a welcome change. The office had felt stuffy and uncomfortable today. Her mom's house was beginning to feel the same. As usual, her walk home was over in only a few minutes. The first thing she saw after going inside was her mother napping in bed. Julie looked so thin and pale. Her cheeks, once rosy and full, now fell hollow and pale across her protruding cheekbones.

Hannah had left home feeling good about herself, but something had changed in her during the day. Patrick had returned, but not in the way he had left her. He was guarded and distant. This summer had been confusing and challenging. On the other hand, it had also possibly been the most profound time of her life. Sometimes she felt as if the feelings she had experienced this summer opened parts of her she didn't know existed. Her relationship with her mother had blossomed. Knowing Patrick had moved her in ways she couldn't explain. Now she felt like her world was starting to narrow again. The end of her summer in Hope was approaching. She could feel it in her bones. She started to tear up, but then heard movement from the kitchen. Hannah moved from the hallway and walked into the kitchen. She was grateful to see Jane cooking dinner.

"Oh, thank goodness you're here!" Hannah exclaimed. Her voice was full of emotion.

"My girl, what is wrong?" Jane threw her arms around Hannah.

"Everything," Hannah responded.

Jane sat outside with Hannah all night as she clumsily tried to explain what she was feeling. Jane just listened. Hannah wanted to tell her the full truth, but it wouldn't be fair to burden Jane with her secrets about the past or Patrick. She did explain, however, how she felt rushed into the wedding because her mother was so ill. She explained that she did love Noah, but that, with things in such a state of flux, she couldn't tell whether she was marrying him because she wanted to or because she wanted to make her mother happy and keep herself from being alone. Without confessing the whole truth, she told Jane how close she had become to Father Patrick. She told her how that was making her question many things in her life.

There was little Jane could say to make any of anything better. She could think of nothing else to do but pull Hannah in for a tight hug. As Hannah quietly cried into her chest, Jane held her and slowly rubbed her back. For Jane, this summer had been a beautiful thing in so many ways. She had gotten to see the girl she loved like a daughter reconnect with her mother. They had all shared laughs, meals, and several good cries. Jane was very proud of the woman Hannah had grown into. She had selfishly been excited for the wedding, just like Julie was. It was a bright spot on the horizon that was sure to end in sorrow. It was clear that Julie was getting very close to the end, and the wedding had given her a concrete date to hold on for.

Jane also knew that there was so much Hannah was holding back. Hannah had changed almost overnight so many years ago, and now it seemed to be happening again. Despite their best efforts, neither she nor Julie had ever been able to find out what exactly had happened the weekend of the festival so many years ago. She could tell Hannah was holding something back now as well. A thought flashed across her mind very briefly. The hesitating way Hannah had spoken about Father Patrick stood out in Jane's mind. She shook her head and tried to forget it. If that was the true reason for Hannah's pain, there was absolutely nothing that could be done about it.

32

The next few days flew by in a blur. At work, Hannah was rushing around trying to stay on top of a busy week preparing for the wedding and the festival. Her and Patrick's conversations continued to be short and professional. Every time Hannah thought he might start to say something more personal, he'd cut off the exchange and find an excuse to return to his office. She couldn't tell what was going on in his head, but it was gutting her. She needed him more than ever to reassure her that what she was doing was right. Yet he seemed further away than ever.

As Hannah walked home from work on Wednesday evening, all she could think about was Patrick. Why was he shutting her out? Things had been so different between them only a week earlier. She wanted to believe it was self-preservation, but she couldn't help but feel insecure. Had his feelings changed while he was back home? Did starting to repair his family relationships fill the void their relationship had been filling? The uncertainty was eating her alive, and she was running out of opportunities to ask him before her wedding.

Tomorrow would be her last day of work before the wedding. Tomorrow evening, Noah and Katie would arrive. She was looking forward to seeing Katie, but she was also afraid of having another set of eyes on her, analyzing her reactions. When she made it to her mom's front door, she paused to take few deep breaths before going in. She told herself that she would confront Patrick the next day. Tomorrow would be her last chance to be alone with him before the wedding.

Like she had done every day after work for the past few weeks, Hannah braced herself to see her mother. She opened the front door, expecting to see Julie either asleep or reading on her bed in the living room. Instead, she was greeted by darkness. All the lights in the house were off. She started to grow concerned, when all at once, the lights flashed on and she was met with a loud "SURPRISE!" She took a step back and let her eyes adjust to the brightness. It was Noah and Katie.

"We came early to surprise you!" Noah came up to her and gave her a warm hug and a kiss.

Katie followed and hugged her as well.

"Aren't you excited to see us?" Katie looked at Hannah inquisitively. Hannah stood still, not sure how to react. Seconds passed as the expressions on Katie's, Noah's, and Julie's faces all shifted from excitement to confusion.

Hannah saw the shift in their body language. She wasn't sure what her own expression looked like, but she was certain it wasn't one of happiness. She tried to recover from her initial reaction.

"Um yes. Uh…of course I'm happy. Sorry. I wasn't expecting to see you both until tomorrow," she tried to cover up her true feelings.

"I was thinking we can have a girls' morning tomorrow, since you didn't get a bachelorette party," Katie said enthusiastically.

Hannah's mind started to race. If she didn't go to work tomorrow, there was little chance of getting to speak with Patrick before the wedding.

"Thank you, Katie, but I'm supposed to work tomorrow. There are some things I need to finish up before I take my vacation for the wedding." She was struggling to keep her composure.

"I'm sure Father Patrick would be okay with it if you don't go in tomorrow," Julie offered.

Hannah's desperation to talk to Patrick was turning into guilt over the fact that she was so disappointed by Noah and Katie's surprise. This was surely not how a person should feel when their fiancé and best friend surprise them days before their wedding. She was having trouble fighting the urge to cry.

"Sorry, I just need one minute." As she spoke, Hannah's voice began to crack. She ran to the bathroom and quickly shut the door once she was inside. She could no longer hold back her tears. They began to fall, heavy and fast. She wasn't sure if it was the missed chance to talk to Patrick, the guilt over wanting to talk to him in the first place, or her trepidation about the wedding in general, but she was falling apart. After a few minutes, she heard a soft knock at the door.

"Uh...Hannah, babe. Are you okay?"

Noah sounded concerned. She usually told him everything, but not anymore.

"Yeah, sorry. I'm just so overwhelmed right now."

"As long as that's all it is. I have known you a long time Hannah, and I feel like there is something you aren't telling me." Noah sounded unsure if he wanted to know the truth.

She didn't want to hurt him. A few years from now, far from this place and Patrick, Hannah knew she would be happy with Noah. They just had to get there. She tried to compose herself. She took a few deep breaths and dried her face. Looking in the mirror, she tried to prepare herself for the several pairs of eyes that were sure to be studying her when she emerged from the bathroom. She opened the door, and thankfully, it was only Noah waiting for her. He pulled her into one of his warm bear hugs, and she let herself relax into him. He was safe and supportive. He had always been there for her. Even now, when he sensed something wasn't quite right, he didn't pry or pester, he just stood by her. He deserved someone better than her. She swore to herself that after they were married, she would try and live up to the level of support he gave her. Their moment was interrupted when Julie joined them.

"Don't worry about anything, Hannah," she said with excitement. "I just spoke to Father Patrick, and he understands completely. He told me to let you know he could finish the things you were working on today." Julie was clearly proud of herself for handling Hannah's dilemma.

Hannah was glad that she still had her face firmly buried in Noah's chest. It gave her the cover to compose herself again before pulling back. She had thought if she could at least call Patrick and talk to him herself, maybe she could clear the air with him. It felt impossible to move forward without his reassurance that this was still the right thing to do. Now she wasn't sure she would be able to get it.

33

When he heard the phone ring, Patrick's heart jumped for just a second. It shouldn't have, but there was no way to deny that he wanted it to be Hannah on the other end. Before he had left for New York, he had given in to his most base instincts. He told himself he had been overcome by his emotions when he kissed her. That wasn't true. He knew exactly what he was doing. He wanted to kiss her. He still wanted to do more. Too often since it had happened, his mind went back to that moment. The feel of her body pressed to his, the way she grabbed his hair and pulled him close. He knew everything they had shared was wrong. He had repeatedly prayed for the strength to wipe his feelings for her from his mind and heart.

Now, he had accepted that that was not going to happen. This was not some passing infatuation or attraction. His only option was to try to keep his distance from her. If they got too close, he knew he wouldn't be able to stop himself from crossing the line with her. All week he had tried to remain professional. Being distant with her was painful for him, but he could see no other way to navigate their situation.

His heart sank when he answered the phone. It was Julie, not Hannah on the other end. His heart descended further when Julie began speaking and asked if Hannah could start her vacation early. She explained that Noah and Hannah's friend Katie had come into town early. Of course Patrick said yes. He didn't really have a choice. He regretted having been so formal with her all week. He didn't even tell her why. He just came back to Hope acting as if there had never been anything between them. How could he have been so foolish to keep quiet about what was inside his heart? When could he tell her now; at her rehearsal? At the wedding itself? From the beginning, there had been an expiration date to their relationship. He felt it more acutely now. He could be transferred any day now. And as terrible as the thought was, any day might be Julie's last. The only time they had was right now. He wanted Hannah to marry Noah, but he also wanted to tell her how he truly felt. Just once he needed to say it. "Hannah, I love you."

34

In the morning, Hannah woke up to Katie gently nudging her.

"Morning. I brought you breakfast."

Hannah pulled the covers over her head. "What time is it?" she groaned.

"Get up. You need to eat. We have a full day of wedding excitement." Katie looked full of anticipation. She had planned a morning trip to the salon to get their nails done. Noah was going to work on the table layout for the reception in the backyard. The weather was supposed to be clear and sunny throughout the rest of the week, so they could start setting up now.

Hannah slowly got up and began to eat. Katie was going on and on about how much fun they were going to have and how excited she was. Hannah couldn't help but wish she'd had her coffee before this conversation began. Clearly Katie had drunk more than one cup. As Hannah ate and the caffeine finally started to kick in, she began to experience some of the excitement Katie was exuding. In a summer of facing past trauma and illness, it felt good to have her best friend with her. They finally emerged from her bedroom, dressed and ready for their trip to the salon. Noah, Julie, and Jane were already in the backyard working. Hannah went out to chide Julie about overexerting herself.

"Mom, sit down! Why are you moving chairs? Let Noah do it, and we can help when we get back!" She knew her mother wanted to be useful, but they had a long three days in front of them, and she wanted Julie to make it through all of them.

"I tried to tell her, but she insisted." Noah shot her a warm grin. He walked over to her and pulled her in for a quick kiss. It was different from the kisses she had shared with Patrick. She and Noah were free to kiss in front of their friends and family. There was no shame or guilt woven through every touch. It was tender and reassuring. She should have been grateful for this, but part of her couldn't help but wish it was Patrick kissing her instead.

When Hannah and Katie finally left for the salon, they were already running late. Katie insisted on driving, but Hannah wanted to walk. Hannah won. They briskly walked down the street on their way downtown. As they passed the church, Hannah held her breath with anticipation. She said a silent prayer that she would catch a glimpse of Patrick. When they turned the corner and had passed by the church completely, Hannah softly exhaled with disappointment. She thought the sound had been soft enough to be inaudible, but Katie heard.

"Why don't you just tell me now what is going on? I know you Hannah, and you have only acted like this one other time. I can tell you're holding something back, just like you did the summer after senior year. You're being uncharacteristically quiet. You're normally an open book. Just please...please tell me what is going on. I'm worried about you."

Hannah was caught off guard. She knew she probably seemed off to everyone, but she had hoped those closest to her would just assume it was because of her mother. Hearing someone call her out so directly put her into a state of panic. Her mind was racing, and she started to feel lightheaded. She looked around for a place to sit but didn't see anywhere and plopped down in the grass instead.

Katie looked even more concerned now.

"Okay, that is IT! You need to tell me what is going on right NOW!" Her voice was loud and demanding.

She was staring right at Hannah. There was no place left for her to hide. Hannah was scrambling to come up with some version of the truth that would satisfy Katie's demands. Honestly, she could use some support right now. She wanted to tell her the whole truth but also knew that would change things forever.

"You're right. I'm a mess—I don't know why I am marrying Noah. I feel guilty all the time." Hannah was fighting back the urge to cry and breathing slowly between each word. "Am I marrying him to make my mother happy, because I don't want to hurt him, or because I actually want to? I honestly can't decide, and the shame is eating me alive." Hannah lay her head in her hands and finally let the tears fall. The words she spoke were true, every one of them.

"Oh Hannah. I know it's confusing with everything happening with your mother, but you had already said yes to Noah before your mom was sick. I was there. You were so excited when he proposed. I had never seen you so happy. Do you remember that?" She gently rubbed Hannah's back.

"I do remember, or at least I am trying to."

She did remember, but then she had met Patrick, and everything she had been so sure of was completely swept away. Hannah sat quietly for a few minutes with Katie at her side.

"But even with that said, if you changed your mind, Hannah, you HAVE to say something to Noah. I will be with you either way, but you shouldn't marry him if you are this conflicted." Katie's tone was supportive but also firm.

Hannah knew she was right. She should tell Noah the truth, but she also knew that she wasn't going to.

"No, I do want to get married. I think it's just a lot to process at the same time as my mother's illness. Please, let's forget we talked about this. Let's go get our nails done." She tried to sound enthusiastic.

Katie looked at her skeptically. "Okay, as long as you're sure, Hannah."

Hannah flashed her most convincing smile. "I am."

Hannah stood back up. They continued their walk to the salon, both still feeling uneasy about the situation, although neither of them said anything else about it.

35

On the rest of the walk into town, Katie tried to make some small talk and lighten the mood. She was still processing seeing Hannah in such a distressed state. She knew that this summer had been overwhelming for her, especially because she had to move home. Since high school, the very mention of Hope had made Hannah go white. Katie had tried for years to find out what had happened to Hannah, but she was never willing to share. It felt like that was happening all over again. Clearly there was something going on, but what? Noah and Hannah were perfect for each other. Noah was one of the best men Katie had ever met. She was often a bit jealous of Hannah, if she was honest. In turn, Hannah was a great partner for Noah; she was the practical to his impractical. They complemented each other so well, and she had been ecstatic when they got engaged.

Something had changed. She just couldn't figure out what. Hannah seemed different. Obviously, she was handling her mother's illness, but it was more than that. On every phone call the past summer, Katie could tell that something had been shifting with Hannah. She seemed calmer and stronger, surer of herself. This just made her current behavior even more confusing. All summer, Hannah had seemed to be gaining her voice, and now she was full of uncertainty.

By the time they reached downtown, the awkwardness in the air had started to lift. Perhaps Hannah had just been overcome by emotion. She was going through multiple life events in a condensed time frame. Katie couldn't shake her unease but decided to move forward and try to get Hannah to have some fun and relax. Right before they reached the nail salon, they were stopped dead in their tracks. The door swung open in front of them and Jackie emerged, laughing, followed by two other women they had gone to school with. Katie and Hannah held their breaths as Jackie and the first woman, Maggie, turned onto the sidewalk, walking away from them. Unfortunately, the last of the women to come out, Jessica, caught sight of them and immediately squealed a loud enthusiastic hello.

"Ahhh! Hannah and Katie! It has been so long!" She walked over and gave Katie a hug before moving on to Hannah. It was an unwelcome and unwanted reunion.

Jackie and Maggie turned around and joined them, and soon all three women were face-to-face with Katie and Hannah.

Jackie tried her best to fake a smile. "Katie, what are you doing in town?" she asked.

"I'm here for Hannah's wedding. It's this weekend." Katie beamed and put her arm around Hannah's shoulder.

Hannah smiled and added, "Yes, my wedding. It's Saturday."

"Wow… I didn't realize you were getting married so soon. Interesting." Jackie's tone was accusatory.

"You never asked. I would have told you," Hannah quipped, preventing Jackie from saying anything further.

Jackie looked visibly annoyed. After a long pause, she finally added gruffly, "Congratulations."

"We have to be off, schedule to keep and all that," Katie interjected playfully. "Nice to see everyone."

They all exchanged farewells as Katie steered Hannah past the group and into the nail salon.

As they sat getting their nails done, Hannah couldn't shake their run-in with Jackie. The day Jackie had seen Patrick consoling her replayed on a loop in her mind.

"She is so awful. What does interesting mean?" Hannah couldn't stop herself from wondering out loud. Katie wasn't sure if she was talking to her or not.

"Listen, you don't have to explain anything to me. Jackie is rude, she always has been. Don't let her ruin the day," Katie tried to play off Jackie's snide comment, but after Hannah's breakdown in front of the church, she couldn't help but wonder if Jackie knew something that she didn't.

36

The last day and a half, Hannah had been surrounded by a whirlwind of wedding preparations. After they got their nails done, Hannah and Katie had helped Noah transform Julie's backyard into a beautiful event space for the rehearsal and reception. Hannah hadn't seen her mother so alive since she had come home. Julie had fussed over every detail, with Jane following her around and constantly reminding her to take it easy. Their antics had helped to lighten Hannah's mood, reminding her why the wedding was so important. It wasn't just about her.

Noah's family had come into town, as well as a few of their friends from Chicago. It would be the same group attending the rehearsal and the reception, but Julie had insisted on both. They had decided on a casual meal from a local diner for the rehearsal, but the reception was being catered by a fancier restaurant in a larger town a short drive from Hope. The florist would come in the morning to set out the centerpieces for the reception, and Katie, Julie, and Jane had put together small lanterns and flowers for the rehearsal. Hannah's nails were done, and her dresses and accessories had been selected. There was little left for her to do but get dressed, walk down the aisle, and say "I do."

She began to think that perhaps she could handle all of it. The last forty-eight hours away from Patrick had been filled with love, support, and excitement. It had helped relieve some of the heaviness she felt. She felt more at peace about her decision. The burst of life it had given her mother made it all seem worth it. The past month Julie had been fading fast, looking more tired and sick day after day.

This week, however, the color had returned to her cheeks. She still needed her afternoon nap, but she was up more than she was asleep during the day, which was a big change. No matter Hannah's reservations, she couldn't imagine taking away Julie's happiness for her selfish desires.

Julie had been feeling weak and tired the few weeks before the wedding. She also had started to lose her appetite, which had contributed to her lack of energy. She knew that this was the course of the cancer her doctors had laid out for her. The end was approaching, and she could feel it in her bones. The wedding was giving her a temporary boost, but she felt anxious about what would happen once the excitement was over. She had treasured every moment of the summer. Hannah had come back for the first time in years, and now she would get to see her married. They would celebrate the wedding in the backyard of the house she had shared with her husband. Her heart hadn't been so full since the first years after Hannah was born, before Matt had passed. She felt content, grateful even, that she had chosen to live out her last months as fully as she could in her own home. There was no point in living her last days sick from medication and far from home. The memories she had made this summer were a testament to that.

The morning of the rehearsal, Julie woke up excited, but she couldn't fight the nagging suspicion that something wasn't quite right with Hannah. As the wedding approached, Julie had noticed that Hannah seemed on the verge of tears almost every moment. At first, she had written it off as a symptom of the heightened emotions related to her illness and this major life event. Then, when she saw Hannah's reaction to Noah and Katie arriving early, she had known it was more than that. The look of sheer panic on Hannah's face and her retreat to cry in the bathroom had cemented Julie's suspicions. Something more was going on with Hannah.

She still wasn't 100% sure what had happened to her all those years ago with Colton and Jackie that had driven her away. She wondered if it could be related to that, or if it was something else. Was she only marrying Noah to make Julie happy? Her mind raced with these thoughts, giving her pause. Of course, she wanted Noah and Hannah to get married. She loved Noah and thought they were a great couple, but only if it was what Hannah wanted.

Julie had tried to build up the courage to ask Hannah what was happening more than once, but she had decided to give her space. Finally, the morning of the rehearsal, she knew it was now or never. She had never forgiven herself for not pushing Hannah into revealing what happened so many years ago, and she wouldn't make the same mistake again.

37

Hannah awoke early the day of the rehearsal. She felt excited, nervous, and full of dread all at the same time. She was still so conflicted about the decision she was making. After stretching and taking her time, she finally sat up in bed, ready to face the day. Shortly after, there was a knock on her door.

"Hannah, are you up?" Her mother's voice was soft and low on the other side of the door.

"Yeah, come in," Hannah responded.

Julie entered, carrying a cup of coffee. She placed it on the bedside table and then took a seat on the end of the bed. Hannah sat up straighter and picked up the coffee. Julie had a troubled look on her face. Knots began to form in Hannah's stomach as she braced for what her mother might say.

"Hannah, you know I'm very excited about this wedding. I love Noah, and I think you are a great match. I always have. I just…I want to make sure this is what—YOU—really want. These past weeks, I feel like something has been different with you."

Hannah was taken aback by her mother's honesty. She fumbled with the sheets and took a sip of coffee to buy some time as she formulated her response. She appreciated her mother's gesture. Part of her desperately wanted to be honest about everything. She quickly gamed through how that would look, though. The joy and excitement she had seen in her mother the last week would turn to confusion and possibly even disappointment in Hannah's choices. She was sure there was no way her mother, a devout Catholic, would understand her falling in love with a priest. Telling her was selfish. It would devastate Noah, it would throw her mother's last days into upheaval, and it wasn't fair to Patrick, who hadn't agreed to revealing their secret to anyone. Yes, she wanted to unburden her conscience, but not at the expense of the people she cared about. After she swallowed her sip of coffee, she said the only thing she could bring herself to say.

"Mom, I appreciate that very much. It has been a lot. I feel guilty about putting all this wedding stress on you when this should be a peaceful time. I just have a lot of mixed emotions..." Hannah trailed off.

"Oh honey, please don't feel guilty. This has given me a beautiful event to look forward to. Knowing you will have Noah after I'm gone has given me so much peace." Julie put her arms around Hannah and kissed her forehead.

Hannah wanted to cry. She wanted to scream. It was all too much for her to handle. The peace she had felt the night before had been fleeting. It didn't hold up to even the slightest scrutiny. The expectations of her friends and mother weighed heavily on her. How could she destroy the bubble of love and happiness she had been enveloped in the last few days for a man that could never be hers? She already knew the answer before she could think on the question. She couldn't. She wouldn't. Her mother pulled back from their hug and got up to leave.

"Okay, then eat and get ready. We have a lot left to do before the rehearsal." Julie smiled warmly at Hannah.

Hannah gave her the best smile she could muster. Julie turned and walked out of the room. As soon as she heard the door shut, Hannah rolled over in her bed and silently screamed into her pillow.

38

Noah woke up to the sound of a vacuum cleaner in the room next door to his. Hope had its charms, but nice hotel lodgings was not one of them. On past visits, he had stayed in the basement on the pull-out sofa at Hannah's mom's house, but that bed had been taken by Katie. It also made more sense for him to stay at the motel so that he could be with his family and the couple of out-of-town friends that had come for the wedding. Hannah was busy putting the final details together to get the house ready for the rehearsal and reception. The least he could do was be a good host to their guests. This hotel left much to be desired, however. He rolled over to look at the clock. It was only 8 a.m. He grabbed the spare pillow and put it over his head. What kind of a motel starts cleaning this early?

He started to feel the excitement of the day and realized that trying to go back to sleep was pointless. He sat up and threw a T-shirt on. He needed coffee. He walked to motel lobby to get one. On the walk back to his room, a strange feeling came over him. He couldn't explain it, but something reminded him of the afternoon two days earlier when Hannah had come home from work. He had expected her to be overjoyed to see him and Katie. They had been so proud of themselves for the surprise they planned. When Hannah walked through the door and made eye contact with him, he was the one who had been surprised. She had looked panicked and completely unhappy to see him. He had never seen her look at him that way. Of course, she said she was just surprised and overwhelmed by the wedding, but he hadn't been able to shake the feeling that something wasn't right.

The last few months, he had felt her pulling away. He often wondered whether that was why he was so determined to have the wedding this summer. The longer they waited, the less likely it was to happen. Hannah was the love of his life, and he didn't want to lose her. He knew things would be different with her living so far away for the first time, but with each visit and phone call, he had felt more and more like he was intruding on her life rather than being a part of it. He couldn't get the way she had looked at him on Tuesday night out of his mind.

When he first met Hannah, he thought it was odd that she never talked about home. She would mention her mother, but she never went back for long weekends or holidays. Her mother always came to see her. As their relationship progressed, he had tried to bring it up a few times, but Hannah never disclosed much. She told him her father died when she was young, and that she and her mother never fit in. There was no reason for her to go back to Hope. When he and Katie started to become friends, she told him after one long night of drinking that something had happened to Hannah one night right at the end of the summer after their senior year. She told him not even she knew what really happened, but a couple of classmates had spread a lie that Hannah had pushed a boy named Colton, causing him to fall down the stairs. Katie knew that wasn't true because Hannah would never have done something like that, but she could never get the truth out of Hannah either.

At first it bothered him that Hannah had secrets, but then he started to realize that it was one of the things he liked about her. Most girls he had been with were almost too open, but Hannah had a little mystery. He liked the idea that he could continue to uncover new things about her over the course of their life together. She had never given him a reason to question her. Even though he felt something had changed this summer between them, he tried not to overthink it. She had been home, in a place she never wanted to come back to, watching her mother slowly getting sicker. The complete upheaval of their lives had to be very hard for her. That was most likely the cause of the distance he felt between them.

Sometimes suspicious thoughts would creep into his mind, suggesting that it was something more that was causing the disconnect. But Hannah never saw anyone other than Jane and Julie. He knew she spent time with Father Patrick at work, but the thought that Hannah could have feelings for a priest was a ridiculous notion. He told himself there was no reason to worry. He took a deep breath and finished his coffee.

39

The backyard had been transformed from an empty yard to a beautiful event space. There were two long tables with chairs down both sides, large arches covered with greenery at the front and backyard entrances, and string lights strung from the trees on one side of the yard to the other in a zigzag pattern. For the reception, they would adorn the tables with long white tablecloths and beautiful flower arrangements. For the rehearsal, they decided to keep things more basic and leave the tables plain with only lanterns and the few small arrangements they had made themselves. Hannah marveled at the change. It barely seemed like the same yard she had spent all summer sitting in. The air even seemed to smell different.

She had taken time to steady herself for the events of the day after her unexpected conversation with her mother. Although she often worried if someone close to her would notice her feelings towards Patrick, being confronted with the reality that her mother and Katie had noticed a change made her feel even guiltier than she did before. Had Noah noticed as well? She would never want to hurt him, even though she was sure her strange behavior of late most likely already had. All she could do was try to take deep breaths and remind herself that this was what she had wanted before the summer began. Marrying Noah had been her greatest desire, and now it was happening. Staying present in the moment would be her main goal for the day.

As she stood in the middle of the backyard, eyes shut, trying to focus on her breathing, she heard a commotion coming from the house—yells of delight from her mother and gasps of how beautiful the yard looked filled the air. Noah and his family had arrived. Hannah tried to use the last few seconds of alone time to steel her resolve before she was jolted from her solitude.

"Hannah! Oh my God, this looks gorgeous!" Noah's mother Gail exclaimed.

Before Hannah had time to fully turn around, her mother-in-law had thrown her arms around her in a warm, enthusiastic embrace.

"Thank you. So glad you are here." Hannah returned her embrace.

Hannah was sincere in her happiness over Gail's arrival. Over the years she and Noah had been together, she and Gail had grown quite close. Since Hannah never used to visit Hope, she would spend a lot of time with Noah's family over holidays and breaks from work. Gail and Noah's father Dan had become like second parents to her. This was another reason she felt so compelled to go through with her marriage to Noah. She had lost so many people in her life already, and now she was about to lose her mother. She couldn't lose Noah's family as well.

They walked back into the house, where Hannah greeted her friends Stephanie and Erin, who had also arrived with Noah's family. The wedding was becoming more and more real with each guest's arrival. Jane and Julie had set out a simple lunch so they could eat before leaving for the church later in the afternoon. Everyone sat around sharing stories about Noah and Hannah. They all laughed about goofy things they had done as children, gushing about how great they were for each other. Hannah felt surrounded by love and support. But she also felt completely alone. The secrets she carried isolated her from all these people who thought they knew her. There was only one person who truly knew her, and he wasn't here.

40

As the minutes ticked by, bringing him closer and closer to the start of the rehearsal, Patrick grew increasingly uneasy. He had agreed to preside over Hannah's wedding, but now he felt it had been a huge mistake. Surely he could have feigned an illness or other obligation and gotten one of the neighboring priests to perform the service. All the guilt and conflict he felt over his feelings for Hannah were coming to a head now. He knew that they could never be together. He wanted her to marry Noah, but he didn't need to be the one to actually perform the wedding. It felt like the universe was pouring salt on his already aching wounds.

He shaved and combed his hair, deciding on a slicked-backed style instead of his usual casual curls. He got dressed and headed to the church to prepare for the wedding rehearsal. The only way he was going to survive this was by keeping his distance from Hannah. Today and tomorrow, she had to become like any other bride in the dozens of wedding ceremonies he had performed since becoming a priest. He had accepted the invitations to the rehearsal dinner and reception, which he also regretted. He was afraid it would have drawn more attention if he had declined. He would go and do his best to detach from the fact that he would be witnessing the love of his life marry someone else.

As he flipped the last light switch on, he heard the doors open at the back of the church. He looked up and saw the wedding party come streaming in. Some faces he recognized: Jane, Julie, Noah, and Katie. The other faces were new. The last person to come in was Hannah. It took a moment for him to find her face in the crowd. She was looking down, searching for something in her purse. He wasn't sure if that was on purpose or not. Maybe she had the same plan as he did—avoid eye contact. She was wearing an off-white summer dress that fell to above her knees. Her hair cascaded around her face and down her shoulders in soft curls. Normally she didn't wear much makeup, but today her cheeks had a red hue to them. He had never seen her look more beautiful. The sight of her looking so gorgeous was painful.

As the group approached the altar, Patrick took a deep breath and began his usual pre-wedding speech. After introducing himself to each guest and making small talk for a few minutes, he moved on to explaining the ceremony and giving directions on the procession. When it was time for Hannah's walk down the aisle with her mother, Patrick looked only briefly at her before averting his eyes and looking down at his notes. He wasn't sure whether Hannah had tried to meet his eyes, but he couldn't bear looking at her.

After they had finished, he thanked everyone and ushered them out to head to dinner without him. He still needed to turn off the lights and lock up. He assured them that he would follow later. Once everyone had left, he let out a sigh of relief. One wedding event was done. Now he just needed to survive the next three.

41

Everyone was excited on the walk home, chatting cheerfully and carrying on. Hannah fell to the back of the group again, purposefully walking a little slower to process her feelings. She had been so nervous to see Patrick, but he hadn't even looked at her. Yes, when she first got to the church, she wasn't ready to see him, but during the rest of the rehearsal service, she kept glancing up at his face. He never looked her in the eye, not once. He was almost cold to her. She wanted to run away and cry. How was she going to keep herself together? Noah slowed down to walk with her. He put his arm around her, and she did her best to smile and relax into his embrace. Noah's pace slowed even further, and the group pulled ahead of them. As the distance grew greater, Hannah became uneasy. When they reached the end of her mom's driveway, Noah stopped while everyone else went inside. He turned to face her.

"Hannah, I just want to make sure you're okay going forward with everything. I don't want you to feel pressured—" Noah tried to continue, but Hannah spoke over him. She couldn't have this conversation again, and definitely not with Noah. He would see right through her. She needed to end it.

"I know I've been a little off. I can just tell my mother is getting sicker, and it's a lot to process. Sorry I've been distant. I promise I don't feel rushed." She flashed her best reassuring smile, then quickly grabbed onto Noah, burying her head in his chest.

He held her for several seconds before pulling her back to kiss her. When she looked up at him, he looked much lighter, and a smile lit up his face.

"Alright then! For the next two days, let's just live in the moment and try to enjoy everything we can!" he exclaimed.

She nodded and followed him into the house.

42

Jane had stayed behind to set out the dinner and drinks while the rehearsal was taking place at the church. She carefully set out the food, arranging it artistically across the long table in Julie's backyard. Then she switched the string lights on and sat down to admire the overall effect. This summer had been so unexpected. When she first received the news that Julie was dying, she had been devastated. A darkness had settled around her. Hope had never been the warmest place for Jane, but she always had Julie. Julie had always been the brightest part of her life here. Then, as her relationship with Hannah had grown, that added even more color to her life. The sadness she had been feeling about Julie started to lift the second Hannah set foot in town. It was a cruel thing that it had taken Julie's illness to bring Hannah home, but if there was any good to be found in the situation, that was it. Now Jane was sitting in Julie's backyard waiting for her best friend, her goddaughter, and all their friends and family to come and celebrate a wedding. She would have never guessed that so much joy could still be found when she was bracing for the imminent loss of her best friend. Nonetheless, she had found it.

She was brought back to the moment when she heard the patio doors open.

"We are back Jane!" Julie called happily.

"I'm ready for you all!" Jane replied. She was ready for the rehearsal dinner, but thanks to the past summer, she was also ready for the less joyful things that were soon to come.

43

All the guests gathered outside, each grabbing a drink and settling into conversations. Julie had told Hannah to have a good look around and soak up every detail. In many ways, Hannah felt that this was the type of wedding Julie had always wanted but never got. Their parents hadn't supported her and her husband. No family members had attended their courthouse service. Hannah was happy that she could give this gift to her mother. Noah's family also seemed very happy. She was surrounded by laughter and love.

She grabbed herself a drink, quickly gulping down a few sips, steadying herself for the night ahead. Patrick had said he would come. He had called to RSVP yes to the reception and the rehearsal dinner. She wanted him to come, of course. She always wanted to be near him. Yet, she couldn't help but wonder if having him there would make things that much harder. Instead of enjoying herself, she was waiting with bated breath for him to walk through the door. Would he ignore her? Embrace her? She wasn't quite sure.

Katie called her over, and she welcomed the distraction. Jessica, Stephanie, and Katie were all telling the story of the night she and Noah met. Jessica and Stephanie were Hannah's friends from college, who had also become friends with Katie over the years of her visiting Hannah. When they all decided to move to the city after graduation, living together had seemed like a natural fit. The first weekend in their new place, they all decided to go out to the bar and celebrate their new independence. Two drinks later, Hannah had turned to get the next round when she bumped into Noah, who was also headed to the bar for his next drink. The next several hours, her friends had watched in awe as Hannah and Noah hit it off immediately. They had never seen her connect with a guy so well in all the years they had known her. When Hannah told them on the walk home that they had exchanged numbers, the girls knew that their summer was not going to be quite as planned. Maybe it wasn't love at first sight, but it was as close as any of them had ever witnessed.

Hannah blushed as Katie continued.

"We all knew from that night, if you weren't going to marry him, it was at least going to be an important relationship for you. And of course we were all jealous," she said with a laugh.

"Noah is so handsome and sweet," Jessica added, winking at Hannah.

Hannah had always had trouble taking any kind of compliment. "Thank you," she mumbled quietly. She was hoping the conversation would shift to something else entirely when Stephanie spoke up.

"I mean, speaking of handsome, did anyone else notice the priest at church? What was his name, Father Paul…Pat?" She was trying to recall his name.

Katie finished her thought for her. "Father Patrick. Yes, I think we all noticed," she said, laughing as she shook her head in delight.

"Really Hannah, how did you manage to work with him all summer and never mention anything about him to us? His gorgeous curly hair, his smile, nothing? If he wasn't a priest, I would… Well, I guess I shouldn't say out loud what I would do!" Stephanie said, laughing as she made the sign of the cross.

Hannah felt her cheeks begin to burn. Patrick was beautiful. No one with eyes could deny that. If she tried to force a denial, her friends would know she was lying. There really was no option but to admit that yes, she had noticed too.

"I mean, yeah, I noticed..." She trailed off as she noticed that Stephanie's eyes had grown wide. Suddenly she realized that someone was standing behind her. Her cheeks flushed a brighter shade of red.

"What did you notice?" Patrick asked with an amused voice.

Hannah's stomach dropped. How long had he been there, and how much of their conversation had he heard? She took a deep breath, trying to calm the color that had risen in her face.

"Just how beautiful the backyard looks this evening, " Hannah said as she turned around.

Patrick gave her a bemused smile. It was the most expressive he had been with her in the last week. Her heart did a summersault. She forget where she was for a moment, focused only on his face.

"Glad you were able to come," she offered.

Patrick started to respond when he was caught off guard by Hannah. Almost reflexively, she leaned in and kissed him on the cheek. As soon as she had done it, she realized how ridiculous it was. As she pulled back, she could see the surprise on Patrick's face. She heard Stephanie gulp behind her, and she was pretty sure she caught Jessica elbowing Katie in the side.

For so long, she had been carefully hiding her feelings. She felt sick that she had exposed herself so obviously now. Maybe it was because she had been thinking about Patrick as the gorgeous man he was, or maybe she really just was so happy to see him. She didn't want to analyze it. It wasn't worth dwelling on now. She had to move past it before it could occur to anyone that there was an issue.

"I thought the rehearsal went well. Thank you for that," Hannah offered.

Patrick shook his head ever so slightly, seemingly regaining his bearings.

"Yes, it did go well. Thanks to you, Noah, and your wedding party. Thank you all for making things go so smoothly." He smiled at Katie, Jessica, and Stephanie. Hannah could see each woman blush as his glance fell on them.

"I'm going to go see if Julie or Jane need anything. I just wanted to say hello."

"Yes, of course. They are in the house." Hannah pointed in the direction of the kitchen.

Patrick reached out, touching her arm ever so briefly, smiling, then turned to walk toward the house.

Once he was finally out of earshot, Jessica playfully pushed Hannah's shoulder.

"Hannah! I mean what was that? I have never seen you greet anyone like that?" she asked, amused but also with a hint of accusation.

Hannah paused for several seconds. When she finally opened her mouth to answer, she was saved by the sound of Julie's voice.

"Please everyone, come sit. Dinner is ready."

44

As they shuffled to their respective seats, Hannah breathed a sigh of relief that she didn't have to answer her friends right now. It would give her time to formulate an answer. When she set out the table cards, she had made sure to seat Patrick at the head of the table. It would be too difficult to sit next to him. And after what had just happened, she knew that had been the right decision.

Hannah took her seat next to Noah. Julie and Jane were on Hannah's other side, and Katie, Jessica, and Stephanie were directly across from her. Noah's friends John and Christopher were seated next to them, and at the head of the table was Patrick. When Julie realized where he was seated, she immediately protested.

"Father Patrick, we can't have you all the way down there. Would one of you girls mind switching?" she asked, motioning toward Jessica, Katie, and Stephanie.

Stephanie, who had always had a thing for Chris, jumped at the opportunity.

"Yes, no problem, I can!" she exclaimed. She was up and out of her chair, moving towards the end of the table before Hannah or Patrick could offer any rebuttal.

Patrick grabbed his wine glass and walked over to take his new seat directly across from Hannah. She was afraid to look at him. As far as she could tell, besides their brief interaction earlier, he had been keeping her at arm's length. He never made eye contact with her at the church, and he was not looking at her now either. He spoke with Katie on his left and John on his right, even Noah occasionally, but he had yet to direct any conversation her way. In turn, she did not say anything to him either. Dinner continued from the salad to the main course. When it was time for the speeches, Hannah fidgeted anxiously.

First to stand and offer a toast was Noah's father Dan. He gushed about how perfect Hannah and Noah were for each other. He recounted the first time he met Hannah and how he had known that she was different from any girl Noah had ever dated. He went on about his gratitude that Julie could be part of the wedding, even mentioning that he wished he could have met Hannah's father. Hannah felt detached as he spoke. She knew this night was about her, but it was as if she was on the outside looking in, watching the scene unfold. Almost everyone around the table was watery-eyed, even Noah's friend John, who Hannah had never seen get emotional. She refused to look directly at Patrick, but she could see there were no tears in his eyes. His jaw looked clenched and uncomfortable. He was looking down and fumbling with his watch, then with his shirt-sleeve buttons. It seemed to Hannah like he was trying to distract himself from everything that was going on.

Noah spoke next, briefly thanking everyone for coming and for all their support. He then turned his attention to Hannah.

"I just want to tell you how honored I am that you chose me. I knew from the first night we met that you were the girl for me. I love you and can't wait to marry you. Now, if everyone would raise their glasses with me! Cheers!" Clinking glasses with Hannah, he then leaned down and kissed her.

Patrick shifted uncomfortably in his seat. Hannah should have been focused on kissing her fiancé, but she couldn't help but think about Patrick. She wondered if Noah's choice of words, that she had "chosen" him, hurt Patrick. She wanted to speak to him so badly. It was wonderful to hear all the kind speeches and to be surrounded by so much love, but there was still so much unresolved between her and Patrick. Being so close to him, literally within arm's reach, yet so distant was painful.

When Julie got up to speak, it was Hannah who was now shifting uncomfortably. She had hoped her mother wouldn't speak, but now she had to hope it would be short and quick. Hannah was barely keeping it together, and she wasn't sure she would survive if her mother got too emotional.

"I wanted to first thank you all for coming to my home. And thanks to all of you who helped transform this place from a dingy backyard to such a fairytale scene. I have never been so moved. Jane, Katie, and Noah, you outdid yourselves." She paused as the rest of the group applauded them. "I also want to say how grateful I am to be here for this wedding. I wasn't sure if I would make it to see this day, but now that it's here, I'm so pleased. Noah, I love you and your family. Knowing that Hannah will have you all when I go makes me feel much more at ease with what is happening to me."

Hannah could feel that her emotions were about to overwhelm her. The tears began to well up in her eyes. Noah put his arm around her, but it wasn't stopping the tidal wave that was building up inside her. She grasped at the hem of her dress, her eyes fixed downward. Then, under the table, she felt a leg brush against hers.

Patrick.

It was Patrick. He knew this would be too much for her. He didn't look at her, but she knew it was him. She took a deep breath and let her leg lean against his. He didn't move away. The feeling of his leg against her skin distracted her enough to keep her from losing control while Julie spoke. She could focus on their secret under-the-table touch.

"I also wanted to say that I wish Hannah's father Matt could be here tonight. He would have loved this. He would have loved to witness all your milestones, Hannah. He loved you so much. I know he is here with us. I don't know if you would have ever come back here if I weren't sick, especially to have your wedding. In some way, that makes me grateful for what has happened. Your father is here in every space in this house, in this yard. Now he gets to be a part of your wedding."

Even with the distraction of Patrick's touch, Hannah couldn't hold back her tears anymore. She felt his leg move away. It was replaced by his hand reaching out to rest on top of her knee. She looked up at him, desperately searching for some kind of acknowledgement, but he kept his eyes fixed on Julie as she spoke. Hannah could see that there was no longer a dry eye around the table. Jane was practically sobbing. Julie reached down and put a hand on her shoulder. Hannah should have expected this, but somehow, she was still caught off guard.

"I also wanted to thank one more person." Julie turned to look directly at Patrick. With the attention now on him, Hannah felt Patrick's hand slowly slide off her leg. Once again, she was untethered.

"Father Patrick, I just want to thank you for helping Hannah get adjusted to being back in Hope, for letting her work with you, and for always being a friend to me. I know this town isn't easy on newcomers, and your kindness has been a great blessing to all of us. I'm so glad you are marrying Hannah and Noah. I couldn't imagine it any other way. Cheers!" Julie raised her glass.

Patrick, who had been trying to remain stone-faced, finally let a tear fall as well. He clinked glasses with those around him, taking a final large gulp of champagne. Hannah was busy offering a cheers to Noah and her mother, hugging them both. After she pulled back from Noah, she noticed that Patrick was no longer in his seat. She scanned the length of the table in both directions, and he was nowhere to be found. Everyone else was recovering from the emotional speeches, hugging, and talking. Hannah told Noah that she needed to use the restroom and would be right back. He kissed her forehead. She quickly walked back into the house, barely breathing the entire way.

As she moved through the kitchen, she heard the front door open, then shut. She sprinted through the living room and into the front hall. When she reached the front door, she threw it open. From the front stoop, she could see Patrick. He was already at the end of the driveway, walking briskly as he turned onto the sidewalk that would lead him back to the rectory.

45

"Patrick!" Hannah yelled from the front stoop. She saw him slow his stride and come to a halt. He kept his back to her, his fists clenched at his sides.

Hannah made sure she shut the door, then moved quickly to reach him. She had become frantic when he left the table, and the panic was still rising inside of her. There were so many things left unsaid between them, but she didn't know how to start or what answers she needed the most. The sounds of laughter, conversation, and music from the backyard filled the air around them. It should have put her at ease, but it only increased her desperation. The wedding was approaching so quickly, and she was not ready. Hannah kept her eyes locked on Patrick, trying to focus on only him. She could see his body grow more tense with each step she took towards him. He was still standing with his back turned to her, like he was bracing himself.

"I'm sorry to stop you, but—"

"Please don't do this, Hannah," he cut her off. His voice sounded pained.

"Do what?" she asked, confused.

"THIS. Whatever THIS is going to be right now. I don't think I can take it." He sounded curt, almost angry with her.

His tone hurt her deeply. She intuitively knew what he meant. He didn't want to rehash their relationship on the eve of her wedding to someone else, but she couldn't let it go. In her mind, this was a conversation they had to have. Reaching out, she placed her hand on his shoulder. He pulled back slightly, stiffening at her touch. She should have moved away, but instead she walked around to face him, placing her hands on his.

He continued to look at the ground, but his tone softened from anger to hurt.

"Please, just let me leave," he pleaded.

Hannah wanted to let him go. The pain in his voice struck her to her core. She tried to get the words out to release him from this conversation, fighting every instinct in her body. She wished she could give him what he wanted, but she couldn't.

There was silence between them for several seconds before Patrick began to speak.

"What do you want to hear from me?!" he asked, again raising his voice. He dropped his head and pulled his hands away from hers.

She tried to answer him but barely got out a sound before he started speaking again, raising his voice even louder.

"Do you want to hear that I'm absolutely gutted, that I can barely breathe when I'm around you? Do you want to hear that marrying you to someone else is the most difficult thing I will ever do…that I think not throwing myself at your feet and begging you to choose me instead of him will be the biggest mistake and regret of my life? Do you want to hear that I'm desperately in love with you? Is that what you want...?" He trailed off, lifting his face to lock eyes with her.

Hannah could see the pain in his face. She could hear it in his voice. She wasn't sure if she had ever stopped crying after Julie's speech, but she was crying again now. The tears fell furiously down her face. It was wrong to put him through this, but hearing him confess his true feelings was everything she had been hoping for. Seeing his pain somehow lessened hers. They were in this together. She wanted him to know why she couldn't let him walk home, why she had to stop him. She wanted him to know how she felt, hoping that maybe that would relieve his anguish as well.

"I didn't want to hurt you, but this week you have been so distant. The silence has been making me crazy. I can't go through any of this without you. I know I shouldn't—but I need you. I had to know what you are thinking. I had to hear that this is still what you want me to do. I wanted to talk to you at work, but then Noah showed up early and..." She trailed off as she started to cry even harder.

Patrick pulled her close. She buried her head in his chest, hoping no one would see but also unbothered if they did. He held her tight, and she him. They remained that way for several seconds, until Hannah had control of her breathing again. Then he moved back from her to look her straight in the eyes.

"Of course I still love you, but I should never have agreed to preside over your wedding. All of this, the ceremony, the speeches, it's all killing me. The distance...it was...self-preservation. I can never be fully yours. I gave myself to the church. You deserve someone who can make their first vows to you. I see how Noah feels about you, how he treats you. He is the right man for you." He gently wiped the tears from her right cheek.

She nestled her face into his palm, kissing it softly. She was still unsure if his words made her feel more secure in her decision, but it was clear that he had already made his mind up. There was nothing more she could say besides, "I love you too."

He kissed her ever so lightly on the forehead, then he pulled his hand back from her face. He gave her the best smile he could muster.

"I think you'd better go back to your party now."

She nodded, resigned.

He moved past her, pausing briefly to squeeze her hand before continuing to walk. She waited several seconds before turning around. By the time she did, he was gone, leaving only darkness on the sidewalk in front of her.

46

When Hannah finally rejoined the party, she didn't feel like celebrating. She wanted to run back to her room and cry. She had gotten the opportunity to speak with Patrick. Now she knew exactly how he felt. There was some relief in knowing that he was suffering just as much as she was. However, it also made her feel as if she were going even crazier. He loved her as much as she loved him. How did any of this make sense? She loved Noah and Patrick. They both loved her. Patrick had already vowed his life to the church, but Noah was free to give himself fully to her. She wasn't sure that she cared about that technicality, but Patrick seemed resolute in his decision. Taking a deep breath, she grabbed her wine glass off the table. She rejoined the conversation with her wedding party, trying her best to hide the storm that was churning inside of her.

Julie left the party first. She was tired, and Noah had to carry her up the few porch stairs into the house. Jane shooed Hannah off as she tried to follow and help put Julie to bed.

"Go. Say goodbye to the rest of your guests. I will stay with your mom." She gave Hannah a reassuring smile.

Hannah would have preferred to retreat back into the house and avoid more forced smiles and feigned excitement. She begrudgingly returned to the backyard, pleasantly surprised that everyone else was gathering their things to leave for the night as well. First, she hugged and thanked Noah's family. She moved on to Noah's friends, and then finally hers. Katie and Stephanie hugged her and told her to make sure to get a good night's sleep. When she went to hug Jessica, she gave her a sly grin.

"You know, I haven't forgotten. You never answered my question about what is going on between you and 'Father' Patrick," she said with a laugh.

The redness started to rise up in Hannah's cheeks again. She really didn't know what to say. Part of her wanted to blurt out the whole story. She needed support and counsel, and who was better for that than her best friends? If she were to tell them, though, they would never look at her the same way. They loved Noah, everyone did. What would she say, that she was in love with a priest? It was ridiculous. All the scenarios played out in her head at the speed of light. She again chose to lie.

"I mean, what about us? He is a priest." She tried her best to chuckle like it was a joke. Her friends all laughed along, pretending to believe her. They each gave her a hug and left together.

Hannah was finally alone. Standing in her backyard, surrounded by the remnants of her rehearsal dinner, she was finally free to cry as much as she wanted. The seat Patrick had been sitting in was still at the angle he had left it when he got up so abruptly. When she closed her eyes, she could still feel his leg pressed against hers. She let herself drown in her emotions for several minutes before coming up for air. There was a lot of cleaning to be done before she could finally go to bed. Jane had offered to help, but she was still in the house with Julie, and Hannah did not want to bother her. Hannah went into the house and grabbed a basket, then came out and started to gather up all the dishes. As she moved from place setting to place setting, her mind drifted, her future playing out before her eyes.

Noah's presence was familiar. He was like a favorite pair of jeans. They fit so well together that it didn't make sense to try on any other pairs. From the day they met, the ease of their connection had been undeniable. He was kind, safe, and warm. She never had to pretend around him, and he always put her first. When she was around him, for the first time in her life, she felt like she truly belonged. He had become her home, a soft landing she had not experienced before. In truth, she still felt that way about him. She longed to tell him everything that had happened with Patrick, because Noah was her best friend. Given that she felt so strongly about him, the reason she had never told him about what happened with Colton eluded her. It had never felt right. Maybe she was afraid he would look at her differently, or maybe she was afraid saying it out loud would make it real again. She was not sure why she never told him. Six months ago, when he had asked her to marry him, she had no reservations. She loved him and could not see any end to that. It had been the easiest yes of her life.

Her feelings for Noah were real, but it was also true that, from the moment she had seen Patrick in the front lawn of the church, Hannah's whole perspective had changed. She only had eyes for Noah for so long that she had forgotten other men even existed. The night Patrick saved her, a new part of her being came alive. She not only felt safe with him, but something much different. He challenged her and saw her in a way no one ever had. It was as if he saw straight through her to her very being. Even the thought of being near him made the heat rise under her skin and her heartbeat quicken. When he touched her, she could barely breathe. The longing she felt when they weren't together, when she wasn't able to touch him, was almost overwhelming. It was making her crazy and desperate. How could she go on without him? She had no idea.

The battle between her head and heart was tearing her apart. Her head knew that she should marry Noah. Her heart was screaming at her that she could not be without Patrick. As she washed the last dish, she was stuck in the same deadlock she had been in for weeks. What was the best course of action? Should she honor her commitment to Noah and do what would make everyone, including her mother, happy? Or should she blow up her entire life, including Patrick's, to follow her heart regardless of the damage? She was too tired to decide tonight. As she moved from the kitchen into the living room, she stopped to catch a glimpse of her mother. Jane had fallen asleep in the recliner next to her with her hand on top of Julie's. Hannah walked in and covered Jane with a blanket. Seeing the friendship between the two women touched her deeply, even after all these years. She wasn't ready to admit it to herself yet, but she was pretty sure her head was going to win the battle the next morning.

47

Patrick woke up before the sun. He rolled over in bed to glance at the clock. 4:45 a.m. Why couldn't he have just slept through this whole day? His alarm was set for 6 a.m., but he woke up well before that and now had even more time alone with his thoughts before Hannah's wedding. Everything that could ever have happened between them had already been decided before they even met. Maybe if his cousin wasn't a priest, maybe if his father had never cheated, maybe if his mother was still alive—the list of things that had led to these exact circumstances could go on and on. If any one of those things were different, maybe they could have had a chance. Perhaps Patrick would have found a different vocation; perhaps they would have met in a different way. There was no point in considering all the events and decisions in his life that led him to the place he was in today. He had made his choice ten years ago, and he had said his vows.

He got out of bed and threw on some clothes. The only thing he could think to do was pray. He walked to the church and asked God for the strength the get through the day, the peace to accept how things must be, and forgiveness for his desire to blow it all up.

***

Hannah woke up to the clinking of dishes. When she opened her eyes, Katie was sitting on the end of her bed with a tray of breakfast. Hannah tried to give her a convincing, happy smile. Katie responded in kind.

"Happy wedding day!" she squealed as she moved to Hannah's

side and gave her a hug. "You need to get up so we can start getting ready!"

Hannah thanked her for the breakfast and asked for a few minutes alone before the chaos of the day began. Katie obliged and left singing, "We're going to the chapel and we're going to get married!"

Once the door was shut, Hannah finally let out a huge sigh of relief. She needed to gather her thoughts before she could face the day. While falling asleep the night before, she had begun to feel a new emotion about her situation that she hadn't grappled with before. Anger. She was angry that her mother was sick, angry about what had happened fourteen years ago, angry that what she felt for Patrick was overshadowing what she had with Noah, and angry that Patrick hadn't waited for her. She knew it was irrational to think in such a way. The reasons why Patrick had become a priest had been laid out in front of her over these past months, but he had still never told her directly why he had chosen it. Not knowing gnawed at her. Maybe that was the missing piece. Maybe understanding his reason fully would help her accept what was. She wouldn't know until she asked him, and she absolutely had to ask him before she walked down the aisle.

48

The next few hours flew by in a haze of hugs, kisses, and well wishes from all the family and friends that occupied Julie's house. The smell of hairspray and perfume filled the air as hair and makeup were taken care of. By the time Hannah had been declared sufficiently made up to put her dress on, she felt completely numb to what was happening around her. The fake smile she had plastered on her face was now accented by the deep peach lipstick Katie had insisted she wear. She walked back upstairs to her bedroom to slip into her dress and seriously considered turning around and running deep into the woods, where no one would find her until it was too dark and too late for the wedding to take place. The only thing stopping her was the look of excitement on her mother's face.

Despite Hannah's detachment from the chaos of wedding preparations around her, one thing stood out—the renewed color and animation on her mother's face. If Hannah bolted now, all the life would once again be drained from Julie's rosy cheeks. She knew she couldn't do it. She and Patrick had no future anyway. As she approached her bedroom, she heard the sound of feet on the stairs behind her.

"You didn't think you were going to try and put your dress on by yourself, did you?" Katie asked playfully. "You will ruin your hair!"

Hannah tried to smile her way out of answering, but when her eyes locked with Katie's, she knew she had been caught.

"Hannah, what is going on?" Katie demanded with authority. "You need to tell me right now what is happening with you. You haven't been yourself since I got here. I can't shake the feeling that it isn't just about your mother. Do you not want this?"

She stared at Hannah, trying to read her expression, waiting for any response or explanation that would clarify why her friend had seemed like a completely different person the last several days. Hannah had always been secretive, but this was more than even Katie could tolerate.

"Hannah, you need to tell me NOW! You're supposed to get married in two hours. I will do whatever you need me to do, but you have to talk to me." Katie's tone turned to pleading.

Hannah wanted to tell her. The words were on the tip of her tongue, but when she opened her mouth, nothing came out. She had kept so many secrets for so long that she didn't know how to reveal them. When she tried to speak again, words finally came, but they weren't the truth.

"I'm sorry, I don't know what is going on. It's like I told you a couple of days ago. I just feel guilty. I feel guilty for making Noah have this small-town backyard wedding when he wanted a big, formal reception. I feel guilty for having my mother do so much work when she is sick. I still feel nothing but guilt. It's overshadowing my happiness." Speaking the last sentence brought her some relief. At least that part was true. She did feel nothing but guilt, even if it wasn't for those particular reasons alone. She had already told Katie about her guilt once. She hoped it would be enough of an explanation for Katie to accept again.

"Hannah, you need to let all that go. They both love you. Have you not seen them the last few days? I have never seen Noah or your mother so happy. I was so worried it was something more than that." Katie reached out, grabbing Hannah's shoulder and pulling her in for a hug.

"Just try to enjoy the day. We can worry about Julie tomorrow, but for today, just let her be happy."

Hannah was grateful for Katie's encouragement but also gutted. There was so much more on her mind, but she didn't know how to begin to express it.

49

After spending most of the morning in prayer, Patrick had returned to the rectory and showered. He got dressed and again slicked back his curls. He wasn't sure why, but he felt an overwhelming need to look his best today. When he had finished getting ready, he went to the church. He walked the aisle of the church one final time to make sure that everything was in place. He turned the lights on and lit the candles on the altar. The church always looked lovely this time of day, illuminated by streams of colored light from the afternoon sun shining through the stained-glass windows. He couldn't believe that this day was finally here. Soon, Hannah and Patrick's guests would file in. He would watch Hannah walk down the aisle, and he would marry her to someone else.

Just as he was starting to lose himself in thoughts of Hannah and everything they had shared this summer, he heard the back door open.

"Father Patrick, it looks beautiful in here!" Katie exclaimed.

He turned to face the voice, grateful for the distraction. Katie was followed in by the other bridesmaids, who were carrying their bouquets and a stack of programs for the service. Soon after, Noah's family and a few other guests came in and took their seats. It was really happening. The church organist, Mrs. Dell, had arrived and had begun playing some pre-service songs. Patrick had tried his best to prepare for this moment, but now his head was spinning and his heart racing.

Hannah had arrived at the same time as Katie, although she didn't go into the church. She headed into the small room at the back of the church used for weddings, baptisms, and funerals. Inside was a small table with chairs and a large window that overlooked the church parking lot and rectory. She planted herself firmly in front of the window, trying to center herself. The organ music had begun, and she started to feel lightheaded. The notes floated through the air around her, making what was about to happen even more real. She stood gazing out at the front of the rectory. The glimpse of it sent a wave a pain through her body. The sight of Patrick sitting at his dining table, the feel of his hand under hers when she reached for it the day he told her about his mother, burned inside of her. As the heat rose up, spreading across her whole body, she was startled by the door swinging open.

"Hannah, it's about time. Most of the guests have arrived!" Katie exclaimed cheerfully.

Hannah wanted to sound excited, but she could barely speak. She kept her back turned to the door so that Katie couldn't see the desperation on her face.

"Katie, could you do me a favor? Would you ask Father Murphy to come here for a minute?"

A few seconds of silence followed as Katie considered Hannah's request. Father Patrick was already lining up the bridal party and altar servers for the procession into Mass.

"Father Murphy?" she asked curiously.

"Yeah, I just wanted to have him say a quick prayer with me. If you wouldn't mind."

She tried to sound calm so that Katie wouldn't get suspicious and held her breath as she waited for her response.

"Sure Hannah, I guess that would be fine. Give me a minute."

50

Hannah knew it was wrong. Everything about the last few months had been wrong. Every kiss. Every touch. Every glance. Every time one of them stared too long. Every time they thought about each other. It had all been wrong. Asking Patrick to come see her seconds before she was to be married was wrong, but none of that mattered, because it was also absolutely worth it. She wouldn't change a single thing that had happened. She would not regret or wish away a single touch or moment. Now, however, their time had run out, and she had to know why. She couldn't walk down the aisle without him telling her why. WHY. Why he hadn't waited to meet her.

The organ continued to play as Hannah waited for Patrick to come to her. She stood with her back to the door, trying to breathe. After what seemed like an eternity, she heard a light knock.

"Hannah, it's Father Murphy. May I come in?"

"Yes, please." Her voice shook as she responded. She thought she heard trepidation in his voice as well. The door opened and then thudded shut. The sound of Patrick's footsteps behind her gave her such relief.

When Katie had asked him to come and see Hannah, Patrick wanted to say no. What was left to say between them? They had spoken the night before, and that was all the resolution they would ever reach. He had reluctantly agreed because selfishly, he wanted one more moment with her as well. As he moved towards her in the small back room of the church, he almost believed he was in a dream. The sunlight streamed around her as she stood in the window, illuminating her silhouette and the soft white lace of her dress.

The light shimmered in the waves of her brown hair. He thought she had looked beautiful yesterday, but today she quite literally took his breath away. When she turned to face him, her eyes full of longing, he thought his heart might leave his chest. He wanted to tell her that she was the most beautiful thing he had ever seen or would ever see, but all he managed to say was, "You look stunning."

She blushed for a second before responding, "Thank you."

They stood staring at each other for a few more seconds. Hannah thought he looked the most handsome he had ever looked. His hair was slicked back and his face freshly shaven. He was in his finest white robe, and every detail of his appearance was perfectly in place. She felt honored that he would go to so much trouble for her.

"You look handsome as well." It came out almost as a whisper, but Patrick heard her. It was his turn to blush.

"I wanted to look nice for your day."

"Patrick, I'm sorry for asking you to come here. I don't want to hurt you, but I have to know why?"

He looked at her, slightly puzzled. "What do you mean why?" He couldn't resist the urge to move closer to her. She was shaking a little and kept fidgeting with the front of her dress. He reached out and grabbed her hands, holding them tight.

"Why didn't you wait…why did you become a priest?" Her cheeks flushed red as she spoke. He was so caught off guard by the question that he dropped her hands and took a step back from her.

"Hannah, I mean…you know why..." He trailed off as he spoke. This time it was his eyes that looked down as he considered what more to say.

"I mean, I know about your mother, and her cousin, but you have never said specifically. It all seems like such a mess. If there is a God, why would he have us meet? Why would he put us in each other's lives for this to be the end of it? I can't understand it. I need you to make sense of it for me, Patrick. I love you so completely. I can barely breathe at the thought of having to marry someone else."

As the words came out of her mouth, she felt free for the first time in months. They had said it to each other only once before, but today it was different. She was certain about how she felt, and even though she had lied to everyone else around her, Patrick knew her whole truth. She wanted to throw herself in his arms regardless of the fact that he was wearing Mass vestments.

Patrick saw the desperation on her face. He felt the same exasperation and longing. Why hadn't he waited? How could he have been so foolish? All the good and bad in his life that had led him to her were the very things now pushing her away from him. The reasons that had felt so compelling to him when he went to the seminary and took his vows now seemed to crumble around him, exposing what was left—his badly broken heart.

"Hannah, I'm so sorry. If I had even imagined I could feel like this for someone else, I would have done everything so differently. My God, how I have messed everything up..."

He put his face in his hands and couldn't hold back the tears. Falling to his knees, he tried desperately to string the words together to make her understand his decisions.

"When my mother died, I was so lost. I was furious at my father for what he had done. I was furious at her for leaving me. My cousin was the only family I had that I could talk to. My mother had always taken me to church to see him preach. Even though I had always hated it when she was alive, after her death it was the only place where I felt truly close to her. It was a place where I found peace. My cousin was such a source of support for me. When it was time to decide what to do after college, there were two reasons I chose to pursue becoming ordained. It would allow me to turn my nose up at the materialistic, money-first world my father cared about, and it was a way to honor my mother, by offering the same comfort and support I had gotten from the church to others. I never once questioned my decision until the night I first met you."

Hannah kneeled beside Patrick. She finally had her answer, but her hopes that it would make things easier were dashed. The things that happened to Patrick had been out of his control. He had made his decision of his own free will, but he was influenced by the results of decisions others had made. It just made their situation seem more tragic to her. If he had a father who didn't cheat or a mother who got the help she needed, maybe Patrick could have been hers. Or maybe they would never have even met. Fate was funny that way. She put her arms around him and tried to pull him close. He moved back.

"I'll get tears on your dress."

They both just stared at each other, unsure what to do next.

Finally, Patrick leaned forward. He kissed her with all the passion that had been building up inside him all summer. Their hands intertwined in each other's hair, both pulling the other closer. After several seconds, they slowly pulled away from each other.

"So what are we going to do?" Hannah whispered. She waited with bated breath for Patrick to decide their fate.

"I can't decide for you. I know I asked you before to marry Noah, but I don't think that was right. Honestly, nothing will stop me from wanting you. But even if you don't marry Noah, I don't see a way we can be together. Not in the way we want. I already committed myself to the church."

Hannah considered his words. He was a man of his word, and as much as they loved each other, he wouldn't break his vow. If she walked out now and called off everything, not only would she be hurt, but so would everyone else. Imagining the look on her mother's face at hearing the news was more than Hannah could handle.

They helped each other up. Patrick smoothed out Hannah's dress, and she his hair. They stood holding hands for several seconds, trying to figure out how to say goodbye to the future between them that never could be. They exchanged no words, but Patrick knew what she had decided.

He spoke first. "I will never stop loving you."

Choking back more tears, Hannah nodded. "Neither will I." He leaned forward and kissed her forehead. She took in a last deep breath of him. When he stepped back, she knew that whatever had happened between them was truly over. It had to be. She was about to walk down the aisle. He gave her a small smile and turned to leave. As he walked towards the door, Hannah couldn't help but feel that nothing would ever be the same for her. A part of her would always be with him, and she would never get it back. Truthfully, she didn't want it back. She wanted it to belong to him.

51

Only a minute had passed since Patrick had left the room before Katie charged through the door.

"That was a long prayer," she said jokingly. "Now it's time to get you married."

Hannah did her best to smile and quipped back, "Let's do it."

She walked out of the room and into the vestibule at the back of the church, where she lined up behind and Katie and Dan. Pachelbel's Canon in D began playing. Soon it was her turn to head down the aisle. Julie, who had been sitting in a chair off to the side, stood up and locked arms with her.

"You look so beautiful. I'm so proud of you Hannah." Julie put Hannah's hand to her mouth and kissed it. Then they began to walk towards the altar, where Noah and Patrick were waiting. Noah had begun to tear up. Hannah tried to focus on his face. She smiled at him and worked hard to slow her breathing and stop her tears. Right behind Noah was Patrick. Hannah was quite sure he had tears in his eyes as well. Halfway down the aisle, she could no longer stop her own tears. There was no point. This was one of the happiest and saddest days of her life. She needed to feel all her emotions.

When she finally reached the altar, Noah came down and took her arm from her mother. Patrick asked Julie who was giving this woman away, and Julie said she did on behalf of herself and Hannah's father. Julie began to tear up at the mention of her husband, and Hannah turned to hug her mother. Knowing how much this meant to her mother gave Hannah the strength to continue with the ceremony.

They took their seats and listened to the readings, sang the songs, and when it was time for the wedding vows, stood back up in front of everyone. As Hannah took her place next to Noah in front of the altar, she stumbled on her dress, and it was Patrick who caught her arm to steady her. The feel of his touch literally burned her skin. She tried to breathe through her feelings, but as Patrick spoke, giving them each their vows to repeat, it was impossible for her not to imagine it was Patrick saying them to her, and her to him.

Finally, the moment arrived for Patrick to announce, "You may kiss the bride." Everyone began to cheer, and Hannah was relieved to have survived without breaking down. She kissed Noah and hurried him back down the aisle as quickly as possible. With each step she took, she realized that she was moving farther and farther away from Patrick. What they had shared was now a thing of the past. They were now both committed to something besides each other.

Noah was buzzing with excitement. As soon as they reached the vestibule at the back of the church, he pulled her close. He kissed her neck, cheek, and forehead. When he pulled his face back, there was a huge goofy grin on his face.

"I wanted to be the first to call you Mrs. Bailey," he exclaimed proudly.

"Why, thank you Mr. Bailey," Hannah responded. She was trying her best to appear as happy as she ought to have been on this occasion. Her head was still spinning, and part of her wanted to run back into the church and into Patrick's arms. She would have to learn to live with that feeling, as she was quite sure a part of her would always feel that way. The rest of the bridal party had made their way down the aisle and were now surrounding Hannah and Noah. Everyone was giddy with excitement. They waited for the guests to file out and then went back in to take a few photos before the reception.

As they arranged themselves in different formations for pictures, Hannah couldn't ignore the new thought that came into her mind. She couldn't stay in Hope. She couldn't be so close to Patrick and not want him. Everything in this town reminded her of him. Even her encounters with Jackie and Colton this summer hadn't made her want to flee this place, but with Patrick, it was different. Now she desperately needed to get out of Hope.

Thankfully, they hadn't hired a professional photographer. Jane had volunteered to take pictures with a nice camera she had. She knew Hannah hated photos and made the process quick and to the point. They captured a few simple poses of her and Noah, the bridal party, their families, and one shot of Hannah, Noah, Patrick, and Julie.

After the last picture had been taken, Katie yelled, "It's time to party!" The whole bridal party started cheering as they filed out of the church. Dan, Noah's friend, had snuck a boom box into the back of the church, and as they walked outside, he played music for their walk to the reception. They all danced down the sidewalk, oblivious to any onlookers. Hannah let the music fill her head as she held hands with Noah. The afternoon summer sun shined down on them, reflecting off the satin of the bridesmaids' dresses. She looked up at Noah and saw the pure joy on his face. Behind her, Julie was holding hands with Jane, dancing right along with everyone else. She would always love Patrick, but she had to let go.

52

Patrick was once again alone in the nave of the church. The commotion of only a few minutes ago was followed by total silence. The organ had stopped playing, and the chatter of wedding guests was gone. He looked around and wondered why life had brought him to this place. Why it had brought him to this small town in the middle of nowhere, and to this dying country parish. He had been in much more elaborate churches, but he felt instantly at home the moment he walked through the doors of this church. Simple, stained-glass windows lined each side of the church walls. A large crucifix adorned with gold and red hung behind the altar. A statue of Mary was in the alcove on one side of the altar, while a statue of the disciples adorned the alcove on the other side. The flooring was stone and wood. The altar was a simple wooden table.

Holy Trinity had been built in the 1960s, when Hope had been in its heyday. A tractor-parts factory had been built one town over, and it brought people from all over, sparking a small economic boom in the once sleepy farm town. The town tripled in size in only a few years. Unfortunately, the factory closed in 1977. Many of the people who had come for the new jobs moved out as the opportunity for work disappeared. The families that remained were primarily those that had been here for generations, and the town returned to its smaller size. Holy Trinity had been built to accommodate the new influx of parishioners during the boom. It was twice as large as it needed to be for its congregation.

Repairs were needed everywhere Patrick looked. The paint was peeling in a few spots along the ceiling, several kneelers were broken, the floors needed refinishing, and the roof had a small leak that left water stains every time it rained heavily. There simply was not enough money for so much work on a building of this size. He had started a repair fund when he was put in charge of the parish, but almost a year later, they were at only 5% of the money needed. Hope was a not a wealthy town, and he knew the people gave what they could afford.

Before he met Hannah, restoring the church had been his greatest desire. He wanted to give both the building and the parishioners a jolt of energy and new life. This summer had certainly distracted him from that. Now his greatest desire was to be with Hannah. He needed to refocus. This was his purpose, no matter how he felt about her. She was now Mrs. Noah Bailey. As soon as her mother passed, she would leave Hope and be out of his life forever.

Patrick slowly made his way to the back of the church and switched off the lights. Locking the back door, he tried to prepare himself for the rest of the evening. It would be painful, but he needed to let her go.

***

The reception began as soon as the wedding party walked into the backyard. Noah's parents had come back right after their pictures were taken and lit the candles, opened the wine, and turned on the music. Everyone was toasting and chatting happily. Hannah stood side by side with Noah, accepting congratulations and well wishes. The food was set out family style on the long table they would all sit at. Eventually Patrick arrived and chatted with Jane off to the side.

When it was time to eat, Julie asked Father Patrick to say grace. He kept it short and sweet. Once the meal started, Hannah began to get a bit nervous, as she knew speeches would be next. Thankfully, tonight Patrick was seated at the end of the table next to her friends. He was quite a distance from her. She tried to avert her gaze from him, afraid to look into his eyes. Something in her knew that when she finally did, it would be different. Everything was different now.

The first to speak was Julie, who thankfully kept her speech brief, admitting she had shared quite enough the night before. Katie's maid-of-honor speech brought Hannah to tears as she again recounted how they had known he was the one for her as soon as he and Hannah met. Hannah tried to remember how she felt at that time. Maybe with time and distance, she could be that sure of Noah again. Dan's best-man speech mostly made fun of Noah.

Hannah had survived yet another obstacle of the day without giving herself away. The sun had almost fully set when the music came on for the first dance. Hannah had finally begun to relax for the first time all day. It may have been due to the two glasses of wine she had drunk, but she was grateful for the relief. Elvis's "I Can't Help Falling in Love With You" started streaming through the speakers. Noah took her hand and led her to the open space that would serve as the dance floor. They slowly rocked back and forth, Noah kissing her forehead, cheeks, and finally lips. She blushed with embarrassment.

"Why are you nervous? It's just our family," he teased. *If he only knew*, Hannah thought. She was embarrassed to kiss him in front of Patrick. It seemed cruel, even though he was her husband. She caught a glimpse of Patrick during one of the spins Noah had insisted on. He was sitting in his spot at the end of the table, wine glass in hand, looking away. Once their song ended, more upbeat music came on, and everyone got out of their chairs to dance. The string lights overhead and the stars shining in the night sky made for the most magical setting. Hannah was having fun for the first time all day.

After a few songs, she went to check on her mother. Jane was sitting next to her, both of them enjoying a glass of wine.

"How are you doing Mom?" Hannah asked, kissing her on the forehead.

"I'm wonderful. I hope this evening is everything you wanted." She smiled up at Hannah, who nodded. Before she had time to make her way back to the dance floor, she felt a hand on her back. She didn't need to see who it was to know who the hand belonged to.

"Hannah, I was wondering if I might ask your mother to dance with me?" Patrick offered quietly. Julie's face flushed red. Hannah turned to face him. "Fine by me," she said with a laugh. She looked into his eyes, and it was different, but not in the way she imagined. She could still see that he loved her, but it was softer, less pained. Maybe they both could survive this.

"May I, Julie?" he asked, extending his hand. Julie shot up out of her seat so quickly that Hannah was sure she would get lightheaded.

"Thank you, Father Murphy." And with that, he led her to the grass. Hannah followed and found Noah. The four of them danced to a fast song. The next song was a slow one. Noah looked at Julie and asked her if she would dance with him. Then he looked at Patrick.

"Father Murphy, would you mind switching partners with me?" He held Hannah's hand out to Patrick.

"Of course." Patrick took Hannah's hand. She moved to face him, placing her other hand on his shoulder. They swayed to the music, staring at each other, and slowly moved a little away from the crowd.

"Are you okay?" he asked.

"I wasn't before, but now I'm starting to have a little fun. I'm glad this day is almost over though. I'm sorry if—"

"You have nothing to be sorry for. We both have to do what we can to move on with our lives. I would never change anything that happened between us, but I also want you to be happy."

Hannah knew he was right. A part of her wanted him to hurt for her forever, but she loved him too much to wish that he would never be happy again. They had to try to get on with their lives. She wasn't sure what would happen between them once she left, but she hoped maybe they could be friends. Unsure if she would ever be held by him like this again, she tried to savor his touch and his closeness for the last few moments. When the song ended, they both hesitated a few seconds before moving away. He took her hand and kissed it. "Thank you for the dance, Mrs. Bailey." He gave her a small smile, and then he walked away.

53

The rest of the reception passed quickly. Hannah danced, drank, and cried more than once. Jane had taken Julie in about an hour before the other guests left, but she had made it through most of the day. Hannah was grateful for that. Katie and her other friends were the last to leave. They promised to come back the next day to help clean. The backyard was finally quiet, except for the sound of her friends' distant laughter as they walked to their car. The whirlwind of sounds and activity that had overtaken the last few days had finally ended. It was now quiet and empty. She looked down at her left hand, at the rings that would now always be there. She was lost in thought when Noah came up from behind her and put his arms around her. The sudden contact made her jump.

"Sorry to scare you, babe. Are you ready to leave for our honeymoon?" She could hear the excitement in his voice. Although she was unsure how she felt about leaving her mother for three days, it would be good to get a break from everything happening in Hope. She needed a chance to clear her mind. Her feelings the last months had been confusing and exhausting. Now all the decisions had been made, and she needed to learn how to live with them. As Patrick had said, they needed to move on with their lives, and her life now centered around Noah.

"Yeah, let me go change my clothes."

Noah kissed her on the cheek, and she headed into the house. As she made her way to her bedroom, she walked by the living room. Jane had fallen asleep in the chair next to Julie again. She went in and kissed both her mother's and Jane's foreheads.

Noah had already pulled the car into the driveway by the time she got outside. It would only be a short drive to their destination. They were staying at a small campground about an hour away. There was a lake to swim in and woods to hike through. The campground offered a few cabins, and they had been lucky to snag one last minute. Hannah had been concerned about leaving Julie, but Noah insisted they take a few days alone together. He had gone to the campground the day before to stock their cabin with groceries and drop off their luggage. Everything was set for their arrival.

Even though it was only a short drive, by the time they reached the cabin, Hannah had fallen asleep in the passenger seat. Noah had planned a big romantic gesture for when they arrived, but as he watched her eyes grow heavier with each mile marker they passed on the interstate, he knew he would have to abandon his plan. She had been through so much the last few months, and putting the wedding together so quickly while also taking care of her mother had clearly taken a toll on her. He was happy to have her to himself again after so many weeks apart. Although they had just gotten married, he couldn't help but feel that this was the most distant they had ever been. It was more than the actual physical distance between them. Hannah's mind always seemed to be somewhere else lately. He was hoping that their few days together would set things right and let them reconnect.

Noah gently nudged Hannah's shoulder, and she opened her eyes. "Oh, we are here already. Sorry I dozed off."

"No problem. Why don't we just get some rest tonight?" he asked. Hannah was relieved he had suggested it. She had enough to feel guilty about without adding not having sex on her wedding night to the list. She nodded. "Actually, that sounds perfect. I'm so beat."

Noah leaned over and kissed her on the head. He put his arm around her as they walked into the cabin. She had never been so grateful to settle into bed. The day had been a crazy whirlwind. When she woke up that morning, she hadn't even been sure that she would make it to this point. Her thoughts of Patrick had been so overwhelming that she could barely think to get dressed or make it to the church. Even now, the taste of his kiss was still on her lips. She could still feel the warmth of his body on her skin from their dance at the reception.

When Noah lay down next to her, he moved towards her and kissed her. They had been alone so rarely in the last few months; this was their first real deep kiss in a while. Hannah couldn't help but notice the difference between kissing Noah and kissing Patrick. When her lips met Patrick's, it was as if they could never be there long enough; no amount of time would suffice. Kissing Noah was less intense but also less desperate. It was kind, loving, and warm—the kind of kiss you could count on and build a life around. It wasn't frantic. There was not such deep passion, but there was also so much less pain. Hannah had already lived through so much pain, she thought it was time she tried to move beyond it. Tonight, she needed to sleep. Tomorrow would be a new day. It would be another chance for her to move towards Noah and away from Patrick.

When she woke up the next morning, Noah had already gotten up and made breakfast, but she could tell by the look on his face that he intended to do something else before they ate. They made love for the first time since she had come to Hope. At first, Hannah felt so guilty she thought she might be sick, but eventually, they settled into their familiar rhythms, and she began to enjoy herself. By the end of the first day, she had started to relax more in general. This was her life, and being with Noah was not betraying Patrick.

They swam in the lake and cooked dinner by campfire. Noah tried to get more details from Hannah about how things had been for her over the summer. He told her how he had been worried about her when she originally decided to come back to Hope. Katie told him once that something had happened with Hannah and a few other classmates one summer. He asked Hannah if she had ever run into the people she had issues with in high school. At first, she was hesitant to share anything about Jackie and Colton, but eventually she told him that she had seen them over the course of the summer. She also told him how Patrick had stuck up for her, and that he had put them in their place. She told him about her nights in the backyard, talking and laughing with Julie and Jane. He was curious about her work at the church, and she recounted tales of dealing with parishioners, planning the summer festival, and holding down the office when Father Murphy had to return to New York.

The last night as they lay on the bed, her head resting on his chest, Noah was unusually quiet. She had been talking about the work she still had to do for the festival when she got back to Hope and mentioned that she hoped Father Patrick hadn't been too busy while she was away. It seemed to her like an innocent enough comment, but Noah moved away from her and sat up. He looked her square in the face.

"Hannah, I know it has been a weird and lonely last few months for you. I'm glad that you had Father Patrick in your life. I really am. I know it hasn't been easy with your mom and coming back to Hope. I just think it's a little weird that the two of you have been together so much."

Hannah wasn't sure if he was asking a question or making an accusation. She was having trouble reading his tone and expression. She carefully calculated how to respond.

"I don't think it's weird. My mother asked me to take her job. Father Murphy is from out of town, and so was I. Neither of us really had anyone else our age to spend time with. Also, my mother had been having him over for dinners before I came back. We are just friends."

Her eyes drifted downwards as she finished speaking. She didn't want to protest too much, but she also didn't want to completely gloss over his concern. She hoped this was enough for him. He could never know the truth.

"I guess. I know it's hard with your mom, but I do miss you at home. I also won't be sad when you don't have to spend all day with him anymore. I know he is a priest, but he is a good-looking guy." Noah laughed and put his arm back around Hannah.

She tried to laugh too and joked, "Oh really? I hadn't noticed."

Noah tickled her, and then kissed her. "You think you're funny, huh?" he asked playfully and continued to kiss her. Hannah had wondered if Noah would ever ask her about Patrick. Now he had, and she prayed it would be the last time.

54

Hannah and Noah's three days together went by quickly. As they drove home on Tuesday night, Hannah started to feel nervous about returning home. With the wedding excitement over, how would her mother be? How would she and Patrick interact? She hadn't wanted anything to change between them, but it needed to be different now. She was married.

As they pulled into the driveway, Hannah thought the house looked different. The constant flow of people who had been in and out the previous week had given it such life. Now, it seemed subdued and empty. Noah put the car in park and then switched it off.

"We're back. How do you feel? Are you sure you don't want me to stay tonight?"

Hannah was certain about her decision to have Noah go back tonight. He had work the next day, and she needed some space. She was worried about so many things, and having Noah around would only mean hiding her emotions from one more person. However, seeing the house as dark and quiet as it was made her reconsider for just a moment.

"Yeah, I'll be okay. I need some alone time with my mom after last week." She leaned in and gave him a kiss.

Noah unloaded her bags from the trunk as Hannah walked to the house. When she opened the door, the stillness was unnerving. It was only 7 p.m. The sun had only just started to set, but the house was quiet and dark. Hannah took a few steps into the hallway and could see her mother already asleep in her living room bed. She looked smaller than when she had seen her just three days ago.

However, curled up under a blanket with an open book across her chest, she looked peaceful. Hannah moved closer and gently removed the book. She rearranged the blanket and took the glasses off her mom's face.

Now closer, Hannah could see that her mother did in fact look thinner and paler. The burst of excitement the wedding had given her appeared to have drained her energy. She winced as her hand brushed her mother's. It was ice cold. She moved it under the blanket.

The front door opened again, and Noah came rustling in with Hannah's luggage. She moved quickly to keep him quiet. In a whisper, she called to him, "Noah, Mom is asleep already." He slowed his movements and gently set Hannah's bags down on the floor.

"Are you sure you don't want me to stay?" he asked again.

"No, please go. I don't want to wake her up. I'm just going to shower and probably head to bed myself. I have work in the morning." She leaned in to hug him.

He kissed the top of her head. "Okay. I'll talk to you tomorrow then. I don't want to call and wake up your mom. Goodnight, Mrs. Bailey," Noah said with a huge smile.

"Sounds good. Goodnight, Mr. Bailey." She returned his smile, and he left.

Hannah carried her bags up the stairs and plopped down on her bed. She was tired, even though the trip had been fairly relaxing. As she lay in bed, staring up at her ceiling, the weight of what was left to come this summer felt as if it was about to suffocate her. The wedding band on her finger felt heavy. Alone with Noah on their honeymoon, things between them had almost felt the way it used to before she came back to Hope. Now back at home, she was once again forced to face reality. Tomorrow she would go to work as Mrs. Bailey. Patrick would be even less hers than he was four days ago. Her mother was closer to the end than not. The doctors had only given her a few months to live, and it had already been almost two. The situation was almost more than Hannah could bear. Instead of unpacking or even undressing, she opted to shut her eyes, block out the world around her, and fall asleep.

55

Hannah awoke to her mother's voice.

"Get up Hannah. You are going to be late!" Julie called from downstairs.

Hannah slowly oriented herself. The sun was brightly shining through her windows. She hadn't even closed her blinds before she fell asleep. Rubbing the heaviness from her eyes, she looked over at the clock beside her. Eight a.m. Hannah shot out of bed and headed downstairs. She had overslept. Julie was standing at the bottom of the stairs, waiting for her.

"How was your honeymoon? I hope you had a nice time. I didn't hear you come in last night." Julie's tone was impatient.

"It was very nice, actually. We had a good time. Sorry, I didn't want to wake you." Hannah smiled. It was the first time she had told Julie the whole truth in a long time.

"I'm so glad. Tell me all about it," Julie pressed.

Hannah gave her mother the abbreviated version of her weekend away as she helped her back to the kitchen. They sat drinking their coffee across from each other. Hannah couldn't help but notice how much Julie had changed in only a few days. She was shaky and thin. Her face looked waxy and pale. The house also felt changed. She knew that what waited for her outside wouldn't be any better. Everything in Hope had changed in four days' time.

Going to work with Patrick had been the singular highlight of every day that summer. Now she dreaded it. The distance between them was growing every second, and seeing him in person would only make it more real. Additionally, once she got to the office, she was going to be busy with the finishing touches of planning the festival. Then, in a week and a half, she would have to work at the festival. The thought of attending sent a shiver down her spine. She had vowed she would never come back to Hope—and most definitely not to the event that had ultimately driven her from the town. The number of vows she was breaking made her head spin. The vows she made to herself about staying away from Hope. The vows she made to Noah of loving and cherishing only him. When this summer was finally over, she would have to reconcile her notion of herself with who she had become. Today was not that day.

Hearing Julie go out on the back porch made Hannah feel a little better as she prepared to head off to work. At least her mom still had the energy to go outside and read. She went outside to say goodbye, and Julie grabbed Hannah's arm and pulled her in for a hug.

"I'm so glad you had a nice trip and that you're back. I missed you. I love you, honey."

Hannah returned the hug and sentiments, kissing her mother on the forehead before wishing her a good day.

The short walk to the office had never seemed so quick. She wanted it to last a few blocks longer so she would have more time to collect her thoughts. The night of her wedding when she danced with Patrick, it had felt like their final goodbye. In some ways, that would have been easier than this long, drawn-out farewell. For however long she would remain in Hope, she would have to be near him, but not with him. Now she had a new reason to feel guilty. She was wishing away her time here, even though she knew that meant her mother would be gone.

Heading up the steps to the office, Hannah was thrown off by the sound of conversation and laughter. At 8:30 a.m., the office was typically completely empty. Patrick usually didn't arrive until 9 a.m. She opened the door and almost dropped her purse. To her surprise, the laughter was coming from Jackie. She was sitting at Hannah's desk and touching her things. That would have been enough to send Hannah into a panic, but Jackie was also talking to

Patrick in a casual, familiar way that made Hannah want to scream. As soon as he heard the door open, Patrick looked at her. She knew he could see the displeasure on her face. He quickly moved back from the desk and Jackie. Hannah stood frozen, unsure how to react.

"You're back! How was your honeymoon?" Patrick tried to sound normal.

"It was fine. What's going on here?" She attempted not to sound angry.

"I've been helping Father Murphy while you were away. I came early to clean up my work. Sorry, I thought I would be done, but then we started chatting…" Jackie trailed off.

"I was only gone a few days. You didn't need to do anything." Hannah's tone was curt and tense.

The three of them stood in awkward silence for several seconds before Patrick finally spoke up.

"Jackie volunteered to help with a few things, and I thought it would make things less stressful for you when you came back. I should have asked you, but I didn't want to bother you last week." He looked at her apologetically.

"No problem. Thank you, Jackie, but I can take over now." Hannah couldn't hide her disdain. She knew she should try to sound grateful, but that wasn't going to happen today.

Jackie was clearly annoyed by her response. "Of course. Let me know if I can help with anything else. Father Murphy, you have my number." She gave Patrick a large smile and collected the last of her work from Hannah's desk.

Jackie walked away from the desk to leave the office. As she passed Hannah, she leaned in and whispered, "He doesn't belong to you anymore."

Her voice had been so low that Patrick didn't hear Jackie say anything. Hannah was still frozen from what she had seen a minute ago. Now she felt sick to her stomach as well. Had she heard Jackie correctly? What did she even mean? Patrick had never been hers. Once the door closed behind Jackie, Hannah finally took a breath. She had no right to be angry at Patrick, but she was furious.

"Really? You let Jackie replace me?" she yelled at him. The sight of them together, laughing and talking, was almost more than she could handle. It occurred to her for the first time that when she left, she would not only be leaving Patrick behind but would be leaving Jackie here with him. She knew that nothing would happen between them, but she was jealous...jealous of Jackie. She would get to see Patrick, speak to him, and help him with work. They would see each other at Sunday Mass and in town shopping. She might even someday drive by while he was mowing the church lawn and see his skin glistening in the hot summer sun. The thought that she had reason to be jealous of Jackie made Hannah want to scream again.

Patrick could see that she was struggling. He finally offered an explanation.

"I'm sorry, Hannah. I wasn't thinking. This last week has had me a little out of my mind. And then you were on your honeymoon…" He looked away from Hannah as he trailed off.

"I know. I realize I don't have a right to be mad at you, but it's Jackie. Anyone but her, please." Her voice was pleading.

"Hannah, she's just volunteering. Nothing is going on with Jackie. How could you even think that?" He moved closer to her, but she held out her arm to stop him from coming any closer.

"I know. I'm sorry for getting so upset. I was just taken aback. To see you with her...I just wasn't expecting that." She felt guilty for having lost her temper. As hard as things had been for her, she couldn't imagine how hard it would be if the roles were reversed. Patrick had to live with the fact that she had gotten married to someone else and went on her honeymoon with a different man. She could barely handle seeing him talk to a different woman.

Patrick's jaw clenched as Hannah spoke. She could see the pain flash across his face. She hadn't meant to make him feel guilty. In fact, he had done nothing wrong at all. She had married another man. What right did she have to shame him for asking for help at work? Trying to walk her obvious displeasure back, she attempted to change her tone.

"It really is no worries, though. I'm glad that things are caught up around here. My mom doesn't look all that great, so it will be good to get out of here on time." She walked over to her desk and took a seat. The chair was still warm from where Jackie had been sitting moments ago. The urge to squirm out of it was almost unbearable, but she resisted. She smiled warmly at Patrick. He looked cautiously at her, still contemplating what else to say, if anything.

"Truly, it's fine. I need a few minutes to get settled, and then we can go over the status of everything."

Patrick still seemed unsure how to react to her. He was fidgeting with the collar of his shirt when he responded.

"Okay. I'll be in my office when you are ready." He gave her a guarded smile and turned to go into his office.

56

The to-do list Hannah had left for herself had been almost entirely checked off. Jackie had ordered the signage, confirmed the catering service, and called a final time to confirm all the vendors. She had sent out the volunteer instruction letters and the DJ's playlist. Hannah felt relieved but also annoyed. All summer, she had prepared for this. She and Patrick had worked so hard. Jackie inserting herself in the process, especially now, was upsetting. Hannah could imagine what things would be like the next summer. Her mother would be gone, Hannah would be back in Chicago, and Jackie would be at this desk spending her days with Patrick. She shuddered at the thought.

***

Patrick sat down in his office chair. The last few days had been a whirlwind. He had married Hannah to someone else, watched as she left on her honeymoon, and had to come back to the place where they had spent so much time together alone. The first time he walked through the door and saw her desk sitting empty, it felt as if he had been punched in the gut. He could still feel the warmth of her body and the feel of her lips pressed against his from when he kissed her by the desk a few weeks earlier. The happiness he had felt in that moment was now a void in his chest. He felt as if he might be sick.

He had quickly gone into his office and shut the door. At least inside he could pretend that she was there, sifting through mail and answering the phone. When Jackie turned up after church on

Sunday morning, he had been annoyed at first. He knew Hannah would not want Jackie anywhere near her work, but the silence in the office had been almost unbearable. Jackie had brought him a coffee, and he felt he had no choice but to agree to let her help. They worked together some of Sunday, all day Monday, and then again on Tuesday. When things ended up taking longer than expected, Jackie had asked if she could come in early on Wednesday to tidy things up for Hannah instead of staying any later on Tuesday. He had agreed, but he should have just done it himself. He had planned to tell Hannah after she was settled in, but things hadn't gone as he planned. The guilt he felt when he saw Hannah's face a few minutes earlier made it clear that he had made the wrong decision.

***

Hannah shuffled through the papers on her desk, trying to sound busy. She was still furious at Patrick for letting Jackie anywhere near her things, but she was also furious at herself for feeling so betrayed. She had literally married someone else, yet she was mad at Patrick for letting someone else help with church business. It was monumentally unfair of her, and she knew it. All summer, she had tried to prepare herself for this moment, and it had all been in vain. She was a mess. She didn't even know which emotion to try and process. Guilt, anger, love, despair, and desire all swirled around inside of her. She wasn't sure which one would erupt first. The sound of an ambulance outside jolted her out of her contemplation. She looked out the window and caught a glimpse of it speeding past the church. That meant the ambulance was headed in the direction of her house. All the emotions she had been feeling only a moment earlier were instantly replaced by fear. She picked up the phone to call her mother. Patrick had heard the ambulance as well and was now standing at the edge of her desk.

"I'm calling right now," she told him with a look of panic on her face.

They stood staring at each other. The sound of the line ringing echoed around the room. After the seventh ring, Hannah hung up. The concern she felt was overwhelming. She had only been gone for thirty minutes, but things can happen in an instant.

"Hannah, why don't we just go to your house?" Patrick suggested.

"Yeah. I think you're right." She jumped up from her chair and was out the door and down the stairs before she had time to give it a second thought. She could hear Patrick's footsteps right behind her. They didn't speak, but she was glad he was there. By the time they had made it halfway down the block, they could see that the ambulance hadn't stopped at Hannah's house but at their neighbor's. Julie was standing with her arm around Mrs. Allen as the ambulance loaded her husband into the back of the ambulance.

At the sight of her mother, Hannah could no longer contain her emotions. She dropped to her knees and started to cry. Patrick wanted to go and see if the Allens needed anything, but he couldn't leave Hannah in this condition. He put his arms under hers and pulled her to her feet.

"Let's go back to the office." She nodded and collected herself enough to walk back. Once they were inside with the door closed, Hannah sat down on the couch. She couldn't tell whether she was more relieved or terrified. Her mother was in hospice, so no ambulances would be called when she passed, but if a neighbor saw her collapse outside, they wouldn't know not to call one. Today the ambulance wasn't for her mother. Julie was okay, but for how long, Hannah didn't know.

Patrick sat down beside her. He wasn't sure what to say or do. Before, he would have reached out and held her, but things were different now. He looked down at the ring on her left hand, sitting motionless as he waited for Hannah to set the tone.

"I thought my mother...I thought she was gone." Her voice sounded weak and shaky. She knew that they were supposed to keep their distance, but she needed him. What harm could there be in a hug? She settled into him, and he put his arm around her. She buried her head in his chest and sobbed.

In all his years as a priest, Patrick had been quick with words of advice and comfort, but with Hannah, his mind was blank. He had no idea what to tell her, so he just held her and rubbed her back. Even at this moment, having her so close but unable to really be with her was almost unbearable for him. He wanted to kiss her tears away. He wanted to hold her and touch her without the limitations of their circumstances dictating what they were allowed to do. He knew she needed him, and he needed her. How could a feeling so pure and true be prohibited, forbidden, and off limits? It went against every instinct in his body. It was their reality, however, so all he could do was hold her. They embraced silently for a couple of minutes as Hannah tried to collect herself. Just as her tears were starting to slow down, the sound of the door opening echoed through the office.

Patrick instinctively pulled back from her. Hannah was caught off guard and fell forward off the couch. When she finally pulled herself up to look at who had entered, she was met with Jackie's flabbergasted face.

"I forgot my planner here. I came back to get it." She walked past them and grabbed a book from the desk.

Patrick tried to offer an explanation. "We heard an ambulance. Hannah thought—"

Jackie cut him off. "I don't think I want to know, Father Murphy." She seemed surprised and annoyed at the same time, leaving quickly.

Hannah had reached her breaking point. She couldn't pretend that everything was okay anymore. What happened to her fourteen years earlier had been wrong. Having conflicted feelings about Noah was wrong. Her mother being sick was wrong. And soon, she would have to walk away from Patrick. She had dreaded this day, and it was turning out much worse than she could have imagined.

She got up off the couch. "I'm sorry, but I need to go home." She looked straight into Patrick's eyes, seeing confusion and pain there. He wasn't to blame for how she felt, but right now, she couldn't be near him.

"No problem, I understand. Will I see you tomorrow?" he asked timidly.

"Can I let you know?"

He nodded yes, and she grabbed her purse. She was halfway home before she even had time to think about all the events of the last hour. When she arrived home, she was relieved to be away from the church, Patrick, and Jackie.

"Hannah, you're home? Did something happen?" Julie sounded concerned.

"No. I just wanted to spend the day with you. Jackie helped Father Murphy while I was gone, so things are pretty caught up. Besides, I want you to fill me in on what happened at the Allens." She tried to sound convincing.

"Okay, I would enjoy that. It has been very quiet around here while you were gone."

57

Hannah and Julie spent the rest of the morning on the back porch, catching up and reading in the shade of the porch awning. Their Adirondack chairs were perfectly parallel to each other, giving them a view of the backyard. After a few hours, Julie set her book down and declared, "I finally finished the mystery I was reading. When I started it, I didn't think I would like it so much. I really wanted to finish it before…" She trailed off before she could complete her thought.

At first, Hannah wondered why she hadn't finished speaking, but then it dawned on her. Julie meant she was glad that she finished the book before she died. The thought sent a shock through Hannah. She knew that the end was near, but hearing it from her mother made it all the more real. She wanted to change the topic of conversation as quickly as possible.

"Let's go in for lunch." Julie nodded in agreement.

Hannah put together a few tuna salad sandwiches and brought them to the living room, where Julie had settled into her bed. She put the lap tray on her bed and served Julie her lunch. They ate mostly in silence, both seemingly lost in thought. When they finished, Hannah took the plates to the kitchen and began to clean up. It was nice to be home, back to the quiet routine they had established that summer. The last few weeks had been so busy and loud. There had been so much going on. Between the wedding and work, she hadn't had much alone time with Julie. She was looking forward to the afternoon and being distracted from all her thoughts of the past and future. She wanted to be in this moment with her mother.

By the time Hannah had washed the last dish and made her way back to the living room, Julie had dozed off. She covered her with a blanket and decided to take a nap as well. Pulling up a chair and grabbing a blanket, Hannah settled in next to her mom. She put her hand over Julie's arm and quickly dozed off as well.

Hannah woke up to the sound of Julie's voice. "Hannah dear, get up. We slept the whole afternoon." Her voice was weak but warm, and it roused Hannah from her slumber. She opened her eyes and was met by the sight of the sun setting outside the living room window. They had indeed slept the entire day away. She sat up in her chair. "How are you feeling Mom?"

"A little better now after such a long nap." She gave Hannah a small smile. Seeing Julie lying in her bed, surrounded by books and plants, Hannah couldn't help but think that she looked even smaller than when she had fallen asleep. "Are you hungry Mom? I can make us some dinner?"

Julie didn't have much of an appetite lately. "No, I think just some tea." Hannah nodded and went to make it. While she waited for the water to boil, Hannah grabbed herself some cheese and bread from the fridge. She ate her sandwich quickly before returning to Julie's bedside. She expected to find her mother nestled in reading a book, but instead, she was sitting upright with a very serious look on her face.

"Hannah, the last few days I've been feeling very tired. I don't want to upset you, but each time I wake up from a nap or in the morning, I'm thankful that I did. I'm not sure how much time I have left. I just wanted to be honest with you."

Hannah was taken aback by her mother's frankness. She had seen the truth in Julie's face this morning. She had known it was coming all summer, but somehow, it still felt as if she had been blindsided.

"I'm so sorry Mom," was all she could think to say. She set the tea down on the end table and took a seat next to her mother on the bed.

"I'm so grateful we were able to spend this summer together."

Hannah laid her head down in Julie's lap and began to cry.

"Oh, my dear girl, don't be sad. I'm at peace. I have lived all these years without your father, and now I will finally be with him again. I have felt closer to him these last weeks than I have in years. At first, I thought it was because of you and the wedding, but now I think he is letting me know that everything will be okay; that he is waiting for me. I was able to see you get married. I know you will be loved and taken care of. It seems like you have made peace with whatever kept you from this town for all those years. I'm happy." Julie stroked Hannah's hair as she talked. "I do have one regret though, Hannah."

Hannah shuddered a little at Julie's words. She knew that her mother had remained in Hope all these years because it made her feel close to her father, but surely their lives could have been better if she had left. She often wondered if her mother ever regretted that choice.

"My biggest regret is that I should have tried harder to make you tell me what happened to you that night before the summer festival. I didn't want to push you, but I should have. I didn't press you then, but I'm going to now. Tell me what happened."

The assertiveness and force in Julie's voice reverberated around the room. Julie had never demanded anything from Hannah like this before. She had always been respectful of Hannah's privacy—most likely in opposition to her own parents, who had dug and pried into every aspect of Julie's life. This was different, however. She had waited too long to extract the truth from Hannah, and she knew her hesitancy had caused more harm than good. Her time was limited, and she was done waiting to know the truth.

Hannah hesitated before saying anything. So much time had gone by. She wasn't sure what good burdening her mother with her trauma would do now. She fumbled with her shirt and tapped her foot nervously.

"Hannah, it's time. I don't want to have to say this is my dying wish, but it is." Julie looked Hannah square in the face and reached out to calm her fidgeting hands. "Just tell me."

It took Hannah a moment to process. She would have to tell her mother the truth. All the years of hiding and deflecting had led to this moment. Seated next to her mother's bed, holding her hands, she suddenly felt like a terrified eighteen-year-old girl all over again. Telling Patrick had come so easily. Perhaps because of the instant connection she had felt with him. Perhaps because he had seen what Colton was truly capable of. Telling Julie seemed so much harder. Hannah knew the truth was going to hurt her mother more than it had hurt Hannah when it happened. She took a deep breath and began.

58

Hannah had trouble making it all the way through the story. She had to stop several times to catch her breath and steady her tears. Julie sat patiently absorbing the full reality of what happened so many years ago. She had often imagined that Colton had simply drunkenly fallen down the stairs and blamed it on Hannah to cover his own mistake. She felt sick at the new knowledge that the truth was even daker than what she had imagined. Once Hannah had finished speaking, Julie pulled Hannah's face up from her lap so they could speak face-to-face.

"I wish you would have told me. I should have tried harder to get you to. I should have known something was very wrong. I'm so sorry Hannah." Now it was Julie who could not hold back the tears. She held Hannah, and they both cried together for several minutes. Eventually Hannah pulled back.

"It isn't your fault. I didn't want anyone to know. I was so ashamed, and then so much time passed that it felt wrong to bring it up."

"You had nothing to be ashamed of. Colton and Jackie do, however. I can't believe I have always been kind to them. How could they look me in the eye, knowing what they did to you? I will never understand…" Julie trailed off as she recalled all the Mondays Jackie had come in to help process the Sunday offerings, working side by side with her knowing what she had done to her daughter. How could she have let Julie be the coordinator for their wedding or their children's baptisms? She had sat next to them in church and greeted them at the grocery store. For weeks after the summer festival, when

Jackie declared to everyone that Hannah had pushed Colton as retaliation for him rejecting her advances, Julie had endured cruel gossip. Yet Julie and Colton had said nothing to clear Hannah's name. Their vile misdeeds had kept Hannah away from Julie, away from her home, for fourteen years. She knew she should forgive them, but she wasn't sure that she could.

"So you never told anyone about what happened, Hannah? Not even Katie or Noah?"

Hannah considered omitting the truth once again, but it seemed futile at this point. Julie now knew her worst secret. Didn't she also deserve to know part of Hannah's best secret?

"No, I never told anyone. Well, that was until the first night I came home this summer. Colton saw me downtown when I went for groceries. He started harassing me, and Father Patrick stepped in. He saved me. I didn't know who he was, but for some reason I told him everything. I told him the whole story from beginning to end."

Julie looked puzzled for a second. "But if you met him that night... The next day when he came here for lunch, you two already knew each other. Why didn't you say anything?"

"I think Patrick...I mean, Father Patrick, wanted to keep my secret. I told him that no one knew, not even my mother. I was embarrassed because I thought he was a stranger I would never see again, and I think he was embarrassed because he never told me he was a priest." For a brief second, Hannah considered telling her mother how she felt about Patrick, but she decided she had dropped enough bombshells for one evening. At least Julie now knew just how important Patrick was to her.

"I'm so glad then, that you and Father Patrick found each other. From the first time I saw you together, I knew you would be good friends, but I never imagined how good. I'm happy that you found someone to talk to."

Hannah couldn't help but start to cry again. She laid her head in Julie's lap once more.

"Don't let what happened define you anymore, Hannah. The

life you have built for yourself is so much fuller and richer than what Jackie or Colton will ever have. Noah loves you immensely, and you have two good friends in Katie and Patrick."

Hearing her mother refer to Patrick by his first name for the first time caught Hannah off guard. The way Julie's voice lingered on his name gave her the impression that her mother might have more of an idea about her feelings for him than she gave her credit for.

"I hope you will keep in touch with Father Patrick even after you leave Hope. He doesn't talk about it much, but I get the impression he needed a friend as much as you did when you first arrived."

Hannah wanted to tell Julie the truth; that once she left here, she would never be able to see or speak to Patrick again. She loved him too much. It wouldn't be fair to him or Noah. She would always be tempted to cross the line. She would always want to linger too long, whether with looks or touches. There would never come a day when she wouldn't want him. The only way for them to both move forward with their lives would be to stay apart. There could be no half measures between them. It was wrong to lie to her mother, but in a way, she would be keeping her promise. She would think about him and love him forever.

"Yes, of course," Hannah muttered under her breath.

"I want you to promise me one more thing." Julie's voice again had a firmness to it. "I want you to promise that no matter what happens to me, you will stay and attend the summer festival. You worked so hard on it all summer, and with Father Patrick by your side, I want you to reclaim that night for yourself. I know the last one you went to was awful, but the first one I went to was the best night of my life. It was the night I danced the sweetheart dance with your father in front of everyone. I know once I'm gone you most likely won't come back to Hope, but I want you to say goodbye to all the bad that happened here and try and imagine the good that your father and I saw. I know it's a weird request, but it would mean so much to me, and I think to your father as well."

Hannah was taken aback by her mother's request. She had already planned on attending. She had to work it, after all.

"Mom, the festival is less than two weeks away. You will be coming with me." Hannah tried to sound confident in her declaration.

"I know it's soon, and I hope so, but just in case. You go and hold your head up high and be proud to be Matt Marshall's daughter." At the mention of Hannah's father's name, she could feel Julie's body tense. Hannah nodded, her head still in her mother's lap.

"Thank you, Hannah, and thank you for sharing everything with me. I love you so much. I'm so proud of you." Julie leaned down and kissed Hannah on the forehead.

"I love you too Mom." Hannah sat up and hugged her mother, holding on for several seconds before Julie pulled away.

"I'm sorry, but I'm feeling very tired. I think I need to lie down." Julie settled back into bed, and Hannah covered her with a blanket.

"I should have told you everything earlier, Mom. I'm sorry I kept it in so long, and that it kept me away so long." Hannah kissed Julie on the cheek as she clicked off the lamp. She turned to walk away but felt Julie reach out for her hand.

"I'm so happy you came home this summer. It has meant everything to me."

"Me too, Mom," Hannah whispered into her mother's ear as her eyes closed.

59

Julie lay contemplating everything Hannah had told her. So much time had passed since the summer Hannah had left. Something had changed in Hannah the last week she had been home. Julie hadn't been sure what happened to her at Jackie's party, but she was sure it was something much different than the story Jackie and Colton were offering. She could feel Hannah withdraw from her, and she wasn't sure she would ever get her back.

For weeks after Hannah left town, Julie endured being the target of gossip and sideways glances. Women at the store or salon would intentionally begin to talk louder about what a shame it was that Colton had been hurt and was now at risk of losing his scholarship. She tried to mostly ignore them. Sometimes she would confront them, all the while knowing in her heart that the events of that fated evening had not played out as Colton and Jackie claimed.

By the end of the summer, it was clear that Colton would in fact never play football again. He lost his scholarship and decided not to go to college at all. He started working on his dad's farm and soon after married Jackie, who had also withdrawn from school. Julie had done her best to avoid the Hayes and the Jenkins. She only interacted with them at church, where they had to remain civil.

Colton never filed charges against Hannah. Julie had always taken that as proof that Colton and Jackie were lying. If he had lost his scholarship because of Hannah, there was no way he would not have sought justice. Especially after his parents' and friends' insistence that he should. After several months, Hannah was discussed less and less. The story of that night was soon drowned out by new town scandals and happenings. Julie was grateful when, after about a year, she could enter a public space without feeling the glare of eyes on her. She tried to tell Hannah that no one was talking about her anymore and that it was safe to come home, but she wouldn't hear it.

It did not take long for Colton to dominate the town chatter again, however. This time it was at his own expense. He was always drinking and getting into trouble. The discussions changed from Hannah ruining Colton to Colton ruining himself. Julie did not take any joy in his downfall, but she was happy that people had moved on from talking about Hannah.

Although she never pressed Hannah to come home, she wished that she would. She also wished that someday, they could try to reclaim the summer festival. It had always been one of Julie's most cherished memories with her husband, but now she dreaded the association it had with what Jackie had done to Hannah. Someday, she hoped she and Hannah could go back and sit in peace where Julie and Matt once had.

Now knowing the truth, Julie felt as though she had failed her daughter. Why hadn't she pressed her harder? She should have asked her what had happened every day until Hannah was ready to talk. So many years they lost together, years Hannah had suffered alone. The only consolation was that Hannah had finally found someone to confide in. Julie was so grateful that Hannah had been able to tell Father Patrick. As she fell asleep, her mind was filled with thoughts of gratitude and peace that she finally knew the truth and that Hannah would be okay.

***

Hannah went to the kitchen and finished washing up the lunch dishes. As she ran her hands under the warm water in the kitchen sink, she felt the stress of everything she had been holding in over the years slowly releasing from her body. She imagined it streaming out from her fingertips and moving into the drain along with the water. For fourteen years, she had held onto the pain of that night, afraid to reveal the truth. Then, in a few months, she had told the two people who meant the most to her.

When she had finished with the dishes, she dried her hands and said out loud to herself, "Enough. It's time to move on."

She went up to shower, feeling more at peace than she had in months. She finished unpacking her bags from her honeymoon. Her room needed to be cleaned, as it was still a mess from all the wedding preparations. The laundry had piled up in the basket by the time she finished tidying up, so she started a load as well. Finally, she was ready to take a shower. Hannah had just started to wash her hair when she thought she heard a knock on the door. Waiting a few moments to see if she would hear it again, she was startled when the knocking turned into the ringing of the doorbell. She quickly rinsed her hair, jumped out of the shower, and threw a towel around herself. Julie was sleeping, and Hannah didn't want her to be disturbed. She ran down the stairs, still dripping from her unfinished shower. When she reached the front door, she switched on the light. She was glad to see that it was Jane, given the state she was answering the door in. However, the relief she felt quickly dissipated after she opened the door and saw the look on Jane's face.

"Sorry I didn't answer. I was showering. Mom is sleeping, but come in." Hannah smiled, but she felt uneasy.

"I'm sorry to barge in like this, but I just had a feeling I needed to come here. It was the weirdest thing. I was sitting reading a book, and an uneasiness came over me. Is everything okay?"

Jane's tone of voice made Hannah nervous. Everything had been alright, but the fear in her voice scared Hannah as well.

"Yeah, I think everything is okay. Mom fell asleep after dinner. We had a nice day together, but you can check on her if you want." Hannah wasn't sure if she was trying to convince Jane or herself.

"That's good to hear. But I'll just look in on her before I go back."

Hannah nodded and moved aside so Jane could come in. She took a deep breath and tried to calm her nerves as they walked into the living room, where Julie was sleeping. The lights were off, so she couldn't see Julie at first. She appeared to be sleeping just as Hannah had left her, covered in the quilt she had knitted Hannah as a baby. As they approached Julie, Hannah reached out her hand to nudge Julie's shoulder. As soon as she touched her, she knew. Julie was lifeless and colder than any living person should be. Julie didn't react, and Hannah shook her harder, this time also yelling out, "Mom! Jane is here! Mom, please get up!" Still no response.

Hannah turned back to Jane with a look of terror on her face. Jane had already begun to cry.

"I'm so sorry Hannah. I don't know how I knew, but I just did. I knew before I even stepped foot inside the house. It was as if I felt her leave." She took a few steps towards Hannah and caught her right as she collapsed onto the floor.

The world was spinning, and Hannah couldn't get her bearings. Everything had been fine. They had a wonderful day together. It had felt as if the conversation they had was only the beginning of them knowing each other better. Now it was over. She was truly alone. She was crying hard and having trouble catching her breathing. Jane sat with her for several minutes until she calmed down enough for Jane to ask her a question. She asked Hannah if she should call Noah.

Not much was making sense to Hannah, but there was only one person she wanted to see, only one person who could tether her back to the earth and help her breathe again. She looked up at Jane and shook her head no. Then, with the strength she had left, she whispered, "Call Father Patrick."

60

The day had been harder than Patrick had anticipated. Seeing Hannah's face as she left the office earlier that day had broken him. Her getting married had seemed like the right thing to do, it had to be, but it was so much harder than he could have even imagined. No matter what prayers he said or peace he searched for, he couldn't reason how their situation made any sense. He had planned on spending a quiet day in the office adjusting to the new nature of their relationship, but instead, it had been a traumatic and stressful day.

He also left the office early and had spent the rest of the afternoon reading and trying to focus on his sermon for Sunday. Thankfully he hadn't gotten any calls or visits, and after a late dinner, he poured himself a glass of whiskey and sat out on his front porch. He was three sips in when he caught a chill. The air seemed to shift, and a strange feeling of apprehension overtook him. The sound of the phone ringing startled him even further. Setting his cup down, he went inside to answer.

When the voice on the other side of the line tried to speak, all he could hear were sobs. He recognized the voice, however.

"I'm coming, Jane." She hadn't said it, but in the pit of his stomach, he was afraid that Julie was either close to passing or had passed. All he could think of was getting to Julie—and to Hannah. He grabbed his bag and ran out of the house without even locking the door. By the time he got to their house, he was out of breath. He tried to center himself before walking in, but Jane was already at the door.

"Please hurry. Hannah is inconsolable." Jane looked concerned and had obviously been crying herself. He followed her into the living room. Hannah was curled up on the floor, red-faced and sobbing. Her body was shaking and she was half naked, a towel half draped over her body.

"Oh Hannah, let me cover you up," Jane gasped when she realized how exposed Hannah was.

She rushed to Hannah's side and rewrapped the towel around her body as best she could. Patrick waited until Jane was done and then kneeled on the floor next to Hannah. He tried to lift her up to sit, but she collapsed into his lap. He put his arms around her and tried to keep her covered. He wasn't sure if she even realized it was him who was holding her. She hadn't acknowledged him, but she did hold on to him as she cried into his chest.

Patrick wasn't sure what to say or do. Jane was crying against the wall next to them. Then he saw Julie. She was still and waxy. He looked back at Jane.

"Is Julie already gone?" he asked quietly.

Jane nodded her head yes.

Hannah wasn't sure how long she had been on the floor before Patrick got there. It felt like it had been only seconds, but it also felt like an eternity. Jane had tried to calm her, but she couldn't breathe. The room had been spinning, her heart racing, and she had felt like she was going to puke. She had thought she heard the door open, and then her next memory was of being picked up by Patrick. She didn't even have to look at his face. She knew his smell and his touch. She buried her head in his chest and tried to steady her breathing. Patrick was talking to her. She couldn't hear the words, but the rhythm of his breathing and the sound of his voice helped as much as anything could.

"Jane, did you call Noah?" Patrick asked. This time, Hannah did hear his words clearly. She wanted to scream please don't call him, but she couldn't speak. Thankfully Jane responded.

"She told me not to call Noah. She wanted me to call you." For a second, Patrick considered calling Noah anyway. But then he nodded in agreement and turned his attention back to Hannah. He let her cry, scream, even fight with him a bit when he tried to calm her down. Even though this was what she knew was going to happen, it still seemed like a shock. After some time, Patrick was able to finally sit Hannah up, and he asked Jane to go get her some clothes from upstairs. She returned with some sweatpants and a T-shirt.

"We need to call Julie's hospice nurse," Patrick said quietly. Jane nodded.

"I will do it," Jane said as she walked towards the phone in the kitchen. When Jane was gone, Patrick slowly dressed Hannah.

"Hannah, I need to leave you here for a second. I want to say a few prayers over Julie's body. Is that okay?" His tone was soft and concerned. She nodded yes.

Hannah sat quietly as Patrick prayed over Julie. She wasn't even sure what she was looking at. The whole room looked blurry, like a photo that hadn't developed properly. After a while, the doorbell rang. Jennifer, Julie's nurse, had arrived. After doing a few assessments, she came over to Hannah and gave her condolences. Seeing that Hannah was in no shape to handle the situation, she took Patrick and Jane to the side and explained the next steps. Hannah couldn't hear their conversation.

Patrick came back in and crouched down in front of her for a second.

"Hannah, we called the funeral home. They are going to come and pick up your mother. Do you want to say goodbye?"

Hannah could do nothing but sit and stare. It seemed like things were moving in slow motion. Yet, there could never be enough time before the funeral home would come and remove Julie's body. Jennifer and Patrick both asked Hannah if she would like some time alone with Julie before they took her, and she couldn't even process the question. Eventually, she had Patrick help her up. She kissed her mother on the forehead, then leaned back against the wall and slumped down onto the floor again. Jane sat down next to her.

Patrick checked on her frequently, but he was also dealing with the funeral-home staff. Hannah remained sitting against the wall until the stretcher was taken away and everyone else had left as well. The house was quiet again. Patrick sat down on the floor across from Jane and Hannah. She was still staring into space with a glassy-eyed expression.

Jane had been doing her best to comfort Hannah, but Hannah's ears were ringing, blocking out all the words Jane was saying. She couldn't process anything. Patrick put his hand on Hannah's leg, and she fell into his lap again. She had kept silent when they took Julie away, but she couldn't hold it in any longer. She began to sob again. Patrick held her and stroked her hair as Julie had done only a few hours before. He looked at Jane.

"It's getting late. I can see you are tired. Why don't you go home and get some rest?" he suggested.

"I don't want to leave Hannah." The weariness in her voice broke through Hannah's daze for a moment, and she pulled herself up, trying to stop the tears.

"Please Jane, I'm alright. I need to be alone now anyway. I'll call you when I wake up."

Jane tried to argue, but Hannah insisted.

"Really, I would feel better knowing you were home getting some rest."

Jane was too tired and upset to put up any more of a fight. She gave Hannah a hug before standing to leave. "Please call me if you need anything. I will come right back." Hannah nodded.

Patrick got up and walked Jane to the door.

"Father, promise me you will make sure she's okay before you leave." He agreed and watched from the front porch until Jane had made it into her house at the end of the block. When he went back inside, he found Hannah standing next to Julie's bed, staring at the empty space where she had been lying earlier that night. He walked up and put his hand on her back.

"Do you want me to call Noah now? I can stay with you until he gets here."

Not much was clear to Hannah at this moment. Her head was spinning, her heart was broken, and she didn't think she had ever felt more exhausted. When she tried to take a breath, it physically hurt. The pain in her chest was constant and felt like it would never go away. She loved Noah and she would call him tomorrow, but she did not want him to know now. If Noah came over tonight, Patrick would have to leave.

"I'll call him in the morning. I don't want him to have to drive in the middle of the night." Patrick considered insisting but decided to honor her request instead.

"Can I do anything for you or get you anything?" he asked as he put his arm around her shoulders, pulling her closer to him.

"Take me up to bed."

He helped her up the stairs and sat her down on the side of her bed. Her shirt was covered in tears.

"Do you want a dry shirt?" he asked.

Honestly, Hannah hadn't noticed that the one she had on was wet. She looked down and saw the snot and tear stains. A new shirt seemed like a good idea.

"Yeah, that would be nice." The words fell flat as they left her mouth.

Patrick rummaged through her dresser until he found one. He held the shirt out to her, waiting for her to take it from him. She didn't move or even look up. He waited a few more seconds before deciding to help her change. He carefully removed her wet shirt over her head before placing the new one on her, averting his gaze from her bare skin. Then he helped her lie down and covered her with a blanket. She turned onto her side and clutched at the blankets, covering her face. She was completely exhausted, but she had no idea how she would actually fall asleep. Her body felt heavy in the bed, but it also felt like the room was spinning around her.

Patrick came around the bed to face her. He leaned in and whispered, "Can I get you anything else? Are you sure I can't call Noah before I go?"

She shook her head slightly. He got up and turned off the

lights. Once the room had gone dark, he hesitated at the door for just a second. Hannah removed the blanket from her face. She could see that his back was to her. When he began to walk forward and further away from her, she started to panic. She wouldn't survive this night without him. It was inappropriate for her to ask him to stay, but she didn't care.

"Patrick," she called out to him.

His body tensed as he stopped. He turned to face her.

"Yes Hannah." She had been worried about his reaction, given that she could see the change in his body language. His voice, however, was soft and sweet.

"I don't want you to call Noah because I need you to stay with me." As she spoke the words out loud, she could hear just how selfish she was being.

Patrick took a deep breath while he considered his answer. The expression on his face was hard to read. He looked relieved and anxious at the same time. She waited for a response, but he didn't speak. After a few moments, he walked around to the other side of the room and sat down in the chair in the corner. Hannah didn't want him to be that far from her. Tonight, even the few feet that separated them were too much. She felt guilty asking him again when he was clearly uncomfortable, but she really didn't care, not tonight. She needed his touch. She needed to hear the sound of his breathing and his heartbeat. She felt lost, as if she was floating outside her body. She knew he was the only anchor that could bring her back to reality. So, she asked him more directly.

"I need you to hold me."

He stared back at her, contemplating her request. Again, that conflicted look flashed across his face. She wasn't sure how he would respond. Had he not understood what she meant when she initially asked? After what felt like an eternity, he stood up and moved to the bed. He slid off his shoes and slipped under the sheets, moving his body close to hers and putting his arms around her. She settled into him as close as she could get, holding on to him with all she had. The tears began to fall again, but eventually she steadied herself.

With all the pain of the evening, she tried to focus on Patrick instead. This was why she needed him. He was the only person who could have broken through her grief. She studied the sound of his breath, the weight of his body against hers, the warmth of his skin pressed to hers. She almost felt grateful for their situation. Maybe this was why they had come together, so that tonight, one of the worst nights of her life, she could hold on to him, and it would mean so much more. Once her crying had completely ceased, she turned so she could see his face. He looked as pained as she did. In his expression, she saw all the emotions she was feeling as well. He kissed her forehead and gently whispered, "Let's try to get some sleep."

She wasn't sure how, but at some point, she fell asleep. When she woke up, the sun had already begun to rise. She reached to feel for Patrick, but he wasn't there. Her eyes flew open, and she sat up, frantically looking around. He was again sitting in the chair in the corner of the room.

"I think I need to go before anyone is up to see me walk home." He didn't sound worried, but she knew it was true. He had come over in shorts and a tank top. That was enough to cause gossip that would spread through the town like wildfire. She nodded in agreement. He got up and walked over to her. He kissed her on the forehead, lingering longer than she expected. She took the opportunity to breathe him in one more time. Today she would call Noah. He would come over, and Julie's death would be real all over again.

Patrick pulled back from his kiss and whispered, "I'll be back later."

His footsteps echoed down the stairs and into the hallway. She heard the front door click open, then closed. The house was eerily silent. It had always seemed empty, even when her mother had been there, but now it was deathly quiet. She lay down and rolled over to the side of the bed where Patrick had been just a few minutes earlier. The smell of him lingered in the sheets, and she didn't want to move. She tried to savor the last seconds of his remaining presence before she would have to face the day. She knew he had to leave, but as she faced the reality of having to walk downstairs to an empty living room, she had never longed for his company more.

61

Patrick briskly walked the short block from Hannah's house to the rectory, feeling a mix of sadness, shame, and guilt. Julie had been the kindest, most welcoming person to him in this whole town. She had almost made him feel as if he was her child. She gave him advice, listened to his hopes, and counseled him through his difficulties. Now she was gone, and soon Hannah would be gone too. The last time he had walked home embarrassed of his actions the night before had been in his youth, but the circumstances of his walk home this morning left a pit in his stomach. He felt terrible leaving Hannah before dawn, like she was some dirty secret. They had only slept next to each other in her moment of pain. He couldn't help but be glad that she had wanted him to comfort her, which only made him feel more guilty. When he reached the rectory door, he breathed a sigh of relief, but he also felt a sense of dread. The closeness he and Hannah had shared the night before was over. When he remerged, he would be Father Patrick again, with all the formality the situation required.

***

Noah was jolted from sleep by the sound of his phone ringing. It scared him, and his first thought was of Julie. No one would call him at 5:30 a.m., unless they had bad news. As soon as he heard Hannah's shaky voice on the other end of the line, he didn't need her to finish her sentence.

"I'm on my way."

She could only utter, "Okay," before hanging up.

He scrambled to pack his things and get out the door. He couldn't remember another time he had driven so quickly, but he didn't want Hannah to be alone. He had tried to call Jane before he left, but she didn't answer. He didn't know who else in Hope he could call to go and be with Hannah until he arrived. Then it dawned on him. Father Patrick. He had the church rectory number in his address book from calling Hannah when she was at work. *It's worth a shot,* he thought.

***

After changing in the rectory, Patrick headed up to the church office. He needed to grab the documents Julie had left with him at the beginning of the summer. She hadn't wanted Hannah to worry about anything when the time came. At first, Patrick thought it was premature to make any such plans, but he had agreed, and now he was grateful that he had. Seeing Hannah last night, it was clear she could not have handled the slew of funeral decisions that needed to be made. Thankfully, because of Julie's preparation, he could now let Hannah know that her mother had taken care of everything.

The sound of the phone ringing startled him. He glanced at the clock. It was only 6 a.m. A wave of concern ran through him. He thought it might be Hannah calling, or worse, someone else needing his attention. He only had the strength to handle what was happening at the Marshall house this morning. He picked up the phone and was surprised by the voice on the other end.

"Father Patrick, it's Noah Bailey. I'm so glad I got hold of you. Hannah just called me and told me that Julie had passed away. I tried to call Jane, but she isn't answering."

At first Patrick wasn't sure how to respond. He wasn't sure how much Hannah had told him. The sound of Noah's voice made Patrick feel even more guilty that Hannah hadn't wanted to call him last night, or that she had chosen to be with Patrick instead.

"Yes, I unfortunately did get that news. Jane called me last night. I went to the Marshall house to offer my support." It was the truth; if only part of it.

Noah was confused hearing that Julie had passed the night before. Why would Hannah not call him right away? He realized he had spoken his thoughts out loud when Patrick responded.

"Hannah was pretty upset last night. I don't think she was thinking very clearly," Patrick tried to explain to Noah. At first this made sense to Noah, but then he thought of Hannah all alone in the now empty house, and he started to get a little angry.

He snapped at Patrick. "So you left her all alone after her mother died? Someone should have called me!" It was Patrick who felt taken aback this time.

"Hannah insisted she wanted to be alone, so I honored her wish. Jane and I made sure she was okay before we left."

Noah felt bad for getting angry with Patrick. It wasn't his fault. It was simply a terrible situation. Julie was gone, Hannah was alone, and Noah was the last to know. He couldn't be mad at Hannah, so Patrick got the brunt of his hurt.

"Sorry Father Patrick, I'm just a little overwhelmed right now. The reason I actually called was to ask if you could go stay with Hannah. She just called me, and she could barely speak on the phone. I won't be there for another two hours. It would make me feel better if someone went to her now."

Patrick let Noah know that there was nothing to apologize for, and that yes, he would go to Hannah right now. As he hung up the phone, a new wave of guilt washed over him. It was the first time he had actively lied about his relationship with her, and it didn't feel good. It wasn't right. She should need her husband, not him. Admittedly, he had been so wrapped up in his own feelings that he hadn't given much consideration to what Noah must be feeling. However, hearing the hurt in Noah's voice on the phone made it impossible to ignore.

62

Patrick knocked on Hannah's door several times before he decided to go in. She didn't answer, and it was still unlocked from when he left earlier that morning. When he walked into the foyer, the house was completely quiet. He called for Hannah a few times before taking his shoes off and going to look for her. He checked the living room, kitchen, and backyard. The quiet was unsettling, and he started to get a little nervous. It only took him a second to get upstairs, but it seemed like an eternity. With each step he took, a new fear entered his mind. What condition would he find her in? By the time he reached her doorway, he had convinced himself that something terrible had happened to her. When he saw that she was simply asleep in bed, he exhaled a sigh of relief so loudly that it woke Hannah.

She quickly turned over in bed.

"Patrick?" she asked, not sure if her eyes were playing tricks on her. "Are you okay?"

"Sorry, it was so quiet in here, I started to think…"

She finished his thought. "That I hurt myself?" She couldn't help but grin a little at what was a most inappropriate time for grinning. He was not sure how to respond.

"Why are you smiling?" he asked, unsure that he wanted to hear the answer.

"To be honest, I have no idea." She was having trouble stopping herself from laughing now. The absurdity of everything that was happening around her was overwhelming. It was tragic, but so tragic that the only thing she could do was laugh about it. She had cried all the tears she could for now.

At first Patrick was alarmed by her unexpected reaction, but after a few seconds, he couldn't help but laugh as well. The situation was unbelievable. The things that had happened between them and to them in the last few months were like something out of a movie, not real life. They sat on her bed, laughing so hard that they both began to cry. After a few minutes, Hannah found herself cradled in Patrick's lap again. Their laughter slowly died out, and they sat in silence. Patrick slowly stroked her hair, and Hannah tried to center herself for what was to be the second worst day of her life.

"Hannah, Noah is on his way. Do you want to get ready? I can give you some privacy." Patrick didn't want to be found in Hannah's room when Noah arrived.

"I will get ready, but can you help me?" Her voice was soft and sad. He wanted to say no, but he couldn't. Instead, he nodded yes. He stood her up and helped her to the bathroom. He sat her on the side of the tub and turned the hot water in the sink on. There were clean towels in a basket on the side of the vanity. He took a small one out and put it under the flowing water, soaking it. He grabbed the face soap from the counter and slowly washed Hannah's face, then wiped it clean with the wet towel. He brushed her teeth and then washed her hands. He found her face lotion and gently applied it for her. Then they walked back to her room. He considered leaving again so she could finish getting ready on her own but couldn't bring himself to do it. He had found his way around her dresser the night before, so he went back in to find some clothes for her.

He set the clothes down on the bed next to her and again waited for her to move and change herself, but she just sat there, blankly staring ahead. He told himself he was only taking care of her, that it was nothing more. As he had done the night before, he pulled her shirt off over her head, trying to avoid looking at her, as hard as that was. He slipped the clean shirt on her. Asking her to stand, Patrick then took her pants off, one leg at a time. She was completely vulnerable to him at that moment. It struck him that this was the closet he would ever be to another person. The intimacy they shared was far beyond anything he had ever experienced before. He couldn't help but think how hard it was going to be to walk out of her room and know that he would never feel like this again. The way she needed him, the way he needed her—their relationship was so much deeper than just physical attraction. She trusted him completely.

Once Patrick had finished dressing her, he sat down beside her on the bed. He placed his hand on her knee and sat in silence with her. When he heard a car pull into the driveway, he took a deep breath. Noah had arrived. Giving her a kiss on the forehead, Patrick stood up to leave Hannah's room. She reached out and squeezed his hand, preventing him from going.

"Thank you," she mouthed.

He nodded and smiled, then went downstairs to let Noah in. With each step he took away from her, he felt as if his heart was breaking again. Each time he thought he was ready to move on or be done hurting, something happened to bond her closer to him and wound him even deeper.

He had just turned the corner at the bottom of the stairs when Noah came through the door.

"Oh good, you're here. How's Hannah?" Noah asked frantically.

"She isn't saying much. She wanted some alone time in her room, but she did get dressed, so that's a good sign. When she's ready, I'll be in the kitchen." Patrick tried to sound concerned but detached.

"Thank you, Father," Noah said as he patted Patrick on the back and quickly leaped up the stairs.

Patrick could hear Noah talking to Hannah. Just a few moments ago, it had been him sitting next to her, comforting her. That was all he could think about, and it was enough to drive him insane. He had to get out of his head, or he might not be able to handle everything that needed to be done. He went and grabbed his bag and tried to focus on Julie rather than Hannah. She had been his friend, and he had promised her he would take care of everything that needed to be done after she passed. He had to focus on that now. Julie's memory deserved his full attention.

63

Hannah was still having trouble focusing. She remembered everything that had happened in the last twelve hours, but it was as if her brain couldn't fully understand it. Noah was there, talking and trying to comfort her, but it seemed like he was speaking a foreign language. She couldn't understand any of the words he was saying. Now that Patrick was gone, all the sounds garbled up in her mind, and the ringing had returned to her ears. Eventually, she realized that Noah had led her down the stairs. She was now standing in the kitchen. She looked up and saw Patrick sitting at the table.

Noah had walked to the sink to get Hannah a drink of water. Being downstairs was disorienting. Before she had time to react, she suddenly felt lightheaded, and her vision was narrowing to black. She expected to feel the impact of hitting the floor, but instead, she felt Patrick's arms around her. He had noticed that she was about to faint and had caught her. He gently lowered her to the ground. Noah rushed over. Patrick tried to pull away from her now that Noah was by her side, but she refused to let go. The only thing that lessened her pain at all was his touch. She heard Patrick making some excuse to Noah, trying to explain that she must be in shock, but she didn't care. She held on to him as if her life depended on it.

After some time, she felt as if she could sit up on her own again. Patrick was holding on to her, although not as tenderly as he had last night. She knew she should be grateful that he was remaining as professional as possible. She really wasn't trying to create a scandal. It was as if her instincts had taken over, and her body was making decisions her mind would never make. When she finally pulled away from him, the first thing she saw was Noah's face. She thought he might be mad, but instead she saw genuine concern. Of course, Noah had always been too good for her. He wasn't concerned that she had been in the arms of another man, only that she seemed so out of sorts. When she shifted her gaze to look at Patrick's face, she saw the same expression—concern. He wasn't upset with her either. She didn't deserve either of them.

Noah helped her up, and she took a seat at the table. Patrick sat down across from her and handed her the funeral plans Julie had dictated to him. He went over what readings there would be, how she had asked Jane to give her eulogy. She would be buried in the plot next to Hannah's father. Hannah heard and understood everything that was being said, but it felt like it was happening to someone else. She was grateful that her mother had done this ahead of time. If she had to make the decisions now, she would not have been able to. She would have let Patrick and Jane choose everything, and then, after some time passed, when she finally emerged from the fog of grief, she would have been wracked with guilt. When Patrick finished speaking, the room was silent. Both Patrick and Noah were waiting for Hannah to say or do something. She sat quietly, her eyes cast down, staring at the papers Patrick had put in front of her. She wanted to move, to react, to agree with what her mother had planned, but she couldn't find the words. Patrick got up from his chair and announced that he wanted to give them some time to look over everything in private.

"If either of you need anything, please call me. I will take care of all the church details, but if there is anything you want to change, just let me know." Noah got up and shook his hand. Patrick moved to walk past Hannah but paused to put his hand on her shoulder for just a second. He didn't say anything, but she knew what he meant.

The next two days flew by. Hannah was surrounded by a house full of casseroles, cakes, and cookies. Neighbors and fellow parishioners—most of whom she was sure had never even spoken to her mother—came out to pepper her with their condolences and tell her how wonderful her mother had been. She stood with Noah by her side, glassy-eyed and nodding as they insisted on hugging her and offered their help if she needed anything. More than once, she wondered where these people had been when her mother was alive. They were the same people who didn't like her simply for not being from Hope. The same people who had believed Jackie and Colton's story even though it didn't make sense. Where were these people when her mother was a young widow with a young child? Where were they when Julie was sick? The irony.

Jane had spent most of the last two days at the house, and Noah had been great. He strategically removed her from conversations he could tell she did not want to be in. He sorted through the food that was delivered, throwing out the things he was sure no one would actually eat. One particularly questionable dish that arrived on her doorstep was a casserole of mayonnaise, tuna, and what appeared to be raisins. Whoever had brought the monstrosity clearly didn't want to be identified and left it on the doorstep to bake in the hot afternoon sun. By the time Noah discovered it, he wasn't sure if it was supposed to be warm or if the sun had heated it. He didn't even bring it into the house, as the smell of spoiling tuna was already overpowering.

The finest of Midwest cuisine cluttered her kitchen and dining room. Pound cakes, chicken and noodles, and ten different salads with either mayonnaise or Cool Whip overtook her fridge and covered the dining room table. It was enough food for five families, and too much for her, Noah, and Jane to eat. She had her first coherent thought in days when she asked Noah to reach out to Patrick and see if he knew of any people in the church that could use the food.

An hour later, Patrick was at the house with a cooler and several grocery bags. Hannah watched as Noah and Patrick loaded up the food. There was very little talking, besides the odd comment about a dish or when they asked Hannah if she wanted to keep anything for herself. Noah took the first load of food out to Patrick's car. For just a minute, they were alone in the kitchen. Patrick stopped loading food and quickly walked over to her. He put his arms around her, and she laid her forehead on his chest. She wanted him to stay with her. She was so grateful for Noah, but there was just something about the calm she felt near Patrick.

He knew how she was feeling without asking. When they heard the front door open, Patrick briefly kissed the top of her head and quickly moved away. By the time Noah came back into the kitchen, Patrick was once again sorting food several feet away from Hannah. The brief respite from her pain was over as fast as it began. Patrick loaded the last food up, and Hannah and Noah walked him to the door. They said their goodbyes, and he drove away. She knew the next time she saw him would be at her mother's wake the next day. She had tried her best to block the thought from her mind, but it was really happening, and there was nothing she could do to stop it.

64

When Noah and Hannah arrived at the wake, Jane and Patrick were already there waiting for them. Katie had driven in from Chicago, as had most of Noah's family and a few of their mutual friends. It was comforting to see them but also a reminder that they had all been together only a week earlier celebrating their wedding with Julie. Hannah winced at the memory of her mother's smile that day. The doors to the reception room were closed, but Hannah knew what awaited her inside.

The funeral director approached her, offering his condolences and explaining a few logistics to her. He asked if she would like a few minutes alone with Julie. She did, but she wasn't sure how she would manage it. Noah put his hand on her back and led Hannah towards the doors. Right before he reached out to open them, Hannah stopped. She didn't want to hurt Noah, but she needed Patrick if she was going to get through this.

"Would you mind if I went in with Father Patrick first? I want him to say a prayer with me." At first Noah seemed reluctant, but he agreed.

"Of course, whatever you need." He let go of her and moved aside. Patrick walked forward and led her into the room. Once the doors closed behind them, he put his arm around her, and she did the same.

"Hannah, I'm sorry I stayed away the last few days. I wanted to give you and Noah space." His voice cracked as he spoke.

She knew it was best that he kept his distance. There was no way she could have hidden her feelings with everything going on.

She would have had to be close to him, much closer than would have been appropriate for a parishioner and her priest. She was grateful he made the decision, and that she wasn't forced to ask him to stay away.

"I know. Honestly, it was for the best."

As they slowly moved towards Julie's casket, Hannah started to panic. She had imagined this moment, but she was still not ready for it. Her feet stopped moving, and she froze in place.

Patrick gave her a few seconds before he intervened.

"I'm with you. It's going to be okay."

For the first time, she wasn't sure if Patrick was right. Would things ever be okay again? She was truly alone, with no family of her own. Noah was her husband now, but with all she had kept from him, she wasn't sure if she deserved him.

"I don't think I can do this." Anxiety started to rise in Hannah's chest, and she tried to turn back. Patrick kept his arm around her, holding her in place. She wanted to fight him; in all honesty, she wanted to hit him and scream. She wanted to blame someone, anyone, and she was most comfortable with him. But as soon as she tried to protest, her anger dissipated, and she dissolved into a mess of tears. He held her and tried to comfort her. He was worried that the sound of her crying would bring others into the room, complicating an already awful situation.

"Hannah, look at me. You will regret it if you don't say goodbye to your mother. You can stand by the door the rest of the wake. But you need to go to her side now. You don't even have to say anything if you don't want to. I can just say a prayer, and we can walk away. Please."

She heard him and knew he was right. It was still so overwhelming to face, but she grabbed his hand and started to walk forward towards her mother. As they arrived at the casket, she felt the same overwhelming wave of grief that she had experienced a few days earlier. She tried to steady herself, and Patrick put his arm around her again.

"You know that night, the night she passed, we had a really

good conversation. I told her all about Colton and Jackie. I told her how you helped me. It felt so good to finally get it off my chest, but now…I wonder if I had waited, maybe she would still be here. I think she was waiting for me to tell her. If I had told her the whole truth about us, perhaps she would have felt she needed to stay to help me figure it out. I just don't know…" She trailed off as she battled with her conflicting feelings of guilt, anger, despair, love, and grief.

Patrick waited a moment before trying to comfort her. "Hannah, there was nothing you could have done to stop what happened. Your mother was sick. It was out of your control. I'm sure she was so happy that you finally felt comfortable sharing everything with her. She was so proud of you. I know that because she lit up every time she talked about you."

Hannah tried to believe what he was saying, but it was impossible to process anything other than the fact that her mother was lying dead in the casket in front of her. Patrick and Hannah stood next to each other, saying goodbye to Julie in their own ways for a few minutes, before the doors behind them opened. They instinctively moved away from each other.

Hannah remained facing Julie while Patrick walked over to greet everyone as they walked in. She didn't move from her spot, silently staring down at the face of the woman who had always been there for her, who had loved her more than anyone else. She looked at peace. Hannah imagined her mother and father reuniting after so many years. They were happy together, watching over her. At least, she hoped they were. Her own faith in what comes after death was shaky, but she knew her mother believed, so she had to hope for her sake that she was right.

Noah came up behind her and put his arms around her. She winced for just a second, the feel of his touch reminding her that Patrick was no longer holding her.

"Are you okay babe?" he asked. She had hoped he hadn't noticed, but clearly he had. "Yeah, you just startled me." She paused for a long time before adding, "I can't believe this is really happening."

Noah pulled her closer and whispered, "I know."

The rest of the wake went by quickly as Hannah was hugged by neighbors, fellow parishioners, and even some of Julie's childhood friends whom Hannah had never met. Apparently, news of her passing had made it back to her mother's hometown. She was grateful that a couple of her coworkers had come down from Chicago. It was a welcome surprise.

She greeted person after person, enduring their condolences and sympathies, but she couldn't help but wonder once again where some of these people had been for the last thirty-something years. Jane and Noah stood beside her, guiding people along, especially when they felt that someone had overstayed their time. She was thankful for that. Patrick stood by the entrance, greeting people as they came in. He looked her way a few times. The looks of reassurance she tried to send him must have been convincing enough for him to keep his distance.

Maybe, with all the support around her, Hannah thought she would be able to endure this day and the next. She was getting well versed in accepting people's condolences while remaining detached. About halfway through the wake, her defenses were put to the test. Patrick saw them arrive first. He had tried to come up with some way to stop them from seeing Hannah, but he didn't have any ideas that wouldn't make a scene. They had been there a few minutes by the time Hannah noticed them.

It had been bad enough when Jackie's mother Barb had shown up. Jane had tried her best not to tell her off when she came through the reception line. Now Jackie and Colton were here as well. Hannah wondered how people could have such little shame. She could barely stand to see them under normal circumstances. Of course, in this town where everyone knew each other, it again made them look like the bigger people in the situation—the injured parties still coming to offer their sympathies to the woman who had wronged them so.

Hannah's instinct was to run. As they got closer in the line, she knew Noah had no idea who they were, and there was no way to tell him in front of so many people. The panic rose inside of her, starting in her stomach, then going up through her chest and into her head. She felt lightheaded and was struggling to hide her feelings. She absolutely did not want to have to hug or shake hands with them. She did not want their kind words.

Even though she had begun to move on from what had happened, dare she say even forgive what had happened, she could not forget that they were the reason she had lost so much time with her mother. She was so angry with them that her whole body was vibrating. When they were only a few steps away, Hannah saw Patrick walking towards her.

"Hannah, can I grab you for a minute? The funeral director had a question for you. Noah and Jane, would you mind?" They both agreed to continue the reception line without her.

Patrick put his hand behind her back and quickly steered her away. He could feel the tension in her body.

"Just breathe, Hannah." His words and touch comforted her. What would she do if he weren't there? How would she have endured this summer, this day, without him? Once they were safely in the friends and family room, Patrick shut the door.

"I think you need a break." Hannah couldn't have agreed more.

"Thank you. I wasn't sure how I was going to handle speaking to them—today of all days. What nerve they have coming here!" Now that they were alone, she could release some of the anger she was feeling.

"Just let it go. There is no point in letting them get to you today," Patrick offered.

Hannah knew that was the best option, but it wasn't going to be that simple. On the table in front of them was a tray of brownies. If she couldn't let go of her feelings, at least she could eat them. She grabbed the largest one on the tray and took a huge bite. Patrick followed suit, and they ate together silently. Eventually Patrick offered to check if Colton and Jackie had left. Once he gave her the all-clear, they resumed their positions in line.

When the wake was over, Hannah felt like she had been hit by a bus, then run over repeatedly. She wasn't sure how much more she could take. It was eight in the evening, so Noah took Hannah home. She was too tired to eat, so she went upstairs to shower and go to bed. Noah said he needed to unwind, so he stayed downstairs and watched TV for a bit.

The funeral Mass was early the next morning. Hannah woke up before her alarm clock. Noah was still asleep next to her. She snuck out of bed to head downstairs. She needed a few minutes alone to prepare for the day. As the coffee brewed, she grabbed a quilt from the living room and wrapped herself in it. It was the same quilt her mother had been using the night she passed. Once the coffee was finished, she went out onto the back porch to sit where she and Julie had so many times this past summer.

It was still August, but the early morning air had the slightest coolness to it. There was even some mist rising from the yard. It was a beautiful sight, and one she knew Julie would have enjoyed. Hannah closed her eyes and imagined herself running around the yard as a toddler, her father chasing after her, her mother splashing in the sprinkler. She pictured her mom as a woman dancing at her wedding. Wrapped in her mother's blanket, she could swear she still felt Julie there with her.

Thankfully, the church service was concise. Jane gave the eulogy, but Patrick also shared some remarks, all of which filled Hannah's heart. It was as personal and meaningful as any funeral she had ever been to. Julie would have been happy with how everything went. After the service, everyone filtered down to the church basement for coffee and pastries. Julie had requested no graveside service. Hannah wasn't sure if it was because she had known Hannah would already be overwhelmed at this point, or if she had wanted to be reunited with Matt by herself. Either way, Hannah was grateful that it was all over.

As the brunch reception was wrapping up, Hannah and Noah said thank yous and goodbyes to the people who had come. Julie's body was still in the church, and Patrick asked Hannah if she wanted to stay until the hearse arrived to remove Julie's casket. As much as she felt she should, she just wanted to go home. She was bone tired and didn't want to wear a strong face anymore.

"Thank you, but I think I need to go home."

Patrick could see her exhaustion. He had to stay with Julie anyway, so there was no need for Hannah to stay too.

"Of course. Please go and get some rest. I will be here with Julie. Please call if you need anything."

He wanted to put his arms around her and not let go. He could see the pain in her eyes, but he had no choice but to simply let her walk away. So many things about his relationship with Hannah filled him with joy. Their connection made him feel more alive than he ever had. The last few days had been so challenging. In her worst moments, she had wanted him, needed him, more than any other person in her life. He liked how that felt. He savored their closeness. His experience with romantic love was very limited, but he was also sure that what they felt for each other was rare and precious. He loved her so much. He would do his absolute best to do whatever was best for her. He wanted to feel jealous of Noah or possessive of her, but he truly was only concerned that she was alright. As he watched Hannah and Noah walk out of the church, he wasn't sure if the realization made him feel better or worse.

65

The moment Hannah made it through her front door, she could no longer contain the emotions she had been suppressing since the morning. For hours, she had been snuffing down her waves of grief each time they tried to crest over. Now, finally alone, she didn't need to hide her emotions. She could feel whatever she needed to feel. She barely had one shoe off before she dropped to the floor in a puddle of tears. Noah had been half expecting it, since Hannah had been putting on a brave face since the day before. There was no way she was really that okay, he had thought to himself. He helped her take off her other shoe and helped her into the chair in the living room. He left her for a few minutes to make her some tea and bring her something to eat. The day had been exhausting for them all, and he was sure she hadn't eaten, even though they had been surrounded by food at the reception.

Hannah sat quietly in the chair where she had spent the last few months sitting next to her mother. So many nights she had come downstairs and sat for a few minutes, just watching her sleep, observing the gentle rise and fall of her chest. Now the room was empty and quiet. The sounds of Julie were gone. Noah switched on the light and set a tray of food besides her. He was talking, but she didn't comprehend the words. She felt like she was underwater again. She could see his mouth moving, but by the time the sounds reached her ears, they had been muted. He had put the sandwich he made up to her lips, and she decided it was easier to take a bite than argue against it. Once she had eaten enough to satisfy Noah, he helped her upstairs.

Noah helped undress her, wash her face, and brush her teeth. With each brush of his skin against hers, a part of her longed that it was Patrick who was with her again, gently lifting the shirt over her head, wiping the makeup from her face. Would she never stop wanting him? Even in this state of grief and numbness, all that broke through was her thoughts about Patrick.

Noah had been so supportive, so loving. It made the guilt she felt for wishing she was with Patrick instead all the more intense. They lay down for a nap. Hannah could do nothing but hope things would be easier when she woke up. She prayed that the ache she felt missing her mother and her need to be close to Patrick would both diminish. She had to hold on to those hopes. If the pain and longing she felt now lasted forever, she wasn't sure how she would survive. Survival meant never losing hope that those sensations would lessen.

By the time she woke up, it was early evening. Noah had gotten up before her. She could hear running water and a commotion in the kitchen. She headed downstairs to see what was going on.

"Hey babe, sorry to wake you, but I wanted to get this all cleaned up." Noah walked over and kissed her on the forehead. He had started to clear the house of the last of the sympathy food. She was grateful for that. Staring at the piles of stale baked goods was only another reminder of Julie's passing.

"Noah, when were you planning to go back to Chicago?" she asked. They hadn't discussed his plans yet.

Things with her mother had happened so quickly. She suddenly realized she didn't really have a game plan for what to do now. Her mother had told her she should sell the house, as she didn't have any other significant assets to leave her.

Julie had said, "Hannah, I know you don't want to be in Hope. It was my choice to stay here, but I want you to finally be free of this place."

At the time, Hannah had brushed her off without fully considering her words because it had been too painful to process the thought of her mother no longer being here. Unfortunately, now she would have to make these decisions while her mind was overwhelmed by grief.

"I wasn't sure when to bring this up, but I think you should come back to Chicago with me, Hannah," Noah said. "We can come back on weekends to take care of the house, or get it ready to sell, whichever you want. I don't want you here alone, and I know that you never wanted to be here in the first place." Hannah raised a hand to stop him. The thought of leaving right now was unimaginable.

"I can't go back to Chicago, not now! I have work, and I promised my mother I would stay until at least the summer festival." Hannah sounded almost desperate.

"Why do you have to stay for that? Haven't you been through enough? I think it would be better if you came home. And you have work at home too. If we go back now, you can probably still teach the fall term." Noah was being more forceful than normal. He had clearly made up his mind that this was best.

"I'm sorry Noah, I can't. It's out of the question. I promised her on her deathbed. The festival is next weekend. I have to stay until then. Besides, it will give me time to get the house up for sale." She tried to sound convincing. She had promised her mother, but there was also no way she could say goodbye to her mother and Patrick in the same week. Her mind had only begun to process the loss of Julie. She could not bring herself to leave without having a chance to adjust to the loss of Patrick as well.

"But Hannah, without Julie you will be alone here," Noah pleaded.

"I'm not alone. I have Jane, and—"

"And you have Father Patrick," Noah cut her off curtly.

Hannah was caught a little off guard, but it made sense that Noah wasn't oblivious. Of course he had sensed something between them.

"Well yes, Father Patrick and my job. I know it doesn't seem like a big deal, but I spent all summer planning the festival, and I want to see it through," she put her foot down.

"If that's what you want, Hannah. I was going to stay a few days to help you get sorted, but if you aren't going to come with me, I might go back tonight so I can work tomorrow." She could hear the disappointment in his voice.

They spent the rest of the evening cleaning up the house. Noah arranged for the medical equipment that Julie had been using to be picked up and moved Julie's things from the living room back to her bedroom. Both of them tried to keep as busy as possible, rarely speaking. Her refusal to go home with him had hurt Noah. She hoped he wouldn't press her on it any more. She was barely keeping it together as it was. Maybe just leaving all the confusion behind would be better for her, but she couldn't make herself do it.

After dinner, they cleared the table together, and the guilt Hannah was feeling started to overwhelm her.

"Noah, I'm grateful for all your support and help this last week. I'm sorry that I'm not ready to go just yet. I will be back with you in only two weeks, and then we can put this place behind us. You should get on the road so you'll reach home with time to get ready for work tomorrow." She tried to sound reassuring, but the look on his face told her that her acting skills were sorely lacking.

"Hannah, are you sure there is nothing else going on? I thought you hated it here and couldn't wait to leave. I'm so confused. Why don't you want to come with me?" She could hear the pain in his voice. She steadied herself to respond.

"Nothing is going on, and I don't like it here, but like I told you before, I promised my mother. It was one of the last things she asked me. She wanted me to stay and go to the festival just like she and my father had." Her voice was quivering.

"I understand that, but you do realize that I won't be able to come back here next weekend? I've missed too much work already. So I won't be able to go to the festival with you. How are you going to handle that on your own?"

Noah was starting to get exasperated. He couldn't make sense of her sudden need to stay in Hope, even if she had promised Julie. Hannah had barely spoken to him in weeks. She had even been uncharacteristically quiet on their honeymoon, almost withdrawn. He had attributed it to Julie's illness, but now his gut was telling him that it was something more.

Hannah waited several seconds before she responded.

"Noah, please don't worry. Jane will come with me, and I'll be alright. Then I'll go back to Chicago to be with you, and we will never have to look back." She reached out and ran her fingers through the back of his hair. The simple gesture seemed to reassure him.

"Okay Hannah. If that's all it is." He kissed her on the forehead and went up to pack. She breathed a sigh of relief and began to clear the dishes. In one week, she would be free of this place. She had just one week to say goodbye to Patrick and move on from all the things that had happened to her here.

66

When the alarm went off the next morning, Hannah was startled from her sleep. The past months, she hadn't worried about waking up on time because her mother would wake her if she forgot to set the alarm or slept through it. Its shrill sound was yet another reminder of what she had lost. She tried to prepare herself for the day ahead. It was hard to imagine going to work and not coming back to have lunch with Julie, or not seeing her after she got home in the afternoon.

The house was so quiet now that Noah had left. She could hear every creak and clunk of the floor and walls when disturbed by the wind or her footsteps. The house was old, built sometime in the forties, but she had never noticed how noisy it was before. Its sounds had been masked by her mother's movements and voice.

She considered not going into the office today. After all, her mother's funeral was only the day before, but staying home alone in the empty house seemed worse. By the time she had finished getting ready for work, she had half convinced herself that it was a huge mistake not to go back to Chicago with Noah. It felt wrong for her to be in Hope without Julie. She tried to convince herself that it was the promise she had made to Julie that was keeping her here, but the truth lurked behind that promise. She wasn't ready to leave because she wasn't ready to say goodbye to Patrick.

Even during the last few trying days, her longing for him had only moved to the background, not dissipated. The nagging ache was always present, even amidst the worse pain of losing her mother. Now, however, facing the prospect of seeing him again, she wished she had just gone to Chicago. Even the thought of spending time with him made her feel guilty. Without Julie to keep her here, she was simply betraying Noah.

She took a steadying breath and promised herself that she would remain professional and would try not to wish for Patrick's touch every time he looked at her. She had made similar promises so many times, however, that she knew it was unlikely that she would be able to keep them. Grabbing the lunch she had prepared, she headed out the door. Even in the bright morning sunshine, the world around her looked duller. Everything had been fresh and full of life when she had first returned home. The grass had been thick and green, the flowers and bushes freshly blooming.

Now, at the end of summer, the grass was yellow and crispy. The flowers were mostly withered, and the air was heavy with humidity. The promise of the new season was gone, and she couldn't help but pray for fall. She needed the change, and it appeared the world around her needed it just as much.

She had a good deal of work to keep her occupied and her mind busy. She started right away, finishing all the vendor number tags for the festival and making sure they were all accounted for on the layout map she had created. By the time Patrick got to the office, she'd had a few precious minutes of forgetting. The sound of the door opening brought her back to reality. Before she even looked up, she could smell him. He always smelled like cool woods with a hint of citrus. She had wanted to ask him many times what cologne he wore, but what would have been the point? Scent was one of the strongest senses, and if she knew what it was, she would have wanted to smell it again. She imagined herself back in Chicago, secretly sniffing a bottle of cologne in her bedroom, and the image was too sad to contemplate.

"Hannah, I didn't expect you in this early." He sounded genuinely surprised. She wished she could keep her focus on what she was working on. The moment she looked up, she would have to deal with the chaos the sight of him would create in her.

"I wanted to get a head start, since I've been out for a few days."

Patrick opened his mouth to interject, but Hannah already knew what he was going to say. She didn't need to hear it. She knew she didn't HAVE to be here doing this. Of course Jackie could come and take over earlier than planned, or someone else from church would volunteer to help. But this was her job, her responsibility. It was her promise to Julie, and she would see it through.

"Patrick, I need to do this."

The certainty in her tone silenced Patrick. He just gave her a nod and went into his office. Hannah wasn't exactly sure what had changed between them. Yet today, for the first time since the beginning of the summer, she sensed that she didn't belong in Hope anymore. With Julie gone, she had no reason to be there. Even Patrick knew it.

The rest of the day went by without any major issues. They had a few work-related conversations. She ate alone at the picnic table near the church playground, and when the work day was over, she knocked on Patrick's door to say goodbye. He looked as if he wanted to say more than, "Thank you, see you tomorrow." But she closed the door and walked away before he had a chance. She couldn't handle another one of their "moments." She was barely keeping herself together as it was.

When she walked into the house, Hannah was relieved to see Jane in the living room surrounded by a pile of boxes. She had no intention of ever coming back to Hope once she left. She had asked Jane to come and help her pack up everything in the house. She planned to put it up for sale at the end of the week. Jane had argued some, but in the end, Hannah had won. The responsibility of maintaining the home would be too much when she was so far away, and she had no intention of ever living in it again.

"I'm happy to see you." Hannah smiled warmly at Jane.

"I already finished your mom's room, and I have the Salvation Army coming on Friday morning to take whatever you don't want to put it in storage." Hannah walked over to Jane and gave her a big hug.

"Thank you so much. I couldn't do this without you," Hannah

whispered. Jane had been puzzled why Noah hadn't stayed to help, but then again, she had been puzzled by Hannah's behavior all summer. She had known her all her life, and she had never seen her so off balance. Obviously, it had been a difficult and painful time with Julie and her illness, but it also seemed like something else was at play that she couldn't quite pin down. It seemed like the same thing that happened to her fourteen years ago was happening again. Hannah had changed overnight. Jane didn't know how to press her as to why.

***

The next week and a half went by in a blur. During the day, Hannah worked tirelessly on church business and the final preparations for the festival, helping to build booths and coordinate the vendors. She only saw Patrick for short moments, and the distance that had begun growing between them seemed to be getting bigger. He would enquire how she was doing, always keeping her at arm's length. In the evenings, she and Jane would pack and reminisce. By the time the Thursday before the festival came around, Hannah felt good about all the progress she had made. Noah had called every night, and when she updated him on her accomplishments, he appeared to grow more comfortable about her decision to stay in Hope.

Thursday afternoon, she took a break from the festival setup to check on a few things in the office. As soon as she sat down at her desk, the phone rang. Hannah answered.

"Good afternoon, this is Cardinal Keane. Is Father Murphy available? I need to speak with him as soon as possible."

Patrick was still outside, so she took the cardinal's information and promised to relay the information immediately. The call was a little out of the ordinary, and something about it felt off to Hannah. She quickly went off to find Patrick.

He was in the middle of setting up the entertainment stage, but when she told him who had called, his face went white. He took the cardinal's number from her and headed back to the office.

Hannah was unsure if she should follow him or not, but her curiosity got the better of her. Patrick was already in his office on the phone when Hannah got back inside. His door was closed, but she tried her best to eavesdrop on the conversation. The only part she could understand clearly was what Patrick said right before he hung up.

"Yes, I understand, this Sunday. Thank you." His tone was uneasy. She waited for him at her desk until he came out.

When he saw her sitting there, he looked startled. "Sorry, I didn't know you were in here." He dropped his eyes and stared at the floor.

"What did he want? He said it was urgent," Hannah pressed. He clearly wasn't going to offer the information on his own.

"Well...a while ago. Um, after that first night we met, I asked for a transfer from Hope." He was unsure how to continue. Hannah was unsure what he was trying to say.

"So what does that mean?" she asked, bracing for his answer.

"After we almost kissed, my feelings for you scared me. Even though I didn't know who you were, I thought it would be best if I removed myself from here as quickly as possible. I knew I felt about you the way I had never felt about anyone else, and I was afraid I wouldn't be able to control myself around you. Sometimes transfers can take years. I didn't expect..." He trailed off, and he still hadn't looked up to face Hannah. She didn't know whether to be furious or grief-stricken. Perhaps she was both.

"Why, after everything we have been through, have you never told me about this?" Her voice had an edge to it he had rarely heard from her, and certainly not when it was directed at him. He felt guilty that he hadn't told her, and ashamed for making it seem as if she was some insurmountable temptation instead of taking responsibility for his own thoughts and actions. She deserved better from him.

"That night seems like a lifetime ago. So much has happened with your family, with my family, and between us. Part of me forgot that I had even sent the letter in, but that's no excuse. I should have told you." His voice rang with sincerity.

Hannah could see it on his face as well. She knew that she

would be leaving after the weekend, and that would change things between them. However, she had imagined he would still be in Hope. There was still a chance she would bump into him on a visit to see Jane or at least see him say Mass on a Sunday. Surely she couldn't go to some other town to seek him out. Now when she left, she would certainly never see him again.

Before she had time to question him any further, he looked up at her. There was sadness and trepidation in his expression.

"Hannah, the transfer…I mean, it's happening soon. The other parish is quite large, and their priest died very suddenly. They are going to have Father Simmons cover here because we are so small. They want me to take over the other parish essentially immediately because it's too busy for the diocese to cover without someone there full time." He was still holding back. Hannah could feel it.

"When is almost immediately? A few weeks?" she pressed. His hesitation made her believe it would be sooner than that.

"I protested, but I have to leave this Sunday after Mass." Hannah's head felt light, and her chest felt heavy. She sat down in her desk chair.

"This Sunday," she repeated the day out loud to herself. She was leaving on Monday. She was supposed to drive away from Patrick. She thought she could handle that, leaving him in the place where she had grown to know him. She would be able to imagine him at his desk working or saying Mass on the altar of Holy Trinity. She could see him sitting on the stones by the creek they had been at together. Now he was going to drive away from her to a place she would never see him in.

"I know. I'm so sorry. This is not how I imagined these last days before you left—me packing, trying to tie up my life here so quickly—especially when we have the festival on Saturday evening. I don't even have time to tell anyone before Mass on Sunday. I fear it would cause too much upheaval. And you and I… I don't even know what to say." His voice shook as he finished speaking.

Patrick felt a panic rise in his chest; a feeling he was becoming too familiar with. The thought of leaving this place, where he had shared so much with Hannah this summer, was like losing her a second time. He too had imagined being able to walk where they had walked, seeing the desk where she had sat, sitting under their tree downtown and feeling her with him. Now he would be forced to leave her behind completely.

Patrick slumped down against the wall behind him, folding his arms over his bent knees. He felt as if the air had been wrung out of his lungs. Each time he thought he had prepared himself for dealing with his feelings for Hannah, some new blow came his way. They should have been able to say goodbye with the hope of seeing each other again, even just in a formal setting. To see how the other was doing by the looks on their faces, for him to get news of her through Jane and vice versa. Now their goodbye would be rushed, and they would have little chance of ever encountering each other again without planning it. They sat across from each other in silence for a minute before either knew what to say next.

Finally, Hannah spoke up. "You have to come to the festival with me. I promised my mother, and I can't face it without you. Even if you're busy packing or whatever you need to do—"

Patrick didn't let her finish. "Of course. I need to go and support the parish. And I would never let you go alone. I promised your mother I would make sure you went as well." He gave her a warm smile.

They both said, "Julie," in unison, chuckling at the ridiculousness of the situation. Patrick eventually got to his feet.

"I think I need to start making arrangements. Are you going to be okay?" he asked.

"Yeah, what choice do I have?" They nodded at each other, and Patrick left the office. Hannah stayed a few minutes before heading back outside. Patrick's news had been completely unexpected. From the night they met, it seemed like things between them were constantly in flux. As hard as it was to handle, maybe that meant someday in the distant future, things could be different between them again. Perhaps one day, they would find each other again. At least she could hold on to that one sliver of hope.

67

The time between Thursday and Saturday evening went by quickly. Both Hannah and Patrick worked tirelessly during the day. Then, in the evenings, they both continued working at their respective homes, packing and cleaning into the early morning hours. They were both exhausted and had barely spoken about anything other than church business since Thursday afternoon. Thankfully, Hannah had most of her work caught up and organized for whomever would replace her. She was supposed to leave Monday midday after the moving company came to put what she hadn't donated into storage.

Admittedly, she still hadn't had the strength to part with many of her mother's things. She planned on tackling it tomorrow after church and after she said goodbye to Patrick. She figured she might as well rip all the Band-Aids off at once. Maybe the pain of saying goodbye to Patrick would numb her somewhat to the pain of saying a final goodbye to Julie.

Patrick had done his best to pack up his personal belongings. Thankfully, he didn't have much. His life fit into several boxes he had placed in the living room. The diocese had told him they would send someone to come pack and clean the rest of the rectory once he was gone. The interim priest would stay at his current residence, so it was unclear when a permanent replacement would arrive. It made Patrick sad to think that they were assigning so little to this community, when he had seen how much the church was so vital for the people of Hope. If he wasn't so worn down, perhaps he would have fought harder to stay, but the cardinal had given him very little choice. He had no option but to obey.

When it was time to head to the festival on Saturday evening, Patrick tried to put on his happiest face. He just needed to make it through to the next day, and then he would be able to start again. Even if it wasn't the start he wanted, it was a chance to remake himself. To leave behind the confusion, stress, and sadness Hope had filled him with. Of course, it also meant he would be leaving behind the love, fulfillment, and passion it had given him, but he could sort that out later. He headed to the festival and waited for Hannah at the ticket-booth entrance where they would be working.

***

Hannah wasn't ready for the evening, but she had no choice. As she walked into town and turned right towards the town square, she had a sinking feeling in her stomach. This was the place that had put her trauma into the spotlight, that had made her the villain instead of the victim. None of her interactions with Jackie or Colton that summer had led her to believe they had changed in the slightest. They were still selfish and self-involved. Thank God Patrick had been there the first night she came home. If he hadn't been there, what would Colton have done to her? The thought made her sick, and she quickened her pace to find Patrick.

As soon as she reached the festival grounds, she saw Patrick right away, standing at the ticket booth. He was in his typical black pants, short-sleeved black button-down, and white collar, but he still took her breath away. She walked over to him, and as soon as he saw her, his face lit up with a glorious smile. She instantly felt at ease.

Patrick knew she was apprehensive about coming tonight. He wanted to wrap his arms around her and hold her close. He wanted to tell her that everything would be okay and that he wouldn't leave her side all night. As Hannah approached, he tried to put his thoughts aside. He patted her on the shoulder, saying, "Are you ready for tonight?" She responded, "As ready as I'll ever be."

68

Throughout the afternoon, they worked at the ticket booth together, greeting festival goers as they entered. Hannah's sense of dread began to recede. Patrick was beside her, sitting so close that she could feel the warmth from his body. A few times, their arms became tangled as they were taking money and handing out tickets, and both lingered in place a few seconds longer than they should have. They hoped no one would notice, but as had happened a few times before, they cared less about that than the feel of each other's skin.

The next day, they would lose each other forever, so it only seemed fair to treasure the last few moments they had together.

Patrick was torn, as he had been all summer. He knew it was not right to feel the way he did, but not loving Hannah just wasn't possible. They hadn't really discussed what would come for them after tomorrow. The last few days had been occupied with work for the festival and both of their moves. They had been together almost constantly during the day but also distant from each other. He had tried to remember every moment, her every movement and look. How would what they had shared so far ever be enough? The clarity of what do to, what was right and wrong, had evaded him all summer. He had not found help in prayer or reflection. He was still unsure what the future would hold for them.

Tonight, however, there was one thing he knew he needed to do. Before she passed, Julie had made him promise that he would take Hannah to the festival and that he would dance with her during the sweetheart dance. At the time, he didn't know that Julie had also made Hannah promise to come to the festival and to hold her head up high. She must have known Hannah would try to avoid it, even though she had helped plan it.

At first Patrick had resisted Julie's request, but eventually he acquiesced. How could he deny her one of her final wishes? She had told him the story of how Hannah's father had brought her to town for the first time the night of the festival. She recounted how it had been one of the best nights of her life, even though so many people were not happy that Matt had married her. They danced the sweetheart dance in front of everyone, even though they got nasty stares. She remembered it with great fondness.

Julie knew it wouldn't be the same for Hannah and Patrick, but she wanted Hannah to see that she fit in this place just as much as anyone else did. Julie wasn't sure if Noah would be able to attend, and that besides him, only Patrick could get Hannah to go. Even though it turned his cheeks red to admit it, he knew Julie had been right. Hannah and he shared a bond that not even Hannah and Noah had.

The festival continued, and as far as they could tell, everyone was having a good time. There were games and rides for the kids, food stalls with pierogies, corn, brats, and beer, bingo, as well a small stage with a live local band and a DJ. It was the same as it had been for more than twenty-five years. Hannah had to admit that, despite her trepidation, she did feel at ease with Patrick at her side. No one seemed to notice her, and luckily, she hadn't seen Colton or Jackie. Hannah and Patrick's relief for the ticket booth arrived, and they were finally free to wander the festival themselves.

Patrick pulled her by the arm to bring her a bit closer to him. At first, she was startled, not expecting him to touch her so intentionally. When their eyes met, she knew he was going to say something she didn't want to hear.

"I know you will not want to, but your mother made me promise to dance with you during the sweetheart dance. Would you do me the honor?" he asked.

Hannah was taken aback at first. She really had no interest in being on display in front of the whole town like that. However, the opportunity to be that close to Patrick when their time together was so near its end was hard to resist. Also, her mother had asked. How could she say no?

Hannah replied with a smirk. "Seems my mother was using her last wish card."

They both laughed for a second, but then Patrick was once again holding his breath as he waited for her answer.

"Patrick, I'm not sure it's a good idea. I—" She tried to continue, but he stopped her.

"Honestly, I don't care what anyone says. I think this meant a lot to your mother. She felt like this was the night she lost you and you lost a piece of yourself. She wanted you to reclaim it for yourself. I will stay with you the whole time." Patrick smiled reassuringly and added playfully, "I wouldn't let anyone else dance with you anyway." The way he said it sent a wave of heat through Hannah's body, erasing all her uncertainty and fear. All she could do was smile and nod in agreement.

The dance wasn't until the end of the night, so they had time to walk around. They moved through the crowd, greeting people and receiving congratulations on how well the festival was going. So far there had been a record turnout, and the church was raising a good amount of money. Hannah began to let her guard down and enjoy herself. She had even briefly seen Jackie and Colton chasing their kids in the children's area, but with Patrick by her side, they didn't upset her.

They played a few games, and Hannah watched in wonder at how Patrick connected with everyone around him. She had been so focused on her connection with him that she hadn't really accounted for how good he was at connecting with everyone. She had seen him interact with people at baptisms, weddings, and funerals, but out amongst the community, he really shined. It made her sad that not only was she losing him, but Hope was losing him as well. The town had benefited greatly from his positivity and energy, and soon he would be gone—all because of her.

69

Towards the end of the night, an announcement was made over the loudspeakers. "Ladies and gentlemen, please gather at the main pavilion for a Hope tradition, the sweetheart dance."

Couples young and old began to make their way to the dance floor, filling it up rather quickly. Patrick reached down to grasp Hannah's hand, and he led her onto the floor. Her cheeks flushed with excitement and embarrassment. What would people think? Could they really be this close and keep hidden what had blossomed between them? They stood next to each other for a few anxious moments before the music started. Since the first festival in 1962, the same song was played every year, Elvis's "Can't Help Falling in Love." When the first notes hummed from the speakers, Patrick turned to Hannah and locked his hands behind her back. She put hers around his neck, and they both took a step closer, slowly swaying back and forth. She wasn't sure if the heat she felt was from the glares they were most definitely receiving or from being so close to Patrick. It was most likely both.

A part of Patrick regretted having agreed to Julie's request. He could not be so near Hannah and not want her. How could anyone look at them together and not see it? How could they not see that he loved her, and not in the way a priest loves a member of his congregation, but in the way a man loves a woman?

Hannah felt her whole body flush, and she resisted every urge to run her fingers through his hair, to wrap her hands behind his neck and pull his face closer. They were both aware that they were on display, yet neither noticed anyone else. They were floating across the dance floor as if they were the only people in the whole world. As the song began to end, Hannah began to panic. This could not be it. One short dance could not be the culmination of everything they had experienced this summer. She didn't know what to say or do, but there had to be something beyond this. Being so close to him, feeling his arms around her, made all the tension they had felt this last week fall away. They were meant for each other, even if they couldn't be together in this world.

The last note of the song faded away. They didn't move, still intertwined. This was the first time they noticed that the couples around them had backed away, and they were standing alone in the center of a circle. When the realization kicked in, they both dropped their arms and quickly backed away from each other.

Jackie moved through the crowd and came to stand front and center, facing off with Patrick and Hannah.

"Are you kidding me, Hannah?!" she screamed. Hannah stood still, stunned, just as she had on this same night fourteen years earlier.

"Colton wasn't enough? Now you're trying to seduce our priest? Do you have no shame?" she continued. The crowd gasped, and Hannah felt a hundred eyes burn into her. Patrick tried to speak, but Jackie cut him off.

"I know you're innocent in this, Father Patrick. Hannah has a history. We all know what she's like. She wants things that aren't hers to have. I hate to say this, since her mother just passed, but we all know her mother was the same way." There was another audible gasp from the crowd gathered around the dance floor.

Patrick was furious over Jackie's outburst. He hadn't seen this side of her before. He knew she had it in her because of everything Hannah had shared with him, but to see the ugliness firsthand was another thing entirely. Patrick was standing with his back turned to Hannah, face-to-face with Jackie. By the time he started to speak, Hannah had already turned to leave.

She was sprinting away from the festival, from all those people, and from Patrick. How could she have been so naïve to think that she could have peace in this town? Of course their dance was a sight to see, maybe something to whisper about later, but for Jackie to shame her in front of everyone, to shame her mother, was unforgivable. As she rounded the corner onto her block, she was thankful for one thing about this town—that the run home was not far. She fumbled with her keys and finally got through the front door. She slammed it shut and threw the deadbolt closed. She had tried to let go of the past. She had fulfilled her mother's wish, which was all she had to hold on to. Just when she let herself believe things could be different, reality had reminded her otherwise.

No one spoke up for her. All the people who had been hugging her, bringing her food and offering condolences just days ago had stood silent while she was slandered. No one told Jackie to stop. It was history repeating itself, and she was furious at herself for letting it happen. This time might have been worse than all those years ago, though. This time, her mother was not there to comfort her. She was completely alone. She sat down on the bench by the front door and cried.

***

Patrick was furious. He paced back and forth a few times, trying to put his thoughts together. Thankfully, after he had yelled at her to stop, Jackie had ceased spewing her vile accusations, but the crowd that had gathered was still watching intently. Everyone was waiting for Patrick to respond. After he yelled at Jackie to stop, he turned to check on Hannah, but she was already gone. He wanted to chase after her, but he couldn't leave before setting the situation right.

He had promised Hannah he would stand by her all night. He knew what these people were capable of because she had told him. It was at this moment that he realized he hadn't fully accepted what she had experienced. Now that he had seen the disgusting behavior with his own eyes, he knew he had to act.

Hannah was not guilty of anything. She had not seduced him. He had been in love with her from the first moment they spoke. But saying that would not help her, it would only indict her further.

The story she had told him about Colton's assault and Jackie's lies spun in his head. She didn't want anyone to know, but how could he let this go on any longer? After all, he was supposed to be the moral voice of the community. Patrick stopped pacing and looked Jackie square in the face. For the first time in weeks, he was completely clear on what he had to do.

"Jackie, this stops tonight. Where is Colton?" he yelled into the crowd, searching for Colton's face. "Why don't you come stand next to your wife?" Patrick demanded. Colton slowly emerged from the crowd, people parting like the sea to allow him to move forward. He came to a halt next to Jackie. They looked defiant but nervous, clearly unsure what Patrick was about to say.

"I've been a member of this community for almost a year now. I've been through baptisms, first communions, and funerals with all of you. I know that there is a lot of good in this town, but I've also seen a lot to repent for. Julie and Hannah Marshall are good people. Julie was as kind and humble as anyone I've ever met. She loved her husband and her daughter and never held a grudge, although she would have been justified to." As Patrick said this, he looked at Jackie's mother Barb. Her face fell, flushed with embarrassment.

Patrick continued, "Hannah was ostracized because of her mother. Julie was a woman who committed no crime but to love a man from this town. From what I've learned, Matt loved her in return. I'm sorry you were hurt by this, Barb, but even today, thirty-five years later, I could feel how much disdain you had for Julie. I have no doubt that Jackie noticed it as she was growing up and took it on. That isn't even the worst part of this situation. Jackie told all of you that Hannah pushed Colton down the stairs all those years ago because she was angry that he rejected her advances. No one ever questioned that story. You all just accepted it without asking Hannah what happened. Most of you continued treating Hannah and Julie with disdain. I have kept my mouth shut for too long. Tomorrow is my last day as pastor for this community, but tonight I'm still obligated to speak the truth. Jackie and Colton lied to all of you."

Jackie tried to interject, but Patrick cut her off. "Just stop, Jackie. I think you have said quite enough for one night." He looked around and took a deep breath, knowing that once he told the truth, things would never be the same with Hannah. If he was being honest with himself, he knew it wasn't his truth to tell. But he loved her, and he couldn't let Colton and Jackie get away with what they did to her for one more day. Everyone needed to know what really happened, and Jackie and Colton needed to face the consequences. He would tell Hannah what he had done. He would face the consequences of his actions. But he couldn't leave Hope letting everyone think the worst of the woman he loved.

"I was going to announce this tomorrow at Mass, but I've been transferred to a different parish, and this is my last weekend in Hope. I can't leave without speaking the truth about what really happened at the party where Colton hurt his arm so many years ago. Hannah didn't push him because he rejected her. She pushed him to get him off her. He pinned her against a wall and attempted to…well, I'll let you all imagine those details for yourselves. Jackie saw it all. The next day, Jackie made up the story about Hannah pushing Colton to protect his reputation. Hannah was too traumatized to contradict her." There were murmurs of disbelief in the crowd, and Jackie looked as stunned as Hannah had a few minutes earlier. Patrick considered if she had perhaps begun to believe her own lies after so much time had passed. Hearing the truth out loud must have been jarring.

Once again, Jackie was quick to defend herself and Colton. "That is preposterous, Father Patrick. Colton would never… I saw the whole thing. Of course Hannah would tell you a story like that to make herself the victim. Can't you see that she was trying to win you over? We've all seen how she acts around you. We all know we can't believe anything she says." The crowd started to back away from Jackie, a sign that they doubted what she was saying.

Patrick grew more impatient. Jackie could have finally been honest, but instead, she was still lying. "That might have been true, except that I heard Colton admit it himself."

Colton spoke up, trying to defend himself. "I would never have admitted to something that didn't happen. I—" Patrick cut him off, again preventing Colton from saying anything further.

"On the night Hannah first came back to town, I was walking downtown. I saw Colton push a woman up against the back of her car. When I ran over to see what was going on, I heard him tell her, 'Go ahead and scream. No one believed you then. No one will believe you now.' I pulled him off her. He was drunk, and she didn't want me to call the police, so I told him to go straight home. That was the night I met Hannah, and she told me what really happened. She made me promise to never say anything. I just can't keep it a secret anymore. I can't watch you torture her anymore, Jackie. None of us are perfect, but this is just too much."

The crowd was silent as Jackie and Colton stared at each other. The anger on Colton's face sent a chill down Patrick's spine. For a brief second, Patrick felt a small bit of empathy for Jackie. The glare Colton was giving her scared even him. Jackie had first been influenced by her mother's bad behavior, and now she was trapped by Colton's.

Colton's parents emerged from the back of the crowd, coming face-to-face with their son. "Is this true, Colton? Is this why you refused to press charges against her? Because you actually assaulted her? It never made sense to us back then. But knowing this now, it all makes sense!" his father yelled.

Colton's mother began to sob and looked at Jackie. "Why would you lie, dear? How could you do that to another woman?" Jackie and Colton started rambling excuses. Jackie's mother Barb just stood by, head down, as the Hayes questioned her as well. Patrick knew he had done enough; probably too much. He should have stayed to help the families work through the truths that had just been revealed, but he had only one thought: Hannah. The town could sort this mess out for themselves. He had to find her.

70

Without another word, he pushed through the crowd on the dance floor. As soon as he was free, he ran as fast as he could. With each step closer to Julie's house, the triumph he felt at finally exposing the truth began to turn into guilt and fear over how Hannah might respond to what he had done. When he reached the front door, he tried the handle and realized that the door was locked. He knocked briskly three times before Hannah answered. She was startled by the knocking but relieved to see Patrick on the other side. She unlocked the door, and Patrick stepped inside. She wanted to run into his arms. She wanted to collapse into his lap and never leave, but something in his face gave her pause. She slowly shut the door, bracing herself for what would come next.

"Hannah, I'm so sorry. I should never have..." he began. A queasiness started in the pit of her stomach. At first, she had thought he was only going to apologize for the dance. But the way his eyes were darting to avoid her gaze told her it was something much more. She was already struggling with what had happened and didn't think she could handle anything else.

He tried to continue, but she stopped him. "Just hold me, please." He closed the distance between them in one quick motion. She fell into his embrace and tried to forget everything else. They remained like that for several minutes, her arms wrapped around him, his wrapped around her. For a while, they were suspended above all the heaviness that hung around them.

Eventually, Patrick pulled back from her, putting his hand under her chin and tilting her face up to meet his gaze. "I have to tell you something, Hannah," he murmured. "I did something tonight. I don't know how to tell you. I didn't want to betray your trust… I…I just couldn't let them get away with it anymo—" Hannah cut him off, tensing as her body pulled away from his touch. A look of disbelief took over her face.

"You didn't." The hurt in her voice cut right through him. Her mind raced, and she was having trouble focusing. A hot wave of anxiety washed over her. Who knew? What had he told them? Did everyone know? He was the one person she trusted more than anyone. She trusted him more than she trusted herself.

"Hannah, I'm so sorry, but I couldn't—" He tried to explain himself, but she interrupted him again.

"You couldn't what, exactly? Ask me before you told a whole group of people my deepest secret? All summer, everything that has happened between us, this is how it ends? What exactly did you tell everyone?" She pictured Jackie standing in front of the whole town gathered around the dance floor.

Patrick felt sick at her response and by how much she was clearly hurt. This wasn't what he wanted for them. There was no time to fix it. This was his last night in Hope.

"I told them how Jackie and Colton lied about what happened all those years ago, and how you did nothing wrong," Patrick murmured, hanging his head. Hannah was left speechless. She scooted even further back from him and brought her hand over her mouth.

"So that's all you told them? Or did you also tell them what Colton tried to do?" She didn't want to know the answer.

"I told them everything." His voice was heavy with regret. He braced for her reaction.

"Why? How? That wasn't your decision to make," she muttered. Her head was spinning after the confrontation with Jackie, but Patrick's betrayal was so much worse. She couldn't even process it. He tried to get closer to her, and she pushed him away. He looked shocked, hurt. *What right does he have to be hurt?* she thought. It was all too much. She couldn't breathe. She told him to leave. She couldn't be near him any longer. The feeling of betrayal was about to burst through her skin.

"Hannah, I'm not going—"

"Go, Patrick!" she interjected forcefully. "I can't look at you! Please! If you care about me at all, just go!" He backed away and hesitated for a few moments. Even louder this time, she yelled, "Go!"

Patrick slowly moved towards the door, but he stopped before he turned the handle. "Hannah, I leave tomorrow. This can't be—"

She looked straight into his eyes, and before he could finish his sentence, she exclaimed with no hesitation, "I wish it was tonight."

It felt as if a knife had been driven into Patrick's skin just below his ribs and jabbed upwards into his heart. He couldn't fix the damage he had done. If he cared about her, he needed to honor what she was asking. Even though leaving her on these terms made him feel as if he might literally die, he walked out the door. When he closed the door behind him, he hesitated. He wanted to go back and tell her all the things he had told her before and all the things he had not yet told her. He wanted to tell her that he hadn't lived until he met her, that she was everything to him. Then the look of hurt on her face as she yelled at him to go came into his mind. He turned back towards the street and walked down the steps.

71

Alone again, Hannah sat in the foyer of her mother's house, in the town she hated, covered in her own tears. She looked into the living room, where she had last seen her mother alive. The sheets and blankets from her mother's last day were still in baskets on the floor. The bedside table was the last thing she hadn't put away. It still had her mother's lip balm, glasses, and a stack of books on it. When she turned to look into the dining room, she saw even more reminders of her mother's passing. The last of the funeral flowers were strewn across every flat surface in the room. They were now mostly wilting, another remembrance that it had been almost two weeks since she had last seen Julie.

She and Jane had made so much progress packing and clearing, but they had both shied away from finishing these last two rooms. It was as if the rest of the house had been normal packing. Yet tackling the living room and dining room, where Julie had spent so much time at the end, was so much harder. Every morning before Hannah opened her eyes, for just a second, she could forget where she was. She would think that she needed to get up for her usual job and that she was in her sixteenth-floor condo back in the city. But when she opened her eyes, reality would set back in. She was in Hope, and her mother had passed. After what had happened tonight, there was no chance she could forget where she was, even for a moment. She was irrevocably, painfully aware and surrounded by nothing other than the remnants of her dead mother's illness and dying flowers.

Despair began to set in, and her head swirled with everything that had happened when she was younger, these past few months, and the last few hours. She missed her mother so much. The pain she felt from her mother's passing was overwhelming. A few short months ago, she would have thought nothing could eclipse that pain. But now she had to deal with her feelings towards Patrick. She was angry that he had shared her secret, angrier than she had been about almost anything in her life. She tried to focus on her anger because it blocked out the grief that was buzzing in the background. But after a few minutes had passed, she was having trouble staying angry. There were too many emotions swirling around her head to process.

The white-hot anger that had caused her to scream at Patrick was slowly fading. She tried to process the fact that everyone now knew the truth. She wasn't sure that she ever wanted everyone to know, but now the decision had been made for her. Having had a few minutes to think about it, she started to consider the possibility that she was relieved that the truth had come out. She was free from the shame and secrets of her past. As soon as she started to adjust to the feeling of relief that had started to calm her mind, another sensation started to work its way to the forefront.

At first, she couldn't quite place how she felt, but after a few minutes, she finally realized that what she was feeling was fear. What was she afraid of? She considered everything that had happened in the last hour. It took her a few more seconds to connect all the dots before she finally realized what she was afraid of. She let out a small scream.

She had just told Patrick that she wanted him to leave tonight. She had been so awful to him. That could not be the last conversation they ever had. It didn't matter what he had done, she could be mad at him about it later. The fear of him leaving without there being any resolution between them was so overwhelming. Before she realized what she was doing, she was on her feet. Hannah had been confused and conflicted all summer, but right now, she knew exactly what she had to do.

She had never had more clarity in her entire life than right now. All her focus was on the singular desire to make things right with Patrick. Their story couldn't end with Jackie Hayes getting the last word again. Her feelings for Patrick were all-consuming. She wasn't going to let the opportunity to be with him a final time pass while she cried in her foyer. Without shoes or even checking to make sure that the door closed behind her, she ran down the front steps and sprinted down the street towards the rectory. The urgency inside of her was so strong that it filled her from head to toe. She wanted to scream out in the middle of the street how much she loved him. She didn't care who heard, as long as he did. The church came into view, and behind it was Patrick's house. She stubbed her toe on a rock in the grass, but the pain only slowed her down for a second. Nothing was going to keep her from Patrick, not tonight.

Hannah headed straight for the rectory's back porch. She hoped the door would be unlocked and that he was home. Hannah slowed down for a moment as she approached the screen door. She needed to catch her breath and gather her thoughts. The light in the kitchen was on. She could see inside. Patrick was sitting at the kitchen table, wearing nothing but a tank top and a pair of athletic shorts. He had a beer in his hand. She had rarely seen him in such casual clothes, and it was disorienting. It reminded her of the first time she had ever seen him. He was surrounded by boxes. They were strewn about the room, half of them packed, half still open.

As she took the last step towards the door, the porch creaked loudly. Patrick heard the sound, and his head shot up. When Hannah saw his face, she was taken aback. His face was covered with tears. He had been crying. She put her hand on the handle and turned the knob. As she stepped inside, Patrick stood up.

He tried to speak through his sobs. "Hannah, I'm so sorry. I never…I only wanted to..." He was having trouble organizing what he wanted to say. He had been trying to figure out what to say to her, how to explain his actions to her if he ever got the chance. Now she was in his kitchen, and he had no idea how to make amends.

Before he could continue, Hannah spoke. "Patrick, let me just say this before I lose my nerve." On the run over, she had been so confident in herself. Now face-to-face with Patrick, his face wet with tears, her resolve was dwindling. She was as distracted by seeing him in a tank top as she was by seeing him cry. As she started to speak again, a small glimmer of hope appeared in his eyes.

"Patrick, I know I was unfair to you. I'm sorry. I wish you would have asked me first, but no one besides my mother has ever stood up for me like that."

"I should have asked. I'm so sorry. It wasn't my place—" Hannah help up a hand and cut him off.

"Just let me get this out. Please… It's your last night here, and our last night together. I don't want to fight. I don't even really want to talk." She looked at him with an intensity he wasn't familiar with. She was embarrassed by her bluntness, but it wasn't enough to stop her. She felt as if her heart was beating outside of her chest as she waited for his response. The anticipation was killing her. She hoped she had been clear enough in her desire.

There was silence for several moments. Patrick took a few deep breaths while Hannah stood awaiting his verdict. When he began to talk, she raised her gaze again to meet his.

"Hannah, I know I should have fought harder against it, but I have loved you since the moment our eyes met that first night on Main Street. Every day I have spent with you since has only made me love you more. I had no idea something like this was even possible. I don't know what to do, but I know I've never been so scared in my whole life. How can I feel this way and just walk away from you? All the things we have gone through, how you helped me with my father... Why would God give me this gift just to rip it away?"

As they looked at each other, the chaos of their lives and their circumstances faded away. Hannah wanted only one thing, and judging by the look in his eyes, Patrick wanted only one thing as well. They had no chance to be a real couple, but they had this one night.

Patrick started to move towards her. As he approached, he whispered, "Just for tonight, I want to be completely yours."

Hannah took one step towards him, and when their bodies met, Patrick kissed her with an urgency that caught them both off guard. She grabbed his head and locked her fingers in his hair, bringing his face as close to hers as possible. He pulled her waist into him, desperately grabbing every inch of her, savoring every kiss. They had kissed a few times this summer, but this was different. They had always been holding back, trying to keep things from getting too intense. Tonight was different. They could not be close enough. They could not let go enough. This one time would never be enough, but at least they would have it to hold on to.

Patrick slowly lifted Hannah's shirt over her head, studying every inch of her body. When he had helped her undress a couple of weeks earlier, he had done his best to keep his eyes averted. Tonight, he explored every bit of her body as he uncovered it. Once her shirt was off, she moved to do the same to him. She ran her hands down his chest and abdomen, stopping where his shirt met his shorts. She lifted it over his head. The sight of him was better than she had imagined.

They both tried to remember every look and every touch as they moved from the kitchen into the bedroom. They fumbled up the stairs, tripping over Patrick's half-packed boxes as they tried to get out of the rest of their clothes. By the time they had reached Patrick's bed, it felt like they were in a dream. Hannah laid herself down, expecting Patrick to join her, but he remained standing at the edge of the bed, trying to imprint the image of what she looked like at this moment in his brain.

When he finally joined her, their bodies tangled into a glorious mess. She had only ever been with Noah, but it was nothing like being with Patrick. With Patrick, her whole body shuddered when he touched her. She had wanted him more than she had ever wanted anything. It was like he could read her thoughts. Every need she had, he met. She hoped he felt the same way.

Eventually, they finally fell away from each other, wrapped up in the sheets, both speechless. The moment was too perfect for words. Hannah rolled onto her side and nestled into Patrick's chest. For a long time, that's how they remained, simply holding onto each other. Hannah spoke first.

"How was it for you?" she asked tentatively.

Patrick pulled away from her so he could look her in the eyes when he responded.

"Better than I could have ever imagined." He kissed her on the forehead. "I will never forget this night."

As they settled in to sleep, Hannah held Patrick as tight as her arms would allow. She was exhausted and overwhelmed. Her head was buried in his chest when she drifted off to sleep, the sound of his heartbeat her lullaby.

Patrick was awake all night. He had never been happier in his whole life. What had happened between them was closer to a religious experience than almost anything he had ever experienced. For the first time, he felt like he had a home. Hannah was his home. As the sun began to rise, his happiness turned to dread, knowing that after this morning, he would leave, and this happiness they had found would be over. He was a priest. He had already made that commitment. Hannah was married to someone who had their whole self to give. He had already promised himself to the church.

When Hannah finally woke up, Patrick was already dressed in all black, his clerical collar in place. He was sitting beside the bed, sweeping the hair from his face. He leaned down to kiss her, and she rose to meet him, throwing her arms around him again. She wanted to remain wrapped around him for the rest of her life. As grateful as she was for last night, it made saying goodbye this morning even harder.

She had never known such complete happiness, and she doubted she would ever know it again. He held her and gently kissed her, all the while trying to keep it together. When they finally pulled apart, it was as if they lost a part of themselves.

Patrick spoke first. "Hannah, last night was quite simply the best night of my entire life. But I have to leave, and I..." He wasn't sure how to finish.

"I know... It was the best night of my life too. Let's just leave it at that for now at least," Hannah said as she tried to fight back the tears. Patrick held her close again. It was hard to believe that their time together had truly come to an end.

"Hannah, I need to go to the church now. Mass starts soon. Just wait until it starts, and then you should be able to get back home without anyone seeing you. I will come to your house after I'm done with everything." She nodded. He kissed her once briefly and left to say his last Mass in Hope.

72

Hannah lay in Patrick's bed for as long as she could. The sheets smelled like him. She wrapped them tight around her body. How was it possible that she could have been so completely happy only a few hours ago and now feel so destroyed? She had waited her whole life to feel the type of passion and love she experienced the night before. The memories flooded her mind, and her body burned where she remembered him touching her. When the church bells began to ring and the music of the entrance hymn floated up to the rectory bedroom, she was brought back to reality. The truth was that last night had been a dream. It was neither of their real lives, and today the dream was over.

She got dressed and took a final look around Patrick's room, trying to capture every detail as best as she could. As the music ended, she knew that she needed to go. Sneaking downstairs and out the front door, she looked around for anyone who might see her. The coast was clear, so she went around the rectory and onto the street behind the church. She hadn't worn shoes the night before, so she had borrowed a pair of flip flops Patrick had sitting by the door.

He had promised that he would come to see her before he left, but she wasn't exactly sure when that would be. It was clear that he was not finished packing, and he still had to say the rest of Mass, so she assumed it would be at least a couple of hours until he came by. The foyer of her mom's house was exactly how Hannah had left it the night before, with her purse and shoes strewn about. The living room and dining room were also unchanged, and she knew it was time to finally work on them. First, she needed a shower and some breakfast, but then she would get on with the awful tasks of saying a final goodbye to her mother, and then to Patrick.

Hannah had finished throwing out the last of the flowers from the funeral and managed to pack up the dining room and most of the living room when she heard a faint knock on the door. A pit formed in her stomach. All morning, she knew this moment was coming, but it didn't make it any easier. It was time to say goodbye.

She set down the box she was packing and took a few deep breaths. How could she ever say goodbye when she knew what they meant to each other? She centered herself and went to the front door. When she opened it, the look on Patrick's face was almost too painful for her to see. He walked through the door and shut it behind him.

They reached out for each other and collided into a mess of tears, kisses, and desperation. They were pressed so tight against each other that they could scarcely breathe. Hannah held on to Patrick's hair and pulled his face to hers. She locked both of her arms behind his neck, forcing his face and body even closer to her. He ran his hands up the back of her shirt, feeling more of her, but not enough. There was no amount of her that would ever be enough for him. No touch or words that would make their goodbye any less painful. He slowly released his grip, and she followed his lead.

"Hannah, let's sit down." Patrick led her to the bench in the hallway. They sat angled towards each other, their hands intertwined.

"I don't know how to say goodbye," he began. "I knew this day would come, but now I'm not sure how to walk away." He kissed her hands and began to cry again. It was hard for Hannah to see him so vulnerable. It almost made it easier for her because she knew he felt as deeply for her as she did for him. That knowledge gave her strength.

"Thank you, Patrick, for everything. I could never have survived this summer without you. And loving you, being loved by you, is one of the greatest things I have experienced in my life." She wasn't sure what else she could say.

"I have thought on this, and I have prayed about it so many times," Patrick murmured. "Why would God put us in each other's lives when there is no way for us to truly be together? The only explanation I can come up with is that we have helped each other when we needed it most. You helped me overcome a lifetime of tension with my father, and I hope I helped you with your mother's passing." Hannah nodded.

"I know you will be with me for the rest of my life, lighting my way and filling my soul with passion. I've never known anything like what I have experienced with you. I didn't even know what it meant to be truly alive until you looked at me that first night. I will love you for the rest of my life." He kissed her slowly but deeply, wishing he could suspend time.

When they finally pulled away, they both knew there was nothing more that could be said or done. They had to go their separate ways.

"Do you want to know where I am moving?" he asked. Part of him wanted to tell her. He wanted to write it on every piece of paper he could find so that she would never lose it. The other half of him knew that it was better if she didn't know. There was no way they could be near each other and not be together.

"Of course I want to know, but I have thought about it. I think it's better if I don't." Her voice was filled with resignation. He nodded in agreement.

"I will look for you all the days of my life, Patrick. There will never be a time that I'm not missing you or longing to be near you. There will never be a day that I'm not grateful for finding you and everything that we have shared this summer. I will pray every day that fate makes our paths cross once again, but I have to try and commit to Noah. If I know where you are…" Her voice cracked as she tried to hold back the tears.

"You don't need to explain. I completely understand." He hesitated, trying to figure out what to say next. "I don't think I can say goodbye though, so can I just say until we meet again?" he asked with a smirk, trying to hold back the tears. She did her best to smile at him. She didn't want his last image of her to be a face covered in tears.

"Until I see you again," Hannah whispered.

He kissed her briefly. When they pulled apart, Patrick stood up. He nodded and smiled, then turned his back and walked out the door.

73

Hannah sat staring at the closed front door. Patrick was gone, and so was Julie. There were no words for the sadness she was feeling, and the desperation. Every fiber in her body was telling her to run out the door and chase his car down the street. She wanted to throw herself in front of it and beg him to stay with her, to love her, to just be with her. Instead there she was, sitting alone in her empty house surrounded by the boxes of her dead mother's belongings. There was no order in a universe that would allow her mother, the kindest women she'd ever known, to die so young, for her father to be killed at an even younger age, and for her to meet the love of her life only for it not to be possible for them to be together. The only good she still had in her life were Noah and Jane, both of whom she had lied to repeatedly, and both of whom she had no intention of telling the truth to anytime soon.

She had no choice but to keep moving forward. The past was too painful to think about right now. Someday, she knew she would be able to look back at this summer as a blessing, a beautiful time she spent with her mother and discovered herself more fully with Patrick. She hadn't even tried to process that the entire town now knew about what happened between her and Colton.

Thankfully, the doorbell rang, interrupting her churning thoughts. It was Jane. Maybe the universe wasn't irredeemable after all.

"I thought you might need some help finishing packing," Jane said with a smile. Hannah could not respond with words. She could only grab on to her and hold on for dear life.

Jane did her best to comfort Hannah. She wasn't sure if

they were madly in love, not with the intention of hurting anyone, but wasn't the result the same? Jackie had done objectively terrible things for Colton and her mother's love. Hannah had always known that people were more complex and complicated than a checklist of their worst actions. Now she truly believed it to be true. When she was younger, it was easy to see things in black and white, but in truth, the grey was where most choices lived.

Hannah desperately wanted to tell someone about Patrick. If she could tell someone, anyone, it would serve as testament that their love had happened. She could never tell Katie or Jane. They would try to be sympathetic, but they would never understand. They knew only black and white. All they would see was her betrayal of Noah and her betrayal of them. But Jackie, she would understand, and if she asked her, Hannah was quite sure that Jackie would keep her secret. Jackie lived in the grey, and she was very good at keeping secrets.

"Jackie, I want to forgive you, but I don't know if I'm there yet. I will try to, though," Hannah offered.

Jackie immediately responded. "Yes, of course. That's all I can ask for." She turned to head out the door.

Hannah stopped her. "Wait, Jackie. I do want to tell you something, though. I need you to promise me that it will stay between us. Can you do that?"

Jackie turned back to face Hannah, and with a glint of optimism in her eye, she enthusiastically agreed.

Then Hannah told her everything. The whole story of her and Patrick. She kept a few things to herself, but she wanted there to be a record that they had existed. That there was a summer when she and Patrick had helped each other and grown in love, and that someone besides them knew that it had happened.

Jackie listened intently to everything Hannah said. She held her when she started crying and even started crying herself when Hannah described their goodbye. When Hannah finished speaking, Jackie hugged her tight.

"Thank you so much for trusting me with this. You will never know how much this means to me. I will most definitely keep your secret." Jackie had never looked as kind and open as she did in that moment. Hannah felt so much gratitude that Jackie had listened to her without judgement.

"And Hannah, I'm grateful that Father Patrick was there for you after how awful Colton and I were to you. I'm sorry that you two could not be together, but the type of love you shared is rare. Always hold on to that. Most of us spend our whole lives looking for that."

When Jackie left, they parted with promises to talk soon and stay in touch. As odd as it was, Hannah was sure that they would in fact stay in touch and that their friendship would only grow. It was an unexpected final gift from her summer in Hope. It served as a tie to her past here, everything that had transpired, and a promise that change and growth were still possible.

Soon after Jackie's departure, the movers arrived. Each piece of furniture and all the boxes were either loaded on a truck for donation or storage. Hannah waited outside while they worked. She sat in the sun on the back porch, trying to soak in the last rays of the summer sun in Hope. The air had begun to change in the last few weeks. There was a chill in the morning air that hadn't been there at the height of summer. The first leaves had started to turn colors. It was a fitting end to a summer that had changed her life in the best and worst ways.

Once the last item had been packed into the moving truck, Hannah loaded her car with the bags she would be taking back to Chicago. Part of her wanted to lock the front door and never step foot in the house again, but her more sentimental side won out. She went inside and took a final walk through the house. She paused in each room, trying to only let happy memories come to mind. Birthday cake candles blown out, Christmas presents opened, drinks and laughs with Julie and Jane on the back porch, her wedding with Noah, the touch of Patrick's hand on hers in the backyard. There were so many to process, but she would have time for that later. She had the rest of her life to try and remember all the things that had happened to her in the house on Pace Avenue. After locking up, she started her drive out of town, past the church and rectory that had become an unexpected refuge for her, and past the church lawn where she had first seen Patrick glistening in the afternoon sun.

As she turned onto Route 36, she watched as Hope grew smaller in her rearview mirror. If she didn't look back, she wouldn't be able to see it at all. When she left fourteen years ago, she hadn't even glanced behind her. She had wanted to erase everything that had happened from her mind. This drive out of Hope was much different. This time she knew she would be looking back at Hope and holding on to what happened there for the rest of her life.

75

EPILOGUE

MAY 2020

Hannah couldn't remember the last time she had been so tired. She sat in the lobby of her hotel, slowly sipping her hot coffee, contemplating how she ended up running on four hours of sleep. Chaperoning her son's class trip to New York City had seemed like a good idea when she volunteered. However, after two days of chasing teenagers around America's largest city, she was beginning to seriously question her decision. She had been up past 1 a.m., waiting for the last kid to return to the hotel. They were supposed to have been in bed, lights out at 10 p.m. She was even more irritated to learn that her son Henry had been one of the ringleaders. The group of kids who decided to see Times Square at night had snuck out under her and the other chaperones' noses.

When Henry had first brought up the trip, Hannah had been nervous. He had never been so far from home. She told him she would consider it. The last twenty-five years, she had avoided even thinking about traveling to NYC. Patrick was from New York, and that made it off limits to her. Hannah had tried so hard to be a better wife to Noah after the summer she spent in Hope. She felt that she had succeeded in most ways. She had been attentive, supportive, and loving. She had been faithful to him in the way that he deserved, in a way that she had not been at the very start of their marriage. They had endured ups and downs, of course. They tried for several years before they finally had Henry, which had been very stressful. Yet overall, she had felt satisfied with her marriage. She believed that Noah had felt the same.

Patrick still held the deepest, most secret part of her heart. Over the years, however, her feelings for him had evolved. She now thought of him as a warm glow lighting up her life, keeping her warm when it was cold, embracing her when she needed support. He had become more of a sensation inside of her and less of a real flesh and blood person. It had helped her move on and kept her thoughts from fixating on Patrick. Especially in the moments when she was trying to remain focused on her relationship with Noah. That's why going to New York had always seemed wrong. She had been certain that walking the streets where Patrick grew up and seeing the places he had talked about during their time together would make him all too real again.

It was different now. Noah had been gone for three years. It had taken her a while to move past her grief. She had only recently begun to recover from the trauma of losing him so unexpectedly. Thankfully, she was starting to come out the other side. Henry had begged on more than one occasion to go on this trip. After so many years of repressing her feelings for Patrick, it finally seemed safe to let them come back to life.

As Hannah finished the last of her coffee, she checked the time on her watch. "Henry better hurry up," she said under her breath. She and the other Catholic chaperones had planned to attend Mass the Sunday of their trip. That meant they would have to miss out on going to the top of the Empire State Building with the rest of the group. Hannah had considered letting Henry miss Mass, but after his stunt the night before, he was definitely going to attend. She watched the elevator opening and closing for several minutes. Eventually, Henry and the other students finally emerged, heavy-eyed and tired-looking.

"Guess you shouldn't have stayed out so late," Hannah quipped to Henry. He rolled his eyes at her.

It was a short walk to St. Patrick's Cathedral. *An apt name,* she thought, considering that everything in this place already reminded her of Patrick. The walk had given the kids time to wake up, and some were already back to goofing off and messing around. They took their seats just before the opening hymnal began. The procession started. Hannah didn't have time to look up to watch. She was reordering their seating arrangements to separate a few of the boys who were going to have a difficult time behaving while seated next to each other.

After the entrance hymn had concluded, the priest saying Mass began to speak. He mentioned that they had a visiting priest with them for the service today. Hannah was still not focused on the service as she tried to control the misbehaving teenagers she was in charge of.

The priest continued speaking. He introduced the visitor. "We are very happy to welcome Father Patrick Murphy back to St. Patrick's. Father Murphy's uncle was our previous cardinal, Cardinal Keeley."

Hannah had been in a bit of daze, partly from exhaustion, partly from the distraction of the rowdy teenagers, and partly from the distraction of imagining Patrick in this place. She felt closer to him than she had in years and had been lost in her thoughts since their plane had touched down. Suddenly she was pulled from her fog by the sound of Patrick's name being spoken. At first, she wasn't sure if she had imagined it or if she had actually heard it. She looked up at the altar, her heart racing as she desperately scanned the faces of the men on the altar. She had a clear view of all but one. None of the men she could see were Patrick. The thought that he could be here, so near to her, was almost too much to bear.

She had to remind herself to breathe. Murphy seemed like a fairly common name, but she knew that Patrick's uncle had been a priest in New York. The coincidence was too strong. Patrick never mentioned that his uncle was also a cardinal, but she hadn't spoken to him in twenty years. She stared at the man she could not see properly, trying to discern anything about him that might let her know if he was Patrick or not. As everyone took their seats after the Penitential Rite, Hannah remained standing. She couldn't move. She needed to know. As the priests moved from the positions where they had been standing, she finally caught a glimpse of the hidden man's face before he turned his back to walk further onto the altar.

Patrick.

She would recognize the angle of his jaw and his shaggy reddish-brown hair anywhere. In the morning light that was streaming through the church windows, she could see that his hair was now highlighted by a few grey strands. His face looked a bit older, just as hers did, but it was the same in all the ways that mattered. His face was still kind and handsome.

Having only seen him for such a brief second, she again questioned whether she had actually seen him, or if her mind was playing tricks on her. Even though her head was unsure, her heart was telling her that he was here—without a doubt. She was not sure what to do. Her instinct was to scream out his name and run to him at this very moment. Yet she couldn't even get her body to sit down. The rest of the congregation had all taken their seats, but she was still standing, completely unaware of anything but Patrick.

"Mom, sit down. What are you doing?" Henry asked as he nudged her.

She had been so lost in that moment that she had forgotten about the song hymnal she was holding. Henry's nudge startled her and caused her to lose her grip on the book. It tumbled to the floor. The sound echoed throughout the entire cathedral, drawing attention and glares from everyone around them. Hannah could feel her cheeks go red. When she finally looked up, she saw Patrick's face staring back at her. Their eyes locked, and suddenly she was thirty years old again, sitting under the tree on Main Street.

At first, Patrick's face had gone white, stunned at the sight of her. But after only a second, his shocked expression faded into the warmest, most acknowledging smile she had ever seen. She smiled back and fought off the tears that were about to spill over. Their eyes remained locked for such a long time that Henry eventually nudged her again.

"What are you smiling at, Mom? What is going on?" He sounded more irritated this time.

"Nothing," she said as she looked down and shooed his concern away. By the time she looked back up, Patrick had turned to look at the rest of the congregation, but the seconds they had already shared together were enough. Every feeling and sensation she had so many years ago all flooded back to her at once. Years of blocking out the intensity of her feelings for Patrick—all blown apart with one look from him. It felt like her feelings were exploding through her body, breaking down all her carefully crafted defenses. She had felt it the moment they locked eyes. Nothing had changed between them.

For the rest of the service, she tried to follow along, saying the correct words and sitting and kneeling at the correct times. She attempted not to stare at Patrick, but after so many years, the sight of him was so glorious that she could not look away. His presence drew her in, the same way it had that summer in Hope. Even though she was trying to stay centered in the moment, the world kept going blurry where the edges of Patrick's body ended. He read the gospel and gave a homily, but she didn't comprehend anything he said. The sound of his voice vibrated through her body, awakening areas that had been asleep for years. She hadn't realized how much of herself she had closed off when she left him. It was as if she had been half alive since the last time they had seen each other. He glanced at her a few times throughout the service, and each time it took her breath away.

When Mass ended, Patrick joined the procession down the altar and out of the church. Hannah couldn't even bring herself to look directly at him. He was so close but so far away, and it physically hurt her. When it was time to leave, all the kids wanted to rush off to try and catch their friends at the Empire State Building. Hannah insisted that she wanted to stay and get a better view of the church. She wanted Patrick to meet Henry, but her head was spinning, and her nerves were shot. Her patience with Henry was wearing thin, and it would only strain her conversation with Patrick. She told the other parents that she would meet up with them later. They all hurried away, none noticing that anything was going on with her.

Should she go out the back of the church? Would he be waiting in the reception line? After twenty-five years, she didn't think a thirty-second handshake would suffice. She decided to stay right where she was. He had seen her there, and hopefully he wanted to see her as much as she wanted to see him. Hannah was certain he would come and find her. She sat down in the pew and started to consider what she would say to him. A few minutes passed, and she began to grow fearful that she had made the wrong decision. Should she have gotten up to seek him out? Then she heard the faintest of whispers. It was soft and hopeful, as if it traveled years to reach her ears.

"Hannah?"

She took a deep breath. Then she stood and turned to face the whisper. He was standing in the aisle just behind her. He was so close that she could almost feel the warmth from his body.

"Patrick," she whispered back. They stared at each other for several seconds, appraising the changes and relishing in the things that hadn't changed. Hannah wasn't sure what to say next, this time unable to stop the flood of tears. He leaned forward and put his arms around her as he had done so many times during their summer together so long ago. She tried to remember that she was in a church and that other people could see them, but it was very hard not to get lost in his embrace.

His voice shook as he spoke. "Hannah, I can't believe it's you. There is so much I want to say to you. But we can't talk here. Can you wait? I'll change, and we can go somewhere else. Would that be okay?" Patrick pulled back from their embrace, waiting anxiously for her reply.

Through her tears, Hannah managed to say with a smirk,

"What is a few minutes more of waiting? I already waited more than twenty years."

A smile lit up his face. "I'll be right back. I promise."

She sat back down and tried to compose herself. She had indeed waited twenty-five years for this moment, and she didn't want to be a blubbering mess when Patrick returned. Hurriedly searching through the contents of her purse, she pulled out a Kleenex and the one tube of lipstick she had. The lipstick was much too intense of a color for 11 a.m. on a Sunday, but it would have to do. She blotted her face dry and dotted her lips with a tiny bit of color.

Even through all the excitement she felt at being with Patrick again, a quiet knocking of guilt started to rise inside of her as she waited. Noah had died three years ago, completely unexpectedly. He had been out for a run and had a heart attack. Their neighbor had seen him collapse and immediately called 9-1-1. It had already been too late, though. Noah was gone before the ambulance had even arrived. She and Henry had been completely stunned. It took her a long time to feel strong enough to want to experience any other emotions again. Her grief had been so heavy. Her mother's death had taught her the hard lesson that life was short and unpredictable, but Noah's death had left her beyond shaken.

Having packed her feelings for Patrick away so long ago, it hadn't even occurred to her to actively try to find him. She had spent the early years of her marriage fighting to be a good and faithful partner to Noah, the type of partner he deserved. By the time Henry was born, she had made peace with her decision and was content in her relationship with Noah. They had created a loving family that she was proud of. She loved Noah, he loved her, and they both loved Henry. She had been devastated by Noah's death, but Noah wouldn't have wanted her to stay that way forever. He would want her to be happy. Today she didn't need to feel guilty about the feelings she had for Patrick anymore. She was free to feel them.

Just as she was finishing putting herself back together, she heard his voice again.

"Hannah, are you ready?" Patrick ushered her to join him in the aisle.

She nodded and answered, "Yes, of course." They walked down the aisle side by side and out the front doors of the cathedral.

"Where are we going, Patrick?" She was curious to know.

"I hope you don't think it's inappropriate...but I was thinking my hotel room?" he asked haltingly.

Hannah couldn't help but laugh out loud. "Your hotel room?"

"Well, it's only a couple of blocks away, and I thought we could have some privacy to talk." His cheeks reddened with embarrassment.

It seemed almost surreal to Hannah that she would be following Patrick anywhere. He could have asked her to follow him into a pit of vipers and she would have agreed.

She motioned for him to go first. "Lead the way."

***

On the short walk to Patrick's hotel, they kept their distance from each other on the crowded sidewalk. Their conversation was almost formal and confined to the facts of their current lives. Patrick asked a few questions about why Hannah was in New York. She explained the class trip and about Henry and Noah. He was very happy that she had become a mother, but Patrick was saddened by the news of Noah's passing. She told him how hard it had been and how she was only now learning to live with the grief. He offered his condolences and then went quiet. They walked a couple of blocks, neither of them speaking. Finally, Hannah broke the silence.

"What brought you to New York?" Hannah asked, trying to lighten the somber mood.

"Um...well, my father had surgery." Patrick told her that, after he left Hope, his relationship with his father continued to improve. He was eighty years old now and still doing well, despite having tripped and broken his ankle. Patrick had come to New York to spend a week with him while he recovered. He also wanted to say Mass at the church he grew up in, so he had asked if he could stand in during Mass, which was why he was there today.

The sequence of events that had brought them both to St. Patrick's Cathedral that morning seemed perfectly ordinary—a class trip and a father's injury. Yet, given the fact that those circumstances had brought them together after so many years, they seemed extraordinary indeed.

When they reached Patrick's hotel, they took the elevator to the fourteenth floor. The elevator didn't stop once on the way. The tension between them was building with each floor they passed, even though their conversation had died down. When the doors opened, they were both glad to escape the small space. Hannah followed Patrick down the hallway, stopping behind him as he opened his room door. Patrick went inside first, and Hannah followed. She turned to make sure the door closed. When she turned back, Patrick was standing a few feet from her with the most pained look on his face.

"Patrick, what's wrong?" The way he was looking at her almost scared her.

"I promised myself if I ever saw you again, if you were happy with Noah, I would wish you well and walk away. But now you are on your own. There is nothing I have wanted to do more these last twenty years than kiss you." His tone was passionate and determined.

She didn't even have time to respond before he had closed the few feet between them. His hands moved to the sides of her face, and he pulled her close to him. He kissed her gently at first, as if waiting to see how she would respond. When she returned his kiss with greater intensity, he pushed her back against the door. Twenty-five years apart ended in an instant. They were hardly two separate people as they intertwined, turning into a frantic mess of kisses and touches. By the time they pulled away from each other, Patrick's coat was on the floor and Hannah's shirt was half off.

"Wait, sorry, we were meant to talk," Patrick joked. "We should take just a minute."

"Yes. Talking," Hannah replied with a laugh as she pulled her shirt back into place.

"I want to tell you something, Hannah. It's something I wish I had understood sooner. A few months after we left Hope, once I could finally think of you without completely losing myself, I realized I had been so wrong. I told you I couldn't be with you because I had already given myself to the church. I told you that you deserved someone who could give all of themselves to you. But the truth was that the church only had part of me. I wasn't complete until I met you. I wasn't whole until I met you. I became a better, more empathetic priest because of you. I became a better person because of you. I should never have left you..." he trailed off, and his eyes began to well up with tears.

Hannah gently wiped his tears away with her hand.

"Don't apologize. We were young. We did the best we could. The things that separated us seemed insurmountable at the time. I've spent all this time we were apart trying to convince myself that I imagined how I felt about you. Sometimes I would think that I felt the way I did because I was overwhelmed by being back in Hope and because of my mother. Seeing you again, touching you again, I know without a doubt that this is real. It was never just a summer infatuation."

They moved close together again, standing forehead to forehead, both contemplating what to say next. Hannah felt as if her soul had come back to life, like her true self had been in hibernation all these years. She had been happy with Noah before he passed. Her life was full. But this was her second chance at a happiness she could barely put into words. She couldn't lose the love they had only just begun to rediscover.

"If we were wrong to leave each other all those years ago..." Hannah's voice was full of anticipation, "What are we going to do now?"

Patrick took a deep breath. "No matter the obstacles, this time we are going to face them together. I'm never walking away from you again."

Printed in Great Britain
by Amazon

61100497R00190